Cross
Currents

Cross Currents

Barbara Whitnell

A Critic's Choice paperback
from Lorevan Publishing, Inc.
New York, New York

Reprinted by arrangement with St. Martin's Press.

ISBN: 1-55547-235-4

First Critic's Choice edition: 1988

From LOREVAN PUBLISHING, INC.

Critic's Choice Paperbacks
31 E. 28th St.
New York, New York 10016

First published in Great Britain by Hodder & Stoughton Limited under the title *The Salt Rakers*.

Manufactured in the United States of America

Foreword

From the latter part of the seventeenth century, Bermudians sailed to the Turks Islands for the purpose of raking salt. They regarded the islands as their own special preserve, and as years went by a permanent settlement was established, first on Salt Cay and then on the island of Grand Cay, now known as Grand Turk and the seat of Government of the Turks and Caicos Islands. So much is history; the story of Zachariah and Dorcas Hardiman, however, is totally fictitious.

There were many who helped me in my efforts to make this novel as authentic as possible. I wish to record my grateful thanks to Mr. Charles Hutchings, late of South Caicos, who generously put books and manuscripts at my disposal, to Doug and Angela Gordon of the Salt Raker Inn, Grand Turk, and to Finbar and Anne Dempsey for hospitality, help and encouragement.

Appreciation is also due to Mrs. Stella Frith of Grand Turk and Bermuda, Mr. Herbert Sadler, the local historian, Mrs. Elizabeth Frith of the St. George's Historical Society, and the many residents of Grand Turk who were happy to talk endlessly of old times and times beyond that – particularly Mr. Oswaldo Ariza, Countess Helen Czernin, Mr. Leon Godet, Miss Helena Robinson and Mr. Ken Sparkes.

My thanks to them all.

B.W.

One

Dorcas Foley, eighteen years old and quite as comely as any girl has a right to expect, sat before her mirror and regarded herself with a certain amount of satisfaction, tempered only by a long-standing regret concerning her nose.

Papa undoubtedly had much to answer for in that matter. However, there it was, bold and dominant, and wishing it different was plainly a waste of time. Better to give thanks for the glowing complexion that the Bermuda sun had done nothing to mar. Not yet, anyway. Her expectations for its long-term future were not high. Grandmama never tired of repeating compliments paid to her in her youth concerning the velvety texture of her skin, but look at her now! Old parchment was never so yellow or wrinkled. Still – cheering a little – no one could deny that Dorcas had been lucky with her hair. She would have hated the pale, sandy colour that had fallen to Fanny's lot, even though her older sister's smooth and silken locks were without doubt easier to manage than her own chestnut mane.

As if summoned by thought, Fanny fluttered into the room like an agitated moth, already dressed in her best brown silk that fell from a high-waisted bodice in the style that had been in vogue since the end of the Revolution in France. She gasped in horror at the sight of her sister.

"Oh, Dorcas! Just look at you! You're not near ready yet, and Father says you are to come at once."

Unruffled, Dorcas smiled at her sister in the glass and began, without any visible sign of urgency, to brush her unruly curls into the ringlets and tendrils that fashion demanded.

"Well, then," she said, all sweetness and innocence, "I can only suggest that for the good of his soul you go at once and point out that patience is a virtue."

Fanny lifted exasperated eyes to heaven, but otherwise ignored this patently absurd proposal. One did not offer unwanted advice to Josiah Foley, nor treat his commands lightly, not unless one totally lacked the instinct of self-preservation. He was an irascible man, without warmth. It was Fanny's contention that he would have been different had their mother lived, but Dorcas had never been able to agree. His was such a strong character, she argued, that he could never have been influenced by anyone, least of all a woman.

She could not remember her mother clearly, though she cherished a vague impression of scented warmth and soft laughter. She and Fanny had been brought up by their grandmother – an amiable and well-meaning woman, who nevertheless raised Mr. Foley's blood-pressure all too frequently by her inconsequent chatter. Despite his frequent bouts of bad temper, he could do no wrong in her eyes. She had done nothing, since the day of his birth, to challenge the view that the women of his household had no purpose in life other than to serve him. He addressed them always, Dorcas thought, as if they were some minor sub-committee of the Bermuda Assembly, and a troublesome sub-committee at that.

He did not take kindly to troublesome sub-committees. Generally his speeches in the Assembly were listened to with respect: and quite right too, in his opinion. There had been Foleys in Bermuda since the days of the first settlers in the mid-seventeenth century, and none more incorruptible and public-spirited than he. Which was, as he never tired of stating, more than could be said for *some*.

Fanny was growing more agitated.

"Do hurry, Dorcas," she begged. "Mr. Amberley arrived several minutes ago and Grandmama is in a pother about supper being so late."

Dorcas gave a private smile but made no further comment on this. The unaccustomed lateness of the evening meal had caused no little inconvenience to herself, but this was not a matter which she intended to discuss with Fanny. Year in, year out, supper was served promptly at five o'clock, and any delay was treated by her father as a malevolent and sinister conspiracy on the part of family and slaves alike. The fact that on this day it had been postponed a full hour was entirely due to Mr. Amberley's previous engagements and was some measure of his importance in Josiah Foley's eyes.

"And what is this famous Mr. Amberley like?" Dorcas, still unhurried, was fastening her necklace. "Is he indeed the most handsome man to come out of Jamaica, as we've been led to believe?"

8

"Well –" Fanny struggled for honesty. "Not handsome, perhaps, but well set up, and most affable. He is quite tall with dark hair and is wearing a remarkably fine plum-coloured coat."

"Why," Dorcas murmured reflectively, preening a little so that the light fell on the emeralds and seed pearls that now circled her throat, "do I suddenly not care for affable, well set up men in plum-coloured coats?"

"Oh Dorcas, you're not going to be difficult, are you? Papa sets so much store by this meeting."

"I? Difficult?" Dorcas looked over her shoulder towards her sister with such an exaggerated expression of outraged innocence that Fanny burst out laughing. It was a weakness of hers and the cause of considerable annoyance that no matter how solemn the occasion, how serious and responsible she might wish to appear, Dorcas still retained this infuriating knack of reducing her to schoolgirlish giggles – giggles that were only intensified by her sister's own perfectly maintained gravity. Sometimes no words were necessary to set her off; a quick grimace, a fleeting expression, were sufficient to trigger the shameful mirth which seemed to Fanny well beneath the dignity of a young woman of twenty, betrothed to none other than Silas Tranton. The Trantons were, after all, every bit as respected and old-established as the Foleys, and far more wealthy besides.

"Well, *I* thought Mr. Amberley most agreeable," she said, making a great effort to speak soberly.

"For my money," Dorcas replied, smoothing an eyebrow, "he may take his agreeable person and cast it from the deck of one of his own merchant ships, preferably in mid-ocean and surrounded by a shoal of hungry sharks. If Father thinks I am to be dangled before him like a piece of juicy bait –"

"I do wish you would wait until you have seen him before setting yourself against him." Fanny came up close behind her sister so that for a moment there were two faces reflected in the mirror, alike yet strangely unalike, as if a gifted artist had, by the inspired use of colour and insight, transformed the pale and pretty sketch that was Fanny into the glowing masterpiece that was Dorcas. "You cannot know that you will not like him."

"I know that I cannot love him," Dorcas said.

For a moment she was tempted to confide – but no! They had shared most things in their life, but not this. Fanny was

9

too conventional, too fearful of their father's wrath, altogether too virtuous, particularly now that she was to be Silas Tranton's wife.

"Love can grow," Fanny said gravely. "You are so foolishly romantical, Dorcas."

"Do you love Silas?" Dorcas was equally serious. She knew that Fanny had been flattered by the interest of this socially acceptable young man and that she was anxious to marry, but could she really be in love with him? He was pleasant enough, Dorcas admitted to herself, and not ill-looking, yet there was something about him which made her uncomfortable. He disapproved of her, she felt certain, considering her frivolous and light-minded. Where others laughed at her sallies, Silas merely looked at her in a cold, assessing sort of way.

"Of course I love him." Fanny turned away, embarrassed, and began to pick up the clothes that were strewn on the floor. Dorcas stopped her with an irritated gesture.

"Oh, leave those, Fanny. Bathsheba will see to them. Tell me, would you love Silas if he were not a Tranton? Say he belonged to one of the families that father detests so much. Say his name was –" Head on one side, she gave the appearance of selecting a name almost at random. "Say he was a Mallory. What then?"

"Then he wouldn't be Silas, would he? Oh, stop wasting time, for the love of heaven, Dorcas! I was supposed to tell you to present yourself at once."

"Why, certainly! You should have made that plain before."

Clad only in her undergarments, Dorcas rose immediately and made for the door, ignoring Fanny's shriek of horror and turning only when her hand was on the latch, eyes once again wide with innocence.

"What's to do, sister? Why so shocked? Don't you think the affable, well set up Mr. Amberley would care to see me this way? At least he would have a chance to inspect the goods before purchase. After all, you know how women outnumber men on these islands! Can we afford not to be matter-of-fact about the whole transaction? In my view we should put all my assets in the shop window."

Her patience at an end, Fanny came towards her sister with determination, turning her around and driving her in the direction of the clothes-press as if she were a calf being driven to market.

"Stop playing the fool, Dorcas, I beg you. Do hurry, or we shall both be in trouble. Which gown are you going to wear? The green silk, I suppose, since you have nothing else suitable. One thing is sure," she went on, taking down the dress in question and shaking it out. "You would have a wardrobe full of dresses if you married Mr. Amberley, there's not the smallest doubt of that. They say he's as rich as Croesus, and heaven knows this family could do with a few riches. Here, let me help you. Where is Bathsheba, anyway? Honestly, I don't know what's got into that girl these days; she's missing more often than not. She ought to be helping you, not I."

Bathsheba's absence was yet another topic Dorcas was unwilling to pursue.

"She'll be here directly," she said. "I sent her on an errand. Pray, go and make obsequious apologies on my behalf, Fanny, and say I'll be there in five minutes. Go on with you! Look, here's Bathsheba now, so you have no reason to doubt me."

Only the tightly clenched hands grasping the green dress betrayed her nervousness as she watched Fanny leave the room, but the instant the door was closed with her sister safely on the far side of it, she let the dress fall to the ground in a whisper of silk as she clutched the plump and pleasant-faced negro girl by the shoulders.

"Did you see him?" she asked urgently.

Bathsheba nodded, her breath short as if she had been running.

"Yes'm, Miz Dorcas, I done see him. And don't you never ax me no more, for dis de last time, for true. It ain't right, Miz Dorcas, an' you know dat fine. Hebe done see me come in from de street an' ax me where I been."

Hebe was old Mrs. Foley's personal slave, thin and watchful and suspicious. "You didn't tell her?"

"I tell her you send me on an errand, but I don't like it, Miz Dorcas. If she tattles to de Master, and he find out –"

"Oh hush, Sheba! How will he find out if you don't tell him? Never mind that. What did Mr. Mallory say?"

"Jes' he be waitin'. Come, Miz Dorcas, we get dis dress on now. You said Miz Fanny you ready in five minutes –"

"He wasn't put out that I had changed the time?" Dorcas's voice was muffled through several layers of green silk. "Did you explain we had a guest and would be eating late?"

"I tell him all you say, Miz Dorcas, but like I say, dis de last time. You mind me, now! You may be a lady and I jest a slave girl, but I know fine what's right and what's wrong and I know it's shameful to act dis way. Hold still, now. How I fasten dis dress wid you twistin' and turnin' like a fish on a griddle?"

"You took so long! I couldn't leave this room until you got back. I had to know –"

"Dis a bad business, Miz Dorcas. Will you hold still now? If Master find out about you and Mr. Mallory and me runnin' back and forth between the two of you, he'd beat me for sure and ain't no one in dis world would blame him for it. I deserve beatin' and dat's de truth. Dere, now you done."

The last few words were spoken in a different tone, quietly and with pride, for there was nothing that gave Bathsheba more satisfaction than seeing Dorcas dressed in her best. The relationship between the two girls was one that went back to childhood and it defied analysis. They were much of an age, but age was of little importance for to Dorcas there were times when Bathsheba seemed like the mother she could not remember. Equally there were times when she seemed like a child.

"You mind me, now!" Bathsheba said again, unwilling to be disarmed too quickly.

"Don't I always mind you?" Dorcas smiled at her. "And nothing bad will happen to you, I promise. Tell me, how do I look?"

She twirled on the spot, knowing the answer that Bathsheba would give before it was spoken. The green silk dress belled out around her to reveal her flat kid slippers. Jewels sparkled in her ears and at her throat.

Bathsheba did not reply for a moment, then, smiling, she shook her head as if in baffled wonder.

"You look like always, Miz Dorcas," she said. "You'd dazzle a blind man and dat's de plain truth."

The meal was unusually lavish and Dorcas tucked into it with unabashed zest. Stuffed roast chicken, boiled mutton with capers, cassava pie; it all made a delightful change from the salt fish that, for reasons of economy, formed their more normal diet. It was yet another indication of the importance that Mr. Foley attached to the visit of the wealthy ship-owner.

Covertly Dorcas raised her eyes and looked at the stranger. He was a dark, sleek man who would one day be stout. He was sipping his wine and listening with polite attention to her father who was complaining bitterly about the acres he had once owned in Georgia, taken from him after the American War of Independence with no compensation, even though he had protested to Mr. Washington himself about the matter.

"It seems quite unbelievable that you should be without recompense," Mr. Amberley said, at the same time waving away a proffered dish with a plump hand.

The girls' grandmother leapt into the conversation.

"Quite, *quite* unbelievable, Mr. Amberley."

From their separate sides of the table both Fanny and Dorcas cast anxious glances towards her, knowing from experience that once embarked on this topic she was likely to continue for a disproportionate period of time. She, too, was dressed in her best for the occasion, the silk for her dress carried in one of her late husband's ships from France, the jewels around her wrinkled throat and on her fingers brought many years ago from the East. These were relics of a more prosperous past, for her son was more interested in his political career than the shipping business so painstakingly built up by his father and grandfather.

"Yes," she went on, shaking her head so that her lace cap trembled. "*Quite* unbelievable! We have been allowed to clear the timber, but nothing more. I am just a poor old lady, my time on earth almost run, and it is not for my own sake but for my son's and my granddaughters' sakes that my heart bleeds, Mr. Amberley. I thank God that my poor, dear husband did not live to see the day when the fruits of his labours could be taken from him so arbitrarily, and he so pleased and proud to think that he had provided handsomely for his family by wise investment. It is not right, Mr. Amberley, say what you will, and if Mr. Washington were alive today and sitting in your place I would say the same. It is not right and no good will come of it. My dear son might have expected to live in comfort on the inheritance from his father, but instead it's a case of pinch and scrape —"

"It's nothing of the kind!"

Josiah Foley seemed to swell with rage. He was a large, ponderous man with impressive features, the nose so deplored by his daughter being dwarfed by a bulldog jaw and massive head. He had cold, slate-grey eyes that whenever he looked upon anything that failed to meet with his approval hooded themselves in a manner so menacing that strong men quaked. They were so hooded now as he directed his gaze towards his mother and she faltered into silence, aware suddenly that pinching and scraping were not words he wished to hear bandied about his table that evening. Had he not insisted on the best food and finery for the express purpose of establishing his position as head of one of Bermuda's foremost families?

"The circumstance can hardly endear America to you." Mr. Amberley was smoothly tactful, glossing over this petulant outburst.

"Mr. Amberley, this family has ever been loyal to the Crown." Josiah Foley succeeded in mastering his anger and now spoke in the measured, sonorous manner more usually employed to address the Assembly. "His Majesty commands my allegiance now as he did during the revolt of the American colonists, though there are those in these islands, as I am sure you must be aware – heaven knows there was enough talk of it – who would have thrown in their lot with the enemy, given their head."

Fanny and Dorcas exchanged a speaking glance. The independence of the American colonies and the loss of their land had taken place twenty-seven years earlier, before either of them was born, yet their father still talked of it as if it were yesterday.

A feeling of despair swept over Dorcas and all at once the rich food was less to her taste. Her father would never forget his hatred of the Mallory family which had begun in those far-off days. She was deluding herself if she thought otherwise. Kit Mallory would never be an acceptable suitor.

He had explained his family's position. The American colonies had, after all, been Bermuda's chief trading partners before the war, and there had been many occasions when the hand of Whitehall had lain just as uncomfortably upon the islanders as it had upon the colonists in America. It was a point of view which Dorcas felt had a great deal to be said for it, and the Mallorys were certainly not alone in having sympathy for the rebels.

Her father looked on this as rank treachery, but it was not for that reason alone that he regarded the Mallorys with contempt. Sterling Mallory, Kit's father, also sat in the Assembly where the two men disagreed on every matter that came before them, from the building of a new Town Hall in St. George's to laws governing customs and excise. They could not even agree, Dorcas remembered with grim amusement, on the need to rid the town of stray dogs! What chance, then, had she and Kit?

"How goes the salt trade?" Mr. Amberley asked when at last her father fell silent. "You have long been concerned with it, I believe."

"That is so, sir." Mr. Foley dabbed his lips with his napkin and gestured towards his slave, smartly dressed in knee breeches and a cut-away jacket with a new peruke upon his head, who stood ready to refill the wine glasses. "Not so much as in the past, for these days I am occupied more with Assembly business than with that of shipping, but it is true to say that salt is Bermuda's life-blood. For generations, Bermudians have sailed each year to the Turks Islands, landed salt rakers, gone about their business in the Caribbean, then returned to pick up both salt and rakers to bring them back home. *And yet –*" He was swelling with a barely controllable rage again – "And yet the Bahamians are claiming those islands, sir! They are ours, *ours* I say, by usage and tradition, but we have been forced to bow to their claim, outrageous though it may be. Turks Islands now come under the jurisdiction of the Bahamas Government. It is a travesty of justice, and a poor reward for Bermuda's loyalty to the Crown to see these salt islands wrested from us."

"But surely," Mr. Amberley said, "as I understand it, Bermudians are still permitted to continue with salt raking? Geographically those islands are part of the Bahamas chain and administratively must be more easily controlled from New Providence. Logic seems to demand –"

"Logic – fiddlesticks!" Josiah Foley sent his peculiar hooded stare in Mr. Amberley's direction before recalling that this was a man on whom he hoped to make a good impression. Dorcas bit her lip and stared down at her plate to prevent herself smiling at the effort he was clearly having to make to control his anger.

"The salt trade is traditionally Bermudian," he said in a more moderate tone after a few moments. "To be allowed to continue in it merely by the kind permission of the Bahamas Government is galling to say the least, when their only interest in the Turks is the excise duties they may exact."

"Such things are sent to try us." This was Mrs. Foley again, shaking her head dolefully. "We in Bermuda are accustomed to annoyances and hardship, Mr. Amberley. Why, during the war when the importation of food was impossible – and for

15

many years after, too – we were forced to tighten our belts, though you would be surprised, I can assure you, at the tasty dishes we were able to devise with nothing more than dried fish as their main ingredient. Today's housewives are pampered in comparison, as I tell my granddaughters –"

"Bermudians are nothing if not adaptable." Mr. Foley stared at his mother as he spoke with a kind of concentrated ferocity that caused her to subside deflated once more. "Our history has made us so. We can rise above misfortune and have proved it, over and over. Many of our young men have been forced to emigrate and are living successful lives elsewhere."

"I had heard so; many to Canada, I collect."

"Ay, and others to the Turks Islands themselves. This very morning I chanced to meet a man who had once been a captain on one of my schooners, home on a short visit from Grand Cay. There is a growing permanent settlement there, it seems, and he assured me that there was a good future for those prepared to deny themselves a few comforts."

"Oh pray, who was that, dear?" Mrs. Foley had rallied from the snub she had received and had brightened at the thought of receiving a morsel of news that might be of interest to her card-playing cronies.

"No one, I surmise, who will interest you in any particular. I speak of Captain Hardiman."

"Oh!" Mrs. Foley subsided again. "You are right. He is a most ordinary person, so squat and grotesque. I do dislike *small* men, Mr. Amberley. Now you yourself must be close on six feet tall, and broad with it. It is all, I feel certain, a matter of breeding and good nourishment. Captain Hardiman is, I have always thought, a very *low* kind of person. By no means a gentleman. Why, whatever ails you, Fanny? Take a sip of water, child. If I have told Carrie once, I must have told her a hundred times to grate the coconut fine, but I might as well talk to flintstone as talk to that girl, and now here you are in a choking fit."

"No, no. Please, I beg you to excuse me, it is nothing." Fanny was scarlet with mortification as she bent her head over her dessert, but not before she had cast a furious look at Dorcas who was gazing at her with wide-eyed concern. There was no hint in her expression that she had known full well when she had squinted her eyes and pushed out her bottom lip with her tongue at the mention of Captain Hardiman's name that it would provoke the giggles that Fanny despised so heartily.

It had been a wicked reminder, that fleeting grimace, of the days when the girls had considered the swarthy captain had looked more like a monkey than a man, and – in the manner of heedless children – had made fun of him behind his back. Dorcas had not thought of him for years, but had caught sight of him in the street herself a few days previously and had noted the fact that though they had exaggerated his ape-like appearance, he was indeed an unprepossessing man.

Fanny, angry that she had once again been trapped into behaving in this childish way, managed to take control of herself again.

"I heard that he lost his wife," she said.

"So he told me. She took some kind of fever and left him with two young children." From Josiah Foley's voice one might have thought this just the sort of low trick a woman might play on a man. "He's done well, I gather, since he took up holdings on Grand Cay. He returned here to bury his mother –"

"A very ordinary little woman, but good of heart and never called on in vain for works of charity. Little did she think," Mrs. Foley continued mournfully, "that when her son left for the Turks Islands she would never see him again."

Dorcas had ceased listening. Her interest in Captain Hardiman was so small that he could have sailed to Timbuctoo without causing her to raise an eyebrow. She looked up at the clock on the wall above Mr. Amberley's head, and as she did so she found his eyes on her and, with a sinking of the heart, she recognised the gleam in them. It appeared that in this matter, as in so many things, her father seemed set to have his way. His instinct was unerring. She could tell that this man, mature and sophisticated as he was, was hers for the taking if she but cared to give him one smile of encouragement.

Men had been looking at her in that way ever since she had turned fourteen and she knew that she would be deceiving herself if she did not admit that she enjoyed the power it gave her, finding it both exhilarating and amusing. This time, however, she would have welcomed an active repugnance, for where this man was concerned she sensed a hardness of purpose in her father that frightened her. Amberley was just the kind of match that he would wish for her and she knew

17

from bitter experience how impossible it would be to hold out against his wishes once his mind was set on a particular course of action.

The meal seemed to be going on interminably. Could anyone blame her for enlivening it by trying to make Fanny laugh, she asked herself? The men were talking now of Grand Cay where most of the salt was raked, and she groaned inwardly. Who cared a fig about the place? Certainly not she! All she wanted was for this endless meal to be over so that Mr. Amberley would leave – he with his smooth, fleshy face and knowing eyes, and the beginnings of a paunch so cleverly disguised by the cut of his plum-coloured coat.

Dorcas had another, leaner, figure in her mind's eye; a man whose mouth was not flaccid with self-indulgence but was hard and demanding. Would he wait? Oh, he must, he must! The thought that he might not was nothing short of agony.

The wind had got up. She could hear the shutters banging on the outside of the house, and the candle flames were stirred so that the silver and glass gleamed and the shadows at the edge of the room beyond the small lighted circle flickered and deepened and changed their shape.

"Come, girls." Her grandmother's voice jerked her back from her reverie. Mrs. Foley had risen to her feet. "Let us leave the men to their tobacco and brandy." Roguishly she tapped Mr. Amberley on the arm with the folded ivory fan which had been lying beside her plate. "But pray do not leave us too long to our own devices, for there is nothing we care for more than intelligent discussion. I can assure you, Mr. Amberley, I have made it my business to see that these two motherless girls have had every advantage in the matter of education. They are well versed in affairs of the day and read naught but good literature. Not that I have neglected more practical matters. I can truthfully say that Dorcas can sew and embroider as well as anyone I know, and is well able to take care of a household such as this with upward of twenty slaves –"

Dear heaven, Dorcas thought, casting a despairing glance at Fanny. Perhaps she should have come down in her shift after all if her other saleable qualities were to be paraded quite so blatantly.

"You were, I collect, about to retire?" Mr. Foley said icily. This, it appeared, was a little too obvious even for his taste.

Mr. Amberley rose to his feet and bowed, his eyes seeking Dorcas's before he turned towards Mrs. Foley.

"The meal was a delight, ma'am, and the company even more to my taste. I shall look forward to rejoining you shortly."

Before he had finished speaking Dorcas sensed that he had looked towards her again, and she could feel his eyes, searing hot, boring into her back as she and Fanny followed their grandmother towards the door.

Fanny showed a distressing desire to gossip rather than go to bed. The evening had finally come to an end, as all evenings must, but Dorcas had been forced to give a series of theatrical yawns before she could dislodge her sister from a position immediately outside the bedroom door. When at last the hint was taken and goodnights said, she whirled into her room and closed the door behind her before starting frantically to unhook her dress.

"Help me, Sheba! Wake up! Fetch me that dark blue lawn."

Bathsheba, who had been dozing in a chair, sat up and rubbed her eyes.

"Miz Dorcas, you ain't never goin' now?"

"I most certainly am! Oh, do help me with these wretched hooks! Truly, it's been a perfectly dreadful evening. I thought it would never end."

"It ain't safe to go out now, Miz Dorcas. If your daddy catches you –"

"He won't! How can he? I'll go out the back door – make sure it's left open for me, won't you? If I work my way round the back of the Bailey house –"

"You's plain foolish, Miz Dorcas." Wide awake now, Bathsheba stood glaring helplessly at her mistress, not aiding in this rapid change of dress.

There was a chance that Mr. Amberley would not have recognised this whirling, glowing, vibrant creature as the same demure girl he had admired downstairs. Buttoning herself into the dark blue lawn dress she smiled brilliantly at Bathsheba.

"Don't fuss so, Sheba! There's no one about. You know I have to go."

"I only know you love dat man so, you lost all your senses and all your shame. Miz Dorcas, you know dere ain't no good can come from it."

The feeling of despair had passed. Now Dorcas was all excitement and eagerness.

"I know no such thing!"

"You jest love Mr. Mallory to spite your daddy."

"That's not true; that's not at *all* how it is."

"All your life, your daddy say white, you say black. He say black, you say white. He hates de Mallorys, you got to love Mr. Kit no matter what trouble he bring, no matter he a wild young man."

"He's not wild!" Hotly Dorcas disputed the fact, then paused in the tying of her cloak, catching her lip between her teeth as she remembered times when his wildness had been matched and surpassed by the wildness in herself. She gave Bathsheba a small and mischievous smile. "Well, not very wild. Oh, what are you mumbling about, you aggravating creature?"

Bathsheba was muttering under her breath as she turned away to fold clothes and bang drawers.

"He wants to court you, he should be man enough to face de Master."

"Much good that would do!"

"Miz Dorcas, you listen here." Bathsheba's head was only on a level with her mistress's shoulder as she came to stand close to her, clasping a shawl in her hands as if it were some votive offering. "Miz Dorcas, you be sensible, now. You be a lady. Don't you do nothing bad, you hear me? I got to speak so, for you ain't got a mother to do it. Don't you forgit what's right and what's wrong. Men take dere pleasure where dey find it, and Mr. Kit, he ain't no diff'rent."

Impatiently Dorcas brushed her words aside.

"You don't understand *anything*, Sheba. Kit loves me just as much as I love him. Don't worry about me! I'm quite capable of taking care of myself."

It was clear from Bathsheba's expression that her misgivings were as strong as ever, and doubtfully she shook her head.

"I surely hope so, Miz Dorcas," she said. "I surely hope so."

The house where Dorcas had spent all her eighteen years had been built by her grandparents at a time when the family shipping business was doing well, when St. George's was a thriving little port. It was in a narrow street not far from St.

Peter's Church, north of King's Square and the waterfront, which was the heart of the small town.

Its front door was impressive, approached by a flight of walled steps which was known locally as a 'welcoming arms' stairway, but the back door was altogether more discreet.

Dorcas let herself out silently and stopped to listen. The outside kitchen was dark and silent but there were lamps and a fire burning in the slaves' quarters and she could hear the sound of voices.

In her dark clothes she was one more shadow among many others. She eased herself into the narrowest of alleys at the back of the adjacent house where purple bougainvillaea, its colour quenched in the moonlight, spilled over a white painted wall. She was sheltered from the wind here, but once she moved away from the buildings it tore at her cloak and whipped branches of bushes and trees across her face. Even the sturdy boughs of the cedars close to the road were bending with the force of it and as the path towards the cliff climbed more steeply her breathing became laboured.

Clouds scudded across the sky, hiding the moon. There was a stand of stunted cedars at the top of the path where she had met Kit once before, and for a moment in the darkness she could see only their solid mass. She could have wept with disappointment. She was too late, after all. He had not waited.

Below the beach gleamed whitely and the curling waves threw themselves on to the sand. Her heart was pounding, not only from her hurried flight and the battle against the wind, but also from the eager madness that had her in its grip; for it was madness, she recognised that. She could not imagine one other young woman of her acquaintance behaving in such an abandoned and – yes, shameless way. There were rules laid down for the courtship of girls of her class, and by sneaking out in this manner she was breaking every one of them.

What did convention matter? It counted as nothing in the face of this obsession with Kit Mallory. He had possessed her heart and mind from the first moment she had seen him at a ball at the State House when he had been newly returned from a protracted voyage to the Indies.

No man had ever affected her as Kit had done, and no man ever could, she felt certain, no matter what small scandals concerning him were whispered behind lacy fans. His voice, his touch, the set of his head upon his shoulders, his slow and rather lazy smile, all delighted her in a way she could never have imagined. She could, she felt, simply look at him for hours. In her head she held imaginary conversations with him, longing always for the touch of his hands and lips. She – Dorcas Foley – who had always been so cavalier in her treatment of the young men who gazed at her with hangdog, love-lorn expressions! The tables had been turned with a vengeance, and she was helpless in the face of this new and overwhelming emotion.

Oh, why hadn't he waited? It was unendurable to have been kept from him for so long, when all evening he had been the only reality for her. She stood for a moment, sick at heart; then suddenly her gaze sharpened. There was, after all, a movement among the trees; a shadow, and then the outline of a man against the sky.

"Kit!"

The wind took her joyous shout and threw it back to her. She began to run towards him and did not stop until she was in his arms, returning his kisses with all the ardour and passion that had been simmering beneath the surface all evening.

They clung together a long time, their kisses punctuated by foolish, incoherent words.

"Three days," Dorcas said at last. "Three whole days without so much as a glimpse of you! I knew I should die if I did not see you tonight."

"You didn't abandon me in favour of the Jamaican, then?"

"How could you even think of such a thing! You know I love only you."

"And you've bewitched me utterly. Dorcas, what are we to do?"

"If we love each other enough, surely all will be well?"

"You're such an innocent!"

"I know, I know!" She pulled away from him and looked up into his face. "I must seem such a child to you, after –"

"After all the women I've known?" He laughed. "Is that what you were going to say? Oh, I know all the gossip!"

"I pay no heed to it."

"In my heart I was waiting for you, my darling. You must believe that."

"I want to believe it." She strained to see his expression in the fitful moonlight. "I *must* believe it!"

"Come, I've found a sheltered place out of the wind."

He took her hand and led her to an indentation in the cliff, in the lee of a rock. Her heart was beating very fast, pounding so hard that it seemed to fill not only her chest but her head as well.

He knelt and pulled her down to him, and she reached up to trace with her fingers the features of this man who had come to mean everything to her. She loved the hard leanness of them; the strong nose, the high cheek bones, the lips that could become so tender and could smile with such beguiling charm. There was a maturity and confidence about him that she found deeply exciting. He was far from the only young man from Bermuda who had sailed away to find fortune and adventure, but she had met no other who appeared to enjoy life with the same panache.

He seemed to have been everywhere, experienced everything. Salt raking, whaling, even treasure hunting along the Bahamas bank where so many Spanish galleons had met their doom. At twenty-five he seemed to Dorcas to embody all the attributes she most admired.

"Surely one can only love like this but once," she whispered.

Love had been a game until the night she met Kit, the tally of scalps something to laugh over with Fanny and her friends. This, however, was no game, but was as serious as life itself. How could she guess that she would ache with the strangest desires? How was it possible that she could feel both more alive than she had ever felt before, yet at the same time quite helpless, as if she were drowning in sweetness?

Below them the waves surged and retreated, and their sound mingled with the wind in the trees and the frantic beating of her heart. Was this a dream?

No, it was real enough. This was Kit's crisp hair she could feel beneath her fingers, his lips that she felt on her lips, her throat, her breast, his hands that caressed her; no dream, but living flesh, seeking and demanding.

He was untying her cloak and reaching to unfasten her dress, his hands cool, strong and practised. And though she shivered and uttered a brief protest, it did not occur to her to do other than abandon herself.

She cried out once, a stifled gasp of pain and panic, but he soothed and gentled her, and afterwards, when all was still, she felt nothing but an astonished wonder. So many mysteries seemed at last to have been explained: yet how could anyone explain this peace?

"That's what married people do, isn't it?" she said at last.

He laughed a little and bent his head to her breast again, and in the darkness she smiled too, knowing that she was bound to him now, and knowing too that once more she had broken the rules.

How foolish of people to say that it was wrong! If it were wrong, then it would *feel* so, like stealing or telling lies, not wonderful and natural and right. Kit was the only reality, the only truth. Just Kit and this indescribable fulfilment, and the beat of the surf against the sand and a closeness she could never have imagined.

For a while they lay without speaking in each other's arms. Kit smoothed the tumbled hair from her face. Suddenly he seemed a little remote and she longed to know his thoughts.

"I was thinking that I must not keep you much longer," he said when she questioned him. "It's very late."

"I don't want to go home. I want to stay here with you, for ever and ever."

He laughed at that.

"If only it were possible! But my darling, can you imagine what your father would say? There's no love lost between our families."

"That's no reason to ruin our lives. We could run away together, Kit."

"My darling, if only we could —"

"Why not, if we love each other?"

"It's a question of money. I'm penniless, Dorcas. The family firm appears to be doing well, building as many boats as ever, but with two elder brothers my father has made it clear to me I must stand or fall by my own efforts."

"I've never been used to money. It's not that important. If I thought it so, I would marry this wretched Mr. Amberley."

Kit, buttoning his shirt, was silent for a moment.

"Perhaps you should," he said at last. "Most girls would give their eye teeth for the chance."

She sat upright and seized his hand.

"I'm not most girls! It's you I love."

"It would be a good match."

"Don't say such things! Don't you care what becomes of me?"

"My dear, sweet Dorcas, of course I care! I merely point out the practicalities, nothing more. Darling, the hour is late —"

"And I must return to my prison. I know! Well, do up my dress, sir – you were quick enough to unfasten it."

He laughed and bent to kiss each shoulder blade so that she shivered again, her longing for him not assuaged at all.

"I could come again tomorrow," she said. "Earlier than tonight."

"What an impetuous girl you are. How can you keep it from your sister?"

"I shall plead a headache – beg that no one should disturb me and go to bed early."

Kit was silent for a moment, his attention on the fastening of her dress. He swore a little at the tiny pearl buttons that needed delicate fingers to manipulate them.

"I don't think I shall be able to come tomorrow," he said at last. "I have business to attend to. It may be a day or two before we can meet."

"You're not going away again?" Dorcas twisted around to look into his face, eyes wide with anguish.

"I may have to. Darling, I have a living to make if I am to be of any use to you, and for the life of me I can't see how I can make it here. You must trust me. I shall get word to you somehow, rest assured. Haven't we always managed to communicate, in spite of everything? Come – smile for me, and give me one more kiss."

"A hundred, a thousand if you like. Just tell me you're not going away just yet."

"How could I leave you?" He reached towards her one last time, and it was the memory of his slow, sweet smile that she took with her as she hurried towards home.

Oh, he was wonderful! Her heart sang within her. Kit was wonderful and love was wonderful and being eighteen was wonderful, and there was nothing and nobody now who could come between them. They were one flesh, she told herself, just as surely as if some fat old parson had prayed over them.

She was glad, though, to find that Bathsheba had not waited up for her. She could not avoid the feeling that with one look, her slave girl would be able to penetrate all her secrets, and she knew that the sight of her accusing, sorrowful face would haunt the dreams that she intended to devote exclusively to Kit Mallory.

25

Two

"Such a *civil* man," Mrs. Foley enthused, the hand that had been moving with rapid dexterity over her embroidery stilled for a moment as she pondered on the excellence of Mr. Amberley's behaviour. "Do you not think so, girls? He has shown himself most agreeable, in my view, calling so promptly to thank me for the supper party and inviting us all aboard his brigantine. I declare, I'm as excited as a girl myself at the prospect. There is no doubt in my mind that he is much taken with you, Dorcas."

"Then I wish he were not." Fiercely Dorcas stabbed a square of silk with her needle. "And I wish very much that you and father would not encourage him, Grandmama."

"Oh child, child!" Sorrowfully, Mrs. Foley shook her head. "Fanny, speak to your sister, there's a good girl. Surely you can make her see how foolish it is to set her face against a man of such charm, such looks —"

"And such wealth," Dorcas finished dryly. "Let us not forget his wealth."

"Indeed not." Her grandmother was unaware of any irony. "Material comforts cannot be lightly disregarded, as you would know well had you ever been seriously deprived. Why, I remember during the war even small luxuries were non-existent, and how we longed for them! Not that we didn't make the best of things, as you can be sure. But be that as it may, Dorcas, your father and I are agreed that Mr. Amberley would make a most enviable suitor."

"No, no!" Dorcas's movement of rejection was so violent that her work-basket was sent flying and silks and pins were scattered everywhere. "I refuse to think of him as a suitor. I refuse, is that clear to everyone? Why, we have not exchanged more than a dozen words! Fanny, I have your support, surely?"

Fanny, down on her hands and knees to help Dorcas retrieve the scattered silks, did not meet her eye.

"I don't know, Dorcas," she said. She was concentrating

very hard on the task in hand. "He seems kind and not ill-favoured, after all. He was telling me about his estate in Jamaica when he called yesterday and it sounds quite magnificent; a mansion, no less, set in scenery so glorious he said it defied description. I cannot think of anyone here who could offer you half as much."

"So I'm to be sold to the highest bidder!" Dorcas snatched angrily at the last of the pins on the polished cedar floor, flung them into the basket and scrambled to her feet. "Anyone would think I had no more feelings than a cargo of salt fish! I consider the whole business sordid and despicable."

"How you exaggerate." Mrs. Foley trembled with indignation. "I knew my own dear husband no better when we were married, but I had regard for the opinion of my parents who considered him an excellent match and I never had cause to think different. I really must speak to you about the immoderate tone of your speech, Dorcas. I had thought you beyond such childish outbursts, but these past days your ill-humour is little short of disgraceful. I have made allowances – the south wind has been blowing and we all know how trying that can be to the nerves – but you go too far! We have hardly had a civil word from you since the night Mr. Amberley came. When I think how your poor, dear father strives to do the very best for you –"

"Then I wish he would not! I wish everyone would leave me alone and stop trying to arrange my life for me as if I were a child."

"If you are treated as a child, it is no more than you deserve when you persist in behaving like one. I suggest you go to your room until you are in a better frame of mind."

Dorcas went from the room without another word, her head held high, but once she had reached the sanctuary of her bedroom she sank down in the chair next to the window and covered her face with her hands. She felt ashamed and miserable. Her grandmother, she knew in her heart, was perfectly justified in her complaints against her; she had been in the worst possible humour for the past three days.

Why had not Kit been in touch with her, as he had promised? The day following their meeting, she had been buoyed up by love and hope, confidently expecting that the moment his business was done she would hear from him by one means or another. But she had not heard, and now she was a prey to all kinds of doubts and fears, and being eighteen and in love was not wonderful at all but an agony beyond bearing.

She had invented any number of errands to justify her walking through the square to the shops and even on the wharf, but there had been no sign of him. Of course, he had not said that his business was in St. George's; he might have gone to Hamilton – but even so, he surely would have returned by this time.

She cared nothing for Mr. Amberley and his invitation to visit the brigantine, now riding so proudly at anchor in the harbour. All the excitement generated by the event flowed over her head and she entered into none of the discussions about the most suitable dress for the occasion. She pleaded a headache on the actual day of the excursion and begged to be allowed to stay at home, but though this request was totally ignored she might, for all practical purposes, have been elsewhere. All of Mr. Amberley's pride in his vessel, all his hospitality and conversation, was received with indifference, and though her father's thunderous face warned her of his anger at her attitude, she could not rouse herself from it. She could think of nothing but Kit and his strangely inexplicable failure to let her know his whereabouts.

Bathsheba, protesting, was persuaded to go to Mallory's Shipyard to see if she could discover what had happened, but the news she brought back was of no comfort.

"He done gone away," she said. "Dat all I know, Miz Dorcas. Dere ain't no more I cin tell you. I spoke t'rough de gate to one of de men, but de overseer shout at me to go away, jes like I some harlot."

"Gone away *where*?" Dorcas had no time at that moment for Bathsheba's wounded feelings. "When is he coming back? Didn't you ask?"

"Like I say, dere weren't no chance, Miz Dorcas, not wid dat no-good white man abusing me like he done. Miz Dorcas –" The indignation she had felt at his treatment subsided as she looked at her mistress and saw her misery. "Miz Dorcas, he ain't wort' no tears. Don't you fret for him. You'll forgit him real soon and find some nice, rich man who'll look after you good –"

"Never, never, never!" Dorcas whirled away from her and began to pace the room. "Never in a million years, Sheba. He'll come back, you'll see. If he has gone away it's because he wants to make money so that we can get married – so that he can offer something that even Father will be delighted to accept." Some measure of hope was restored to her as this version of events took hold of her imagination. "Yes, that's what it is, you can depend upon it. He'll come back from wherever he has gone with the means for us to marry and then not all the family feuds in creation will keep us apart. It's all so childish and irrelevant – just because our fathers differed all those years ago before we were born about the stupid war and have taken every opportunity since to snarl at each other in the Assembly, why should that affect Kit and me? We shall defy them, Sheba. Kit will come back. I know it, here in my heart! His message must have miscarried in some way. Oh, do stop looking at me so! What is the matter with you?"

"Ain't nothin' the matter with *me*, Miz Dorcas."

"Well, I can assure you there's nothing the matter with me!"

"I right glad to know dat, Miz Dorcas. It just I cain't help thinkin' –"

"Thinking what?" Dorcas glared as if daring her to put her fears into words, and Bathsheba sighed and turned away, shaking her head. In her own good time Dorcas would tell her, if there were anything to be told.

As the weeks went by she was not the only one to harbour doubts about Dorcas's health.

"What *is* amiss with you, child?" Mrs. Foley demanded one morning when Dorcas had listlessly pushed aside her breakfast, plainly heedless of plans for Christmas dinner that her grandmother was set on discussing. "I declare you have lost weight and I have never known you so mopish. I shall send for Dr. McClosky –"

"No, no." This was the last thing Dorcas wanted. "I am perfectly well, Grandmama; it is merely that I hardly slept last night. It's upsetting, being at such loggerheads with my father."

"No more upsetting for you than it is for him." Dorcas had still not been forgiven for her attitude towards Mr. Amberley who had now left Bermuda and presumably was back enjoying all the comforts of his Jamaican mansion. "He was greatly disappointed in you."

Fanny's fiancé, Silas Tranton, was back from a business trip to Nova Scotia in time for Christmas, and Dorcas watched with a somewhat jaundiced eye as Fanny whirled through the festivities encased in her own little bubble of happiness. How astonishing, Dorcas thought, to see her sister so flushed and animated, and all in honour of such a dull man. Set beside Kit, he would have seemed quite colourless, with his small-featured face and the mousy-coloured hair that looked as if it would feel like dried grass to the touch; but where was Kit to set him against? There had still been no word from him.

There was talk of a house to be built for Fanny and Silas on land owned by the Tranton family just outside Hamilton, and for a while those unbuilt walls seemed to mark the limit of Fanny's vision: but even she became anxious when she found Dorcas bent double over a basin in her bedroom towards the end of December having brought up her breakfast.

"Oh, you poor dear!" There was a note of compunction in her voice, for beneath the happiness she had been aware that all was not well with her sister. She ran to support her and to bathe her sweating face with a damp cloth. "Was it the fish, do you think? Yet we all had it and felt no ill effects."

Dorcas steadied herself against the wash-stand and took a few experimental breaths.

"I feel better now," she said. "I expect it was the fish – or Carrie's lime cream pie. I made a glutton of myself yesterday."

"You don't look better." Unhappily Fanny peered into her sister's face. "I think you should rest, dear. You're deathly pale! I'm sure you're not well enough to come to Hamilton with me – oh, *such* a shame! I so wanted you to see the plot of land Silas has chosen."

Dorcas took a few dragging steps and sat down heavily on the bed.

"Will you give my apologies to Mrs. Tranton? I should be glad to rest, I must confess."

Mrs. Foley was engaged to play cards at the house of a friend that afternoon. She made a generous offer to cancel the arrangement in order to bear Dorcas company, but Dorcas refused her firmly. She had felt better as the morning progressed, she assured her grandmother; so much better, in fact, that she might even take the air.

"Some exercise cannot but be beneficial," Mrs. Foley agreed. "But only a short walk, Dorcas, I beg you. It would be folly to become overtired."

A short walk was all Dorcas had in mind; down the lane, across the square, and a few yards up King Street to the Mallory house. Desperation had driven her to this plan. It was many years since the two families had done more than exchange cool nods when forced to meet face to face and Dorcas had little stomach for calling on Mrs. Mallory who was a pale, dark-haired woman – delicate, so people said – with a thin, unsmiling mouth.

She dressed carefully in one of her better dresses of white lawn, tied a straw hat with pink ribbons upon her head, took a deep breath and went purposefully forth the moment she felt sure that her grandmother had gone from home.

She was shown into Mrs. Mallory's presence and greeted with an air of faintly hostile bewilderment.

"What a surprise, Miss Foley." No sign of a smile. "Sit down, pray. Such a warm day, is it not, for the time of year?"

Dorcas sat down on the edge of the chair indicated by Mrs. Mallory, nervously clutching her reticule in both hands.

"Indeed it is," she agreed. "So warm, in fact, that I did not need my shawl, which is most unusual in early January. We have hardly suffered this winter at all, so far."

"Last year, I recall, was a great deal cooler, was it not?"

Dorcas assented eagerly, but having done so could think of nothing more to say. All her prepared opening gambits had flown from her mind like birds released from a cage, and Mrs. Mallory was of no help at all. She sat silent and straight, dark brows drawn together, hands clasped in her lap.

"Does your father know you are here?" she asked abruptly after an uneasy silence. "Did he send you for some reason?"

"No, not at all." Dorcas was aware that shyness had caused this denial to sound vehement to the point of rudeness and felt the colour rushing to her cheeks. "This was entirely my own idea, Mrs. Mallory. I felt it high time there was more friendship between our families."

"Really?" From her expression it was clear that this idea met with little enthusiasm on the part of Mrs. Mallory.

"It is, after all, a small community. Would it not be better if we could live in harmony? A feud such as exists between our families seems regrettable, and a bad way to start yet another New Year."

Mrs. Mallory permitted herself a wintry smile.

"If such a feud exists, it is none of our making, I assure you. It is your father's intransigence in the Assembly which prevents social accord – that and the slanderous way he speaks of my husband's attitude towards the Crown. This family has suffered much from your father, Miss Foley, and can hardly be expected to disregard the past."

"No – no, I see that." Dorcas spoke hesitantly and humbly. "My father is not the easiest of men, and holds strong opinions."

"We, too, are a proud family." Mrs. Mallory seemed to straighten still further her already straight back. "We do not forget easily, Miss Foley."

"I should not expect you to; but is it necessary to maintain enmity from one generation to another?"

"Ah!" Mrs. Mallory sat back in her chair a little and lowered her head so that she seemed to peer at Dorcas from beneath her heavy brows. "It is the next generation that concerns you, is it?" She smiled thinly, without warmth. "Not Stephen or William, I take it, since they are both married with growing families. Can it be my son Kit who interests you?"

"He – he has, I believe, left the islands –" Dorcas stammered, feeling the colour once more rush to her cheeks. It was clear from the expression of amusement laced with a dash of spite on Mrs. Mallory's face that she now realised the precise purpose of Dorcas's visit.

"You surely did not imagine he would settle here, did you? Marry a local girl, perhaps?" The Mallorys had scored over the Foleys and she was extracting much satisfaction from it. "What opportunities are there here for a man such as my son? Anyone with ambition and spirit must look elsewhere. His departure on this occasion was sudden, but not unexpected."

"But where has he gone?"

"He has gone privateering, Miss Foley, in one of my brother's ships. He is sailing against the French, but hopes that before any such engagement he will have the chance to visit his cousin in England."

"He will return at some time, surely?" She was being too open, she knew, but was beyond caring now.

"I very much doubt it." Mrs. Mallory seemed to find great pleasure in this statement. "The last time he was in England he reached an understanding with a young woman whose estate lies next to that of my cousin – a delightful girl, we are told, with a considerable fortune, sadly left an orphan when her father was killed in the Battle of the Nile. I need hardly say what a joy it would be to his father and myself to know that he was settled in a marriage so advantageous."

"Marriage?" Dorcas could do no more than echo the word.

"Have you not heard me, child?" Mrs. Mallory was growing exasperated. "It is my sincere hope that at any moment we shall hear that already the wedding is arranged, if not actually solemnised. I sincerely hope, my dear Miss Foley, that you have wasted no time in tender thoughts of him, though you would not be the only young woman in Bermuda to have her head turned by his pleasing looks and nature. I am persuaded he cannot possibly have given you cause, bearing in mind the nature of his understanding with Miss Charman."

Her voice seemed to reach Dorcas from a long distance, echoing and reverberating. She had never fainted in her life and had, until that moment, felt nothing but scorn for those who took refuge in what she had always considered stupid affectation, but as the room slipped sideways it was only with the exercise of a massive degree of self-control that she found it returning to normality once more. She even managed to give a stiff and unnatural smile.

"You misunderstand me," she said. "Kit and I were acquaintances, nothing more. I'm sure I wish him every happiness."

She could not afterwards remember how she left the room, or what — if any — civilities she exchanged with Mrs. Mallory before emerging into the sun-baked street.

Some kind fate decreed that she should reach home without meeting anyone, and she was thankful for it as the tears ran uncontrollably down her cheeks. It was a relief to throw herself on her bed and weep, away from the eyes of all but Bathsheba who had come into the room to enquire after her mistress.

The slave girl said little, but tutted and clucked over the distraught girl, patting her shoulder and fetching her tea. Then, when the weeping was over, she stood by the bed and looked at Dorcas with a face every bit as worried and woebegone as Dorcas's own.

"What we do, Miz Dorcas?" she asked.

Dorcas looked swiftly up at her, then bent her head, scratching at some imaginary stain on the bedspread.

"You know, don't you?" she said quietly at last.

"Miz Dorcas, you cain't hide nothin' from me. I know I ain't had no rags to wash —"

"God in heaven, Sheba!" Dorcas buried her face in her hands. "I shall kill myself, I swear it."

"Don't you talk that way." Bathsheba cuffed her none too gently on the shoulder.

"Then *what*, Sheba? What am I to do?"

"You not de first, Miz Dorcas, and you won' be de last. Didn't I say —"

"Yes, yes, you told me so!" Dorcas spoke with bitter impatience, taking out her anguish on the slave girl, but immediately put out her hand and touched her with compunction. "Oh Sheba, I'm sorry! What are we going to do? There's only you to help me."

"What cin I do, Miz Dorcas? Soon you have to tell you' grandmammy —"

"I can't, Sheba! I just can't!"

"Then maybe Miz Fanny —"

"What about Miss Fanny?" Fanny herself danced into the room, full of excitement and pleasure after her day at the Trantons'. Discreetly Bathsheba slid away. "How are you feeling, Dorcas?" Fanny went on. "Oh —" not waiting for an answer — "how I wish you could have been with us today. Mrs. Tranton sent her best wishes to you and said she hoped you would soon be fully restored, and so did Mr. Tranton. He was not near so awe-inspiring as usual. He must be accepting me as a proper member of the family, I suppose. We made all sorts of plans for the wedding." She took off her chip straw hat and tossed it on the bed, turning to preen a little in the mirror as if to confirm the admiration she had received from the Tranton family. "We talked of the bridesmaids. Mrs. Tranton said she has two nieces I ought to ask, otherwise feelings would be hurt, and I said I was perfectly agreeable just so long as I had you and my cousin Phoebe as well. Silas thinks that late September would be the best time to be married, for then the hurricane season will be over and I can go on a trip to Jamaica with him; it will be our honeymoon, you see, as well as a business venture."

Dorcas watched her dumbly, seeing her happiness, her own misery intensified by it. Fanny whirled about the room for the sheer joy of being alive.

"Isn't everything wonderful? We drove up to the site of the house and had the greatest fun making plans. You have no idea how comical Mr. Tranton can be in the right mood! He absolutely insists, he says, on a really large nursery because he wants ten grandchildren, of whom five must be girls as pretty as you and I —" She stopped abruptly, as if for the first

34

time aware that Dorcas was not looking pretty at all. Her expression changed and swiftly she came across to the bed.

"Oh, my poor sister! What a heartless wretch I am to chatter on so when quite plainly you are still feeling seedy. Did Grandmama fetch the doctor to you? Are you feeling worse?"

Dorcas lay back against the pillow and did not look at Fanny.

"I am going to have a baby," she said, her voice flat.

There was no sound in the room other than a stifled gasp from Fanny. When Dorcas looked towards her sister she saw that Fanny was frozen in mid-action, one hand stretched towards the bed, eyes and mouth circled in astonishment.

"What on earth can you mean?" she said at last.

Dorcas laughed at that, short and harsh.

"I know of no way to make it plainer," she said. "I'm pregnant, Fanny."

Fanny continued to stare at her dumbly, mouth open. Blindly she fumbled for the bedpost and clung to it as if for support.

"You talk such nonsense!" She spoke angrily, but her eyes were frightened. "It's impossible! Oh, why do you always have to act so dramatical? You have some foolish fancy in your mind, nothing more. Of course you are not pregnant! How could it be so? Don't you know how nature contrives for babies to be conceived? I suppose you see yourself as another Virgin Mary – how wicked and profane! I don't believe one word of it."

Dorcas turned her head away and closed her eyes, tears seeping from under her lids.

"I'm sorry, Fanny. You must believe what you like."

"Dorcas?" Fanny's voice was small and anxious now as she broke the silence that followed. "Dorcas, it isn't true, is it? Tell me it isn't true?"

Dorcas moved her head on the pillows once more, looked at her sister and tried in vain to speak. Dumbly she shook her head.

She saw the colour leave Fanny's face, all the happiness of the day drained away.

"Who was the man?" she asked in a whisper. "Not – not *Amberley*?"

"Of course not!"

"Then, who?"

"I can't tell you; not you nor anyone else."

"But he must marry you."

Dorcas struggled to a sitting position.

"No – I don't want him to. Anyway, it's impossible."

She hated Kit, she felt certain of it. How he must have laughed inwardly at her protestations of love and her gullibility in believing that he returned it. No doubt he despised her. He had used her no better than transient sailors used the loose women that thronged the tavern by the wharf.

To have him hauled back against his will – forced to marry her! No, that was unthinkable. No power on earth would make her speak his name, not even to Fanny. Least of all to Fanny, for she had never been able to stand up to their father and would confess all at the slightest pressure.

"What do you mean, it's impossible? Is he already married?"

"Yes." It was the simplest excuse after all and might well be true. Perhaps by now the wealthy Miss Charman was already Mrs. Mallory. "Married and no longer in Bermuda."

"Oh, Dorcas!" Fanny turned away and sank down on the chair by the window. "Oh, the disgrace! How could you? What possessed you?"

"Love." Dorcas spoke without expression. "Love possessed me. Surely you can understand that. You're in love with Silas, aren't you?"

"Yes, but we would never . . . Silas is a gentleman . . ." Fanny had blushed bright pink and for a moment was speechless until the enormity of Dorcas's sin caused her to rise agitatedly from the chair to cling once more to the post at the foot of the bed.

"Yes, yes, I am in love with him." She was half-weeping now, her face contorted by anger and grief, her stunned horror swept away as all the implications of Dorcas's condition occurred to her. "I may not have made such a dramatic song and dance about it as you would have done – I may not even have felt it at first – but I love him now. I love him and want to marry him. Oh, what have you done, Dorcas? How can I expect him to marry me now? You never stop to think of anyone but yourself."

Dorcas stared at her blankly.

"It's not *your* tragedy!"

"Not my tragedy? Not *my* tragedy? How can you be so

36

infuriating? Can you not see any point of view but your own?"

Her face white with anger she leant towards Dorcas and spoke with exaggerated clarity as if to a child.

"I am betrothed to Silas Tranton. The Trantons are a respected, proud family. Oh!" She whirled away from the bed as if too distraught to find the words to explain her case adequately. "Can't you see what you've done to me?"

Dorcas stared at her speechlessly.

"Never a thought for anyone else," Fanny said, the words emerging in brief, angry spurts. "It has ever been the same. What Dorcas wants, then Dorcas must have. *I* have to be content with what's left over!" She turned and pointed an accusing finger towards her sister. "The music box," she went on. "Remember the music box? Uncle Harmon gave it to *me*, but you cried for it so that Grandmama insisted that you should have it. And when Father brought home those two pieces of silk – the green and the brown – it was you had the green and I the brown, like some old dowager, even though the green would have suited me –"

"Fanny!" Dorcas was aghast at the huge reservoir of grievances that had apparently accumulated over the years. "The music box incident was years ago. I was a child."

"You still are – as thoughtless and selfish as ever."

"Oh, please!" The tears which had been stemmed through sheer surprise now began to flow again, and Dorcas groped for a handkerchief. "Fanny, I never meant –"

"You never *mean* anything! You merely do exactly as you please and the devil take anyone who stands in your way."

"I'm sorry." Dorcas's voice was stifled behind the handkerchief. "I – I cannot explain, but truly I'd never hurt you willingly. Please don't turn from me, Fanny. I was wrong and I know it, and now I shall suffer for it; but nothing will hurt me so much as losing you. We've always been close and I need you now more than ever."

"Can you imagine what Father will say? How disgraced and betrayed he will feel?"

Dorcas bowed her head, for she could feel the weight of his disgrace in addition to her own, and it was not to be borne.

"I'm disgraced and betrayed too," she said.

The undoubted truth of this statement brought Fanny to Dorcas's side to sit beside her on the bed.

"Oh, Dorcas," she said again, but quietly and sadly this time. "You are quite sure? It is possible to be mistaken, I believe."

Dorcas shook her head dumbly.

"Bathsheba knows," she said. "She guessed even before I did."

"Oh, Dorcas. What are we to do?"

Dorcas, once more in tears, could only shake her head. With a sigh compounded of love and exasperation, Fanny put her arms around her.

"There, don't cry; you'll make yourself ill. I'm sorry I spoke so harshly. It was the shock —"

"You had every reason. But you will stand by me?"

"Dearest, of course I will."

For a while they clung together, then Dorcas disengaged herself.

"Don't worry about Silas," she said earnestly. "Papa will be as anxious for me to go away as I am myself. He will be even more aware of the disgrace than you or I."

"When will you tell him?"

For a moment they stared at each other, speechless at the thought of this impossible task.

"We can keep it from him for some time yet," Fanny said at last, but Dorcas shook her head decisively.

"No, Fanny. This much at least I can do for you; I can leave before there's the slightest whisper about me. The — the nettle has to be grasped sooner or later." Her expression showed how greatly she feared the grasping of it.

"Listen." Fanny took her sister's hand and held it tightly. "Suppose I break the news to Grandmama tonight? She might take it better from me, since at the moment I'm the one to bask in her favour —"

"And likely to continue to do so," Dorcas agreed, with a touch of rueful humour.

"We can leave it to her to tell Papa."

"Oh, Fanny, you're so good! You're the best sister anyone ever had — far, far better than I deserve. Believe me, I'd throw myself off the cliff rather than put your happiness at risk."

Fanny stood up, sighing with exasperation.

"You and your dramatics!" she said. "I suspect suicide will be quite unnecessary once Papa hears the news; murder will be much more the order of the day. Do me the favour of making a will and leaving me your green dress."

"You can have it anyway," Dorcas said dolefully. "I shall soon be so monstrous big, it will never fit me."

Tears filled her eyes again as she contemplated this last and insupportable tragedy.

Three

Disgrace!

To Dorcas, alone in her room and condemned by her father to a diet of bread and water (secretly augmented by tit-bits smuggled in to her by Bathsheba and Fanny), the air seemed full of it as if it were some foul miasma rising from a putrid marshland, seeping in through cracks in the stonework and running down the walls.

Everything was very quiet. Even the slaves seemed to be going about their duties with bated breath, and Mrs. Foley, Fanny reported, had taken to her room in a state of nervous collapse.

Her father had stopped short of physical violence, but his fury had been awe-inspiring. Dorcas's refusal to divulge the name of the baby's father seemed to fuel his anger as much as anything else, but though she trembled and grew pale in the face of his rage, she kept to her resolve, knowing that the revelation that a Mallory was to blame for her condition would only make matters worse.

"There is no point in telling," she said wearily to Fanny. "Marriage is out of the question, believe me."

"How you must have loved him, to want to protect him so," Fanny said. "Do you love him still?"

Dorcas could not reply, for it was a question to which she hardly knew the answer any more. She only knew that when she thought of Kit she felt a blush that seemed to begin inside, at the very core of her being, and then spread through her veins so that her whole body seemed to tremble with the shame of it. Had he laughed with his brothers about her, so that when her name was mentioned it was with knowing smiles and lewd jokes? Did the whole town know her as a girl of easy virtue? Oh, the love was gone, she told herself.

But if that were so, then why did she cry for him each night, stifling her sobs in her pillow? Why could she then think of a dozen excuses for him? Had she been too possessive that night, too ready to leap to the conclusion that he wanted to marry her? Or perhaps he loved her just as passionately as she loved him, but could not bear the thought of a protracted farewell, knowing that he was committed to the girl in England. Or perhaps the whole thing was a lie from beginning to end. Mrs. Mallory was a spiteful woman, that much was clear from her face, and she had enjoyed Dorcas's discomfiture. Then again, he could have written to her, and the letter miscarried . . .

Sometimes she could believe any or all of these alternatives, but always, when morning came, she was faced with the dreary fact of his betrayal and the knowledge that she would have to endure alone.

Physically she felt low, the sickness of early pregnancy affecting her not only in the mornings but throughout the day. It was after a particularly wretched bout that Fanny appeared to tell her that Mr. Foley wished to see her downstairs in his study.

He was standing on the hearth-rug, facing the fireplace, his back towards her as she entered the room, and he spoke without turning towards her.

"Close the door, if you please." He sounded cold and remote. Dorcas did as he told her, and stood silent waiting. For a while he said nothing, shoulders hunched, hands clasped behind his back, his huge head thrust forward, then turning, he flung himself down in the chair beside the empty grate and stared at her with hard, hooded eyes.

"I have made plans for you," he said. "Pay close attention while I acquaint you with them."

She was to marry Zachariah Hardiman.

She couldn't believe it; it simply was not possible! Were it not for the fact that her father never joked, she would imagine it to be a macabre hoax. Not Zachariah Hardiman – not that little dark, swarthy man she and Fanny had always laughed at!

"Father, no! I refuse! I shall kill myself first –"

Her voice faltered and died as she looked at her father and saw that his expression had not softened one iota.

"Father, please." She spoke humbly and penitently now, not frantically as she had done before. "Please, I beg you, don't ask this of me."

"I am not asking." He had crossed one leg over the other and was swinging his slippered foot up and down as if

41

impatient that she had not leapt for joy at his plan. "All is arranged, and you will do exactly as I say."

"I *cannot*!"

"Hardiman's not a bad fellow." It was as if she had not uttered a word. "No gentleman, of course, but reliable. The ceremony has been arranged early on Saturday morning, after which you will sail with him to the Turks Islands."

She stared at him, her horror mounting. It was impossible to talk to him, impossible to communicate her horror at being banished with this man she barely knew – this grotesque peasant.

"Father, no, no – I beg you!" Her voice trembled. "Send me away – send me anywhere, but do not force me to marry Captain Hardiman."

In one impatient movement he raised his bulky form from the chair and towered over her.

"Silence, miss." He brandished a fist as if he would strike her. "For over a century our family has occupied a respected place in these islands. There is no man who could accuse me of immorality – no finger that can be pointed at me. All my life I have stood for rectitude and now you, miss, bring dishonour and disgrace, besmirching a name that has ever been a proud one. Don't talk to me of what you can or cannot do. Be thankful I have found you a man who is willing, for reasons of his own, to give a name to you and your child."

He flung himself down in the chair again, leaving her pale and trembling.

"You could have married Mr. Amberley if you had chosen," he went on, almost sulkily. "You could have brought honour to this family, just as your sister has. Instead you have brought disgrace." He reached out and took some papers from the table at his side. It was some government document, Dorcas could see, with columns of figures. "Now leave me, if you please. I have affairs of more importance to deal with."

The matter was, it seemed, concluded. He leafed through the papers as if his interest in Dorcas were at an end, but she was incapable of leaving the room. She stood silent, numb, trying to think of the right words to say that would move him to some compassion.

"Father, please," she whispered at last. "If you have ever loved me, do not make me do this. Let me just go away. I'll go anywhere you wish, but I will not marry Zachariah Hardiman."

42

He slapped the papers down on the table so hard that the sound made her jump.

"And I am to keep you, I suppose? I am to pay out good money for a passage to England or America, and continue to support you and your bastard for the rest of your life – for who else will you find to do it for you? Answer me that!"

"I will work –"

"Work – bah!" He glared at her derisively. "Enough, miss. I'll listen to no more. Money has changed hands and Hardiman and I have shaken hands on the deal. I have spoken my last word on the subject and would be obliged if you would now leave me so that I may get on with my business."

For a moment or two longer Dorcas stood there, unable to move, seeing him narrow his eyes as he looked at the figures, turn to the second page then back to the first to compare one figure against another. She saw then that he was fully engrossed and that he had truly nothing more to say to her.

She did not sleep that night, but sat by her window looking out at the moonlight on the white walls and roofs, at the movement of the branches of the tree that lay between their house and the next and at the striped pattern its shadow made on the pale, colour-washed stone of the house across the narrow street.

It was a prison, she thought. The whole of the islands of Bermuda were nothing but a prison, and the only way she could leave it was under guard, the guard being Zachariah Hardiman. Unless, of course, she threw herself from the cliff, or swam out towards the distant horizon, on and on until exhaustion relieved her of all her troubles.

It was a possibility that had occurred to her more than once but always, almost regretfully, she had abandoned the idea, knowing that she could never bring herself to do such a thing.

So what was left? Only marriage to Captain Hardiman; a man she barely knew, that she and Fanny had joked about, a man she had mimicked countless times behind his back. How old was he? He could be anything between thirty and forty, for she never remembered him looking any different from the way he looked now, even when she was quite small. And – oh, God in heaven! – there were children! No doubt he thought this a way of providing the family with a house-keeper at reasonable cost.

For hours she sat in the darkness, the future stretching even darker before her. Zachariah Hardiman – plus banishment to an island that consisted of nothing but salt, if all accounts were to be believed. It surely was not to be borne – and she would not bear it! She would think of something to save herself. Somehow a way must be found.

There was noise and bustle all about them as they stood on the poop deck of the schooner *Mary Louise*, the moment of sailing very near. Of the two girls, Fanny was the more visibly distressed. She had sobbed throughout the hasty, joyless little ceremony, but Dorcas had moved through the day like a sleep-walker, untouched and apparently unaware.

Now they stood together, looking down at her husband of a few hours. He was on the wharf directing the loading of a few last-minute boxes amid a small knot of negroes come to the quayside to bid farewell to the slaves that Hardiman was taking with him to the salt islands. Dorcas remembered, as from a long distance, that he had told her he was doing well and was taking on more slaves. She had not been interested then and was not interested now, too numb even to feel gratitude that included in his purchases was Bathsheba.

"Dearest, you will send word of your safe arrival, won't you?" Fanny clutched a handkerchief that was already damp. "I shan't have a peaceful moment until I hear – and Grandmama, too. She implored me to tell you of her prayers for your safety, even though she did not come to the ship."

"Wouldn't a French man o' war and a cannonball amidships settle all our problems? Perhaps she should divert her prayers into other channels."

"Don't talk like that!"

"Well, I imagine she will include a word of thanksgiving for my removal from the scene. God bless the worthy Captain Hardiman!"

"We shall miss you every hour, as you well know."

"Can you keep a secret?" Dorcas clutched at her sister's arm and lowered her voice. "Promise me you won't say a word of what I tell you."

"Of course I promise."

"Well then, listen to this. I have no intention of completing this voyage, Fanny, and that's the truth. No, no –" at Fanny's horrified expression. "I am too cowardly for suicide; if I had not been, I should have taken that course weeks ago. Nevertheless when this ship arrives in the Turks Islands I shall not be aboard, of that you may be certain."

"What can you mean? Where do you intend to go?"

"My dear ape-husband was bemoaning the fact that on account of the war with France, we were being forced to travel in convoy to Nassau before proceeding to Grand Cay. It adds to the voyage, of course, but at least it will give me a chance to leave the ship."

"Dorcas, for pity's sake –"

"Why on earth do you think I have gone through this ridiculous charade of allowing myself to be married to that creature? Simply to give myself a chance to leave Bermuda, that's all. I could think of no other way."

"But what will you do? Who will take care of you?"

"I shall take care of myself – and Bathsheba, of course, will come with me, so I'll not be entirely alone. At this moment I have not the slightest idea how I will live – how, even, I shall get ashore – but I am convinced that somehow I shall find a way."

"Dorcas, the idea is absurd!" Fanny was bright pink with agitation. "How will you support yourself? You have no money."

"I have my emerald and pearl necklace and my garnet brooch. They'll serve to keep the two of us from starvation for a while, I should think, until I can find work as a seamstress or governess. Oh, don't look so fearful, Fanny! I can't see that either alternative is near as bad as living as the wife of the ape-man."

"Dorcas, I wish you would not call him that! That was childish mischief on our parts and ought to be forgotten. You know –" She hesitated for a moment, knowing that her words would not be well received. "You know I spoke to him at some length before we came aboard and was most pleasantly surprised. Dorcas, why not give him a chance?"

She took Dorcas's arm and turned her so that she could look into her face.

"You were ever a courageous girl, far better than me at making the best of difficult situations and – oh, it may ill become me to say this, for I am marrying the man I love – but Dorcas, you are not the only girl to marry a man chosen for her for one reason or another and this morning, as I conversed with Captain Hardiman, it seemed to me that you could have fared worse."

Dorcas tossed her head.

"I shall leave the ship at Nassau and there's an end of it."

"Nassau's a lawless place, they say, full of pirates and all manner of riff-raff. There's your condition to think of, too — the baby —"

Dorcas melted towards her and bent to kiss her cheek.

"Dear Fanny, I know you only have my interests at heart, but you must allow me to act as I see fit. I swear not to be impetuous or foolish, but surely you must see that I cannot be subject to Zachariah Hardiman as a wife must be to a husband."

"I think he is a deal better than you give him credit for. Do you know what he told me today?"

Indifferently, Dorcas shrugged. "That salt was fetching twenty-five cents the bushel?"

"That he has admired you for years and considers you the most beautiful girl in all the islands. He said I was to have no fears on your behalf; that he would cherish you until the day he died."

"Poor fool." Dorcas's lips twisted in a bitter little smile. "He'll have scant chance of that. Why, the very thought of having him touch me makes my blood run cold. Just look at him!"

They both looked down over the taffrail at the dark head of Captain Hardiman, who from this angle looked foreshortened and more squat than ever.

A seaman approached to tell Fanny it was time she left and for a moment the two sisters looked at each other in silence, hearts too full for words; then, tears spilling over, they clung together.

"Go quickly," Dorcas said. "And be happy with your Silas."

"Pray do nothing foolish, dearest. All may yet work out well —"

"Time to go ashore, Miss Fanny." Zachariah himself stood beside them. "Come, wife." He smiled as he offered his arm with exaggerated courtesy to Dorcas, and she realised he was doing his best to lighten the moment with an attempt at humour. "Let us bid goodbye to St. George's together."

She ignored the arm, turning from him to look at the island which she both loved and longed to leave. The white roofs shimmered in a mist of tears.

"Don't you fret, lass." His voice was gentle and coaxing, the sort of voice one might use to a frightened child. "I'll make it up to you, I promise."

She neither looked at him nor made any sign that she had heard.

The cabin under the poop deck measured no more than six feet long and four feet wide. Two people could hardly stand within it without touching, and Dorcas's heart sank at the thought of the unwanted intimacy that this implied. As for the chamberpots that were held in brackets on the bulkhead just above each bunk – she would die, she felt, rather than use one in his presence. She felt sick with horror at the mere sight of them.

She stood beside the bunks, not looking at him, not speaking. She felt numb with exhaustion and despair, at the end of her strength, unable to imagine what he would now want of her. Surely he would not expect to exert his marital rights immediately, the moment they were alone together?

He touched her arm, and fearing the worst she flinched away from him.

"Oh, lass, lass," he said reproachfully, in that same gentle voice. "I'll be good to you. There's no call to be frightened."

He took her by the shoulders and turned her to face him. He was no taller than she was, perhaps slightly shorter. His eyes were on the same level and were dark brown, with thick, tangled lashes and equally thick brows, arched like a clown. His skin was like leather, deep seams running from nose to mouth – to that long upper lip that gave him his simian appearance. She closed her eyes to block out the hateful sight of him.

"Poor lass," he said. "You're worn out, and who's to wonder at it? You've had a hard time, one way and another. Things will look different in the morning, mark my words. I'll get out of your way and give you room to move, then you best get to bed to sleep the sleep of the just –" He grinned at her, baring strong white teeth. "Or the just married, I should say." He chuckled at this small play on words, but Dorcas turned from him, too weary and despondent to show that she had even noticed it.

"Poor lass," he said again. "I'll not disturb you when I come to bed. I must off now to see the children. Nola cares for them as well as she can, but they'll want their father tonight, not a slave girl."

The children! She had, for a while, forgotten them, but now saw again the two small figures at the wedding: the

47

five-year-old boy, large-eyed and overawed by the occasion but somehow giving the impression of vitality; and the girl – older, with a small, dark, watchful face and hostility in her eyes. The thought that she could, in the future, be responsible for the well-being of these two small strangers took her breath away.

Even so, she was asleep far more quickly than she had expected. She awoke at some stage during the night and was aware that the schooner had left calm waters and was pitching a little, the timbers creaking, but neither the action nor the noise was sufficient to keep her awake. She slept again, and when she woke finally it was morning and a shaft of sunlight lay across her eyes.

For a split second her mind was a blank, but this false calm lasted no more than a moment. The next instant realisation flooded back and a wave of sheer panic flooded over her. She lay on her back, her heart pounding, such pressure in her chest that she could hardly breathe. Far from feeling better after her night's rest, it seemed that the new day had brought an even sharper realisation of the horror of her position.

He must be there, in the bunk below. She listened carefully, but could hear no sound other than the rhythmic creaking of the ship's timbers, the splash-splash as the hull rose and fell, and the sound of footsteps on the deck above.

Slowly, cautiously, she leant out over the bunk, only to catch her breath sharply and duck back again. He was there, lying bare-chested, one ankle protruding from the sheet which reached no further than his waist.

With difficulty she swallowed, summoning enough courage to take another look, as if she needed a further chance to confirm that this rough, hairy creature was no figment of her imagination, and this time she was more prepared for the sight of him and studied him longer and with more attention.

She had never seen anyone other than a young child sleep with such – such *abandon*! His arms were above his head, hands loosely curled, and his mouth was gently curved as if his dreams were affording him some amusement. The long jaw was dark with the morning growth that, if left to its own devices, would provide him with a beard as black as any Spanish pirate, and a pelt of dark hair covered his chest which was burnt nut-brown by the sun. The shoulders were massive, but he did not look as fleshy as she had imagined, being hard and well-muscled.

"Well?" There was laughter in his voice. "Are you pleased with your bargain?"

She ducked back again, outraged that he had not been asleep after all, or at least not all the time. He must have been watching her through those thick lashes. She heard the sound of movement from below and in a moment he had swung himself up so that he was sitting at the end of her bunk, clad in nothing but a pair of white cotton pants. She pulled the sheet up to her shoulders and looked warily at his cheerfully smiling face.

"Well, what was the verdict? Will you keep me or throw me back into the sea?"

She could not speak. Now was the moment, she felt certain, when he would throw himself upon her like the animal he surely was. He leaned towards her and she shrank back, but his only intention, it seemed, was to take her hand which he held in both of his, staring at it as if it were the first one he had seen.

"Will you look at that?" he said in an awed voice. "Isn't that the loveliest thing you ever saw? Four fingers and a thumb! Everyone has them, and I've held a good many, but never one as delicate as yours." He bent his dark head and planted a kiss almost reverently in the centre of her palm, folding her fingers around it as if she were a child.

"Are you wondering why I married you?" he asked, smiling at the suspicion he could see in her face.

Dorcas shrugged her shoulders, not knowing what to say.

"It's not easy to tell." He seemed quite at his ease, not at all put out by the unusual circumstances in which they found themselves, nor by her silence which she was powerless to break. "There's more than one reason." He took her hand again and began to chafe it as if she were cold or sick. "You could say, I suppose, that I married you because I was sorry for you, and that would be the truth. Don't forget that I worked for your father for many years before my wife and I came into a little money and settled in the Turks Islands, and I've no love for him. He seems to me a miserable kind of a devil, and I'd not care to be a daughter of his who'd fallen from grace, I can tell you. I knew when he spoke to me that he was eaten up with fear in case any of his fine friends should find out you were in the family way, and from beginning to end I detected not one ounce of the milk of human kindness."

Dorcas stared at him dumbly, still wary.

"Then there was the money, of course. You could say I was glad of what he offered me and that would be the truth too, for I needed more slaves and had to lay my hand on ready cash for them. Last year was a bad one for salt. I was down ten thousand bushels on the year before – but believe me, lass, money alone could never have persuaded me to do aught I felt wrong. Still, any man who says he can't use a little extra is either a fool or a liar or both. *Or* –" He shifted a little on the bunk, banged his head, pulled a face and grinned at her. "You could say," he went on, "that I needed a woman to be a wife to me and a mother to my children, and that is no word of a lie. And touching this matter –" He was suddenly serious, looking down at her hand and for the first time showing some sign of shyness. "Touching this, lass, I'm in no hurry to – to make a proper wife of you, if you understand me. The time will come, and when it does, you'll know and I'll know, and I daresay we'll be able to make each other very happy. But for the moment I'm content if we get acquainted with each other. It'll be as if our courting time has come after the ceremony instead of before, that's all."

Dorcas found she could speak at last.

"I'm grateful to you," she said swiftly, and indeed she was. She felt as if a great weight had fallen from her.

"But there's yet another reason." Zachariah looked at her now, his expression still serious. "And this is the truest thing of all, so mark it well. Years ago when you were nine or ten and I a young man in my early twenties, I saw you come on to the wharf one day with your sister and grandmother. I was checking a load of cedar shingles at the time, I remember it well, and I looked down and saw you there, looking up at the sloop, and I said to myself, there's a lovely little creature if ever I saw one; she'll break a few hearts, I said to myself.

"And then I went away to sea, and came back again, went away and came back again, and every time I came back you were just a little older until suddenly, one day while my back was turned, you grew into the most beautiful woman I'd ever seen. I was married by that time, a husband and father. And a good one," he added, giving her hand a shake as if to underline the fact.

"My Clara was a good, bonny, loving girl and I'll fight any man who says different, but set beside you, she was like an everyday earthenware pot next to cut crystal. I never thought

50

I'd do more than look at you from a distance, and then, suddenly, there was your father *begging* me to marry you and take you off his hands! How could I deny myself a chance like that?"

It was impossible not to feel disarmed. His voice was rough and ill-educated, but not unpleasant; in fact it was deep and resonant and sounded kind. It seemed to Dorcas some time since she had heard words spoken to her in kindness. If only she were not tied to him for life, she thought, she might find him as pleasant as Fanny had done.

"The child," she said awkwardly. "Its existence did not — did not trouble you?"

He threw back his head and laughed.

"Bless you, no! I love children. All children! We'll have my two — young Davey and Emma, you'll get along with them handsomely I make no doubt — and there'll be your little fellow and any number of others belonging to the two of us, and we'll all live together as happy as sandboys, you mark my words."

There was, she thought, something almost laughable about his simplicity.

"I'll not deny there are many who'd spurn you. Men like your father, for example. But it says in the Good Book, 'Let him who is without sin cast the first stone.' Isn't that right? I'm not going to tell you my sins for they'd last from here to Grand Cay and back again and still there would be enough left over to fill a book, but I'm not going to cast stones, either. Men are strange, you know." He hunched himself nearer to her. "They're the same about women as they are about fiddles."

"About *what*?"

"Fiddles. Do you like music? Yes, of course you do! Anyone who looks like you must have music in their soul. Well, there are those who would pay a fortune for a new fiddle but would look with scorn on the old, worn, scratched thing I've taken with me all over the world, from when I was a boy. I had it of a Jew in Malta, and even he thought it of little value." He wagged a finger at her. "But I'm telling you, lass, I would rather have that fiddle no matter how many hands it had been through —"

Dorcas, following all this with a frown and not seeing in what direction he was leading, suddenly caught the drift of his remarks and flashed him a look of outrage.

51

"Well, sir," she said. "*I* haven't been through many hands, whatever you may think to the contrary."

His eyes grew round and he blew out his cheeks like the pictures of the winds in ancient charts; then suddenly his amusement boiled over and he began to laugh, quietly at first with some attempt at restraint, then more and more explosively until he seemed not simply a man who was amused but the very personification of laughter. He was blind with it, helpless with it, his whole being was given over to it.

At first Dorcas looked on coldly at this strange phenomenon, for a man so helpless with mirth was something she had never witnessed before. She found it impossible, however, to keep up her haughty regard for long. So infectious was his laughter that she was powerless to resist and soon was laughing too, albeit with more restraint, for she was not at all certain of the reason for the joke.

"Pray tell me," she said at last. "What was so very funny?"

Zachariah wiped his eyes.

"*You*, my lass. You and your outraged dignity." He tossed his head and pursed his mouth, and in a wicked parody of her manner he echoed her words. "*I* haven't been through many hands."

"Well," Dorcas said, defensively. "I spoke nothing but the truth."

He grew serious and took her hand again.

"I know that. You're not a light-minded girl. You fancied yourself in love, no doubt – no, don't tell me. Don't ever tell me. I'll not ask questions, you can depend upon it."

"What an extraordinary man you are, Captain Hardiman."

"So people sometimes tell me." He grinned at her. "There's just one favour I should like to ask. Could you, d'you think, see your way to calling me Zachariah? Captain Hardiman seems a little formal for husband and wife."

"I'll do my best," she promised, and he patted her hand.

"You do that, lass, and we'll do very well together, you and I."

For a moment he seemed to be studying her, and in return she studied him. Such an ugly, comical man, she thought; but kind and gentle. No doubt she would think him pleasant enough, if only she were not married to him. As it was, she still felt a clutch of revulsion at the thought that her body was at his disposal. Thank heaven she had a reprieve! He had shown himself to be unexpectedly sensitive to her feelings, but for how long would his patience last?

He smiled at her, the brown eyes almost disappearing in the network of wrinkles that surrounded them, then jumped down to the floor and, to the accompaniment of a clear and tuneful whistle, pulled on his trousers and his shirt.

"There'll be breakfast served soon," he said. "And I'm more than ready for it. Will you be joining me?"

Suddenly Dorcas realised two things: the first, that she was ravenously hungry; the second, that she did not feel nauseous.

"I believe I will," she said, surprise in her voice.

She had to cling very tightly to her determination not to be *too* disarmed by him. If only he were a cousin or an uncle, she thought from time to time, it would all be easy. There was a warmth about him that was instantly likeable; a kind of spontaneous enjoyment of life that was new to her and very beguiling. Nevertheless, cling to it she did. Her determination to leave the ship at Nassau was as strong as ever.

Sitting on the poop deck, the breeze cool on her face and the blue sea calm and friendly, she watched him playing with his children and marvelled. It was not merely that Nola, who normally had the care of them, had succumbed to sea-sickness the instant she had set foot aboard the *Mary Louise* that caused him to take such a hand in their entertainment. He actually enjoyed spending time with them.

Seven-year-old Emma was a serious little girl. Not a child who instantly attracted, Dorcas thought, feeling disconcerted by her intent and apparently hostile regard. However with her father she was a different creature, smiling and animated, vying with Davey for his attention. Zachariah treated her with an elaborate mock gallantry in which she plainly delighted.

With Davey he was more boisterous, the pair of them engaging in sham fights and rolling on the deck like puppies. There was something in his expression as he held his son aloft when the fighting was done that caught at her heart.

Had her father ever looked at her with such love? Though she cast her mind back over the years, she could not remember such a time. She had never associated him with laughter or enjoyment, only with stern admonitions and a fearful feeling of foreboding whenever she knew she had committed some transgression – a thing that had never been difficult to do. A summons to her father's presence was more likely to presage punishment than any expression of affection.

"See the flying fish?" Zachariah had left the children to Nola who had managed to venture on to the deck that day. He was dressed in cool wide-legged sailors' trousers and a shirt that was open almost to the waist.

"Where?" She went with him to the rail and followed with her eyes the direction of his pointing finger.

"There! I love to see them." He was as enthusiastic as if this were his first sight of them.

"We seem to have set them in such panic-stricken flight," Dorcas said regretfully.

"For all we know they may welcome the excitement. It does a man good to be jolted from his rut from time to time; why not a fish?"

She laughed at the fancy, and as she did so it occurred to her that thanks to this surprising man she had laughed more in the past few days than she had done for weeks.

"I was thinking," she said, smiling at him, "how very unlike my own father you are."

"Well, God be praised for small mercies!" He leaned his elbows on the rail beside her. "I'm thankful you show little resemblance to him yourself."

"I'm said to favour my grandmother."

He pursed his lips, considering the question.

"Yes, I can see how that might be. She is very handsome even yet – but somewhat talkative, if my observation is correct."

"There are few who would disagree with you there." Dorcas's smile died, and she sighed a little. "Poor Grandmama! She has the best of hearts. I – I was sorry that I caused her so much pain and disappointment and that we parted on terms that were – well, less than affectionate, for she has ever been as kind as a mother to me."

"She loves you as much as ever, I'm certain."

Dorcas knew that if she looked towards him, she would see in his eyes the expression of wondering admiration that she had come to expect, as if he still could not believe his good fortune in having had the chance to marry her. It was impossible not to feel comforted by it and she felt regretful that it was necessary to hurt him – for her desertion at Nassau would do so, she knew. The whole project would have to be carefully planned to prevent his leaving the ship himself to

54

search for her. They were to be in Nassau several days, it appeared, and for the moment she was content to leave any plans until she was able to see the lie of the land.

"Tell me about Grand Cay," she said, more to make conversation than because she was interested. "What can I expect to find there?"

"Salt," he said, grinning at her.

"Is there really nothing more to say of it?"

He was silent for a moment, staring into the gently heaving distance, his smile less broad now and a look on his face that had something of the visionary about it.

"You'll find a flat, barren island, covered in cactus and sea-grape; a few palm groves, some Indian corn, the occasional tamarind tree. We have a tamarind hard by our house, and the children love to eat its fruit." There was a short silence and the furrows on his face deepened as he stared straight ahead of him, his eyes narrowed as if he were trying to bring this strange island into focus.

"There's nothing soft or lush about it," he said after a moment, his words slow and thoughtful. He seemed to be defining it to himself as well as to her. "It's a – a *raw* place, waiting for people like us to make something of it. People have raked the salt for two hundred years or more, that I know, but they have put little into the place, only taken its riches away with them. The soil is nothing. It's thin and poor, and formed of a kind of pitted, broken rock which has some long scientific name I can never get my tongue around."

"Calcareous?" Dorcas hazarded, dredging up the word from some half-forgotten, overheard conversation. Mr. Amberley, she remembered, with astonishment. He had mentioned it, that night a thousand years ago.

"That's it, that's it! Oh, you're a clever lass. I was never great at book-learning. The ocean and the sky were my tutors – and my fellow men. I've met all sorts in my travels, I can tell you; good and bad, and some downright wicked. Turks has had its share of those, but now that wives and families are settling there the old, lawless days are over." He grinned again. "Well, almost. Most of us manage to avoid the Collector of Customs when it comes to a few bottles of rum here and there."

Dorcas accepted that confession nonchalantly, for she knew there were plenty in Bermuda who would say the same.

Instead she pursued the subject of the island, for try as she might, she could not picture it.

"Where do the salt ponds lie?" she asked.

"They are scattered. I have my holdings in the Town Pond which is central, a few hundred yards back from the shore. There are others, mainly to the south."

"And people live close to the ponds?"

"The slave barracks are there, ay – and many of the poorer white workers have their huts in the area. There is one fine street running from the Town Pond directly north and you'll find most of the better houses there, with yards and outbuildings, and trees and flowers planted. Oh, it's wonderful to see what has been accomplished in a few years."

"And that's where your house has been built?"

"Nay, mine is on its own, a little to the south. When we first went there we lived hard by the jetty. The building still stands today, but now I use it as an office, above a store."

"I didn't know you owned a store!"

"I don't. I lease the premises to a wild Irishman by the name of Gilligan."

He hunched his shoulders and contorted his face, and in some miraculous and inexplicable way she received a picture of the wild Irishman named Gilligan, more vivid than if he had painted a portrait. It was strange, this way he had of talking with the whole of him, as if words had never served him well and he had to make up for their deficiencies.

"How close are the other islands in the group?"

"Salt Cay is but nine miles to the south-west. Salt Cay and Grand Cay, plus other small cays of no significance, form the Turks Islands. South Caicos is twenty-two miles to westward, and beyond it East Caicos and Grand Caicos, North Caicos and Providenciales."

"But they are not salt islands?"

"Some is raked on South Caicos, but the rest of them have been settled by Loyalists from the southern states of America. Most of them went in for cotton, but it's not been a success. They are plagued by pests and some of them have already returned to the Republic leaving their fine plantation houses to rot. Some hang on, in spite of everything. I feel sorry for them. We shall do far better with salt, you mark my words. After all, what substitute is there for salt? By what other means can folk preserve food?"

"I know of no other," Dorcas agreed.

"There you are, then. How can we fail? Nay, lass —"
Momentarily he laid his hand on her arm and she suffered it
without flinching, though she still felt wary of him. "It's not
an easy life I have to offer you and perhaps I should feel shame
because of it, yet somehow I cannot feel so for something tells
me that together we can create something grand and exciting
out of *nothing*!" He leaned towards her, his dark eyes glowing.
"There'll be a white beach and a clear blue sea on our
doorstep, and the house is one that I'm not ashamed of. It's
no mansion, but it's solid and made of good timber with
honest workmanship, and with you to grace it, it'll be a place
of joy. And oh, there's so much I want to show you; tiny cays
where no one else goes, where we can swim and fish, and
caves deep under the earth —"

For a moment a shutter seemed to lift in her mind and she
saw a future that was not frightening at all, but filled with
light and laughter. It seemed to beckon like some enchanted
country that she had only seen in dreams. There was safety
there, and comfort, and companionship. There was excitement and challenge, too, and a certainty that here was a man
she could rely on all the days of her life.

Then, as suddenly, the shutter dropped again and the vision
was gone. She saw a small, swarthy man wearing the costume
of a common sailor, his open shirt revealing a mat of dark
hair, his shoulders wide and powerful, his broad face one
that provoked laughter. A peasant, nothing more. And she
belonged to him! He could do with her exactly as he willed,
the moment he willed it! The thought was as abhorrent to
her as ever.

"When do we expect to dock in Nassau?" she asked him,
and even to herself her voice sounded cold, and formal, a
douche of cold water on all his dreams. She could see the high
spirits draining from him. The clasp of his hand loosened and
the light died from his eyes.

"Tomorrow," he said flatly after a moment. "Or perhaps
the day after. Much depends on the wind."

For a few seconds more he looked at her, then swung away
from the rail back towards his children, the disappointment
he felt in her response visible in the droop of his shoulders.
He looked, she thought, as deflated as it was possible for
Zachariah Hardiman to feel, and she was conscious of a
twinge of sorrow on his behalf.

*   *   *

Bathsheba was not happy.

"Miz Dorcas," she said. "Now I know you is out of yo' head. You cain't stay in Nassau all alone, no one to take care of you."

"You'll be there, Sheba. You'll take care of me – we'll take care of each other."

"How come, Miz Dorcas? You want me hunted for a runaway? I belong to de Master now."

"But we've always been together." There was an edge of desperation in Dorcas's voice. "You couldn't let me down, Sheba. I'd see nothing bad happened to you. Haven't I always looked after you?"

"We together a long, long time, dat's for true."

"Then trust me now, and help me, Sheba."

"How you manage for money? Dere be de chile to tend soon." The girl was far from won over, Dorcas could see. She summoned all her powers of persuasion and spoke eagerly and rapidly.

"I've been thinking and planning. You know Mr. Digby? The old, white-haired gentleman who is travelling with us? He is staying in Nassau at the house of a widow who lets rooms, for he told me his only alternative was a tavern by the dockside. Nassau is crammed full of people wanting rooms, he said. Well, I have enough money to rent a house for a while, and I shall let rooms to gentlefolk."

"Dey ain't no gentlefolk in Nassau. Dey all pirates. You end up wid a knife in yo' back and all yo' money gone –"

"No, I will not! Oh, stop thinking of so many objections! I've worked out a plan, Sheba. You must have my clothes ready. Just a few things – there's no hope of taking everything, but it doesn't matter. You know the things I like best. Put them in a basket and take them ashore when the boat docks. Captain Hardiman is going to see some government official, he says; but after that he will take me ashore to see the place. Somehow I'll give him the slip, and you and I will arrange to meet at some central point – a market or church. I'll see if I can find out a suitable location in conversation with Mr. Digby."

"It ain't a good place." Still uneasy, Bathsheba's face was set in the stubborn lines that her mistress knew so well. Dorcas sighed as she took the girl's arm, her expression of determination replaced by one of pleading.

"You won't let me down, Sheba," she said again.

"You think hard, Miz Dorcas. Cap'n Hardiman's a good man —"

"All the more reason to think he won't pursue a runaway — *two* runaways! We'll both be in the same boat, Sheba."

"You think hard," Bathsheba repeated, refusing to commit herself.

Dorcas pressed her lips together.

"My plans are made," she said firmly.

It was a hot night. Down in the saloon where the passengers ate their evening meal there was hardly a breath of air and the smell of the oil lamps and the turtle steaks, combined with the odour of the whale oil that was in the hold on its way to New Providence, all combined to make Dorcas's stomach heave in a way it had not done for a few days.

She excused herself before the meal was over and rushed hurriedly on deck where she stood by the rail, breathing deeply of the sweet evening air. She turned as she heard Zachariah's voice behind her. He had followed her up and now regarded her with a look of concern.

"Is there aught I can get you, lass?" he asked gently.

"No, thank you. I am better now. It was just that I couldn't breathe down there."

"The breeze often falls before nightfall." He came to join her at the rail. "We could hardly have asked for a calmer passage, could we? It is not always so, I assure you."

"It's a heavenly evening." Dorcas spoke wonderingly as the full glory of the sky and the sea dawned on her. "Such colours!"

"And one small star to wish on." He covered her hand with his own. "I have no need for more wishes. I've all the happiness that any man can possibly expect."

But only temporarily, Dorcas thought uneasily, and wished again that it was not necessary to hurt him. He deserves better, she thought, and gave him an awkward smile. He looked searchingly at her and seemed about to speak, but suddenly there were voices and footsteps approaching and soon a cluster of people had joined them on deck — the six passengers, the captain, and two of the ship's officers, all come to take the air and marvel at the golden bowl that the sky had become, rapidly darkening now as night approached.

Soon it was completely dark, with the velvety sky so thick with stars that one could not have placed a finger tip between them, and it was then that the first officer, who had known Zachariah on some previous voyage, suggested that he should play the fiddle.

He needed little persuasion. He discarded the jacket he had donned to eat his supper, tucked the fiddle beneath his chin, and played jigs and shanties until all the ship's hands and the slaves had come out from the nooks and crannies in which they had been passing their off-duty hours and were clapping in time to the brighter music or listening in brooding silence as the more poignant melodies soared above the slapping of the waves and the singing of the shrouds.

Dorcas took the jacket and moved a short distance away, folding it into a pillow and lying back on the boards of the deck with her head resting on it. The beauty of the night was a pain beneath her heart, and the ache in her throat was the ache of unshed tears.

The fiddle sobbed a lament, and all around her was a great hush from the listeners in the darkness.

We are all so small, she thought, looking up into the star-filled sky above her. So small; and ultimately, so alone.

Of what did the slaves think, sitting so quiet and attentive? In spite of what was seen as their outward gaiety and irresponsibility, it had always seemed to her that there was a deep core of sadness inside them which they expressed in their music. Was Zachariah's music calling to it, awakening it? How little she knew of them.

She thought, suddenly, of the girl she had been; wilful, arrogant, certain that she could go on her own way without suffering the consequences, sure that life had something wonderful to offer. Other girls might settle down to humdrum lives with husbands they did not care for, but not Dorcas Foley! Oh, no! For her there would be a Prince Charming, with whom she would live happily ever after.

And in spite of all that had happened to her, she realised with sudden startling clarity, she had not changed. Still she – who was of no more importance in the scheme of things than the smallest grain of sand on the ocean bed – was thinking only of her own desires.

Another truth burst upon her. It was the baby that mattered now; the baby that had hardly seemed real so far, but which was undoubtedly growing inside her. And for him, she thought with a reluctant affection, could there be any better father than Zachariah? She saw again the warmth in his expression as he looked at his children. Would it be different for her child? She felt certain that it would not. There was enough love in Zachariah to spread to all comers.

He had put his fiddle down now and was singing in a tenor voice that surprised her by its clarity and resonance. She sat up so that she could see him dimly, arms circling his knees, head thrown back.

The song was in a minor key; a song of unrequited love.

> In Scarlet Town, where I was born,
> There was a fair maid dwellin',
> Made all the lads sing 'well-a-day',
> For love of Barbara Allen.

The melody was so sweet that suddenly the combination of the music and the night was overwhelming. Tears filled her eyes. There was no one near to see and she let them flow, finding a blissful easement in them, as if they were washing away much of the hurt of recent weeks. She was crying for Kit and for the love he had rejected. She was crying for her father's coldness and for her own foolish wilfulness and the fact that she was far from home.

Still the song rose soaringly, only to fall again. The audience was silent until, at the end of it, the tension snapped and there was applause and some laughter as Zachariah feigned exhaustion and two of the sailors rose to dance a jig.

Unnoticed in all this activity, Dorcas rose from her place on the deck. She felt strangely empty and at peace, as if an unendurable burden had been set down.

On the lower deck she looked around her for Bathsheba, and seeing her sitting on a hatch called her name softly. At once she rose and hurried over.

"You want me, Miz Dorcas?"

"Yes. I've come to a decision, Sheba."

"Miz Dorcas?"

"We shall stay on the ship. We shall not be leaving at Nassau after all."

Bathsheba drew a long, thankful breath.

"Den praise de Lord, Miz Dorcas! Praise de Lord you use yo' head."

"You see," Dorcas said, with a wry smile, "it does happen." Briefly she touched Bathsheba on the shoulder before going to take her place close to her husband.

Four

Tamarind Villa,
Grand Cay,
Turks Islands.
Wednesday, February 13th, 1811.

My dearest Fanny,

By the time this reaches you, I hope that you will long have had your mind set at rest by the letter I sent from Nassau and the brief line I wrote telling of our safe arrival here in the Turks Islands. I am happy to say my health continues good, with no return of the nausea which troubled me so much before I left home.

My decision to continue to Grand Cay was prompted by many considerations, not least the kindness of Captain Hardiman, whose good nature you were able to appreciate far quicker than me and did not underestimate in the least particular.

Since arriving here I have taken up my pen to write to you a hundred times, but have been prevented from proceeding both by the press of events and the difficulty of knowing where to begin my account of this curious island. It is flat and neither so green nor so lush as Bermuda, yet I have to admit that as we approached it I was aware that it possessed a certain charm I did not expect, being fringed with white sand and lapped by a sea the clarity of which beggars description. The vegetation is mainly thorny scrub and cactus. Did you know that the name of this group of islands comes from a variety of cactus known, so I am reliably informed, as *Cactus coronatus*, the crown of which bears a vague resemblance to a Turk's cap? The weather since our arrival has been pleasantly warm without excessive heat, and the air is far less humid than in Bermuda.

The famous salt ponds are set close to the small huddle of buildings that calls itself a town and are at the moment filled with shallow water. The salt comes later when the sun has caused the water to evaporate. The area which they occupy is flat, ugly and desolate. Beyond, the land rises a little towards the north and the east, but close to the ponds there is no redeeming natural feature to please the eye. It is here that the slave barracks have been built and there are also many mean shacks belonging to other workmen, black and white, the blacks being cast-off slaves whose masters cannot afford to keep them.

Even now I find it difficult to write of our arrival, for all was confusion with a crowd of people thronging the jetty, both seamen and idle on-lookers. There was, I think, much curiosity about my own person, and much chaffing of Zachariah who was jokingly castigated as a wily, secretive dog for not making his plans for matrimony plain before quitting the island in December. I learned rapidly that the men of Grand Cay can claim little delicacy in their speech; much was said which I deemed it politic not to hear. Most are living here without wives or families and therefore are wanting the beneficial and civilising influence that a good woman may give.

My main impression, though, was one of rough good humour and little refinement, apart, that is, from the few ladies – in the main the wives of salt proprietors and government officials – who have called to bid me welcome and, I suspect, to cast a critical eye upon me. I will tell you of them in a later letter, for to be truthful, my head was in such a spin that only two remain clearly in my mind: the first, a Mrs. Cecily Fairweather, the wife of the Provost Marshal and the mother of a little girl who is a close friend of Zachariah's daughter Emma; and the second, a Mrs. Grimshaw, a somewhat formidable lady of uncertain years with flaring nostrils and a bosom like a pouter pigeon who is the wife of the major salt proprietor on the island. Zachariah informs me that she is well named, since she is both 'grim' and 'sure'! Certainly it is clear from her grand manner that she considers herself to be the leader of society, which can only cause me to reflect on the adage that in the country of the blind, the one-eyed man is king!

Monday of this week was a truly remarkable day, and provided the reason why Zachariah could not linger in Bermuda. For him and for others like him it is the most important day of the year, namely the annual subdivision and allocation of shares in the salt ponds. The quaint method in which this is carried out quite defies belief! Every resident of the island, be he man, woman or child, slave or free man, has to present himself or herself to be registered, and all are given a share, the only qualification being their presence on the island on that particular day! Children are measured to establish the size of their share, as they are awarded them in proportion to their height.

The shares of the slaves naturally revert to their owners, but as well as slaves there are present here a number of poor white men who own no slaves to work the salt and who therefore sell their allocation to the wealthier proprietors. The day following the allocation, therefore, there was a great to-do as bidding went on for the unwanted portions. I am now in a position to inform you that one share will yield on average three hundred bushels of salt annually, but that all is dependent on the weather, a dry year producing up to half a dozen rakings during the season, and a wet year perhaps not one. I sincerely hope and confidently expect that you are favourably impressed with my grasp of the salt industry after little more than a week on these shores!

Zachariah seems pleased with the number of shares he has been able to procure, but less pleased with the man he engaged to take care of his interests while in Bermuda. There was no actual raking carried out during the winter months, of course, but the slaves were engaged in building a water tank and other public works and it seems there was considerable unrest among them, a fact which Zachariah attributes to the less than wise handling of Mr. Trotman. I confess my first impression of the man is to mislike him thoroughly, but I strive to be as charitable as my husband who attributes his mistakes to his youth and nothing more. One thing I have learned about Zachariah is that he is never harsh in his judgements and treats others always as he would wish to be treated himself.

The house is a good one, built very much on Bermuda lines with three dormer windows and an upstairs balcony. The furnishings are plain and (pray do not mention this in your reply to me) to my mind chosen without taste. I have plans to acquire different when the time is ripe, but like other things on this island, good timber and carpenters are in short supply. However, we have comfortable rocking chairs on the shaded porch where we sit during the day and where a purple bougainvillaea climbs the railings to remind me of home. We are fortunate in that we have a tamarind tree on the north side of the house and several red cordias on the south side, while to the front of us there is an area of waste, sandy ground ending in a clump of casuarina trees and the whitest beach it is possible to imagine. From where I now sit I can see an ocean of the clearest turquoise shading to a blue as deep as sapphires where the reef ends, much as we are accustomed to in Bermuda.

Davey, Zachariah's son, is a dear little boy and I feel sure I shall come to love him as my own. Already he has lost his shyness towards me, but alas, it is a different story with Emma who appears to regard me with hostility and suspicion. It is, I suppose, understandable, for she loves her father dearly and is resentful of my presence. For the moment I am attempting to be calm and friendly, hoping that time will bring a happier understanding between us. I am thankful she is old enough to attend a small morning class where a handful of children gather to be taught the essentials by a Mrs. Palmer, wife of Mr. Grimshaw's overseer. The slave Nola who cares for the children is not, perhaps, the girl I would have chosen myself for she suffers from any number of vague ailments, particularly when there is work to be done, and is constantly calling for potions for this and draughts for that. Bathsheba has no time for her, but I am persuaded that her heart is good and the children undoubtedly love her – perhaps partly because she finds it hard to say 'no' to them!

Speaking of Nola reminds me to ask if you could procure for me some information regarding the treatment of common ailments? There is no doctor here (and alas, so much sickness, particularly of the stomach, and so many quite heart-rending small graves). I believe that there is a bookshop in Hamilton that may well be able to provide me with the information I need, and also, perhaps, a pamphlet on the making of a garden. Apart from the bougainvillaea, this house is surrounded by a sandy waste which I have visions of making blossom as the rose. Mrs. Grimshaw is very proud of her hibiscus and frangipani and Bermuda lilies, and I am resolved that whatever she has accomplished, then I may do the same. Indeed, I am almost persuaded to say that I will do better, or die in the attempt!

My dearest Fanny, I must bring this long epistle to a close, for time presses and the packet will be leaving shortly, before which time I must pen a short letter to Grandmama. I think of you constantly and miss you sorely, yet am comforted in the knowledge that nothing now stands in the way of your happy future with Silas. I pray nightly for your well-being, and beg that you will write to me soon. As ever I send my fondest love.

Your affectionate sister,
Dorcas

Grand Cay,
Turks Islands.
Wednesday, February 13th, 1811.

My dear Grandmama,

I pray that you will forgive a short and hasty note, as the packet is about to leave. I know that Fanny will share with you all the intelligence contained in a letter to her that has taken me all morning to write.

I did, however, wish to say that, together with my dear sister, you are constantly in my thoughts and prayers, the most fervent prayer of all being for forgiveness for the hurt and disappointment which I have caused you and my father. It was a poor way to repay all the love, care and kindness which you have ever shown towards me, and I beg that you will find it in your heart to pardon me and that eventually even my father will think more kindly of his daughter.

As some sort of atonement, I am determined to do my best to be a good wife to Captain Hardiman and mother to his children, and to this end I should be more than grateful if you would be good enough to furnish me with some of your receipts for the preparation of fish, both fresh and dried, which appears to form the major portion of our diet here. Pumpkins, sweet potatoes, and some Indian corn are grown on the island, though in small quantities, but guinea corn is in better supply so that at least the slaves may have their grits. There are several small stores, but they are poorly stocked and their supplies are spasmodic and not to be relied upon.

My dearest hope, dear Grandmama, is that you continue to enjoy good health and that not too many years will pass before we can meet again, face to face. Until then, I hope that you will not think too unkindly of,

Your affectionate granddaughter
Dorcas

With these two letters finished, Dorcas sat for some time staring blankly at the dazzling ocean. Should she write some sort of apology to her father, also?

Reluctantly she dipped her quill once more into the inkwell but, after sitting for some moments with it poised over a fresh piece of paper, she compressed her lips tightly and threw it down.

No, she thought. Perhaps one day, but not yet. After all, what kindness or love had he ever shown her? It had been sheer chance that caused him to choose Zachariah as her husband, and not for his kindness or goodness or humour, merely because he was leaving Bermuda hurriedly and was willing to take her off his hands.

"Miz Hardiman, Master done send me for de letters."

The voice from the rough street beyond the porch made her sigh with relief. Well, that decided it. It was too late.

She sealed the two letters with a wafer and handed them to the tall, broad negro who stood at the foot of the steps.

"You're Joe, aren't you?" she asked.

He grinned and touched a hand to his wide straw hat.

"Dat right, ma'am."

"Captain Hardiman tells me that you and he sailed together, long before you both came to Grand Cay."

"Dat right, ma'am," he said again. "I right glad you come, Miz Hardiman. Master, he happy now."

Was *she* happy? Dorcas considered the question for a moment as idly she stood on the porch, leaning against the post and watching a tiny humming bird hovering by the red cordia blossoms. Could this strange, suspended feeling of calm be happiness? Perhaps it could. It was hard to tell.

"I wish I understood about salt," Dorcas said.

There was a low rumble of laughter from Zachariah. She could not see his face for the night was dark and they were sitting on the front porch with only a dim, diffuse light coming from the lamp in the room behind them.

The children had long since gone to bed, and Dorcas was thankful for it. This had been one of Emma's difficult days; a day when it had been impossible to please her – a day when it would have given her stepmother the utmost satisfaction to put her across her knee and spank her soundly.

Now the slaves had gone to their quarters, so that even they were quiet, and all was still, nothing to be heard but the whirring of the cicadas and the splash of the waves on the shelving beach on the other side of the street.

"There is little to understand," Zachariah said lazily. "It is a natural process."

"Then why, if it is so natural, do not more islands engage in it?"

"Not all have such ideal conditions. Heat, low rainfall, even temperature, the wind that aids evaporation – added, of course, to the fact that the island is low and level and lends itself to the construction of salt ponds . . ."

Dorcas listened with only half an ear to the deep, comforting voice of her husband. Contentment, rather than happiness, she thought dreamily, continuing the train of thought that had begun earlier in the day and had been forgotten during the press of small affairs that had occupied her ever since. Not that she considered Emma a small affair! What was to be done about her? That passive hostility, that implacable, sulky non-co-operation! At least, she thought with rueful amusement, such matters prevented her from thinking too much about herself. Even the thought of Kit had lost its power to hurt her.

But even as she congratulated herself on this point, she felt a small ache, as if she had probed a bad tooth, and knew she deluded herself. The hurt was still there, and always would be; and with it the memory of the ecstasy which prevented her from accepting the present tranquillity as more than second best. Others might think of it as happiness, she mused, but only because they had not known –

Stop it, stop it!

"The sea is brought in by sluice gates at high tide, d'you see, and the pans are filled with brine. Then the sun is left to do its work and the longer it's left, the better for the yield of salt –" Zachariah broke off, adding indulgently: "and you, my lass, are not listening to a word of this! Where are your thoughts? Far away in Bermuda?"

"I'm sorry." Dorcas stretched out a hand in his direction and found that, as if he had divined her intention, his hand was there to meet it.

"I'm very grateful to you, Zack," she said softly. He gave her hand a small shake.

"Come to bed, sweetheart."

He pulled her to her feet and she could sense the heat in him and knew his intention. He stood without moving for a

68

moment, his lips against her hair, both of her hands clasped in his.

"What would I do without you now?" he asked. "You are everything to me, lass. Everything."

He led her then to the bedroom where, shortly after their arrival, he had led her equally gently and with an unexpected skill into a world of love that had fulfilled none of her fearful imaginings. It was a world, she felt, that she could live in quite easily, even though it lacked the heart-stopping excitement she had known with Kit.

Love was not all excitement, she told herself soberly, lying beside Zachariah and listening to the regular breathing that told her he was asleep. Love was not all quickened heart-beats and painful longings, It was also trust, and affection, and friendship . . .

She was growing sleepy, her thoughts losing their shape and substance and melting into nothingness. Soon she, too, was deeply asleep and if in her dreams she seemed to be searching, searching, for some treasure she could not name, in the morning she had no remembrance of it.

Dorcas was filled with curiosity about the rest of the island and begged Zachariah to take her to see it.

"The tracks are rough," he said doubtfully. "In your condition –"

"Oh Zack, I'm as strong as an ox and shall die of frustration if I don't know what lies beyond the bend in the road. Soon the work will begin in the salt ponds, and then you will say you're too busy. We can take the children and make an expedition of it."

"Very well." He laughed at her eagerness and could deny her nothing. "Early on Saturday before the sun is hot I shall take you to the south, where the first settlement was established. We'll harness the old mare and take the coach to Hawkes Nest Salina, then drive to South Creek to eat our picnic. The children will like that."

The whole island measured no more than eleven miles from end to end, with the main settlement somewhere in the middle of it, but the journey to the southernmost area took on the nature of an expedition for the track was every bit as rough as Zachariah had said. On the way they passed two more salinas where they stopped to inspect the work in progress. The time was not yet ripe for the salt ponds to be cleaned, but slaves were busy remaking stone walls which divided the shallow water.

"I've a few holdings over there," he said, pointing with his whip. "Though by far the largest number are in Town Pond."

"That's Joe, isn't it, in charge of the men?"

"Ay, it is."

"You think highly of him."

"I'd trust him with my life. All right, Emma, we'll be on our way directly!" He shook the reins and they set off southwards again, stopping at last on a small hillock which gave them an excellent view, both of the salina which lay towards the tip of the island and the area from where they had come.

Apparently floating on a sea which today was lightly touched with flecks of white foam were a number of smaller cays. Zachariah named them for her.

"That's Salt Cay," he said, pointing to the south-west. "The very first settlement of all was made there. Then there's Round Cay and Long Cay – and that small one close at hand is a place I must take you to one of these days. There's not a soul lives upon it and I find it magical."

"Take me, too!" Davey, busy about his own affairs was not too busy to hear this, and rushed at his father, clasping his arms about his legs and butting him in the stomach with his head. "Take me, too!"

"They don't want *you*!" Emma's small, disdainful voice cut through the laughter and Dorcas could not suppress the twinge of irritation she felt, even though she hastened to contradict the child who seemed determined to cast her in the role of wicked stepmother.

"Such nonsense, Emma, of course we do," she said. "We wouldn't dream of going without the pair of you."

Emma's expression made it clear that whatever protestations Dorcas might make, *she* knew better.

From their vantage point on the hillock they could see a jetty where a few boats were tied, and between there and the salina, a cluster of simple, palmetto thatched huts. Here, too, there were slaves working on the upkeep of the pond, and for a moment Dorcas stood and looked down on them in silence.

"They look a little like a disturbed ant-hill," she said.

"Ants in straw hats!"

"Zack, do you – do you wonder, sometimes –"

"About what, sweetheart?"

"About the morality of it. I was reading the newspapers that came on the latest packet, and it seems the Abolitionists are making a stir in the English Parliament. They are not content, apparently, with stopping the slave trade throughout the Empire. They want to make it illegal to own or sell slaves too."

Zachariah was silent for a moment, his eyes on the men below. The children had wandered off a short distance and were engrossed in trying to catch the butterflies that hovered over the tufty grass.

"In my view," he said at last, "it was a pity the system was ever introduced. I saw slavers a-plenty when I was at sea and I was sickened by them, I can tell you. It was a dirty business and I would have naught to do with it. But now that they are here – well, what can a man do but look after them the best way he can? I treat my slaves fairly, I guarantee you that, and I'll eat my hat if they're discontented. Mark you –" He turned to her, his finger raised. "It is not so everywhere. In the sugar islands where there are large numbers of slaves in the charge of an overseer, and he dependent on getting the last ounce of work out of them –" He drew in his breath with a hiss and shook his head sadly. "Then things can go badly for them. All I know is that without slaves I'd not make a success of my business, and then where would they be?"

"Why are you and Miss Dorcas always talking secrets?"

Emma had come up unnoticed, and taken her father's arm. She had consistently resisted his attempt to make her call Dorcas 'mama', though Davey was happy enough to comply. It was something that annoyed Zachariah, though Dorcas begged him to leave the matter alone, assuring him that it was something that should not be forced. Still, he looked down at his daughter now with something less than his usual warmth.

"We are not talking secrets, sweetheart. We were talking about the slaves."

"I don't like Bathsheba. I wish we didn't have to have her in the house. I think she's insolent. It was much nicer when we only had Nola."

"And we all know why you think that, don't we? Bathsheba tries to keep you in some sort of order."

"Perhaps we should move on to South Creek," Dorcas said,

determined that the day should proceed without upset.

The newspaper reports she had read would not leave her mind, however, and as they drove through the thorny scrub land towards the creek she returned to the subject.

"I've never thought of slavery as other than in the natural order of things," she said. "I've lived with it, from birth. It never occurred to me to think of it as evil, yet the Abolitionists despise us for it."

"Bermuda has quite as many slaves as it can comfortably support, so none have been imported for years. There are no large plantations there, no gangs of slaves in irons. You've not seen the worst side of it."

"I believe you. We have, after all, no slave markets as in Nassau."

That was the beginning of her sensitivity on the subject, Dorcas recognised. They had been walking along Bay Street in Nassau and had chanced to pass Vendue House just as a batch of slaves was about to be sold, placards around their necks stating the price demanded. One girl, priced at two hundred and fifty dollars, had turned and looked right into her eyes as Dorcas slowed her steps to see what was going on, and she had been appalled at the expression of derision and hate on her face. In spite of all the other impressions that had assailed her senses, both then and after, the memory of that girl was something that haunted her.

"Here's the creek," Emma said. "Come and walk with us a little, Papa."

There were mangroves around the shore, and in the soupy green water schools of fish darted among the prop roots. It was very hot and still; claustrophobic, Dorcas felt, suddenly not liking it at all. There was something about the smell of the place that seemed to suggest death and decay.

"It's a useful place, with all the mangroves to shelter it. People put their boats here in time of hurricane," Zachariah said.

"No doubt." Still Dorcas shuddered. "Call it a mere fancy, Zack, but somehow I dislike this place. Davey, come away from that water. Heaven alone knows what you may find there."

"A horned monster with dripping fangs!" Zachariah stuck his fingers up straight beside his ears, gave a blood-curdling roar, and chased his children to the accompaniment of delighted shrieks.

"*We* like it here," Emma said in a manner that defied Dorcas to disagree with her.

"Then I am highly delighted that we came," Dorcas replied evenly. "I was most anxious to see all the island has to offer."

It was some days later that she and Zachariah went without the children to the most northern tip of the island. Emma was having tea with her bosom friend Sophie Fairweather, and Davey had been left uncomplainingly to Nola's care.

"Oh, this is better," Dorcas said softly, gazing with delight at the crumbling limestone cliffs, falling to rocky beaches, and the carpet of yellow flowers beneath her feet.

There was the ever-present sea-grape and prickly pear, too, and beyond them a wide vista of the sea, the waves in their ranks carrying plumes of spray and breaking on hidden coral heads.

"I can breathe here," she said gratefully. "Let us come here often, Zack."

When he made no response she turned to look at him and found him looking out to sea with the eyes of a prophet, his head thrown back, hands clenched by his sides.

"Zack?" She spoke his name softly.

When he spoke, his voice was charged with emotion.

"If I take the wings of the morning and remain in the uttermost parts of the sea; even there also shall Thy hand lead me." He turned to her and grasped her hands in his. "Don't you feel it, lass, that this is where we're meant to be?" He smote his chest. "I feel it here, I have from the beginning." He turned again to the sea and Dorcas, seeing that he struggled against tears, felt a great tenderness for him.

On the way back to town, Zachariah stopped the buggy and pointed his whip westwards.

"See the big inland lake? That's North Creek. Another time I shall take you there, for it's quite different from South Creek which you disliked so."

A large grove of palm trees lay between the creek and the shore.

"Is it some sort of plantation?" Dorcas asked.

"Ay – there's a house beyond the trees, hidden from us. It's called Treasure Bluff and it belongs to a most unusual lady; one you'll enjoy meeting, I fancy, for she will talk to you about slavery to your heart's content. She's been away in the

Carolinas for some time, but yesterday I heard she was back so no doubt you'll be seeing her before too long."

"What is she called?" Dorcas asked.

"Mrs. Bettany," he replied.

Her name [Dorcas wrote to Fanny] is Mrs. Bettany, and I would give much to hear your opinion of her and her views, which are quite extraordinary! She is an American lady in her middle age, a widow, soberly dressed and undeniably plain but with a most attractive personality.

She came here with her husband some ten years ago since he was a Loyalist and would not remain in South Carolina under a Republican government. Many such Loyalists came to the Caicos Islands, but Mr. and Mrs. Bettany chose Grand Cay, for what reason I do not know.

Sad to relate, Mr. Bettany died scarcely more than a year after they settled here. You can imagine how strong-minded she is when I tell you that she stayed on and continued to run the estate her husband had founded, much to the amazement of all. Even more amazing than her determination to carry on in the face of all the difficulties which could beset a solitary woman was the fact that she immediately freed all her slaves, most of whom continued to work for her as indentured servants! If you can imagine the furore that this would cause in Bermuda, then increase it at least ten-fold and you have some idea of how it was received here.

Though these events occurred the better part of nine years since, it is still a matter for comment on the island, and much is made of it though her sweetness of nature is such that there are many who accept her eccentricities even though they deplore them. She has indeed been kindness itself to me and has done much to make me feel at home in this strange place where, apart from Cecily Fairweather whom I have mentioned on previous occasions, I have not yet met a congenial soul. I continue to miss you, my dear sister, more sorely than I can say . . .

Five

With the best will in the world, she found it impossible to put the past behind her completely. There were close friends and relations in Bermuda. What must they have thought at her sudden departure, without a word of farewell? Surely there must be hurt feelings, whispered speculation. What explanation had her family given?

She was not to worry, Fanny wrote. There was some surprise, certainly, that she had married Captain Hardiman so hastily, but in islands where seafaring dominated all, comings and goings were accepted with equanimity – and all understood, she said, the need for a hasty return to the Turks Islands in time for the annual allocation. There was even, she added, a certain amount of approbation for a family such as the Foleys who would deny themselves the pomp of a large wedding for their daughter in consideration of the feelings of a man who so recently buried his mother. (That there were others who said that Josiah Foley was mean enough to deny a crust of bread to a starving beggar she did not bother to report.)

Homesickness and an aching sense of loss continued to wait for Dorcas around every corner, like twin beasts waiting to leap upon her in unguarded moments. The first caused her to write copiously to Fanny, and the second was the cause of shame. Only a fool, she told herself, and an ungrateful fool at that, could still ache with longing for a man who had demonstrated his indifference so clearly.

Her new life was not, after all, unpleasant. She learned to deal with the practical problems of food shortages and to use the available water as if it were molten gold. She was luckier than many, for the larger houses had their own tanks to store rainwater. Poor people were forced to carry the precious liquid from a central tank, for though there were wells to the north and south, the water in them was brackish and fit only for animals.

She soon realised that she had to go quickly to the market

whenever the flag was raised to indicate that fresh meat was available, learned to keep an eye out for incoming sloops from Hispaniola which brought the occasional consignment of fresh fruit and vegetables. She also learned, in the way of small communities, to appreciate the qualities of those who, in Bermuda, would barely have crossed her path. People like Gilligan, for example, the Irishman who kept the store below Zachariah's office. She knew full well that at home she would have dismissed him as a rum-soaked rogue, unworthy of her attention, but now she appreciated the intelligence and humour that concealed itself behind a whiskery and none-too-clean exterior, passing many an enjoyable moment in conversation with him. He had a dry turn of wit coupled with an irreverent attitude to life and those who might consider themselves his betters that struck an answering spark in her.

"Now, isn't it a funny thing how the sight of all that grandeur affects me memory?" he said to her once, just after Mrs. Grimshaw had surged from the store on being told he had no pickling spices to offer her. "Wasn't I after forgettin' that somewheres down at the back I've a small stock left?"

"You're a very wicked man." Dorcas spoke with mock severity.

"Sure, the blessed saints will forgive me, so they will, for didn't herself buy up the whole of me last shipment, with never a grain left over for lesser mortals? Will you be wanting any, Mrs. Hardiman, ma'am? Best take an ounce or two while I have it, for it'd not surprise me if herself doesn't sniff it out like a bloodhound and come back to tear the hide off me."

Without waiting for agreement, he twisted paper into a cone and tipped a measure of spices into it. "Weaker sex!" he snorted derisively. "Sure, that's a misnomer if ever I heard one. If this is a lie, Mrs. Hardiman, may I be struck down where I stand; I am telling you, I've felt safer ever since My Lady Grimshaw came to live on the island, for hasn't she a face that would stop a hurricane in its tracks?"

By April the more slothful atmosphere of the winter months had given way to purposeful activity, for this was the month when the ponds were drained and cleaned preparatory to the opening of the sluice gates which allowed the sea water to flow into the main ponds. The weather was warm but dry, with a good breeze, and Dorcas noted cautiously and with gratitude that the twin beasts seemed to have lessened their attacks on her. Physically she felt well, and the days were pleasantly filled by domestic duties and by mornings spent with her friend Cecily Fairweather, when together they sat and sewed.

Even Emma seemed more amenable these days, apparently brightening with pleasure as Dorcas praised the stitching on her sampler. Dorcas discovered a piece of bright yellow silk in her workbox and helped Emma to cut out a dress for her doll, directing her stitches and offering lavish praise when the girl's efforts produced a really creditable piece of work.

"I do believe I have found the answer," Dorcas said to Cecily. "If I can find activities which we can undertake together, perhaps she will come to realise that I wish her nothing but good."

"Oh, how I hope so!" Cecily was blonde and blue-eyed, very earnest in her manner. "Emma is of an intense and passionate nature, I fear – born to suffer! I have noticed how jealous she can be in her attachment to Sophie, and certainly that is at the root of her antagonism towards you. I hope the arrival of a baby will not present a further set-back."

"I shall have to make sure it does not," Dorcas said vigorously.

Each afternoon she rested, but often, when the worst of the heat was gone from the afternoon, she would walk with the children on the beach, joining with Emma in her search for unusual shells; or on other days they would all go towards the salinas or Zachariah's office, to meet him on his homeward journey. The sight of his short and bulky frame with its rolling seaman's gait caused the children to cry out and run towards him, to be picked up and hugged boisterously and, in Davey's case, to be set on his father's shoulders for a ride home.

It was towards the end of April that they went to meet him and saw, when he came into sight, that he was not alone but was accompanied by Willis Trotman, his overseer.

"A fine family, Captain Hardiman," Trotman said, as the children gave Zachariah the usual greeting.

The words were innocent enough. Why, then, Dorcas wondered, did she suspect that a sneer lay behind the polite exterior?

Perhaps she was being unfair. She had never taken to Trotman – never felt at ease with him, since the very beginning.

There were those who thought him a fine-looking young man. Certainly he was tall and broad, but Dorcas could see nothing to admire in his fleshy face and thick lips with their exaggerated, almost womanish, Cupid's bow. His hair was blond, the wiry curls cropped very short, but rather than any physical feature, it was something far more intangible that repelled her. There was a feeling of violence about him – a streak of cruelty only thinly disguised, a look in his hard little eyes that seemed to say that he would be pleasant and polite only as long as it suited him.

Yet Zachariah thought well of him, at least as far as his business acumen was concerned. With figures he was a genius; with men, he had little talent at all, and in consequence Zachariah was thinking of effecting some kind of reorganisation in the business.

"The children always look forward to their father's homecoming," Dorcas said.

"Sweetheart, our meal tonight can be made to stretch to one more, can't it?" Zachariah asked. "There are matters I wish to discuss with Willis."

"Of course." Dorcas's smile, the more brilliant because of a vague feeling of guilt, gave no hint at the way her heart had sunk at the thought of having Willis Trotman for the evening.

Expansively and with no regard for convention or the interested gaze of passers-by, Zachariah put an arm around Dorcas's shoulder and pulled her to him.

"Isn't she the best wife a man ever had, Willis? What have I done to deserve her?"

His voice which could be soft and caressing or could soar to the stars, seemed to fill the street. Laughing, Dorcas pulled away from him.

"Oh hush, Zack! You embarrass me."

"Nonsense! The world should hear of you. When are you going to find a wife, Willis? You should do so before too long. I little knew the meaning of joy until Dorcas came into my life."

"Ah, but where should I find such a treasure as Mrs. Hardiman?"

Trotman bowed towards her, polite to the point of subservience, but Dorcas knew, suddenly and without any doubt, that her instincts had not misled her. He despises us both, she thought; Zachariah and myself alike.

"Come children," she said, turning to head for home. She held out one hand to Emma and the other to Davey, but although Davey came to her side readily enough, Emma ignored the proffered hand and walked on a few paces ahead, her small face which was usually transformed by the sight of her father, closed and sullen.

Oh, *wretched* Trotman! Dorcas thought, knowing herself to be unfair, for certainly the invitation had been given on Zachariah's initiative. Still, it was aggravating, for his presence was undoubtedly a blight on this normally pleasant hour of the day.

She quickened her pace and caught up with Emma.

"I don't suppose he will stay too long," she said quietly.

"I'm sure he may stay as long as he likes," Emma replied primly.

The talk over supper was impersonal and general, and Dorcas rightly guessed that Zachariah was waiting for her to remove herself and the children before broaching whatever matter he wanted to discuss with Trotman.

Diplomatically she kept out of the way for some time, but hearing the sound of the men moving out to the porch, she decided that the business of the evening must be over and Trotman about to leave, and that she should put in an appearance to bid him a polite goodbye.

Instead she found the two men ensconced outside with the rum bottle on the table between them, a glass at each elbow.

"Come, my dear," Zachariah said, getting to his feet as she hovered uncertainly in the doorway. "Come and join us. Would you care for a tot yourself — or a glass of brandy, perhaps?"

"No, I think not, thank you. You have finished your business, then?"

She took the rocking chair beside Zachariah, setting it gently in motion.

"Oh, it was hardly business." Zachariah sat down again and took a sip of his rum. "More of a chat." He reached out and shook Trotman by the shoulder. "A fatherly chat."

"Oh?"

"Captain Hardiman has been giving me the benefit of his advice on the treatment of slaves," said Trotman.

Didn't Zachariah hear the sneer in his voice, Dorcas wondered?

"You were employed on a sugar plantation in Jamaica before coming here, I believe?" she said. "No doubt there are differences."

"Your husband thinks I am too hard on them." He drawled the words lazily, amusement in his voice. In the dim light

Dorcas could not see his face clearly, but she formed the strong impression that the rum bottle had taken a considerable amount of punishment.

"And are you?" she asked crisply.

"I am a disciplinarian." The way he slurred the word confirmed her opinion. "Slaves need disc'pline, in my view. What's the matter if they're in Jamaica or the Turks Islands? But naturally I defer to Captain Hardiman."

"Discipline is one thing," Zachariah said, "and I myself am in favour of it; but harshness is something I cannot tolerate. Physical punishment must not be used on my slaves without my knowledge or approval or presence."

He reached for the rum bottle and poured another measure into Trotman's glass. "Have no fear, lad. I've said all I'm going to say on the matter and we'll put it behind us. You're young yet and will learn from your mistakes, I make no doubt. Believe me, Dorcas –" He reached out to hold Trotman's shoulder again. "This young man has a grasp of figures better than I've known. He'll have my books in apple-pie order in no time."

"I'm glad to hear it."

Dorcas's voice was politely neutral, but when Trotman was gone she questioned him anxiously.

"What did that wretched man do, Zack? What form did his harshness take this time?"

Zachariah sighed.

"In a way the blame was equally mine," he said. "It was an old man, none too strong. I'd put him on light duties, but forgot to mention it and Trotman refused to take the fellow's word. He should have sought me out to check the truth of the matter, but he's a quick-tempered man. He acted in haste, he said."

"Zack, he's hard and arrogant and cares not a jot for your principles! How much rope do you intend to give him?"

Zachariah sighed again, plainly troubled.

"On this occasion, I have to accept some of the responsibility. I had much on my mind today, it's true, but it was wrong of me to be unmindful of old Tom. I'm troubled at my part of it."

"While Trotman, I am certain, has dismissed the whole matter as trivial. I neither like nor trust him, Zack."

"He's better with account books than with men, it's true. He'll be spending more time in the office from now on."

"Well, keep a close watch on him."

Zachariah gave a rumble of laughter and reached for her hand. How he loves to touch, Dorcas thought. No matter whom he converses with – Trotman, the children, anyone – always he seemed to rely on touch as well as words to convey a message.

"I'm not so stupid as I look, sweetheart," he said. "Never underestimate your poor old husband."

After a few moments' silence she began to laugh as she thought over the past evening.

"A fine way to discipline an employee, bringing him home and filling him with rum. I'm sure he must be shaking in his shoes."

"He'll learn," Zachariah said again.

They sat in the companionable half-light for a little longer, turning over the small change of their day, until Dorcas, pleading tiredness, preceded him to bed. Bathsheba was waiting for her, having turned down the sheet and laid out the lawn nightdress.

"There's a good breeze tonight, Sheba. I shall sleep well."

"Sure hope so, Miz Dorcas."

Bathsheba unbuttoned her dress and helped her now unwieldy body into the nightdress, and yawning, Dorcas sat before the mirror for her hair to receive its nightly brushing. The rhythmic strokes were soothing and for a while she gave herself up to a sensual enjoyment of them. Then a thought struck her.

"Sheba," she said, "what do you think of Mr. Trotman?" She could feel the girl shift awkwardly in reply, as if the question embarrassed her.

"I don't rightly know, Miz Dorcas," she said after a long silence. "I only know what folk tell me."

"And what do folk tell you?"

"He a hard man, dey say. Joe don' tol' me –" She broke off as if suddenly aware that she might be about to say too much. Dorcas laughed at her.

"I know what Joe tells you," she said. "Joe tells you you one good-looking girl, doesn't he? You watch out, Miss Bathsheba! Now it's my turn to give the good advice!"

Bathsheba giggled and ducked her head.

"I don't need no good advice, Miz Dorcas. I know a good man when I see one."

"And Joe is a good man, Sheba." Dorcas was serious now.

"Master thinks a lot of him." She yawned mightily. "Oh, I'm too tired for more brushing tonight, and I'm sure you must be, too. You go off to your bed and get some well-earned rest. Sweet dreams!" she called teasingly, as Bathsheba said goodnight and made for the door.

Joe and Sheba, she thought, as, still smiling, she moved towards the bed. What a happy thing that would be! She could wish for no one better for Sheba than Joe, and there was no doubt what *his* feelings on the subject were. Scarcely a day passed without his calling at the house on some pretext or other and Dorcas had given up being surprised at finding him in the kitchen.

She pulled down the sheet to get into bed, but as she did so, a flash of yellow caught her eye; something thrust down into the bed. She peered more closely, puzzled. What on earth could it be? It looked like yellow silk – like the yellow silk that had been used for Emma's doll's dress. How odd and incomprehensible that the scraps that were left over from it should somehow have transferred themselves to her bed, especially when she knew for certain that Bathsheba made it up thoroughly every day.

She reached into the bed and brought out the material; not one piece but several, she found on inspection, cut into small segments. For a moment she looked at it without comprehension, then suddenly she gasped. These were no left-over scraps of material, but the doll's dress itself, cut into pieces, totally ruined.

Who on earth could have done it, and why? And how would she break the news to Emma, after all the painstaking work that had gone into it? Full of dismay, Dorcas looked down at the scraps of silk and at the tiny stitches still holding parts of the material together, evidence of so much effort and determination.

"Who?" she said aloud. "Who?"

Suddenly she knew, and could not understand how she had not known from the beginning. She went to the bureau and thrust the yellow silk into a drawer out of sight, not wanting Zachariah to see this, the latest evidence of her failure with his daughter. For what else was this but failure?

There was no one but Emma who could have done this thing; no one but Emma who could know how much this would disappoint her.

*　　*　　*

"You look pale, my dear." Marcia Bettany studied Dorcas thoughtfully, a small line between her brows. Her strong, plain face with its beaky nose and square jaw looked sympathetic, but there was a briskness in the manner in which she handed Dorcas a glass of fruit juice. "Drink this, child. I've instructed your good Bathsheba to squeeze the juices of any citrus fruit she can lay her hands on and make sure that you take it regularly. Do you have plenty of exercise?"

"Zachariah and I walk along the shore when the sun goes down. I've given up my daily walk with the children now that it is so hot —"

"And that child is like a furnace inside of you! I know how it is, my dear; mine were born in Charleston in July. The only consolation I can offer is that the end comes eventually and with each day that passes the time grows shorter."

Dorcas nodded and tried to smile, but it was a smile that trembled dangerously on the brink of tears. It was the heat, she told herself; just the heat, nothing more. There was no other reason why her spirits should be so low — no sensible reason, at any rate. Surely the sick feeling of dread she experienced whenever she contemplated the actual birth was not something that any normal woman would feel? It was, after all, a natural process; the true fulfilment that every woman longed for.

She was conscious of the rustle of Marcia's dress as she crossed the porch and came to sit beside her, taking her hand.

"What is it, Dorcas? Tell me your fears."

"Oh, they are such foolish ones! I'm ashamed of myself."

"Do you imagine you are alone? That no one else has ever felt as you do?" When Marcia smiled in that way, Dorcas thought, her face was quite transformed and she looked almost beautiful. "Every woman with any imagination at all must be apprehensive, at least the first time, for no matter how many women have gone through it all before, for each of us it is a unique happening."

"It's not just the pain." Dorcas clung to Marcia as if to a lifeline, and the words, now they had begun, came pouring out as if she could not stop them. "It is, after all, very hazardous, especially here; and oh, Marcia, I don't want to die before I have ever lived! Mrs. Grimshaw was here only yesterday, sitting just where you are sitting now, and she told me that mine would be the third baby to be born on the island since this time last year. Oh, I said, how lovely — I had not known there were other babies, not white babies, that is. No more there are, she said. Both the others died — but really there was no need to have the smallest worry, for in one case the mother survived and was told that there was no reason at all why she should not have many other healthy children. She seemed to think that I ought to find that intelligence most cheering —"

"Mrs. Grimshaw is a fool," Marcia said sternly. "Both women she referred to entrusted themselves to ignorant mid-wives who waved herbs over them and made incantations and had no idea of the rudiments of hygiene. Things will be different for you. I shall take care of you myself and will instruct Bathsheba in the right way to look after you and the child. You are young and strong and there is no reason in the world why, with the right care, you should not produce a healthy infant with the minimum of fuss. You must ensure that you eat sensibly and take plenty of rest and sufficient gentle exercise."

"You sound just like a doctor."

Marcia laughed at that and shook her head ruefully.

"Would that I were! My father and my brother are lucky enough to follow that profession, and two of my sons also. I should dearly have liked to do the same, but naturally am debarred because of my sex. Perhaps one day we shall see lady doctors — you may laugh, but I cannot help but think that women might prefer to consult another woman in matters such as childbirth. Anyway, if it ever happens it will be long after I am dead and buried, you can be sure. Meanwhile, I read books and pick up what information I can from my relatives. Any medical knowledge is of value here."

"What an unusual person you are!" Dorcas was intrigued enough to forget her own problems for a while.

"Because I think that women might one day become doctors?"

"That and other things. Your views on emancipation, for example."

The older woman looked down at the hands now folded in her lap with a small smile. She wondered if Dorcas realised how often she returned to the subject of emancipation. It was true that she herself was vitally concerned about the issue, but she made a point of not pressing the matter until her views were specifically sought. Dorcas, it seemed, was fascinated by the idea and liked to flirt with it.

"Isn't it another side of the same coin?" she said after a moment. "I hate bondage of any sort – the idea that any human soul is the chattel of another. Sometimes it seems to me that women are in no better case than the slaves, for both are owned by their husbands. Oh, I'm not speaking of the likes of Zachariah, whom I recognised long ago as a jewel among men! I was disposed to like you at our first meeting, for I knew that only a woman of common sense and discernment could appreciate his qualities, for as you and I both know, at times he goes to great pains to conceal them!"

Dorcas, remembering the circumstances of her marriage, and her own conspicuous lack of common sense, smiled wryly. Regarding Zachariah, however, she could only agree.

"Indeed he does," she said. "He likes nothing better than to play the fool."

"He is far from that. We have had many conversations in the past, Zachariah and I, and I know him to have an acute intelligence, as well as the soul of a musician. He loves beauty – which, partly, is why he loves you!"

"If ever I was beautiful," Dorcas said, "which I dispute, then certainly I am not so now! I feel like a tub of lard."

"A temporary condition, my dear. All will be well soon. How long do you have to wait now? About the end of August, I believe you said?"

Dorcas smiled and nodded. Never confide, she reminded herself. That had been Zachariah's advice and she had held to it; she had, in fact, never been tempted to do so, not even during her long gossipy mornings with Cecily Fairweather, for she knew only too well how in small communities secrets could become common property.

Now, however, she would have given much to be able to unburden herself. Still she kept her silence. No one knows the date of our marriage, Zachariah had said to her. Everyone knows that babies sometimes come before their time. The matter is of no concern to anyone but us. Forget it, sweetheart, and be happy.

"Yes," she said. "The end of August, as far as I can calculate."

"Think how wonderful it will be when the child is in your arms," Marcia said.

"And when my waist is back to its normal size," Dorcas

agreed. "By the time Fanny comes, I hope I shall be myself again."

"Your sister is coming here?"

"On her wedding trip. Did I not tell you? Oh, it is quite the best news I have had for months!"

"Then I'll permit no more long faces from you, madam! You have a great deal to look forward to – and no need to worry, believe me." Marcia stood and smoothed her skirts. "Bathsheba and I will take care of you, you may be certain. Now, heat or no heat I must go up to the market to buy meat, for I saw on the way down that they were preparing to hoist the market flag. Take care of yourself, and keep up your spirits. At least Zachariah should be pleased with life! I gather the salt harvest is excellent."

"So he tells me. How different and strange the salinas look now that they are all white, instead of that faintly pinkish colour. Isn't it odd that before evaporation they should be coloured, yet afterwards the crystals are quite white? Zachariah tells me the organisms in the water make it so and laughs at me for seeming to find it mysterious and wonderful. The landscape now reminds me of pictures I've seen of Arctic wastes, yet the sun pours down and the pyramids grow ever higher down by the jetty."

"Well, our landscape at Treasure Bluff may not be mysterious, but to me it's wonderful and after the baby is born you must come and enjoy it. It's a different, cooler world up there."

The prospect cheered Dorcas considerably, and it was with a lighter step that she went into the inner room to sit at her desk and take up her pen once more to write to Fanny.

To me [she wrote] Marcia seems everything that is charming, and when we converse I am aware of doors opening one by one, giving light on matters which, in my ignorance, I had never considered before. Take, for example, the plight of the slaves –

She paused, considered her words, then sighed, and shaking her head she scratched them out vigorously.

Fanny, she knew, would read them without comprehension. She hardly knew, herself, how to convey her thoughts on the subject. She merely knew that little by little an abhorrence to the whole idea of slavery was growing within her.

* * *

From her bed, Dorcas watched Bathsheba as she poured precious water from a jug into a bowl so that her mistress could wash before coming downstairs to greet Zachariah on his return from work.

"Sheba," she said idly, "when are you and Joe going to get married?"

Bathsheba smiled as if to herself, and went on filling the bowl.

"He ax me all de time," she said, with satisfaction.

"Then why don't you say yes?"

Bathsheba stood with her head bent, the empty jug clasped in her hands. Then she made a slight movement of her shoulders.

"I don't rightly know, Miz Dorcas. Times I think it right; times I think Joe want too much for comfort."

Dorcas pushed herself upright against the pillow.

"What things?" she asked curiously. "What does Joe want?"

Again the slight shrug.

"More'n he got. De men on de salt — dey work hard, Miz Dorcas. Hard like you never saw." She set the jug down and turned towards Dorcas, her face grave. "De rakes and de shovels and de carts — dey heavy, back-breaking t'ings, and de men jest toil and toil and toil till dey cin hardly stand. Joe's a big, strong man, but times when de work finish, he weak as a baby. He wants t'ings diff'rent."

"If you agree, why do you say he wants too much?"

Bathsheba's face took on a mulish expression that Dorcas knew well. It was a look that was both stubborn and guarded, giving nothing away. For a moment she fidgeted with a towel.

"It ain't comfortable, to want too much," she said at last.

"Sheba." Dorcas's voice was soft. "Joe won't be satisfied until he's free, will he? Is that what you want, too?"

There was a sudden stillness in the room, almost as if Bathsheba had stopped breathing. The sound of the sea came clearly through the half-shuttered windows.

"Why you ax dat, Miz Dorcas?"

"Because I want to know how you feel."

Dorcas could see the movement of Bathsheba's throat as she swallowed convulsively. The girl licked her lips as if they had suddenly become dry and for a moment she did not speak; then proudly she lifted her head.

"I say you how I feel, Miz Dorcas. I born a slave and I

know I always live a slave. Dat's what I say to Joe. I say you is plain foolish, man; how we get money to buy our freedom? Dere ain't nothin' we cin do to change t'ings. Joe want too much. He want his own boat, he want to raise free children; but me – I tell dis for true, Miz Dorcas." She was trembling, Dorcas saw, and her lower lip was caught between her teeth. "I only want one t'ing. I live a slave, Miz Dorcas. All my life I live a slave. But one t'ing I want. I want to *die* free!"

The words came tumbling from her, and when she had fallen silent, still she trembled and breathed heavily as if in the grip of strong emotion.

"Yes," Dorcas said softly. "Yes, Sheba. I'd feel like that, too."

For a moment neither spoke nor moved, then suddenly Bathsheba turned briskly to busy herself again with the bowl and the towel. "Dis water go cold, you don't come and wash real soon, Miz Dorcas. Which dress you want to wear? Master like de blue one, I hear him say so."

She was giving no more away; and perhaps, for the moment, it was better so, Dorcas thought, as she stood clumsy and defenceless as Bathsheba sponged her sweating, swollen body. Later, perhaps, there was something that could be done and she would find the energy to do it. Just now she felt drained, stunned into insensibility by the heat, incapable of sustained concentration on any matter.

"There seems no air at all," she said, weary in spite of the afternoon's rest.

"Looks like there might be a storm." Bathsheba spoke calmly, all passion gone from her voice.

"Well, it's the season for it," Dorcas agreed.

Clouds hung like a pall over the island. Each evening the sun went down like a circle of dazzling silver, making a path on the steel grey sea. The breeze freshened then, and it was possible for a while to breathe freely again before its brief life was over and the air was still once more. Night after night Dorcas lay sleepless, listening to the whine of the mosquitoes, sweat pouring into her pillow, her hair clinging damply to her head.

Sometimes she rose at daybreak for then, too, the breeze stirred the leaves on the red cordia tree and the sky was often a clear, translucent blue. The sea had a pearly sheen on it and it was possible to be tricked by the fleeting freshness into believing that perhaps this day would be different, this day the breeze would not die; but always the purple clouds massing to the south-east told a different story and always, before many hours had elapsed, the leaden stillness had settled on the island once more.

The children were fractious and quarrelsome and Dorcas's head ached with their incessant noise. She was grateful when Cecily Fairweather arrived and removed Emma, Davey and Nola, lock, stock and barrel.

"You're a good friend, Cecily," Dorcas said in heartfelt tones. "I can never thank you enough."

"No doubt I shall be calling on you to perform the same service one of these days. Small islands tend to make us all dependent on each other."

"Never was spoken a truer word," Dorcas agreed.

Zachariah, who had been negotiating the purchase of a ketch from an American in the Caicos who at last was giving up the attempt to grow cotton and was taking himself back to the Republic from which he had fled with such disgust, looked at the weather with a jaundiced eye. He well knew the havoc that storms could play with his salt production.

"And then how shall I pay for this extravagance?" he asked gloomily.

"It's not an extravagance! You need a boat. Anyway —" She smiled at him. "You'll manage somehow, I'm sure. It's been a good year up to now, hasn't it?"

"Ay, not bad, not bad. You bring me luck, sweetheart, that's the truth of it."

It was wonderful, Dorcas admitted to herself, being without the children, though the admission was tinged with a feeling of guilt. Emma was no easier to handle, and she had lacked the energy lately to make any great effort to improve relations. She would do better, try harder, she promised herself, once the baby was born.

She had slept at last, but was suddenly awake in the darkness. The draperies at the windows were gusting inwards and the shutters were banging in the wind, which seemed like some voracious animal prowling around the house, banging itself to pieces against the timbers.

It was hardly surprising that she had woken on such a wild night. The noise, surely, would have disturbed the dead; but even as she listened to the wind she felt the pain that began somewhere in the small of her back and stretched out steel, pincer-like fingers so that for a moment her entire body seemed caught in their grip before they relaxed their hold and allowed the pain to retreat.

Her heart thudded. The pain seemed familiar, as if it were no new thing; as if it had been going on for some time, even as she slept. But perhaps the whole thing had been pure fancy. Where was the pain now?

The rain began, not gradually or gently, but with sudden violence, lashing against the shutters and pouring into the room so that Zachariah woke too, and leaping from the bed rushed to close the windows.

The thunder that had rumbled threateningly all day suddenly came to life and crashed overhead, and the room was lit by a flash of lightning which coincided with a return of the pain, a pain so intense that Dorcas cried out.

"Hush, my love, don't be frightened," Zachariah said soothingly, thinking it was the storm that had alarmed her. "I've known far worse than this."

But as he turned to the bed he saw her distress and reached out to hold her.

"Sweetheart, what is it? Has your time come?"

For a moment she could not speak; then once again the pain ebbed away and she nodded.

"I believe so."

"Then hold on, my lass, and be brave. I shall go and find Bathsheba to stay with you whilst I go for Mrs. Bettany. She promised to come at any time."

"But in this storm, surely —"

"She'll come, whatever the weather, I have no doubt of it. This baby of ours cares not a jot for storms." He was pulling his clothes on as he spoke. "Tell him to slow down and take his time. I'll be back as quickly as I can."

Oh, but he was good, Dorcas thought. This baby of *ours*, he had said, and clearly meant it. She gasped a little as the pain re-established its hold, raising herself from the bed and reaching towards Bathsheba as she entered the room and came swiftly over to her.

"You chose a wild, wild night fo' dis chile, Miz Dorcas."

"Poor Zachariah," Dorcas whispered. "And poor Marcia, too —" She cut off the words sharply and lay back, biting her lips. Bathsheba watched her with shrewd, compassionate eyes.

There was a long way to go yet, in her opinion. There would be plenty of time for help to arrive.

There was no lessening of the storm. To Dorcas, sweating and gasping on the bed, it seemed a fitting accompaniment to her labour. The sea was roaring now, the rain lashing down in torrents, the night sky bleached and livid with the sheet lightning that flashed across it.

"Just listen to the sea," Dorcas said during an interval when the pain was no more than a flickering threat. "It sounds so close."

"We safe here, Miz Dorcas."

In her heart, Bathsheba was not so sure. She had taken a look through the front shutters and even though the night was black she had seen the white-edged waves throwing themselves over the narrow track at the front of the house. She hoped that the Master would not be long – but Treasure Bluff was a good five miles distant and in this weather was no easy ride.

"Is there no sign of them, Sheba?" Dorcas's voice was thin and strained. Bathsheba hurried to her side.

"Dey don't reach yet, Miz Dorcas, but dey come soon for sure."

Sounds, feelings, emotions, kaleidoscoped in Dorcas's mind. She lost count of time. Bathsheba twisted a sheet into a rope and hung it from the bedhead.

"Haul on it when de pain come," she urged, and Dorcas hauled but found small comfort in it; and all the time the thunder crashed overhead and the roar of the sea grew louder.

"Why aren't they here?" she asked fretfully at last. "They've been so long. What can have happened?"

"Dey reach soon, Miz Dorcas. Don't you fret, now."

A hurried trip to the front of the house had shown Bathsheba that the waves were at the very foot of the steps, but she said nothing. Quietly, deftly, she made all ready, as Marcia had shown her; a pile of clean cloths and towels, the cradle for the baby, water set to boil.

Inside, however, she felt frightened and apprehensive. What was keeping them? Again and again she returned to the front windows, wondering if she should go in search of assistance from some other white woman closer at hand, yet unwilling to leave her mistress even for a moment.

"Sheba, Sheba –"

"I here, Miz Dorcas."

"Sheba, I'm frightened. Suppose they have met with an accident —"

"Dey reach soon. Don't you fret."

Calm, comforting words, but meaningless as they both knew. Then, suddenly an outside door opened and the storm entered the house with a roar, bringing with it Zachariah and Marcia.

"The road was washed away," Zachariah began, but Marcia wasted no time in explanations.

She stripped off the oilskin in which she was draped and let it fall to the floor as she came at once to the bed. She dried her hands on a towel, and placed them on Dorcas — cool, capable hands that seemed to transmit a feeling of calm authority.

"Well," she said, with some amusement in her voice. "It seems I was scarcely missed. Bathsheba has cared for you well."

"I praise de Lord you done come, Miz Bettany, ma'am."

"There's nothing wrong, is there?" Zachariah, pale and anxious, tried to edge closer to the bed. "Dorcas is all right?"

"Miz Dorcas jes' fine, Master. You go dry yo'self an' hurry right back. Dis chile goin' to get hisself born right now."

Zachariah was the first one to hold him, for Marcia handed him the yelling boy child wrapped in a small blanket before she turned once again to Dorcas to attend swiftly to her needs.

He had not gone to change his clothes. He was not capable of leaving that room while Dorcas was going through so much; now she lay pale but peaceful and blissfully free from pain, smiling at the look of pure delight on Zachariah's face.

"He's beautiful," he said. "Beautiful! Look at those little ears! Like shells, they are —"

"Let me see." Dorcas struggled to a sitting position and held out her arms. She felt amazement and disbelief and a helpless, all-consuming love as she looked down at the child in her arms.

"He big, Miz Dorcas," Bathsheba said proudly, sharing her delight.

"Is he? Is he big, Marcia! He looks very tiny to me."

"Look at the finger nails," Zachariah said, coming up close to bend over her and the baby.

"You're dripping all over us! Oh, look at you both — how

could I not have noticed how wet you are! Go and get dry, I beg you, before you get chilled."

Zachariah went but Marcia stayed. There were still practical duties to be carried out.

"I'm so very grateful to you," Dorcas said. "And Sheba, too. What would I have done without her?"

"I believe she could have managed without me." Marcia was smiling, proud of her pupil. "Her preparations were excellent."

"Miz Bettany, I never more glad to see a livin' soul."

"It seems the storm has passed." Marcia, with leisure to mop herself dry at last, took time to notice the weather.

"It was all in the baby's honour." Zachariah was back at Dorcas's side. "The heavens were welcoming him."

"Is that what they were doing!" Marcia said dryly.

"We shall call him Storm," Dorcas announced suddenly. There was no doubt or indecision in her mind now, though in all the previous months she had been unable to make a choice. "Zachariah Storm Hardiman."

Six

It was to be the finest party Grand Cay had ever seen; Dorcas was quite determined on that score.

"Sure now, Mrs. Hardiman ma'am," Gilligan said when she went to the store to see if at last the new stock of white flour had arrived. "It's not as if there's ever been a power of competition. Is it a ball you're after havin'? Wid music and the like? Well, well" – at her assent – "may the saints preserve us! There'll be battle done for the favour of an invitation, I'm thinkin'."

They both laughed at that, a laugh of complicity. Among salt proprietors and government officials alike, the Hardimans' stock had not been high of recent weeks, the general opinion being that while it was understandable that Mrs. Hardiman might wish to free the woman who had supported her so well during the birth of her son, to free *two* slaves was surely irresponsibility taken to absurd lengths.

To encourage a visiting whipper-snapper of a Methodist missionary to perform a marriage ceremony over them, just as if they were white and properly entitled to such things, was even more reprehensible! Who, they asked each other, could be trusted to fight the crazy Abolitionists, if not one of themselves?

"Do you think they have forgiven me sufficiently to accept our invitation?" Dorcas asked Gilligan.

"Indeed they have!"

"It's the food that worries me. I'm hoping Joe will catch some enormous fish the day preceding, but how can one be sure?" Since receiving his papers of manumission, Joe had left the salt ponds and was now in charge of *Flyer*, Zachariah's ketch, part of his perquisites being the privilege of using the vessel for fishing, the fish to be sold on the open market. Bathsheba, on the other hand, continued to work in the house as before, but lived with Joe apart from the other slaves.

"He'll do his best for yez, Mrs. Hardiman. I've not the smallest doubt of that, at all."

"No more have I, but fishing's a chancy business. What a place this is! If it's not flour that's in short supply, then it's sugar or onions or any one of a hundred other things. Would you be shocked, Mr. Gilligan, if I said I'd be prepared to commit murder for half a dozen fowls? There's a receipt of my grandmother's I should dearly love to cook for my party, but I can see no hope." She sighed. "And if I managed to find the poultry, I would need rice and saffron."

Gilligan scratched his nose thoughtfully.

"I might manage you the leg of a goat," he said.

Dorcas laughed when speaking of it afterwards to Marcia who had called into Tamarind Villa for a cooling drink, having come into town from Treasure Bluff to visit a family of sick children.

"The tragedy is," Dorcas said, "that I shall no doubt be glad enough to accept the offer when the time comes."

"There's not a soul on the island who doesn't appreciate the difficulties. It's not the food they will come for, but the chance to dress up and meet together. How glad I am that my son may be here for the occasion."

"I shall look forward to meeting him," Dorcas said.

This was no empty politeness. She had heard a great deal about Dr. Hugh Bettany, the son of whom Marcia was so proud, and indeed felt that she knew him already.

"Tell me," she went on after a moment. "What ailed the children you saw, Marcia? It's no epidemic, I hope?" The fear was ever-present, the confines of the island so small. Though the family in question lived in the area beyond the salt ponds, known locally as Backsalina, disease could quickly spread from those mean, palmetto-thatched shacks to the more salubrious part closer to the shore. This time Marcia dismissed her worries.

"It's nothing that better food and housing wouldn't improve. I'm more worried about Cecily, to be honest. There's such a pale, waxen look about her! I don't believe her pregnancy is going well. I shall have to get my son to take a look at her."

"How soon do you expect Dr. Bettany?"

"Any time now. I hope he will stay at least a month — meantime, I've advised Cecily to rest as much as possible."

"I'll try to ensure that she does. You know, Marcia, I cannot imagine what we would all do without you. There must be something I can do to help. I should come with you on your errands of mercy."

"Not while your children are so small. Which reminds me, Dorcas — surely I do not imagine that Emma is happier and more agreeable these days?"

"No, you do not! She's a changed child since Storm was born. She adores him. From the first moment she became his willing slave. The other day she was holding him in her arms and she looked at me with those big brown eyes and said: 'Nobody will *ever* know how much I love him!' Surprisingly, perhaps, it has created something of a bond between us."

"Well, I'm delighted to hear it — and now your sister is due to arrive in just a few days! You must be very happy."

"Oh, I am." Dorcas glowed with the kind of beauty that made Marcia wonder, not for the first time, how Zachariah Hardiman had succeeded in capturing this exotic creature. "I do so hope Dr. Bettany arrives in time for the party, too — that would make everything quite perfect. I'm determined it will be a success. I know it won't be as grand as Fanny is used to, but it will be as good as I can make it. Zack is finding some musicians. He wanted to play himself, but I told him that would never do — he must act the jovial host. We thought we would clear the drawing-room for dancing. It's not near big enough but will hold two sets — perhaps three at a pinch — and we shall put chairs on the porch and under the trees; then later, after supper has been cleared away, we can have several tables of whist in the dining-room. If only I could think what I am to give everyone to eat."

"Bathsheba's conch fritters are always acceptable."

"But so everyday and ordinary!" She sighed. "The matter of food is not my only worry, Marcia; the real question is, who will accept our invitation? Have the worthies of Grand Cay forgiven us, do you think?"

The answer to that was much as Gilligan had predicted. There were coaches and buggies in plenty rolling down the track to Tamarind Villa, and Willis Trotman, standing in the shadow of the casuarinas at the edge of the beach, marvelled at the extent to which the burghers of Grand Cay had dressed up for the occasion. There were silks and satins and velvet jackets that had been tucked away in boxes for months, if not years, to judge by the outmoded cut.

In this company the figures of Mr. and Mrs. Silas Tranton

stood out, for they were by far the most stylishly and expensively clad couple present. Trotman could not take his eyes off Dorcas, however, though the expression in them, had anyone been there to see, would have been difficult to read. She reminded him of his mother, which was no compliment, for the whole of Jamaica knew her to be a whore and himself a bastard. He despised her as he despised all women, especially beautiful ones, but God, how he wanted her; and would have her, he was quite determined about that.

How in the name of heaven had she ever married Hardiman? The situation was ludicrous, laughable! She could never have chosen him, not of her own free will. Trotman smiled, a down-turned, sneering smile. Hardiman was kind, people said; good-hearted to a fault.

There was more than one opinion about that. In Trotman's view 'weak' was the word; even 'stupid'.

But Dorcas – now, there was a woman to be reckoned with. He felt his body stir involuntarily at the sight of her, and his breathing quickened.

He wanted her as he had never wanted another woman. He thought of her constantly, and when driven by need to the stinking whore-house beyond the edge of town, it was Dorcas he lay with, not the sweating, nameless harlots who took his money.

He wiped the back of a shaking hand across his mouth. He would have her, and she wouldn't be unwilling. He smiled his bitter smile again. Women like that were never unwilling. She was built for passion, and once she knew of his desire she would not hesitate, he was sure of that. How could a man like Zachariah Hardiman satisfy her? He was old and ugly, a buffoon, no match for him, Willis Trotman.

The Grimshaws were going in now, and the Friths and the McGoverns, both Patrick and Michael with their respective wives; virtuous women, the pair of them, both as plain as pikestaffs. Who would imagine that the Hardimans scarcely merited the time of day only a few short weeks ago? All was changed now that the high and mighty Trantons from Bermuda had come to stay.

Here was that witch Bettany, and a tall, thin young man who could be no other than her doctor son, for their beaky profiles were identical. He'd heard people express the wish that Hugh Bettany might stay on the island, but for his part, Trotman hoped that his visit was merely fleeting, and that when he left he would take his mother with him. Women like that repelled him – poor, second-rate apologies for men that they were; and she was dangerous besides, spreading heaven alone knew what absurd views among the slaves.

The Hardimans and the Trantons were standing together, smiling and greeting the guests; but the line was thinning now. It was time to go in.

He brushed his hand over his cropped head and pulled down his jacket. He would kiss her hand, he decided; not bow over it like everyone else. And he would look deep into her eyes to convey his readiness to accept any advances she might care to make.

He felt a quiver of anticipation as he emerged from the shadows to go up the path towards the house. In a second or two she would look towards him, he would feel her flesh beneath his lips, the bitch's smile would be for him alone.

Dorcas saw his approach from the corner of her eye.

"And here," she said in an undertone to Fanny, "comes the unspeakable Trotman."

He failed to notice the empty artificiality of her smile or the quickly suppressed grimace of distaste as his lips brushed her hand. Soon, soon, he thought. Soon he would show the bitch who was master.

"Why unspeakable?" Fanny asked curiously when Trotman had gone into the house.

Dorcas grimaced again and shrugged her shoulders.

"Oh, I don't know exactly. He takes Zachariah's wages but looks at him as if he despises him – and me, too, I sometimes think, but then I see *that* look in his eye – you know what I mean – and my skin crawls. I find him repellent. Never mind Trotman! For the sake of good relations, you must come and speak to Mrs. Grimshaw – the uncrowned queen of Grand Cay!"

She led Fanny across the porch to where Mrs. Grimshaw was holding court, pink and plump and encased in purple, nose like that of a rocking-horse, well-upholstered bosom decked with lace. Silas, she noted thankfully, was already in conversation with Mr. Grimshaw. Whatever one thought about her brother-in-law – and personally she found him too stiff and starchy for comfort – he did at least possess all the social graces and could be relied upon to do the right thing.

There was no doubt about it, Fanny and Silas could hardly

have timed their visit more advantageously. Perhaps the good-will engendered thereby would restore Zachariah to favour, since he was so anxious to be elected as a representative on the Board of Assembly. She was aware that it was her pleas on behalf of Joe and Bathsheba that had cooked his goose for the next elections, due to take place after Christmas, but could not find it in her heart to regret it. Bathsheba's joy on being given her freedom was something she would never forget.

"The house looks beautiful, Dorcas." Marcia, unfamiliar in wine-red satin with pearls in her hair, caught Dorcas by the arm.

"And you – I've never seen you looking so well!"

"I felt I owed it both to you and my son to make a little more effort than usual – and how right I was to do so, for there can surely never have been a more glittering occasion! You've made the house look quite magical."

"It was Zachariah's idea to thread lanterns through the trees." Dorcas leaned towards Marcia and lowered her voice. "And would you believe it, I have even managed to procure some chickens – or at least, Gilligan procured them for me. I beg you, if you hear talk of poultry runs being raided, pray do not tell me until after supper! With goat's meat the only alternative I couldn't bear to ask too many questions –"

"Mrs. Hardiman?" Willis Trotman stood before her, a light in his eye which she could not fathom. In anyone else she might have assumed a certain admiration, but in Trotman's case she felt sure that the matter was not so simple. "They are making up sets. May I ask you to partner me?"

No one could have guessed from her smile that she was less than delighted, but once the dance was over she put as much space as possible between herself and Trotman. After all, she was the hostess and had duties to perform. It was something she enjoyed and which came easily to her, she found, speaking to one guest after another, ensuring that no one was left out in the cold.

"What a beauty," Hugh Bettany said to his mother, watching her. "Unexpected, somehow, to find a woman like that in this place. Do I scent some kind of story?"

"If there is one, I have never heard it."

"Captain Hardiman seems an agreeable fellow, but –" He broke off short, looked at his mother and laughed. "What business is it of mine? My curiosity will be the death of me."

"Perhaps it's not such a bad trait in a doctor."

He did not reply, and Marcia saw that his eyes were still on Dorcas. Seeing her like this, at a distance and from a stranger's point of view, she acknowledged that Dorcas had, if anything, grown in beauty since the birth of Storm. There was a ripeness about her that had been missing before, a glow that would have made her stand out in far more fashionable gatherings than this.

"She's like an exotic butterfly in a gathering of moths," Hugh Bettany said appreciatively.

"Well!" Marcia looked at her son sideways. "She is well and truly netted. You must go hunting in other pastures."

"My dear Mama," Hugh replied with a grin. "I am too busy at the moment to go hunting anywhere, believe me."

From the other side of the room Silas Tranton was watching Dorcas, too.

"Your wife looks very well," he said dryly to Zachariah who happened to be standing next to him. "She is clearly happy here."

"Ay, it's to be hoped so." Zachariah's eyes were soft with love and pride as he watched her. "She's brought happiness to me right enough. But you know, Tranton, sometimes I wonder –" He stopped short and chewed his lip, his expression clouded.

"Yes?" Silas raised his eyebrows, but Zachariah did not answer him directly.

"Just look at her," he said. "Grand Cay is too small for her. She should be the mistress of some great house. There are times when I grow fearful, for I know there's no society she couldn't have conquered."

"I'm sure you do yourself and Grand Cay an injustice."

The words were polite but his tone was aloof. Zachariah knew without being told that Silas Tranton was sure of no such thing. There had been an expression of mild distaste on his face from the moment he had stepped on the island, an expression that said all too clearly that nothing was much to his liking, and the sooner he and his bride sailed away from this barren place to more favoured islands, the better he would be pleased.

No doubt, Zachariah thought, he dismissed his brother-in-law as a rough, ill-educated seaman. Well, he wouldn't be far wrong, but who had come off best, Zachariah would like to know, Silas Tranton or Zachariah Hardiman, with all his drawbacks? Fanny Tranton was a nice enough little thing, but set against his incomparable Dorcas – well!

"I'll go and claim a dance," he said, smiling again. "She'll be booked to my exclusion the entire evening if I'm not careful."

Dorcas danced with her husband and with Silas and Hugh Bettany. ("Hugh frightens me to death," she reported to Fanny confidentially between dances. "He looks so intelligent but says little, which makes me babble like an idiot merely to fill the gaps.")

In between dances she moved from group to group, making certain that glasses were filled and that those who wished to indulge in whist after supper knew their partners. And when supper was served, everyone pronounced the chicken dish quite delightful, a truly splendid treat.

"I am gratified but fearful," she confessed to Marcia. "I swear that Mrs. Hickson was regarding me with the deepest suspicion. She asked me where I had procured them and I unashamedly attributed all to Gilligan, so he must take the blame if questions are asked."

"May I advise you to steer the new judge away from the subject?" Marcia suggested behind her fan. "He is the kind to make the clearest conscience tremble with imagined guilt."

"Oh, how I agree! I never saw a pair of more strait-laced killjoys than Mr. Crockford and his wife. I had the temerity to ask Mrs. Crockford if she wished to play whist a moment ago and you would have thought beyond any doubt that I was proposing an orgy of sin. She's had a face like vinegar the entire evening."

"Pay no heed. Everyone else is enjoying the party."

Cheerfully Dorcas did as she was told, but Willis Trotman was more difficult to ignore. He seemed to haunt her, and even when she was dancing with someone else, she would look up to find his eyes upon her.

Her heart sank when she saw him approaching and was thankful that Bathsheba chose this moment to tell her that Storm had awoken from sleep and needed to be fed. She smiled vaguely at Trotman and swept past him into the house, coming face to face with Fanny as she did so.

"I was coming to find you," Fanny said. "We've not ex-changed a word for hours."

"Then come upstairs with me while I feed Storm. It will be a chance to talk, for truly we've had so little."

The baby slept in a crib at the foot of the bed shared by Dorcas and Zachariah. Now two small fists waved in the air and a furious bellow told the world of his hunger.

Dorcas picked him up, bared her breast, and looked down at the red-gold head against her flesh with amused tenderness. There was such fierce determination in the way he sucked.

"He's a handsome child." Fanny looked at them both for a moment before sitting down at the mirror to rearrange her hair. "I'm so glad things have turned out so well for you, Dorcas. When I heard you'd stayed with Zachariah and not left the ship as you threatened, I felt a load had fallen from me, but I was still anxious to see your state for myself. Your letters sounded contented enough, but there is so much that letters can't reveal."

"That's true. I wish you were staying longer."

"Silas is anxious to get to Antigua. Surely you will be coming to Bermuda before too long?"

Dorcas was silent for a moment, her eyes still fixed on the baby.

"What would Father say?" she asked at last. "How would he receive me? Never once have I heard from him, though I have written, as you must know. He seems as cold and unforgiving as ever."

"In his heart he would be glad to see you, I'm sure. I know Grandmama would. She sent all manner of tender messages to you as you know, and has forgiven any hurt long since. Any letter she receives she reads over and over. And as for me – well, I don't have to tell you how joyfully I'd welcome you, do I? I was so sad that you weren't present at my wedding."

"Oh Fanny, so was I!" Dorcas looked up with a smile. "It sounded the most wonderful occasion. Do tell me the last, smallest detail."

"I've already told you the last, smallest detail! I suffered from writer's cramp for days after my letter to you, and Silas complained that he'd unwittingly married a scribe with no time for her husband at all! Did I tell you that Aunt Rose wore that self-same rust-coloured gown she wore for Willy Foley's christening, and he a midshipman in the Navy these past two years? And Cousin Sarah chose to wear green which upset Grandmama dreadfully, you know how superstitious she is!"

"What about Cousin Phoebe? She had a fine new gown, I'll

wager." Dorcas was smiling, enjoying these small revelations, anxious to hear more.

"Oh, she looked lovely, as always, in blue. She quite outshone me. No —" as Dorcas protested, "it is true and I would be a fool to deny it. There is something so stylish about her; there always has been, you remember, even when we were children. She had her gown made up by that little French émigré who came to St. George's just before you left, and she looked so chic and charming."

"Is she engaged to be married yet? There was a whisper some time ago that an announcement regarding Mr. Sinclair was to be made at any moment."

"Mr. Sinclair fell out of favour for some reason, no one quite knows why." Fanny paused in her narrative to press a little powder into her glowing cheeks. "No," she resumed after a moment. "Phoebe seems to have other interests now. Kit Mallory seemed much taken with her at the wedding."

The name, spoken so casually, hit Dorcas like a hammer blow and left her gasping. Fanny took the small, wordless sound she made as a query.

"Kit Mallory. You remember him, surely?" Fanny's absorption with her toilette prevented her from seeing the shock on her sister's face. "Yes, of course you remember him! He is a handsome rogue and very charming when he wants to be, but Phoebe is a fool to take him seriously." Laughing, she turned towards Dorcas whose downbent head gave no indication of her inner turmoil. "You can imagine Father's emotions at having to entertain anyone by the name of Mallory, but the Trantons are related to them by marriage in some vague way and Silas was most anxious that they should be invited. There are business links, too. All Silas's ships were built in the Mallory yard, whilst they buy many of their raw materials from the Trantons — so as the very last thing father wanted to do was to upset the Tranton family, there was little he could do but agree to putting the Mallorys on the guest list. His anguish at having to pay for so much as a drop of liquid or crumb of cake to pass Mallory lips made him almost suicidal."

"I thought," Dorcas said, very casually, putting Storm up against her shoulder and rubbing his back, "that Kit Mallory was to be married. I heard a rumour —"

"And that's all it turned out to be, apparently. It was said that he had gone to England to marry some heiress, but that was proved to be nothing but wishful thinking on the part of Mrs. Mallory. Kit told Cousin Phoebe that there had never been the smallest chance of such a match, though a cousin in England had mentioned the friendship to his mother who immediately jumped to the wrong conclusions. Really, it just goes to prove how little of the idle gossip that passes for conversation in St. George's can be believed! Kit said that the sum total of his stay in England was three days in the port of Bristol! The main purpose of his trip was to go privateering against the French in a ship owned by an uncle. He wanted to make money quickly, it seems, and in that he was successful more than he could have dreamed, for they captured a prize in the first month and now he's back in Bermuda with enough capital to buy his own sloop."

"Will he marry Phoebe?" Dorcas was proud of the way she could speak so evenly and casually, as if the matter was only of passing interest.

"Oh, Phoebe! You know what she is like!" Fanny swung round from the mirror to face her sister. "The foolish girl is quite bowled over, but she never did have the smallest bit of sense. Silas says that when Kit marries, it will be to someone with money — which rules out anyone from the Foley family, doesn't it?"

"I suppose it does."

"Miz Dorcas?" Bathsheba was by her side. "You all done now?"

"All done, Sheba." Dorcas gave Storm a last kiss and handed the baby over so that he could be changed and restored to his crib. Like one in a trance she began to rebutton her dress.

Kit unmarried still, and back in Bermuda.

Had he looked for her, enquired for her? Had he thought to ask himself why she had married so suddenly? Or was she already forgotten — one of a long line of foolish girls who had flung themselves at his head while he, as Bathsheba had warned her, took his pleasure where he found it and gave nothing in return?

Perhaps we should form an association, she thought bitterly, a hard, bright core of anger beginning to glow inside her; all we poor fools who have imagined ourselves in love with him.

She went downstairs again and drank a glass of wine very

quickly so that the colour flamed in her face, and she danced and laughed more recklessly and with greater abandon than she had done before. All eyes were on her and while many of the men responded with admiration, there were ladies present whose stares grew cold and critical, and who whispered to each other behind their fans.

Hugh Bettany looked and saw that she was troubled.

Willis Trotman looked and saw an open invitation.

She was annoyed to find him more ubiquitous than ever and suddenly, after a second glass of wine, she was moved to tackle him on the subject. She had yielded to his request for a dance and afterwards, hot and breathless, she had bowed towards him politely and made her way into the garden in search of a breath of air. Annoyingly, he stuck by her side.

"My dear Mr. Trotman," she said icily. "You are at liberty to seek other partners, you know."

"I don't think you want me to do that."

They were standing in the shadow of the porch with the strains of music and voices coming from behind them, mingling with the sound of the waves and the muted murmur of other, hidden voices out beyond the circle of light which spilled from the house. There were people out there, Dorcas realised suddenly; black faces, watching, gaping, like children outside a toy shop.

"I assure you, I want it above all things."

"Don't play coy with me, my lady."

Her fluttering fan was arrested suddenly, and she gave him a penetrating look. Her head was swimming with the wine she had drunk so rapidly, it was true, but not so much that she was unable to detect the sudden change of tone. This was something ugly and threatening and had nothing to do with the kind of light flirtation that she had indulged in with others.

Emotion and the wine had driven away all caution, all conventional politeness.

"Willis Trotman," she said, her voice low but every word quite distinct. "You are becoming a bore."

"Stop playing games. You know you want me." He spoke harshly and caught hold of her wrist. "I've seen you looking at me. I've seen you smiling at me."

"Leave go of me, Mr. Trotman." She was perfectly sober now, and very angry. Still she spoke calmly and evenly, determined that this ridiculous episode should end without a public scene to shame her or Zachariah.

She tried to pull away from him, but he tightened his grip and forced her away from the house, further into the shadows.

"You have no need to pretend with me. I know exactly what you want."

She laughed at that, short and scornful.

"What I want, Mr. Trotman, is for you to leave me alone. I have no wish to make a scene but if you do not loosen your hold on me –"

"I only want to talk." He brought his face closer to hers, and she saw that he was in the grip of intense excitement. His breathing was rapid and his voice was hoarse. "Listen to me, Dorcas. I've known from the start what a farce your marriage to that fool must be. You're a woman with fire – a woman of passion. You think I don't know? Of course I do! I've watched you night after night, hidden in the trees. I could pleasure you in ways you've never dreamed of –"

"Get *away* from me!" With a powerful jerk of her arm that took him by surprise, Dorcas freed herself. She, too, was breathing rapidly, but with anger, not with lust. Men, men, men! Her head seemed to ring with the word. Did they think of nothing other than the gratification of their senses? There was only one she could trust.

"Let me tell you a few home truths, Mr. Trotman." Her voice shook a little. "You are not fit to black my husband's boots, neither you nor –" She bit back the other name that had filled her mind since her conversation with Fanny. "Nor any other man present," she substituted. "Things like you are found under stones, Mr. Trotman – wriggling, slimy creatures, only fit to be stamped upon. Never speak to me in that manner again, do you hear me?"

She turned from him abruptly, walking almost directly into Zachariah's arms.

"There you are, sweetheart," he said. "I was looking for you. The Crockfords are about to leave –"

He broke off as if suddenly becoming aware that all was not well, and he looked with some bewilderment and a dawning anger from her to the tall figure who stood a few feet behind her.

"Trotman?" he said, a note of query in his voice.

"Mr. Trotman is also leaving," Dorcas stated firmly.

He went quickly, without a word.

"What's to do here? Has he been bothering you?" She had never heard Zachariah speak so harshly.

"Mr. Trotman has bothered me since the day we first met. I have never liked nor trusted him, as you well know, and tonight he has given me good reason."

"By God, I'll deal with the bastard." Zachariah turned to go after him.

"No, don't, Zack. Let's not have a scene. It's not worth a fuss – he'll not try his arm with me again."

She spoke boldly enough but inwardly she felt soiled and ashamed, close to tears. She clung to Zachariah's arm.

"I wish they would all go," she said. "I want only you, Zack – only you, you must believe me. You do, don't you? You cannot think I encouraged the man?"

"Sweetheart, I know that you did not, and of course I believe you."

How strong he was, Dorcas thought. Strong and soothing, utterly dependable, utterly devoted.

She was lucky, she told herself when all the guests were gone and she was lying next to her husband, tired out but far from sleep. There surely was no girl as lucky as she.

Why, then, did she weep so?

The answer to that question was one she dared not face.

Seven

"The first thing we need is a plan," Zachariah said, kneeling in the sand with his face flushed with exertion. "No good just digging away with no idea of what our aim is to be. We want to make a good job of it, don't we, Davey boy? None of your disgraceful shanty towns for me, thank you very much. This has to be a place to be proud of."

"Like Hamilton," said Emma.

"Well now, miss, I don't know about that!" Zachariah was a St. Georgian himself and had never become used to the fact that Bermuda had a new capital. "Still, let it pass! Come on, now, heads together – we need a fine harbour, that's the first thing, and a jetty –"

"And a fort," Davey said. "We must have a fort now we're at war with America again." He had brought his toy soldiers to Treasure Bluff with just this eventuality in mind.

"And a church with a tall spire –"

"Look here, Emma sweetheart –" Zachariah sat back on his heels and grinned up at his daughter. "There is a limit to what you can do with sand, you know. Still, we'll do our best."

"This would be a good place for the fort." Davey had a dogged nature that refused to give up an idea but worried at it, wearing down any opposition. "We could make a hill, Papa, and put it on the top, couldn't we? Storm, go *away*! Papa, make Storm stop it. We can't build anything if he keeps knocking things down."

"Stop being such a great bully, Davey Hardiman!" Emma, eyes wide with outrage, put her arms around the two-year-old boy and held him close. "You're the clumsy one who's always knocking things down. Storm's the best little boy in all the world."

"But perhaps a little young for the business of construction," Zachariah suggested pacifically. "Why not take him back to his mother – ?"

"I'll look after him myself. This is only a silly baby's game anyway."

Marcia and Dorcas, sitting in the shade of a tree outside the grey stone house at the north of the island where Marcia lived alone, looked down on the scene below them.

"How devoted she is still," Marcia commented.

"A little too devoted, I'm afraid. There are times when Storm should be disciplined, not cosseted. Emma is altogether too protective of him."

"He is very young."

"Not too young to realise he gets away with all manner of naughtiness when she is about. He knows he is the centre of her world, and mine as well. I only wish –" Dorcas broke off suddenly, aware of Marcia's sympathetic glance.

"I know what you wish. But truly, you must stop fretting for another child. Two years is not so long."

"Two and a half. Zack would so love more children."

"You both have much to be thankful for. A healthy family, and your own health and strength –"

"Oh, I know, I know!" The death of her good friend Cecily was never far from Dorcas's mind, though it had taken place over two years earlier, not long after the eventful party at Tamarind Villa. Cecily had suffered a miscarriage at the sixth month, and though it occurred during Hugh Bettany's brief visit to the island, not all his skill and devotion had been able to save her.

"It's all in the Lord's hands," Marcia said.

And who can argue that He moves in mysterious ways? Dorcas thought. What but a malignant fate could have arranged that she should have become pregnant so easily when she wanted it so little, yet somehow prevented it when she would have welcomed it above all things? She sighed heavily, then apologised.

"Forgive me, Marcia. I know we have a lot to be thankful for, and sitting here with you at Treasure Bluff is one of them. We all love coming here." She was silent for a moment, then sighed again. "You can't deny, though, that there are days when it's impossible to see any ray of hope for the future. Zachariah is depressed too, in spite of his cheerful aspect. The salt is piling up for shipment, but with this stupid war with America going on we have lost half our markets. Who would have thought that the whole disastrous business would start again? Isn't it enough that we have to battle against the elements to scrape a living, without suffering the results of man's inhumanity to man? Oh –" Penitently she reached to touch Marcia's arm. "I should be ashamed, and I know it. We are in not near so bad a case as some of the smaller owners with no savings at all behind them."

"There's a great deal of real hardship on the island," Marcia agreed. "Stocks of food are running so low, and even if the food were there in the shops, many have no money to pay for it. And the Caicos Islands are even worse hit. I'm told there's no flour at all, though it seems someone has discovered that a substitute can be made by pulverising the root of the sisal plant."

"And as Mrs. Grimshaw informs me," Dorcas said, "there are nine hundred and ninety ways of making the prickly pear edible! No doubt we shall all survive one way or another, if the American privateers allow us to. The Caicos Islands have been much harried, I hear – thank God we have a strong militia here! Davey watches Zachariah dress up in his uniform with his musket and bayonet and mourns the fact that the war is bound to be over before he's old enough to do the same."

She smiled affectionately in the direction of her husband and stepson, now busily co-operating in the construction of the model town. One look at Zachariah's absorbed face showed beyond doubt that his own interest was at least the equal of Davey's.

"That is no game to Zack, you know," she said to Marcia. "He has this dream of building a town right here on Grand Cay that is every bit as good as anything in Bermuda. There is no money now, of course, nor will there be until the war is over, but afterwards he is determined that somehow funds must be wrested from the Bahamian Government to make something of the place."

"Things have improved since I first came."

"Yes, but all the development is so piecemeal and haphazard. Zack has drawn up a plan of a small square and a court house and a fine building to house government offices, and he has tried to get the Board of Assembly to back it so that the whole project, properly costed, can be presented to the Government in Nassau. We've been under their rule for ten years now, and what have they done for us? Nothing but take the revenue from the salt."

"Does Zack have any support for the scheme?"

Dorcas sighed.

"Very little, though of course everyone agrees that the Bahamian Government takes all and gives nothing. I'm afraid that no one takes him very seriously, you see, and that, as I tell him myself, is largely his own fault. He is the best of men, but he loves to play the clown and his enemies make capital from it."

"Does he have enemies? It's hard to imagine."

"Oh yes, he has them! Mrs. Grimshaw contrived to let me know last week during her lecture on the prickly pear that neither she nor her husband have forgiven either of us for freeing Joe and Bathsheba, nor for allowing the Methodist minister to preach in the slave barracks. All *he* did was to spread insurrection and discontent, she said. And of course, ever since his dismissal, Trotman has wasted no opportunity to blacken Zack's name. He works for the McGovern brothers now and is much prized by them, I hear, for his ability with figures — heaven alone knows what poison he drops into their ears along with his accounts! Since they and Mr. Grimshaw are three out of the five Representatives on the Assembly, it is hardly to be wondered Zack is never elected. I wish that he could be. He is an honest, practical man with so much to offer and so much dedication to the good of the island."

"He'll come into his own, Dorcas; I feel quite certain of it."

Dorcas smiled at her gratefully and nodded towards the scene in front of them.

"This day out will do him good. It's kind of you to put up with all of us invading your peace, Marcia. There's something about the atmosphere here at Treasure Bluff that induces a wonderful feeling of ease and relaxation."

"I'm glad you think so. You know you're always more than welcome."

Marcia's home stood in the midst of palm trees in a landscape as different as it was possible to imagine from the area of the island around the quay and the salt ponds. In front of the house was a low bluff and the sea; to the rear, the waters of North Creek. The shores of the creek were protected by mangroves and buttonwoods, but unlike South Creek, it was not open to the sea.

It should be opened up, Zachariah maintained. Then it would be the perfect shelter in time of hurricane.

This notion was not one that was dismissed, as were so

many of his plans, as foolish and unworkable. The other salt proprietors agreed with him, but their representations to the Assembly in Nassau had resulted in a cool communication from the Governor stating that the Representatives were exceeding their duties in writing such a report, their sole function being to frame civil and police by-laws.

The whole matter reinforced the widely held local belief that the islands were in an impossible position, with the seat of government so far away in the Bahamas. They were, in theory, entitled to send one Representative to the Assembly in Nassau, but time and distance made it virtually impossible for anyone to attend on a regular basis; and even on the occasions when a Representative was able to be present, his voice was consistently ignored. North Creek, therefore, remained closed to the sea, its possibilities unexploited.

Such matters were annoyances and caused Zachariah to rant and roar and pull faces indicative of fury. He would dearly have loved a voice in the concerns of the island, as Dorcas had mentioned to Marcia, but year after year his ambitions were thwarted.

Dorcas raged with anger on his behalf, even though she still found it difficult to take the island seriously. There seemed something unreal about it. Surely, she said to herself from time to time, this could not be her home for ever? As a temporary resting place it was tolerable, even pleasant at times, but there was always the feeling in the dim recesses of her mind that sooner or later she would be leaving it. She could not feel settled. How, after the lushness of Bermuda, could she ever feel settled in such a bare and almost treeless landscape?

Another baby would help. It might help in her relationship with Emma, too, for the truce between them following the birth of Storm had proved but temporary. Now Emma seemed to resent her more than ever, challenging her authority over Storm and actively encouraging the small boy to flout her wishes. Emma was, indeed, devoted to him – but unwisely, Dorcas was certain. Yet she hesitated to make an issue over the matter, for surely love and devotion were qualities that should be encouraged?

"Emma should go to school," Zachariah said when, on the following day, he and Dorcas walked on the beach in the cool of the evening. "I have long felt she needs more than Mrs. Palmer can offer."

"I agree with you wholeheartedly; but surely it is hardly possible to send her off the island with this war raging?"

"It cannot last for ever, sweetheart."

"You think not? The war between England and France seems to be doing so."

"Nay, nay! We'll be at peace before too long, I'm convinced of it. Think of the pasting Boney took at Moscow!"

Peace!

The thought of it was wonderful, but there seemed little between the four walls of Tamarind Villa. It was on a morning soon after Storm's third birthday – a hot, oppressive day – that Dorcas took up her pen to write to Fanny, now the mother of two little girls:

> How good to hear news of you [she wrote]. I am always overjoyed to know of your continued safety and good health, and that of your dear babies whom I would give much to see. Storm grows ever more vigorous. There is no doubt that he is a wilful child – much, I imagine, as I was myself at his age and far beyond, and though he is not the most restful of children, he is full of health and intelligence and I am thankful for it. Emma continues to dote upon him –

She broke off and stared moodily at the paper in front of her, not able to think of a single thing to write that would not be unfavourable to her stepdaughter.

Emma had celebrated her eleventh birthday in July. She had a round, small-featured face and a demure air which made most others think she was a good, quiet, biddable child. Only her immediate friends and family could guess at the passionate nature that lay behind the composed exterior, and the intensity with which she fought Storm's battles for him. Already, in spite of his extreme youth, Storm was fully capable of playing off his mother against his stepsister, and Dorcas quailed at the thought of the battles ahead if Emma were not removed from the scene soon.

Dorcas crumpled up the paper, threw it into the waste basket and began again.

> All the children are well, with Storm growing daily in vigour and intelligence. It will not be long now before he is able

to attend morning lessons, for Mrs. Palmer excels with the younger children. Alas, I feel that she cannot provide sufficient challenge for Emma who is scornful of her teaching –

She paused again. Was the girl so much on her mind that it was impossible to write a letter without constant reference to her? She toyed with the notion of yet another fresh start, but decided against it.

I am glad to say [she continued] that Marcia Bettany – so much better educated than I am myself – proposes to draw up a course of reading for her, which will perhaps –

A sudden shriek from upstairs caused her to lift her head, her hand poised over the paper. For a moment there was silence, then the sound of a scuffle, then more angry shouts so loud that the house seemed to vibrate.

Bathsheba, her own small son clinging to her skirts as she dipped water from the tank outside the house, paused in her task before shaking her head and laughing ruefully. She went back to filling the bucket, thankful to be occupied elsewhere. Squabbles between the children were becoming a regular occurrence and she had learned long since that interference did not pay.

Nola, busy tidying Emma's bedroom, hunched her shoulders around her ears and pretended not to hear the noise from next door. Such upsets caused a malady which she described as 'de sickness', and it was not something she proposed to expose herself to unless absolutely necessary; not on that day, anyway, for already she was distinctly conscious of a pain in her back that was something new. She increased in volume the droning lament which was the habitual accompaniment to her labours, but not before she, too, had lifted her eyes to heaven and shaken her head.

Dorcas could not ignore the fracas so easily. For a moment she sat with her eyes closed as if defeated by the noise and the strife; but then, resignedly, she abandoned her letter and went to see what had caused this particular uproar.

She found Emma with Storm on her lap, sitting with her back to the door of Davey's room, while from the other side furious bellows were accompanied by a fusillade of kicks delivered with stout boots. Storm, red faced and weeping, both hands knuckling his eyes, sobbed pitifully comforted by hugs and kisses from Emma, but Dorcas noted that on her arrival he paused in his sobbing for a second while he cautiously looked at her from half an eye as if to assess the situation.

"What on earth is going on?" she asked. She knocked sharply on the door of the bedroom. "Stop that noise, Davey – you'll have the door down. Do you hear me? Stop it this instant."

"He won't take any notice," Emma said with lofty resignation. "He's quite *beside* himself!"

"But why? What's happened? Davey, stop kicking that door this minute. Come out sensibly and tell me what is wrong."

"He can't come out. I've locked him in." Emma delved into the pocket of her apron and produced a heavy key. "I thought he was going to kill this precious baby, my poor darling Storm –"

"I *was* going to kill him! I still will!" The door once unlocked, Davey shot out of the room with his face scarlet with outrage. "You know what he did, Mama? He broke my fort and spoiled all my soldiers –"

"He did not spoil all your soldiers! He moved them, that's all." Emma's voice was equally shrill, her expression equally outraged. "Anyway, a boy of your age shouldn't be playing with soldiers. It's babyish. You should be ashamed."

"It is *not* babyish! They were in battle formation – they were in *special* places – now I shall never get them back right and it's all Storm's fault. He did break my fort –"

"There was no need to hit him. He's much smaller than you."

"Quiet!" thundered Dorcas. "All of you – yes, you too, Storm. Stop that dreadful wailing. That's enough, Emma – just be quiet for a moment."

She removed Storm from her embrace and holding him by the shoulders, she crouched down so that she was on his level.

"Listen to me, Storm. Stop crying and listen. You are not a baby any more. You are well past three, and you know very well that you are not to go into Davey's room and touch his things. You have been smacked for that many, many times before. How would you like it if Davey broke your hobby horse or your toy boat? That would make you very sad, wouldn't it?"

Still choking with sobs, Storm nodded his head.

"He's only little," Emma said disgustedly. "Davey is a great bully."

"Emma, I said be quiet." Dorcas was stern. "Storm understands very well what I say to him. You really must not treat him like a baby, and a half-witted baby at that. What sort of a boy will he grow into if he never has to take responsibility for his actions? Now, go to your room and get on with some of the reading Mrs. Bettany has set for you –"

"I don't see why –"

"*Go!*"

For a moment the air seemed to vibrate with the silent clash of wills, then Emma tossed her head and went away with an angry flounce of her apron. Dorcas turned her attention to the boys, extracted a lisped apology from Storm and sent him downstairs to Bathsheba before lecturing Davey on the folly of resorting to physical abuse. She inspected the fort and was able to reassure him that, mercifully, it had suffered no more damage than Zachariah would be able to put right.

When finally she returned to her letter she found she had lost all heart for it. She tore it up into small pieces and threw it away. Perhaps another day would find her more inspired, with more news to impart. She was hardly prepared for the drama which occurred the following night and which she could hardly wait to relate to her sister.

> Tamarind Villa
> Grand Cay.
> 5th October, 1814

My dearest Fanny,

Yours of the 27th August to hand, and how pleased I was to learn of your continued health and that of your family.

We, too, are in good health, but life has not been without incident. Two nights past, Zachariah and I were awoken by calls from outside the house which proved to be Joe imparting the intelligence that *Flyer* was taken from her moorings. It was then after midnight, and only pure chance had led Joe to the jetty; he said afterwards that he had been restless and having had bad luck in his fishing during the day had decided to put out again at night.

Picture his dismay when he was in time to see the ketch heading south down the coast!

It is a cause of profound gratitude to us that Joe is such an astute being, for at once he connected this occurrence with certain whispered rumours he had heard among the slaves of Mr. Grimshaw, but had not spoken of since his loyalties were divided. However, now that 'his' ketch was involved, he knew at once where his duty lay and ran to rouse Zachariah.

Consequent upon the rumours heard by Joe, they rode together across the island to South Creek, where they were in time to find no fewer than eight slaves preparing to board *Flyer* with the purpose of sailing to Haiti to gain their freedom.

Though all present were black men, it was, however, a white man who took the ketch; Joe was quite certain of that, and certain, too, that it was the same white man who, when Zachariah challenged the party at South Creek, somehow managed to slip away into the surrounding low scrub.

Zachariah was convinced it was none other than Trotman, but by the time he had roused the Constabulary to call at Trotman's lodgings, he was at home and in bed, albeit half-dressed and with a scratch across his face still oozing blood, a circumstance which seems suspicious and not inconsistent with a hurried scramble through thorny bushes.

Trotman has done all in his power to discredit Zachariah ever since the time of his dismissal, and I, too, have not escaped his lies and insinuations since the unfortunate incident at the party, about which I fully apprised you at the time. Zachariah is convinced that this latest escapade was intended to imply that, in view of other liberal actions so deplored by various of the salt proprietors, he would connive to transport slaves to Haiti in his own ketch, thus depriving Mr. Grimshaw of property belonging to him. However, if this were his intention it has come to naught, and instead Zachariah is applauded for his quickness of action in foiling both the theft of his ketch and the escape of the slaves.

The whole matter has, however, left a bad taste in my mouth. I can imagine all too well the sensations of those poor wretches, recaptured when freedom must have seemed within their grasp. Perhaps the loss of the ketch would have been a small price to pay — yet how can I say that when

Zachariah wants so much to be elected to the Assembly for the good that would then be in his power to do? And when we ourselves own upwards of forty slaves still? Life is no simple matter, Fanny.

I am sorry to hear of Father's bronchial trouble and sincerely trust that he has improved by this time. How wonderful that Grandmama keeps so well, considering her great age.

I was glad to hear that Cousin Phoebe has at last married Mr. Sinclair. The poor man certainly displayed the patience of Job in waiting so long for her! I hope and pray that they will prosper in Nova Scotia, and have no doubt at all that she will be far happier than if she had married Mr. Kit Mallory, as I believe was once her hope. Charm and good looks are no substitute for solid worth in a marriage, which is a matter on which I feel I can speak with authority, for though no one can for a moment call Zachariah a dandy, neither can they point to any occasion on which he has been less than the best of husbands.

I can hardly believe that it is three long years since your visit here. When, I wonder, shall we meet again? We talk often of paying a visit to Bermuda and of leaving Emma at school, for we have good reports of Mrs. Fanshawe's seminary. Perhaps you would do us the kindness to tell us its local reputation? I fear, though, there is little chance of Zachariah making up his mind to send her, at least until this war is over, for we have precious little money to spare since sales of salt have been hit so badly.

Undoubtedly, with so many ships of the British Navy in Hamilton and St. George's it is a different story with you. Wealth will be brought to Bermuda in many ways, and I hope Silas contrives to profit by it; but how one's heart grieves for the loss of life! War causes so much bitterness, lasting from one generation to the next, as you and I know to our cost. No doubt the present conflict has given an added impetus to Grandmama's reminiscences of the past.

May God protect us all and bring us through these difficult times. Until that happy day when we shall meet face to face, both Zachariah and I send our warmest remembrances and a thousand loving kisses.

Always your affectionate sister,
Dorcas

To skim across the waves in *Flyer* with Zachariah at the tiller, skirt kilted over bare legs, the sun warm on her face and the ribbons of her hat flying in the breeze, seemed to Dorcas like an escape to girlhood, a return to an almost forgotten time when she had no worries and no responsibilities.

They owed it to themselves, Zachariah said. It had been a long, dreary winter; but now the war was over and the months of summer lay ahead, when surely times would get better.

A marooning party for two, he called it. They were to sail to some unnamed cay where he had never taken her before, there to spend the day in blissful idleness and solitude; to splash like children through the shallows, to spread a rug in the shade of a cliff, to drink the wine and eat the food they had brought with them. Certainly, Zachariah would swim, diving down amid the coral to watch the colourful pageant of darting fish, bright as jewels. Perhaps Dorcas would do the same. She was not committing herself. If she did so, it would not be for the first time, but she could not rid herself of the ingrained feeling that such behaviour was hardly ladylike.

From his place in the stern, one arm draped over the tiller, Zachariah grinned at her.

"It's been a long time since we escaped, sweetheart."

"Much too long! I only hope that Storm –"

"Hush, now! Bathsheba will keep him in order and there's naught you need trouble with today."

Dorcas sighed with satisfaction, knowing he was right. Emma was happily occupied with Sophie and Davey had gone fishing with Mickey McGovern and his father. Today she could enjoy her freedom with a clear conscience.

The winter had been dull and wet, which was excellent for filling water tanks but lowering to the spirits of one accustomed from birth to the blessing of sunshine.

Now the sky was cloudless, apart from a few gauzy trails like diaphanous scarves tossed into the air, and there was no malice in the waves which glinted in the sun. There was a light breeze – sufficient to fill the sails, but not enough to create anxiety in the bosom of the most fearful landlubber.

"Look!" Dorcas pointed delightedly as a turtle swam by, serene and untroubled, his head out of the waves and his shell gleaming, dappled by sunlight through clear water.

"I should catch him and give you turtle steaks for dinner."

Zachariah spoke lazily and made no move to carry out the suggestion. He was enjoying the moment too much; the relaxation from work, the motion of the boat, the sun and the warmth and the sight of Dorcas.

The tiny island which was their destination floated before them. It was fringed with golden sand, white waves breaking on the shore, the azure sea smiling and innocent as if it were quite a different ocean from the one that had lashed the island in recent months. Zachariah ran the ketch on to the beach, leaping out as it touched to pull it higher and holding it steady as Dorcas jumped out after him, the waves catching the hem of her skirt in spite of her efforts to hold it clear.

It didn't matter. Nothing mattered on this golden day. Barefoot, hand in hand, they walked in the shallow water at the edge of the shore, their feet disturbing the ripples of sunlight beneath the surface so that they broke and wavered and re-formed.

"We're alone in the world," Zachariah said.

"We shall stay here." Dorcas spoke imperiously. "Build me a palace; I think – just – *there!*" She circled around as she spoke and ended by pointing at the top of the rounded hummock that rose from the low cliff.

"Certainly, your highness – at once, your highness –" Theatrically, Zachariah mopped and mowed before her, touching his forelock.

"Thank you, my man. I shall appoint you my court jester."

"Well, damn your impertinence!" Hands on his hips, head thrust forward in mock fury, Zachariah stood with his feet astride and glared at her. "Cannot you see, short-sighted wench, that I am the frog who will turn into a handsome prince if you but kiss me?"

Laughing she held out her arms to him and he came to claim his kiss. When it was over, Dorcas still clung to him, her lips close to his ear.

"I wish to know the answer to one question," she breathed. "Tell me, frog, what has gone wrong?"

"Impudent hussy!" He pushed her deeper into the water and splashed her with a thousand droplets of crystal so that she fled from him until once more he caught her in his arms.

They found the ideal place to spread their blanket in a small fissure shaded by a rock, and Zachariah brought the basket which held their food and wine, burying the wine bottle where the waves could wash over it and keep it cool.

"I have plans for you." He was dusting his hands free from

sand as he came back to her. "First, we shall remove this dress and spread it to dry on the rock —"

"Zachariah! I cannot! In broad daylight —"

"We're alone in the world, that's been established. Then we shall swim — oh yes, my lass! It would be a crime if we did not."

The water was like cool, liquid silk against her skin, and while she could not dive as Zachariah did, she floated on the water as he had taught her, her eyes closed against the sun and a kaleidoscope of a million colours beneath her lids.

She knew he would make love to her. Surely this time, she thought, arching her body to meet him — surely this time, on such a day, we shall have a child; and as he shudderingly subsided into quietness, she said as much to him.

His hand was gentle on her hair.

"You mustn't mind so much, sweetheart."

"I want to please you."

"You do please me, every hour of every day."

"But a child is a — a kind of pledge."

"Your presence is pledge enough. You're my life, Dorcas."

For some time she lay silent, then bitterly she spoke.

"Why?" she demanded. "For God's sake, *why*? Life is so unfair."

"Who but a child expects it to be otherwise?" He covered her with small, tender kisses. "Come, smile for me, my darling. This is no day for gloom. Suppose I kiss you *here* and *here* —"

"Then I shall feel even more wanton than I do already."

They laughed like children, at anything and nothing. They ate and they drank and they swam again, and Dorcas laughed most of all at the expression of horror on Zachariah's face when she looked at a point beyond his bare shoulder and said:

"Well, good-*day* to you, Mrs. Grimshaw! How delightful that you could join us."

"You baggage — you hussy —" Laughing, he held her close, but the joke had reminded her that there were, after all, others in the world.

"We have tested our luck too far," she said, reaching for her clothes. "There might be a passing fisherman, after all. I should act in a sober and respectable manner."

"Have some more wine, sweetheart."

Sober was, perhaps, not quite the word, Dorcas reflected as she drank the wine. Tacking homewards once more against the wind, the laughter still bubbled to the surface as she caught Zachariah's eye.

"I've come to a decision," he said, as they neared Grand Cay, the day almost over. "This is the year we shall go to Bermuda. I yearn to show you off to the whole world."

"Bermuda is hardly the whole world!"

"It will suffice. Don't you want to go?"

"You know that I do."

"We shall go after the hurricane season – for Christmas, perhaps. That would please you, wouldn't it?"

"You know it would, Zack."

She smiled at him, and went on smiling as she looked over the bow, seeing the coral heads beneath the glassy surface. She was armoured against Kit now, she told herself, trailing her hand in the water, enjoying the play of light and shade. She could see him and never turn a hair. She was a different person from the girl who had left Bermuda four years earlier.

"The market will pick up again," Zachariah said confidently. "America knows there's no salt like Turks Islands' salt."

Lost markets were not their only difficulty. Climatically things could hardly have been worse. The months from May to August, usually hot and dry, were punctuated by storms that diluted the brine in the shallow ponds so that the precious white crystals refused to form in anything like the quality or quantity that was expected.

Towards the end of August the wind dropped and an oppressive stillness settled over the island. There seemed no colour in the sea or sky, and men sniffed the air and looked anxiously at the horizon.

"It's hurricane weather," Dorcas said fearfully.

"Maybe." Zachariah remained calm. "The glass stands fairly high." He rasped a hand along his jaw. "Even so, I'll get Joe to take the ketch to South Creek for safety."

"What about the house? Are we safe?"

"I shall check the shutters. See that we fill some vessels with water, sweetheart, and look to the food stocks."

For once Dorcas was, without a single reservation, entirely thankful that she could trust Emma to ensure that Storm kept close to the house. He roared with fury as she curtailed his wanderings, but eventually even he seemed overawed by the indefinable threat in the atmosphere and played quite happily on the porch.

"Is it going to be bad?" Davey asked, a hint of excitement in his voice.

"We hope not. It may yet turn away."

It did not turn away. Ominous black clouds massed on the skyline, darker and darker, turning the whole world pewter-grey.

Towards evening the glass fell and the wind got up, whining like a live thing, and on the horizon the clouds writhed and re-formed, poised for the kill before racing inland.

Zachariah closed all the shutters to windward, leaving the others to minimise the damage. Still there was no rain, just the mad, moaning wind that bent stout trees to the ground and stripped palmetto roofs from the shacks beyond the salina. A heavy sea was running and the boats of those who had chosen to ride out the storm were ripped from their moorings and tossed like matchwood on the mountainous waves.

Inside Tamarind Villa, they huddled fearfully, anxious for what the night would bring. The household slaves had been brought inside for their own safety, and eyes gleamed in black faces, silent and stoical, as the rain descended so fiercely that the house shuddered and groaned as if in agony. Hour after hour they suffered this battering until suddenly, in the small hours of the morning, all was quiet.

"It's only the eye," Zachariah said, as they stirred from uneasy sleep and listened to the silence. "It will begin again."

It did, however, give him the chance to check the house. He found that a portion of the upper balcony and the steps leading to it had been swept away, and that some of the timbers beneath an upstairs window had gone so that rain had poured into the main bedroom. He and Joe shored it up again as best they could, then, as the wind rose once more, they struggled to close the shutters to leeward.

For the rest of that night and part of the following day the hurricane raged, though there was no more rain. It was spindrift that battered the house now, and the fine, flying sand; a different sound, but equally destructive.

When at last the storm blew itself out and they were able to emerge into the outside world, Dorcas realised that the devastation and loss of property in her bedroom was as nothing compared to the devastation elsewhere in the town.

"We were the lucky ones," she said, pale with shock.

The hurricane seemed to have struck at random targets: here a house was battered on the windward side, there to leeward. Roofing over water tanks was ripped off while the house close by was undamaged. One shack would stand, while another within feet was reduced to a shambles, its contents scattered. Trees everywhere had been uprooted, but those close to Tamarind Villa suffered only minor damage.

As for the salt ponds, they and the nearby roads were an unbroken sheet of water. Zachariah stood, Dorcas by his side, his face a mask of tragedy, and neither of them could speak.

Immediately, there was work to be done. Stocks of food were assessed and pooled, and it was estimated that there was only sufficient on the island for fifteen days, unless goods were efficiently distributed. A soup kitchen was set up in the gaol yard, a plea for help was sent to nearby islands, and Marcia opened a casualty station to treat the numerous cuts and abrasions caused by the storm. Now we shall see who our friends are, people said. Now we shall see how ready the Nassau Government is to come to our aid.

Drought followed the storm, and for many it was the last straw, these disasters coming as they did after two years of war.

"We've had enough," said the McGoverns and the Barstows and the Hicksons.

"You mean they're going back to Bermuda?" Dorcas asked when Zachariah came home with this news.

"So they say."

"But what will they do there?"

"They say nothing can be worse than scraping a living here, at the mercy of the elements."

She looked at him and said nothing, knowing that the small flicker of hope that was beginning to burn in her heart was nothing less than treachery.

He slumped down at the table and buried his face in his hands. She had never seen him look so defeated, so entirely without hope.

"Oh, Zack!" She went to him and put her arms about him, pressing her cheek against his head. "Oh, Zack –"

Couldn't we go, too? The words were there, aching to be spoken, yet somehow she managed to hold them back. It made no difference. He was conscious of them just the same.

He pounded his fist on the table – once, twice, three times.

"We'll stay," he said, his jaw set. "I can't give up yet. I can't give up, sweetheart."

"No, Zack," she said. "I didn't think you would."

Eight

The visit to Bermuda was postponed, for Zachariah had neither the cash nor the enthusiasm that year. Other families packed up and left the island, but grimly he hung on, refusing to admit defeat, depressed but determined. Sometimes Dorcas remembered the gaiety of the day they sailed to the deserted cay and wondered if they would ever be so carefree again; not until salt fetched more than fifteen cents the bushel, that was certain.

It was Emma who finally pushed them into making arrangements for the trip the following winter, after all danger of hurricanes had passed. The problems concerning her education had not diminished, and her possessive love for Storm was the cause of interminable squabbles, not only with Davey but with an ever-more-independent Storm.

"I have put off this decision long enough," Zachariah said, at the end of a long and strife-filled day. "Emma must go away to school, and she must go now if she is to go at all. Write to Fanny, Dorcas, to see if we may stay at Cedarcroft for Christmas."

The malaise and depression that had weighed on Dorcas's spirits for the entire year seemed to lift as if by magic. They sailed during the first week in December, to be greeted at the port of Hamilton by Silas and Fanny.

The two sisters fell into each other's arms, moved almost to tears, and it was only after several moments that they remembered their manners and the fact that there were others in the party.

"Emma, how pretty you have become," Fanny said, bending to kiss her cheek. "And so grown up!"

Eyes downcast, lashes making neat, dark fans on her cheeks, Emma bobbed a demure curtsey. Dorcas, looking at her a trifle anxiously, hoped that she would be on her best behaviour during their stay at Cedarcroft. The last few days on board ship had, if anything, been more difficult than any that had gone before.

Fanny turned to her brother-in-law.

"Zachariah, how lovely to see you! Oh Silas, is it not wonderful to have them here?" Silas smiled his assent, but did not seem unduly bowled over by the wonder of the occasion. Fanny quickly passed on to Davey.

"Why, you dear boy, you grow more like your father, I declare, and you're shooting up, too – and here's Storm! My, *such* a man! Welcome home, all of you. How we have looked forward to this, have we not, Silas? Oh, *Dorcas*!"

The men smiled indulgently as the sisters embraced yet again.

Later, after Dorcas had duly admired the two little girls in the nursery – Phillipa, aged four, and Julia, two and a half and fat as a butterball – Fanny conducted her to the chamber she was to occupy during her stay at Cedarcroft. It was a spacious, second-floor room, looking out over a grove of cedar and pine, cool under the white roof, the walls constructed of thick stone to keep out the worst of the summer heat. The four-poster bed and the carved chest at its foot were made out of cedar wood. All the furniture, the tables with the silver candlesticks and crystal hurricane shades, were simple but solid and elegant, and Dorcas sighed with pleasure to find herself in such surroundings once more.

"Emma's a quiet little thing, isn't she?" Fanny remarked, bringing her back to her everyday problems.

"Sometimes she's quiet," Dorcas admitted cautiously. "Not always, I fear. Oh Fanny –" as she looked about her at the polished wood and the white bedspread edged in deep crochet – "it's such a lovely home! And you – you've changed! You're more sure of yourself, I suppose. A true mistress of Cedarcroft."

"I've put on a great deal of weight."

"It becomes you. You look serene and dignified. Tell me –" Dorcas turned a little anxiously towards her sister. "When am I to see Father? I confess I am nervous."

"There's no need to be. He is quite subdued these days. I swear he has forgotten the circumstances that caused you to go to the Turks Islands, almost as if age has blunted his memory."

"He's not as old as all that!"

"No, but there's a change in him. You'll see."

Silas had despatched the coach to bring Mr. Foley and his mother to Cedarcroft, and when it rolled up to the front steps, all the Trantons and Hardimans were gathered to greet them.

It was the sight of her grandmother that came as the biggest shock to Dorcas. The years that had passed since their last meeting had taken a toll; she was tinier and more withered than ever, and her head – still elaborately dressed beneath her frilled bonnet – shook as if she suffered from palsy. She had tears in her eyes as she stepped down from the coach, and from that moment it was clear that however angry she had been with Dorcas in the past, all was forgiven now.

"My dear, dear child," she said, holding out her arms. "Such a long time! I was beginning to think we should not meet this side of Paradise."

She felt like a scrawny chicken in Dorcas's embrace, all tiny, brittle bones and paper-thin skin.

"Well, Dorcas?" In his turn her father embraced her, looking at her in such a way that in spite of all Fanny had said, she could see no difference in him.

"It's good to see you, Father," she said.

For a moment he did not speak, his eyes hooded. His mouth made odd twitching movements, then he nodded rapidly and seemed to be making an attempt to smile.

"Keeping well?" he enquired, as if they were chance acquaintances meeting in the street. Dorcas, her arm through his, felt a totally unexpected pang of compassion for him, realising suddenly that even when he wished to be pleasant he found it almost impossible. Zachariah came to her side and Mr. Foley stretched out a limp hand towards him.

"Captain Hardiman," he said. "Keeping well, eh?"

"Father, you must meet the children. Emma, Davey, Storm – come and meet your grandfather."

Mr. Foley nodded and twitched in a general way, but it was on Storm that his eyes rested.

"Your son, eh? Storm, d'you call him?" As if he had only just heard the name – as if Dorcas had not written about him constantly for the past five years. "The Foley looks, I see. A fine boy, Dorcas."

Mrs. Foley twittered inanely.

"Nothing of Captain Hardiman about him ... well, I suppose he wouldn't ... though I must say that he is not nearly so ... I mean, now that I see him again –" She peered at Zachariah short-sightedly, then suddenly seemed to come to her senses and become covered with confusion.

"There are sweetmeats in my reticule for the children,

Dorcas, and for your little girls, Fanny. I have them here somewhere –"

"We are to eat dinner shortly, Grandmama." Fanny came quickly to her rescue, took her grandmother firmly by the arm and shepherded her up the steps and into the hallway. "Come and refresh yourself before sitting down. Silas, I feel sure Father would welcome a glass of madeira."

It was a strange reversal, Dorcas thought, when they were all sitting at the table. It was quite plain that Silas was now the head of this family, with her father deferring to him in all things. He even looked smaller in stature.

"Has he been ill?" she asked Fanny afterwards when he had gone. "I know he has had this bronchial trouble, but he seems so diminished, somehow."

"He has had his disappointments and reversals," Fanny said. "There's a great deal of new blood in the Assembly, and the younger members are tired of being dominated by the old guard like father and Mr. Mallory. Since the war there seems a different spirit abroad here – more optimism and hope for the future. New families have come to positions of importance. There's more prosperity. Silas says it's essential to move with the times, and this, of course, Father is quite incapable of doing. He bitterly opposed the adoption of Hamilton as the new capital which caused a great deal of ill-feeling."

"You can't mean to tell me that he and Mr. Mallory are actually *friendly* now?" Dorcas asked incredulously.

Fanny laughed at that.

"That, I think, would be going too far. Still, they fight no longer. I think I would call it an armed truce rather than friendship – and it's all Silas's doing! He simply would not allow the feud to continue. It would have put us in an impossible position, bearing in mind his connections with the Mallorys."

This revelation caused Dorcas to regard her brother-in-law in a new light. He was a man who said little and to her he seemed to possess little humour and still less presence; a cold fish, in fact. Now she saw that there was more to him than she realised, a steely strength that was not to be disregarded. In his own family his word was law. Fanny, though happy enough, seemed to turn towards him for confirmation of her lightest word.

"She has him on a pedestal," Dorcas remarked with some wonderment to Zachariah in the privacy of their bedroom.

Zachariah's eyes rounded and up went his comic eyebrows.

"And that causes you surprise, wife? You mean that *I* have no pedestal in your eyes?"

"It's worn away with constant polishing," said Dorcas.

She felt it more and more apparent, however, that Silas did not much approve of her — that he considered her too vehement in her opinions and too ready to give voice to them. There was one uncomfortable evening when, at dinner, she ventured to add her contribution to Zachariah's mild defence of the Abolitionists' views in the British Parliament.

"I understand," she said, "that production in fact increases in those places where work is done by free men. The matter has been proved —"

"It is not a subject on which women can have any valuable contribution to make," Silas said coldly. "They are hardly in a position to understand the commercial implications. Of course, if you wish total ruin of the entire West Indian economy, then support Abolition by all means."

"Dorcas was ever one to let her heart rule her head," Fanny interjected hastily, casting anxious glances between her husband and her sister.

"I am quite certain that eventually all slavery will be abolished," Zachariah said. "No matter what our views. The trade is already illegal in the British colonies and for myself I'm glad of it. Freeing the slaves we have is another matter. I regard myself as responsible for them."

Dorcas remained silent, for Fanny's sake and for Zachariah's, but she smarted at Silas's lofty dismissal of women and their opinions.

"I should like to hear him in discussion with Marcia," she said to Zachariah when once again their bedroom door was closed behind them, and he agreed that the occasion might be quite diverting.

"But you are enjoying being here, aren't you?" he asked, when later they lay in each other's arms in the four-poster bed. She drew away from him a little so that she could see the blur of his face in the half-light.

"Of course," she said. "How can you ask? It's wonderful to get away from Grand Cay, if only for a short time. Bermuda will always be my home."

Zachariah was silent for some time after that.

"What would you say," he said at last, "if we never returned?"

She could not see his expression, only the shape of his face and the dark half-moons of his eyebrows, but somehow she knew he was saddened by her gasp of delight.

"What *can* you mean, Zack? Not go back at all?"

"Silas has suggested that we stay."

"*Silas*? But I had the impression that we were here under sufferance! I don't think he likes me very much."

"I imagine Fanny has made representations – but in any case, he seems to think I have something to offer. He knows what a hard time we've had this past year. All Bermuda knows! He's in a partnership that has bought four American prizes as the basis of a trading fleet and he's offered me a chance to go in with them. With more capital they could buy more, he said; they're available for the asking."

"Oh!" Slowly Dorcas let out her breath and turned over to lie on her back, arms beneath her head.

Never to go back to Grand Cay! Never to see that scrubby, dusty little island again, with its stunted vegetation and salt-soured soil. To be able to live graciously – not so grandly as Fanny, of course, not at first – but to live in a society where she felt at home and among her own kind, not cut off from all she had ever known. How could Zack hesitate?

"Who is Silas's partner?" she asked.

"Kit Mallory. Silas seems to think well of him. He's something of an adventurer, he says, but has drive and ambition and knows his business."

She felt, suddenly, an insane desire to laugh wildly. Of all the bizarre twists of fate, this surely was the most absurd? It mattered little, though. Kit was nothing to her now.

"What do you say?" Zachariah asked her. "Would you like it?"

"Zack, you know that I would. How can you doubt it?"

He said nothing, and all at once Dorcas had a memory of him standing on the North Point at Grand Cay shouting his faith in the future to the four winds.

"I would like it," she said more gently. "But would you?"

"I don't know," he said, after a long moment's silence.

She could hear the rasp of his hand along his jaw.

"I told him we would consider the matter together," he said. "I told him that your opinion was of the utmost importance to me."

Dorcas laughed at that.

"I can't imagine," she said, "that his opinion of your judgement remains very high."

She knew that a meeting with Kit was inevitable. It was clear from Silas's conversation that the two men were now deeply involved in business and that Kit had become a family friend.

"Do you like him?" she asked Fanny when they were taking tea on the veranda together in the absence of their husbands and children.

Fanny considered the matter and shrugged.

"Everyone likes Kit Mallory," she said. "Silas finds much to admire in him."

"That's no answer! I asked what you thought."

"I cannot see that my view is of the least importance." Busily Fanny poured tea, but Dorcas was not to be diverted.

"His reputation is that of an adventurer," she said. "You yourself said that Cousin Phoebe was well rid of him."

Fanny looked confused.

"It may be that I misjudged him. He is very charming, there is no doubt whatsoever of that —"

Doubt, however, was somehow implied by her voice and still Dorcas looked at her questioningly. Unhappily Fanny set down her cup.

"I don't know what it is," she said. "I know that Father was — and still is to an extent — unfair in his strictures against the Mallorys. But it cannot be gainsaid that Kit Mallory's father did turn his coat during the Revolution, merely to suit his own pocket —"

"Oh, come Fanny! Surely you are not still fighting those battles. Leave them to our parents and grandparents."

"It is the principle!" Fanny had grown pink in the defence of her beliefs. "Loyalty is something that is important to me —"

"As I've reason to know and be thankful for," Dorcas admitted.

"Kit Mallory's politics are his own business. I have this conviction, though, that he has little motivation beyond his own interests and would stop at little to gain his own ends. He is very ambitious. Silas regards this as a virtue, and I suppose in some ways one has to agree; but I am sure he would cast off Silas or anyone else who stood in his way. Under the charm there is a hardness, a ruthlessness about him. His mother," she added in a more practical and down-to-earth tone as she reached for Dorcas's cup, "is a very strange woman. She seems to have fallen out with almost everyone in Bermuda. Her memory for slights and imagined slights is quite phenomenal!"

"And her son is the same, do you think?" Anyone would have thought Dorcas's attention to be wholly engaged in the stirring of her tea.

"Oh, I can't tell! Perhaps I am quite wrong about him. Certainly I am in a minority, for it seems most women fall down before him like ninepins."

Not me, Dorcas thought. Not me. Never again. I am armed against him.

She shopped in Hamilton, wondering if at any moment they might come face to face; but it seemed they were not fated to meet by chance. However, one day Zachariah returned from town with Silas and said that they had met with Kit in the tavern and had been talking business.

"They're pressing for me to join them," he said, one arm around Dorcas's waist, holding her close to him. "Mallory wishes to be remembered to you."

"How kind," Dorcas said, seething inwardly at this effrontery. Remembered to her, indeed! After all that had happened between them. Yet, in all fairness, he was only behaving as she intended to behave; as if they were no more than old acquaintances.

"Have you decided, then?" she asked.

"It would mean a better life for you and the children." He was staring out of the windows that looked over the carriage drive and the flowering garden, his shoulders drooping a little as if in defeat. "There would be no need to leave Emma at that mincing Mrs. Fanshawe's seminary, or abandon Davey to Reverend Hartwell," for it had been decided that Davey, too, would benefit by being away from Grand Cay.

His voice trailed away, and Dorcas had the feeling that he was seeing another view – not trees and flowers and lush greenery, but bone-white salt ponds glinting in the sun. He shook himself a little as if making a determined effort to put all that behind him.

"The three of us are to dine with a business acquaintance of Silas's tonight; a Mr. Jamieson. He is interested in investing capital with us. Perhaps you know him?"

Dorcas shook her head.

"I don't think so."

"It seems he owns indigo estates in Charleston, as well as a quarry here. He would be an important contact, were we to join together and expand . . ." Again he seemed to drift into silence as if he could not sustain these sudden bursts of enthusiasm.

Dorcas caught at his arm and pulled him round to face her, putting her arms around his neck.

"Dear Zack," she said. "This could be exciting too, you know. There are other worlds to conquer besides the twenty-two square miles of Grand Cay."

"I know, I know." He smiled at her lovingly and gently rubbed her soft cheek with the back of his hand. "My lovely, lovely Dorcas! I care for naught so long as you are with me."

The men were late home that night. Davey and Emma dined with Fanny and Dorcas and after the meal was over a card table was unfolded so that the children could be taught to play whist until Davey's yawns were so intrusive that he could no longer avoid being sent to bed.

"I needn't go yet, need I?" Emma appealed to Fanny rather than to Dorcas. "I'll be very good and quiet."

"You've been a model of good behaviour since coming here," Dorcas said, hurriedly paying tribute to this extraordinary state of affairs. "I think another half-hour might prove acceptable if your aunt agrees."

Fanny had seated herself at the piano. She played a few chords in a tentative way. She was no great musician, but was able to play a simple accompaniment.

"Come and sing to us, Emma," she said. "I have a book of songs here I feel sure you must know."

Emma, a true daughter of Zachariah, had a sweet, clear voice. From her seat by the fire Dorcas watched her standing beside Fanny, gravely bending from time to time to turn the pages, and acknowledged to herself that the troublesome stepdaughter she had fumed over in Grand Cay seemed a different person here with Fanny. She commented on the fact when at last the song-book was closed and Emma had gone upstairs.

"I'm not married to her father and I have no claim on Storm's affection," Fanny said. "You mustn't blame yourself entirely, Dorcas — I can see there are deep passions beneath that demure surface. In my view," she went on, "the fault lies with Grand Cay. In a place so small, emotions are magnified and grievances remembered long after they would have been forgotten elsewhere."

Dorcas thought this over as she prepared herself for bed and acknowledged it to be true. For as long as she had lived there, Grand Cay had seethed with one small crisis after another and hurt feelings seemed almost to be cherished, as if they gave point and colour to existence. St. George's had been bad enough, she reflected, but Grand Cay was many times worse. In her present jaundiced frame of mind, it seemed a small island full of small people with small concerns, and the thought of returning to it sent her spirits spiralling downwards. Heaven send that even now Zachariah was making up his mind to give up the struggle there.

Midnight had struck some time ago, so plainly the men had found much to discuss, but at last the sound of an approaching coach made her put down her brush and go to the window, for no other reason but a wifely curiosity to see if too much rum had made her husband's steps unsteady.

At the sight of the coach, however, she frowned and peered closer. It was lighter in colour than the one in which Silas and Zachariah had gone out earlier in the evening and the horse was quite different, smaller and darker. She clutched the chest-high window-sill and peered out as it came to a halt in front of the steps, slightly to her right and perfectly visible. She felt a sudden clutch of fear that something had gone wrong – an injury, an accident, sudden illness – but this was quickly dispelled by the sound of men's voices raised in friendly banter. The rum bottle, she thought sardonically, had not been entirely neglected. Well, she had little to complain of on that score. Zachariah was, on the whole, an abstemious man.

There was laughter as Zachariah, jumping to the ground, made some remark regarding boats, at least, being unable to lose a wheel, while Silas could be heard offering profuse thanks.

"More than kind," he was saying. "Many apologies for taking you out of your way."

He was speaking to someone inside the coach, and after renewed thanks and repeated 'goodnights', both he and Zachariah turned to enter the house. A voice from within the coach halted them and made them turn back.

"There's yet one more thing I ought to mention –"

A booted foot and tight, white trousers emerged from the

coach, closely followed by the rest of the hitherto unseen owner.

Dorcas, watching from above, felt as if all the blood had drained from her body; as if, suddenly, she had received a mighty blow to the pit of her stomach.

"No, no!" She was unaware that she had uttered the words aloud. Still gripping the window-sill, she turned her head away. She was not ready for this; it was not fair, to confront her with Kit in this way, when she was tired and vulnerable and unprepared.

She thought her heart would burst from her breast, it was beating so. Slowly, fearfully, she looked down again. He was hatless, clearly visible in the light shining from the open door, his hair as glossy and dark as ever, his features as finely chiselled. She remembered the set of his shoulders and the carriage of his head and – oh, God! – the way he stood, back on his heels, one hand on his hip. How could she have thought she was armoured against him? How could she have dreamed for one moment that she could remain unaffected? She saw him laugh and throw back his head, and that, too, seemed as dear and familiar as if she had seen him every day for the six years that had elapsed since their last meeting. She strained to hear his voice, but everything was obscured by this strange rushing noise in her ears.

She saw him look towards Zachariah, who had his back to her. She saw him smile and raise a hand in farewell: hadn't he smiled and lifted his hand in just that manner, the night she left him on the cliff?

For a moment or two she could not move, and she realised that she was trembling, her teeth chattering as if she had a fever. She lifted her shoulders to her ears and wrapped her arms about her body as if for comfort, but there was no comfort to be had, for all was coldness and desolation and misery. Life without him was a wilderness in which she would walk for ever with no sun to warm her.

She heard Zachariah's footsteps approaching along the polished wood floor of the corridor outside their room, and in a flash she was in bed, curled with her back to the door, feigning sleep.

She could not speak, least of all to Zachariah. Another day, perhaps, this pain would ease. Another day she would be able to act the affectionate wife again.

For tonight, she knew that any attempt at words would

emerge as a sob of anguish, a lament for what might have been, and long after Zachariah was asleep, she stared with wide, blank eyes into the darkness while the clock in the hall downstairs faintly marked the passing hours.

By morning she knew what she had to do.

"Let's go back," she said to Zachariah. "We have something that's our own there, a challenge to face together."

Zachariah raised himself on one elbow and looked down at her, his expression one of amazement and delight and disbelief.

"It will be an uphill struggle —"

"I know! But there's satisfaction in it."

"For me, that's true — but for you? Dorcas, sweetheart, what has caused you to change your mind? I want you to think about this."

"I have thought about it." This, at least, was true. She had thought about it endlessly, hour after hour, while Zachariah slept. "It seems to me we are presented with an opportunity to prospe:. Now that others have left the island, this is your chance, surely, to step in and buy up more holdings. Maybe we should borrow to increase our investment — buy a larger boat, perhaps, so that you can export your own salt. Silas might help there. It could tie in with this new business of his —"

"Dorcas —"

"Think of the slaves there who depend on you, Zack. Think of your dreams for the island, the town you're going to build —"

"Sweetheart, these are the thoughts that have haunted me ever since the question of leaving was brought up! Life will be hard, though. I've no wish to be unfair to you."

"In some ways it might be harder here," Dorcas said obscurely.

"I'm used to running things my way," Zachariah admitted. "And I hate to abandon my dream. I didn't commit myself to Silas, Dorcas, even last night, for always at the back of my thick, stubborn head were the criticisms I've made of those who've taken what they wanted from the islands and given nothing. I don't want to be like that."

"That's settled, then."

Dorcas spoke calmly, but eluded his grateful embrace, briskly getting out of bed to pull the curtains and greet the day. She caught sight of her face in the mirror. It looked strange, she thought; set and stiff and strangely pale. She stretched her lips in a meaningless smile before turning back to Zachariah.

"I've much to do today," she said, "for it's Christmas tomorrow and Fanny needs my help. I'll wager you need to rest after last night's debauchery —"

"Not a bit of it! I'm taking the boys to the harbour."

All was as normal, she told herself. Nothing had changed, nothing *would* change, so long as she blocked out the past and kept her eyes solely on the future.

There was no way of avoiding Kit, Dorcas knew. Fanny was determined to make New Year the occasion for a ball to which everyone would be invited. At least she was now prepared for the effect his appearance would have on her and could school herself to withstand the shock of realising that, no matter what, her desire for him was unaltered. She should be thankful for that unguarded sight of him, she told herself.

She dressed with care on the night of the ball, knowing that the fluttering of her nerves only served to heighten her colour and the brightness of her eyes. Zachariah, as she stood before him to tie his cravat, kissed her cheek and told her so.

"My wife is still the loveliest girl in Bermuda," he said, and she laughed and kissed his cheek in return.

"This gown flatters me," she said. "Green was ever a favourite colour of mine."

The house was decked with greenery and garlands of flowers and two hundred candles in a glittering candelabra shed their light on gleaming shoulders, setting jewels ablaze with fire. The swirl of silks and satins and lace composed a mixture that was as intoxicating as the punch that was being offered by the livery-clad slaves. Recklessly Dorcas took a glass and drank down the contents. She needed all the help available, she told herself; how else would she get through the night?

Emma sat amongst a group of young Trantons and Foleys, dressed in white lawn with pink ribbons and rosebuds in her hair. She looked remarkably pretty, Dorcas thought; pretty but apart, in some indefinable way.

Dorcas was dancing with a Foley cousin when Kit entered the room, and she saw, without surprise, that he had a young woman on each arm. The Foxley twins, she recognised; still in the schoolroom when she left Bermuda, but now tall and elegant with blonde hair swept up in two neat, identical knots, and two identical pairs of sparkling blue eyes to laugh up at him. Georgina and Geraldine were their names. She had never been able to tell them apart, and still could not.

They were greeting Fanny and Silas by the door. Kit was laughing, gesturing, looking about him at the decorations. In another second he would be aware of her scrutiny. Immediately she smiled up at her cousin and launched herself on a sea of frenzied conversation. Wasn't this a wonderful occasion? Fanny had surely surpassed herself, for the room looked a perfect dream – and he simply would not *believe* the diversity of the refreshments! She had become unused to such luxuries, for in Grand Cay one took what one could get and was thankful.'

The dance was over. Solemnly Cousin Josiah proffered his arm and escorted her back to Zachariah.

"Your wife is in fine fettle tonight," he said jocularly. "As happy and full of spirits as I have ever known her."

"And why should I not be?" Dorcas clasped Zachariah's arm and looked up at him, the very picture of an adoring wife. "Am I not the most fortunate of women?"

"Then allow me this dance." Zachariah beamed at her fondly. "Excuse us, sir."

Zachariah danced as he did everything else; with vigour and enthusiasm and a total disregard of the figure he cut to the outside world. He felt each beat of the music in every fibre and pore, and though Dorcas normally regarded his style of dancing with amused affection, on this occasion she wished with all her heart that he would perform with more restraint. Was it really necessary for his coat-tails to fly like that? She needed to admire him tonight, and needed others to admire him too, not be amused by him.

Kit, she saw, was dancing with Fanny. He was wearing the pale evening breeches that were fashionable, but his height and slenderness gave them added elegance. *He* was not bouncing like a rubber ball! He moved with grace and dignity, his dark hair gleaming under the lights.

Would he dance with her? She longed for it and feared it, all at one and the same time. When the present dance came to an end, she protested when Zachariah suggested joining Fanny and Silas, for she could see that Kit was still in conversation with them.

"I should like to sit a little, Zack," she said, plying her fan vigorously. "It is exceedingly hot –"

"There is a vacant chair beside Fanny."

His arm beneath her elbow, he propelled her across the room. The time was upon her, she recognised; the moment could no longer be delayed. She would need to summon all her strength to greet Kit with the cool friendliness that was appropriate between one acquaintance and another.

He was still bending towards Fanny as they approached, but turned as Zachariah hailed him.

"Hallo, Mallory! Good to see you again. You know my wife, I believe."

"I had the pleasure of meeting her long ago." Kit bowed, his eyes unfathomable, his gaze holding hers. "I'm delighted to renew the acquaintance. I trust you are well, Mrs. Hardiman."

Dorcas smiled at him above the ivory fan.

"Very well, I thank you." She felt mildly triumphant at the polite chill with which she managed to invest these words.

"May I beg the honour of a dance with your wife, Hardiman?"

"So kind, but really I must decline – I am quite exhausted –"

Somehow, in spite of her protests, he contrived to draw her on to the floor, and for a moment they performed the complicated figure of the dance without speaking. Her head was once more full of that incapacitating, thunderous roar, and her throat was dry. She even forgot to smile.

"Well, Dorcas?" he said at last. She looked at him coldly.

"My father always says that when he can think of nothing else. Is it meant to be a question?"

"Not really." The rhythm of the dance was unbroken: step towards her, step back; glide forward and circle. "More of a comment, I suppose, on the strangeness of dancing with you after so many years. I'm told by your husband that it was your urging that caused him to abandon the idea of staying here."

Step forward, step back, step forward and promenade.

"We discussed the matter together. He would have stayed had it appealed to me, but frankly I can't wait to return."

He inclined his head as if in acknowledgment, his eyes holding hers, his expression unsmiling.

"I suppose," he said after a moment, "I should not be surprised. After all, you were always anxious to run away from Bermuda. This would not be the first time."

"*What*?" Dorcas was so outraged that she missed a beat and had to scramble a little to catch up with it. "*You* accuse *me* of running away?"

"What else would you call it?" He abandoned this topic for another. "Tell me, is your marriage happy, Dorcas? Was it love at first sight?"

"Your impertinence astounds me." Anger was almost choking her, but it was important to keep a bland countenance or there would be talk. Mechanically the dance continued: step and glide foward; step and circle. She managed to regain her expression of polite indifference. "Yes, my marriage is happy."

"Then you are to be congratulated, for such is not common in my experience."

"Your experience is, I understand, still limited to that of an onlooker. Though of course," she added waspishly, "I have no doubt you have consoled yourself plentifully." She heard her voice ringing in her head, thin and vinegary, and was horrified. This was not how she had intended to present herself to him.

Step back, step forward, circle and promenade. Still the ridiculous figure went on. Kit appeared to be smiling faintly.

"I have found diversions, it is true."

"Perhaps it is time you returned to your twin diversions of this evening. How do you manage it, Kit? Do you kiss them strictly by rote, or take them on alternate nights?"

She felt a fluttering sensation as if the bitter words were boiling in the cauldron of her stomach, boiling so hard that she could not prevent them spilling over. Still the music played and still they danced in this ludicrously false accord. Any onlooker would assume them to be discussing nothing more controversial than the weather or the excellence of the orchestra.

"Where is the sweet young thing I used to know?" he murmured, and now she saw amusement in his eyes and the beginning of that smile that was always her downfall. Grimly she clutched at her anger.

"You have the effrontery to ask that?"

"Effrontery is not something I have ever lacked."

The music came to an end at last and politely they bowed. All around them couples were leaving the floor, but they stood unmoving, eyes locked together.

"Dorcas," he said, smiling openly now. "You are magnificent. I could never have believed that you could have become even more beautiful."

"Pray do not say such things!" Love him? Dorcas asked herself. She hated him! He was arrogant and uncaring.

Why, then, when he drew her from the floor, not in the direction of Fanny and Zachariah but towards the double doors beyond which was the dining-room, did she tamely succumb and accept from his hands a glass of punch taken from the tray of a passing slave?

"Your husband, I think, is not of a nature that would object to two old friends reminiscing over the past?"

"I have no wish to reminisce." She turned her head away from him, but she could feel the power of the old attraction pulling at her, infiltrating her defences, dissipating her anger.

"Well, that I can believe." His voice was full of warmth and laughter and carried the caressing note that she remembered so well. "But if I can forgive and forget, surely you can do the same."

"*What?*" She looked at him fully then, eyes wide and blazing. "What, pray, did you have to forgive?"

He smiled deep into those eyes, his expression almost joyful as if her passion was awaking other passions long relegated to the past.

"You are magnificent," he said again, slowly and wonderingly. "Oh, Dorcas, what did you do? Running off like that, marrying the first man that asked you! How do you imagine I felt when I came back and found you gone?"

"Poor Kit!" Dorcas's voice was brittle. "I imagine your feelings must have been ruffled for a full ten minutes."

"You do me an injustice."

"It seems there is no justice when it comes to matters between a man and a woman, and no truth either. *You* left *me*, and with no word of explanation; no word, that is, except that of your mother who told me you were about to marry an English heiress."

"I'm sorry for that. She exaggerated a passing friendship, no more. She was always ambitious — and vindictive towards your family, Dorcas, you must have realised that. It was my word you should have trusted."

"Your word? I had no word! Let it go, Kit. All this talk of the past is quite pointless. It's over and done with."

Was Storm over and done with? she thought suddenly. Storm was this man's son. She ached, all at once, with a mad desire to tell him, but knew that she would not, could not, for the repercussions might well be more than she could cope with.

"I must go back to my husband," she said coldly.

"You appear," he said, ignoring her, "to have conveniently forgotten the letter I wrote."

"Letter?" Dorcas had put down her glass and turned to leave him, but at this she turned back. "You never wrote a word to me in your entire life."

How she had watched and waited and hoped! She remembered again the pain of those days and the slow disintegration of her dreams. It was madness to allow it to be resurrected now.

"I wrote before I left, setting it all down – the sudden offer of a berth on a privateer, the reason I wanted to go, so that I could earn a stake to put into my own business. I asked you to wait for me. Why didn't you, Dorcas?"

Eyes wide, devoid of words, she stared at him. Stillness enveloped them both. From the ballroom beyond the doors came the strains of music and laughter. People out there were dancing and talking and raising glasses, going about the business of enjoying themselves.

Could it possibly be true? She felt herself on shifting sand, not knowing where to put her trust. His eyes looked into hers, bright with sincerity; so, no doubt, he had looked at the numerous 'diversions' he had mentioned.

"I had no letter," she said sceptically.

"I made sure it was delivered. It was given to your slave –"

"Bathsheba?"

Impatiently he made a gesture with his hand.

"Who knows? I did not ask and my messenger merely said it had been delivered. What does it matter?"

"You're right. The incident is of no importance whatsoever." She lifted her chin and smiled at him, brightly and emptily. "What's past is dead and gone."

"What's between you and me is not dead and gone." He had drawn her closer and was speaking softly and rapidly. "Be honest, Dorcas – you feel it, just as I do. Nothing has changed. There's never been another woman to wipe you from my mind, though God knows I've looked hard enough to find one. Why did you do it, Dorcas? Why throw away something that most people spend their lives searching for? Meet me again, just as you did before –"

It was as if she could hear the surf and the wind, as if once more she was a girl of eighteen with love the only reality, as if her very soul cried out with longing for the sweetness he offered her. She could feel herself leaning helplessly towards him, as if his persuasiveness, his passion, drew all the strength from her.

Then, suddenly, from the outer room she heard Zachariah laugh. The sound was unmistakable, and seemed to jerk her back to the real world where life consisted of everyday matters, small and of themselves unimportant, but cumulatively the very stuff of existence.

As if she took strength from the knowledge that her husband was close at hand, she straightened and drew away from him.

"I am not the fool I once was, Kit," she said coldly. "The wide-eyed innocent who believed every word you uttered is gone, believe me. I am Mrs. Zachariah Hardiman now — a wife and mother, with a great deal more sense —"

"Oh, *there* you are!" Fanny's voice was heard from the doorway leading to the ballroom. "I have been looking for you. Dorcas, for the love of heaven, I beg you to come and help me with Silas's Aunt Becky! She's deaf as a post and quite the most cantankerous of creatures. You'll forgive me, Kit, for interrupting your conversation, won't you?" She smiled at him, her expression innocent and without guile. "I'm sure you have found much of interest to talk about."

"Indeed we have." Kit's smile was bland.

Though her arm was through Dorcas's as if to urge her away, Fanny lingered for a moment.

"Do you not think Dorcas is looking well, Kit? She is hardly changed from the old days, when she was naught but a heedless girl!"

All politeness, Kit bowed towards Dorcas.

"She is as lovely as ever," he said.

"You're too kind." Equally polite, Dorcas returned his smile. "But not, I assure you, near so heedless. Pray excuse us, Mr. Mallory."

Somehow, she told herself as Fanny bore her back to the other side of the ballroom, she would get through this evening — and the next, and the next. Soon she and Zachariah would have left Bermuda and she would be out of danger. She had said the right thing, done the right thing. The pain would go before long, the sense of loss would not last.

Aunt Becky couldn't understand it, and said so several

Nine

Dorcas kept to her own room for breakfast the following day, and when she finally came downstairs it was to find Zachariah and Emma sitting on the back porch in silence, Zachariah deep in the *Bermuda Gazette* and Emma sulkily fraying the end of her sash. One look at her expression and Dorcas knew, with a sinking of the heart, that this was to be no easy day.

She felt ill-equipped to deal with it. Though she had been tired to the point of exhaustion by the time she had been able to go to bed, she had not slept. Time and again she had tried to clear her mind of thoughts of the past, willing herself into a more peaceful state, but to no avail. Every detail of those troubled days before her marriage seemed to force themselves before her.

Was there a letter? If so, why did it not reach her? Would Bathsheba have hidden it? No, no – she could not believe that for one moment, for the girl had shared in her distress. Kit had gone without a backward look, never meaning to marry her, and had only now produced this story of a letter to put her in the wrong.

The sooner she forgot him, the better. She had all but forgotten him before this latest meeting, and would do so again. This clamouring of her senses at the sight of him was something that had to be fought, his claim that there was some unbreakable bond between them disregarded. Last night he had seen her as a challenge, that was the truth of it. He had merely been curious to see if he could exert the same influence over her as he had done six years before.

She sat down on the porch and pressed her throbbing temples.

"Where is everyone?" she asked.

"A small army of slaves have been clearing up," Zachariah said. "But as you see, they seem to have finished now. Fanny said she had work to do in the kitchen. Davey and Storm have gone across the hedge to play with the Dickenson boys next door, and Silas rode into town."

"My goodness! How energetic everyone is after such a late night!"

"We're country bumpkins, sweetheart, unused to all these festivities. Still, you enjoyed yourselves, didn't you?"

"Yes, indeed." Dorcas managed to inject some warmth into her voice, but Emma sat silent.

"I must say," Zachariah went on, putting the paper aside. "I was proud of my women-folk last night. Emma, you looked a picture, and I was not the only one to think so —"

"I looked a fright," Emma said through clenched teeth. "My dress was too babyish. No one would think I was almost fourteen."

Zachariah beetled his brows at her and pursed his lips.

"Well now, miss, I should have said half past thirteen myself, but we'll not fall out over a few months. You looked just what you are — a pretty young girl, soon to become a lovely young lady."

"Your father's right, Emma. You looked charming." Dorcas smiled placatingly at her, not underestimating the importance of the matter. "My Cousin Josiah remarked on it and said how proud I must be of you. I agreed that indeed I was."

"Your Cousin Josiah's eyesight must be failing him," Emma said rudely. Zachariah's face darkened and he opened his mouth to reprove her, but quickly Dorcas touched his arm, signalling him to ignore the matter. He relaxed and smiled at her, capturing her hand in his own.

"As for you, lass," he said, "everyone remarked on your looks, almost in surprise, I felt, as if they expected six years of marriage to me to have whitened your hair or lined your face beyond recognition. Oliver Dickenson maintained you are lovelier than ever. He said you were ever the belle of every ball you attended and that plainly nothing had changed." He bent his head to kiss her fingers. "He spoke nothing but the truth, sweetheart."

"It's all right for her," Emma said. "*She* had a new dress!"

In a gesture of uncharacteristic anger, Zachariah brought his clenched fist down hard on the arm of his chair.

"Leave us," he said. "I'll not have your speak to your mother in that way."

"She's not my mother! I'll be glad when you all go back to Grand Cay and leave me here, you and Miss Dorcas and

146

Storm. Nobody cares about me! She has even turned Storm against me now."

"Emma, that's a monstrous thing to say, and quite untrue."

"I was all ready to read to him today, the story we were reading yesterday, the one he begged me not to stop when it was time for him to go to bed. Still he *would* go next door with Davey! 'I want to play with boys,' he said. 'Mama likes me to play with *boys*!' Such a stupid thing! All he will do is race about and get silly and excited."

"I *do* like him to play with boys," Dorcas agreed. "Especially boys of his own age, for at home he has no one he can play with on equal terms. The Dickenson boys are good for him —"

"You just hate him to have anything to do with me!" Angrily Emma stood up and prepared to flounce away, but Zachariah caught her arm in passing and forced her to a halt.

"That's enough, Emma. You'll apologise at once."

"Why should I, when it's perfectly true? Miss Dorcas won't be happy until she makes him stop loving me."

"Sweetheart, you have much to learn about love." Zachariah pulled her closer and spoke gently but with underlying severity. "Have you ever held a bird in your two hands and felt it fluttering and fluttering to get free? The tighter you hold, the more determined you are to keep it, the more frantic its efforts to fly away. People are like that, too. You must learn to give Storm room to grow, room to fly if he wants to. He won't stop loving you; only you can make him do that. Letting go is something all parents have to learn — ay, and big sisters, too. Now, tell your Mama you're sorry you spoke so —"

"I'm sorry, *Mama*!"

The apology was clearly insincere, the last word flung scornfully and defiantly towards Dorcas, and Emma pulled away from her father and ran from the room. Angrily Zachariah rose to follow her, but Dorcas stopped him.

"Leave it until tempers cool, Zack, I beg you."

"But she must apologise to you!"

"Later." Dorcas was ruffled too, but knew that it was more than Storm's independence that bothered Emma. "Zack, can you not see that you do little to help the situation when you insist on praising me so extravagantly in her presence? Can you not see that every time you do so, it's like a nail being drawn across glass? It sets her teeth on edge, so badly does she want your exclusive love, the way it was before."

"Then it's time she learned that everything changed the day you became my wife. I love her dearly, as dearly as any father could love a daughter; for the life of me, I can't see how she could doubt that. But you –" He paused a moment and looked at her intently, his eyes warm with emotion. "You, my love, are part of me – the one thing that makes sense of the whole. Without you I should not care to live."

"You'll never be without me," Dorcas said.

She lay back in the chair and closed her eyes, knowing that Zachariah still looked at her with that same loving regard.

She must never think of Kit again, she told herself. Never, never.

She did not see him before they left Hamilton, for only a few days remained to them and these were spent in attending to the children's needs – buying new gowns, a mantle and two bonnets for Emma; two pairs of trousers and a jacket for Davey.

Emma had apologised with a reasonably good grace once she had returned to a better frame of mind, but although Dorcas accepted the apology with equal grace, she did not delude herself that anything had changed. Emma's resentment burned as fiercely as ever.

Towards the end of their visit, Zachariah returned from town with Silas, agog with news. A distant relative of Silas's, met at the ball, was, like them, only on holiday in Bermuda, Halifax in Nova Scotia being his permanent home. He had gone there when opportunities for advancement seemed non-existent in his native island, and had set up a salt-fish factory.

"If my salt is up to standard, and prices competitive, he's anxious to enter into a long-term agreement," Zachariah told her. "If I can meet his conditions, it'll mean a lot to us, sweetheart, to have a guaranteed outlet."

"And one likely to expand rather than contract," Silas added. "Jonathan Cahill has a good business head on his shoulders and the most modern equipment."

"I'm grateful to you for putting the opportunity my way," Zachariah said, and indeed the knowledge that there was a chance of a regular income seemed to put new heart in him.

*   *   *

Emma cried a little when she parted from her father, but Davey stood straight, bright-eyed and smiling, eager to embark on this new period in his life. He was eleven years old now, with his father's easy-going nature which made him everyone's friend, but underneath with his same steely resolve and tenacity.

He had given up his soldiers. Now it was the sea that fascinated him and he made no secret of the fact that he intended to join the Navy as a midshipman the moment it was humanly possible.

"The boy's crazy!" Zachariah roared, but he smiled nonetheless, and seemed pleased that Davey would follow in his footsteps, even though the life was hard. "He'll go far beyond me," he said. "He's had advantages I never had. Work at your Latin and Greek and Euclid, my boy, and you'll be Admiral of the Fleet."

"I'll do my best, Papa," Davey said solemnly.

"There's no need to worry about him," Zachariah said as the boat pulled away from the shore, leaving a line of fluttering handkerchiefs on the quayside.

"And Emma will rally once we are gone, I am sure. I could tell she was pleased by her first impressions of Mrs. Fanshawe's school, and Fanny will keep an eye on her."

"I'm your only one now," Storm said, without any visible sign of dismay.

"So you are, my son." Zachariah's hand rested on his shoulder as they stood and watched the collection of islands that made up Bermuda slowly recede.

Dorcas felt strangely numb inside; unable, somehow, to react fully to anything that was happening.

She needed time, she told herself. It was one thing to make bold and virtuous decisions about never thinking of Kit again, and quite another to carry them out. The whole episode had been a shock to her system and now she felt as if she were experiencing convalescence after an illness.

It would be different once they were back on the island. Then Kit would truly be at a great distance from her and she could relax in the knowledge that he would not suddenly appear from around the next corner, or be present in the next drawing-room she visited.

She would return to the life she had known before, with all its small concerns – bazaars to raise money for the church for which everyone had been saving for so many years; a concert, perhaps, with Zachariah playing his fiddle and giving a solo or two and Mr. Grimshaw singing gloomily about death and Frank Hickson giving a comic recitation. There would be games of whist, too, and gossip over the tea-cups and meals with friends.

Some had gone, but others remained, and there was still reconstruction to be carried out after the hurricane. Plenty to think about, plenty to make her stop hankering for what might have been.

There were the elections, too. Surely now Zachariah would be recognised as a fit and proper person to be elected to the Assembly?

"Oh Zack, you'll surely get in this time," she said.

"If I do," he replied thoughtfully, "I shall work towards some kind of a break with the Bahamas Government. We need to be able to make our own decisions. We need autonomy."

"Are we not too small, Zack?"

"Ay, very likely, but what could be worse than the dead hand of Nassau upon us? Take, take – that's their only concern. We need a development plan of some kind, financed by the revenue that now pours into the Bahamian coffers. Well!" He laughed and shrugged at Dorcas's sceptical expression. "Maybe it trickles at the moment rather than pours, but it will flow freely again. Times are hard but things will pick up, I'm certain of it. I've said so before and I'll say so again – there's no substitute for salt and ours is the best obtainable."

"We must be grateful to Silas for introducing Mr. Cahill," Dorcas said. "I take back all I have ever said regarding his coldness and lack of regard for us."

"It'll make a difference to us, there's no doubt at all about that. Given a fair wind, sweetheart, all will be well with us now."

"All will be well," she agreed firmly; and said it again to herself, over and over. All will be well. Do the right thing, and all will be well.

She had forgotten quite how damaged and down at heel the little community was. She surveyed it with a kind of rueful amusement in which there was, after all, a touch of affection.

Efforts at repair had been made, it was true, and even now the air rang with the sound of hammer and saw. From the ship's anchorage off the island, she could see that many of the palm trees to the south at Palm Grove and to the north at Treasure Bluff had suffered in the hurricane of 1815 and would never recover. The people that thronged the jetty looked equally battered, she thought, but they were still vociferous in their welcome as the lighter brought the Hardiman family close.

"We were taking bets, Zack! Never thought you'd come back," one man called out.

"You'll not keep me away," Zachariah shouted. "I can see there's work to be done."

"There's a Haitian witch from Backsalina says this is going to be a great year."

"Ay, we'll all be rich men yet."

Joe was there, Dorcas could see, and beyond him and the crowd on the jetty, Marcia was sitting in her buggy behind a grey horse. And there was Mrs. Crockford, the judge's wife, actually smiling and waving as if she were pleased to have them back. Perhaps she was. There was, Dorcas reflected, something of a siege mentality about the place; for good or ill, they were incarcerated together and grew close, like it or not.

Dorcas looked towards the south. The formation of the land prevented a view of Tamarind Villa, but she knew it would be waiting for them, unchanged but for a new coat of paint applied by Joe in their absence. Solid and foursquare, it would still stand guardian over the half-moon beach, looking out on the turquoise and green and deep, deep blue of the sea.

"Mama, Mama, we're home," Storm cried, tugging at her skirt as if the reality of the situation had only just dawned on him in its full glory.

"We're home, sweetheart." Zachariah's voice, as he put his arm about her shoulders and held her close was less shrill but equally joyful.

She looked at him and smiled to see his pleasure.

"Yes," she agreed. "We're home."

Zachariah's optimism was not misplaced, for salt production began to improve due to the dry weather and cloudless skies. The year of 1817 might not have proved quite as wonderful as predicted by the Haitian witch from Backsalina, but at least it marked a turning point for the Hardimans and those other salt proprietors who had chosen to stand their ground.

A year after their trip to Bermuda, Zachariah returned there, on his own this time, for Dorcas, so she said, had a dozen small projects on hand and could not spare the time to leave. So successful had the year been – helped in no little way by the Cahill contract – that Zachariah had entered into an agreement with Silas, whose trading partnership with Kit Mallory was proving equally lucrative. Their vessels now plied regularly across the Western Atlantic; due west to Charleston, north to New York and Halifax, south to Nassau and the Turks Islands, and even further afield.

The ships that brought stone and timber and palmetto for thatch carried salt away. Now Zachariah was to lease a schooner from them so that he could carry his own salt to some of the nearer West Indian islands which it was not worth Tranton and Mallory's time to visit.

The new schooner was named the *Lady Dorcas* – for what other name would do for Zachariah? – and was once in the possession of the American Navy before being captured during the war. She was captained now by a grizzled, weather-beaten Scotsman by the name of Cameron, and Dorcas had a shrewd suspicion that Zachariah sometimes longed to be aboard as it set sail for Haiti and Puerto Plata in Santo Domingo.

With the departure of the McGovern brothers, he had at last been elected to the Assembly. Less pleasing to him was that the fifth Representative from Grand Cay was none other than Willis Trotman, a fact which many regarded with astonishment, taking into consideration his comparative youth and hitherto subordinate status. However, the hurricane and the departure of some of the more influential salt proprietors had left the way open; but there were those who wondered how it had come about that Trotman, once nothing more than a book-keeper-cum-overseer to first Zachariah and then the McGoverns, now seemed in sufficient funds to purchase as many shares in the salt ponds as others far longer in the business.

"It seems suspicious to me," Dorcas commented. But Zachariah shrugged.

"Who knows? Perhaps he has a rich uncle in Jamaica. We know nothing of his background."

"More likely he is every bit as clever with figures as you always maintained. The McGoverns should look to their books."

"Careful, lass! Those thoughts are slanderous – and I do have to work with the man. There's enough salt for all in a year like this."

"Well, guard your back! He'd stick a knife in, if he could."

Trotman's elevation was an irritation, but did nothing to detract from Zachariah's pleasure in other areas of his life. Dorcas, he thought, seemed more settled. He had worried about her when first they had arrived back from Bermuda; she missed her sister, he knew, but now seemed whole-hearted in her determination to cast no backward glances. She tackled her garden afresh, for her earlier efforts had been devastated by the hurricane, and already it was showing results. She also joined forces with Marcia Bettany to visit the sick and help the poor, even starting literacy classes. These mostly consisted of white men – seamen, labourers, the odd riff-raff who eked out a living by fishing or smuggling or both. Ex-pirates, Dorcas called them, and was probably not far wrong in her assessment.

But a handful of blacks presented themselves, too; free men, of course, for slave owners did not look kindly on their chattels being given ideas above their station and official permission for her to give classes in the barracks had been refused.

There were many who disapproved strongly of her activities, but Zachariah found pleasure in her fulfilment and sense of purpose. The longing for another child had not left her, he knew, but it was not now so plainly dominating her thoughts.

Storm was another source of delight. The boy, small though he was, liked nothing better than to ride with Zachariah to the salt ponds, sitting in front of him and held securely in those powerful arms. He asked constant questions, pondered the replies, saw for himself the difference in quality between one raking and the next. His main joy, perhaps, was to see the precious crystals being shipped. He was fascinated by the rapid bagging of the salt in half-bushel bags which were then loaded on to the lighter, four hundred bags making up the load, and could happily watch for hours the constant traffic between wharf and the cargo ships that stood off shore beyond the reef.

They fished together, too, and swam and sailed and held earnest conversations regarding such diverse matters as whether crabs *minded* having one arm longer than the other, and why God went to so much trouble to make shells so intricate. The boy's undoubted good looks, his strength and self-confidence, were a source of great pride to Zachariah.

"He's a one-er," he said admiringly to Dorcas, shaking his head and smiling in disbelief. "There's no other lad like him."

"And no other lad grows out of his clothes so fast, I'll warrant," Dorcas said.

Storm's dearest wish was to sail in the *Lady Dorcas* on a more protracted voyage from those he took in the ketch with Zachariah, and it was in the early summer of 1818, when he was almost seven but as tall as the average nine-year-old, that Zachariah and he took ship to go to Bermuda with the purpose of bringing Emma and Davey back to the island for their long vacation.

"Why do you not come with us, sweetheart?" Zachariah asked Dorcas. "It's some time now since you saw your family."

Dorcas continued to leaf through a book and showed no sign of the near panic that fluttered her nerves at this suggestion. Go back to Bermuda – reawaken all those hurtful, wicked longings that she had almost subdued? Not yet – no, no, not yet.

"It's hardly worth it," she said evenly. "After all, you propose turning round and coming home almost as soon as you arrive. I'm not so enraptured by sea voyages as all that. Fanny has sworn to visit in the winter, so I shall bide my time and see her then. You two men go and enjoy yourselves."

The prospect of having Emma at home again was one she viewed with some trepidation. To say that life was more peaceful without her was to underestimate the case a hundred-fold, yet though Emma's own letters were unrevealing, Fanny reported that, after some initial coolness, she mixed well with the younger Tranton cousins and had matured considerably during her sojourn with Mrs. Fanshawe.

Things will be better now, Dorcas assured herself. Things *must* be better! She was determined on it, and full of the best of intentions went down to the quay to greet her stepdaughter.

Emma had undoubtedly grown and developed. She would never be tall and would never have the long, graceful lines that were such an integral part of Dorcas's attraction, but she had a neat waist and small, firm breasts, and her thick, dark hair, like a cloud around her head, was truly her crowning glory. At fifteen she gave the impression of being poised on the threshold – not of great beauty, but certainly of a passable prettiness. Outwardly she was as quiet and demure as ever, but Dorcas witnessed a few sideways glances at a group of sailors on the jetty and felt sure that inwardly there had been changes. And what more natural, she asked herself?

"Emma, my dear," she said, embracing her as they met. "And Davey! How lovely to have you home again. I declare I feel I am meeting strangers, you have both grown so. Zachariah, what are we to do with them? They are far more elegant than we are!"

Davey's elegance was quickly discarded and he returned happily to the bare-footed, open-shirted boy he had been before he went away, spending days fishing with Joe or his father, basking in Storm's hero-worship, swimming and sailing with friends, often disappearing on pursuits of his own to appear again ravenously hungry and ready to eat anything that was put before him.

At first sight he seemed as cheerful and uncomplicated as ever. He still loved to laugh and had grown into a wicked mimic, but sometimes Dorcas thought she discerned a new thoughtfulness and maturity about him that she had never seen before. She questioned him about his school.

Yes, he said. He was perfectly happy, adding a little disquietingly, "It's all right now."

"Now? It was not all right at first?"

"Well, I was such a dunce, Mama! I knew no Latin and scarcely any mathematics, and Dr. Hartwell called me a fool and made a mock of me. He said I should never qualify for the Navy –"

"He said that?" Dorcas was afire with indignation. "How could he be so unkind! He knew your circumstances, how your education had been curtailed through no fault of your own. He should have made allowances."

"People don't make allowances, Mama. I learned that very quickly. You see, the other boys – well, being short didn't help me, and what with Dr. Hartwell implying I was little more than an imbecile –"

"They bullied you? Oh, Davey!"

"Not now, Mama. I found I could make them laugh, you see, and I worked hard so that they saw I plainly wasn't a fool. Now there's no need for anyone to make allowances."

"I'm proud of you, Davey, and what's more, the Navy is going to be proud of you, too. Admiral Hardiman! That sounds very well, don't you think?"

"Admiral *Lord* Hardiman," Davey corrected her, sticking his nose in the air and pulling a haughty face that reminded her so much of his father in clownish mood that she laughed and hugged him tightly.

It was hard to extract much information from Emma regarding Mrs. Fanshawe's seminary, though the views of a girl called Jane Willoughby were quoted at length on almost every subject, from fashion to the poems of Milton. Clearly her devotion to Storm had been diluted a little by this new friendship, but even so there were a few occasions when she retired to her room, silent and sulky, hurt by Storm's obvious preference for Davey and the occupations he offered.

"She is a great deal better, though," Dorcas assured Zachariah.

"I knew that she would be once she went away and mixed with girls of her own age. She has more to think about now – her music and her lessons –"

"And the opposite sex. I don't think, somehow, that it's the love of a father or brother that is her main preoccupation these days!"

"What?" Mouth agape, Zachariah stared at her. "What can you mean? Please remember she is a child still."

"She's over fifteen, Zack. From what I remember –"

"Nay, nay love, you cannot judge her by yourself for you were born with a certain – a certain *knowingness* I cannot explain. Emma is a child and totally innocent."

Dorcas said no more, for she still trod warily where Emma was concerned. In a way she knew what Zachariah meant, for she recognised that the girl's personality was deficient in the kind of warmth that attracted easy admiration. She seemed to expect rejection and to be on the defensive even before receiving it.

Recognising the problem and having the ability to help her were, unfortunately, two very different things, though as the holiday progressed Dorcas saw encouraging signs of an improvement in the relationship between her and her step-daughter. They shopped together and sewed together; even laughed together, which was something that had never been easy.

A few nights before Emma and Davey were due to go back to Bermuda at the end of the hurricane season, they were all invited to a wedding reception, held in the grounds of a new house to the south, known as Waterloo.

Among all the familiar faces, that of a stranger stood out. Its owner was head and shoulders taller than most of the men, and had the look of a Norse god; blond, blue-eyed, tanned, his charming smile revealing perfect teeth. He was such a perfect specimen, Dorcas said wickedly to Marcia, that he should be shot and stuffed and hung on a wall.

He was, it turned out, some distant kinsman of James Misick, the owner of Waterloo, who chanced to be in Grand Cay on a fleeting visit, being the owner of a small fleet of vessels trading out of Boston.

To Emma he looked like Sir Galahad and Prince Charming rolled into one. She stood to one side of the guests, unable to eat, unable to take her eyes off him, her heart thudding painfully as she desperately tried to summon the courage to approach him so that she could stand near and hear his voice. She knew she would not speak to him; just listening to him speak to others would be enough.

She was on the point of moving when she saw him walk away purposefully in the opposite direction. He had, she saw with a sinking of the heart, seen Dorcas.

After that he could not be budged from her stepmother's side. He smiled down at her with his winning smile, brought her a plate of food, sat at her feet, laughed at her jokes. Then, when the eating and the speeches were done, he begged Dorcas to stroll down to the sea with him, for Waterloo's acres contained the finest beach on the island.

After her initial shock of pleasure at his extraordinary looks, Dorcas found him conceited, tiresome, over-persistent and limited in wit. She instantly forgot him once the party was over and two days later could not have remembered his name.

He spent a total of three days on the island; he had never been before and was never destined to make another visit. In one afternoon, however, he successfully blighted the relationship she was building with Emma and it was the sulky, withdrawn child of previous years who presented her cheek to be kissed as she boarded the schooner for Bermuda.

Ten

It was in January of the following year that Dorcas received word of her father's death.

She had seized upon Fanny's letter, certain that it would contain news of her hoped-for visit, but instead it told of unavoidable postponement.

> For I cannot now leave Grandmama [Fanny wrote]. Papa's death was so sudden that it has been a shock to us all, but naturally most of all to her since she has lived with him and depended upon him for so long.
>
> It is a consolation that he cannot have suffered for more than a few moments, for he was taken by a seizure on the steps of St. Peter's Church and had expired by the time anyone could reach him. His funeral was magnificently attended and many were the fine orations made, praising his devotion to public works in these islands. I enclose a description and his obituary, published in the *Bermuda Gazette*, and am sure that you will be much affected by it.
>
> Our main worry is Grandmama, who steadfastly refuses to leave her home which, she says, has ever sheltered her and will continue to do so until the day of her own death. Between us, Silas and I are convinced that this will not be long delayed, for she is so frail and eats next to nothing. It is strange, is it not, that one so seemingly weak can survive, while her son is taken. Providence is indeed beyond our understanding.

There was, by the same packet, a letter from Emma.

> Aunt Fanny is writing to you concerning Mr. Foley's death. Mrs. Fanshawe sent for me in the middle of French conversation to tell me of it and to give me leave to go to Cedarcroft for the funeral, also to be visited by the dressmaker who provided me with suitable mourning wear (white, high-necked, with black trimming and bonnet).

Uncle Silas was to have sent the coach for me, but was much occupied with Mrs. Foley who insisted on attending the memorial service in spite of being almost prostrate with grief, so as he was prevented, Mr. Mallory came for me and was my escort to the church where we sat through a service during which every famous man in Bermuda rose to praise Mr. Foley. Mr. Mallory whispered to me that there would be no man more surprised than Mr. Foley, were he able to hear the half of it.

The gentlemen proceeded to the graveside and the ladies returned to Cedarcroft where a great feast had been prepared.

"I should have been there," Dorcas said.

"Sweetheart, how could you have been? No one had warning of his death and the funeral was over by the time word reached us."

"I know, I know – still, I wish I had been with Fanny to help comfort Grandmama. Zachariah, what is to become of her if she will not budge? She has a household of slaves it is true, and Hebe in particular is devoted and always has been, but it will be hard for her and even harder for Fanny, for I can imagine her constantly at Grandmama's beck and call. I ought to be there."

"Later in the year you can make a visit."

"My dear Papa," Emma wrote, for her letters bore no mention of Dorcas except as a dutiful afterthought.

I am in the best of health and hope you are the same. I have gained good marks in history and have been chosen to sing a solo at a sacred concert. I am to sing 'Come Unto Him' from the Oratorio by Mr. Handel.

Both Davey and I spent this past weekend at Cedarcroft and enjoyed a pleasant time. On Saturday there was a marooning party to Devonshire Bay. We were twelve in number and we played games and grilled fish and sang catches. Mr. Mallory much admired my voice which I told him I inherited direct from you, to which he replied he had no idea you were such a skylark! The party was arranged because it was his birthday, though I do not know how old he was.

Thirty-three, Dorcas thought, making a swift calculation. Thirty-three, still unmarried and still turning young girls' heads, if Emma's letter was anything to go by.

This intrusion of his name into her accounts of events in Bermuda filled Dorcas with a profound sense of unease, even though so far the cloud was no bigger than a man's hand.

My dear Papa,

All continues well here. My health is good and the concert was a great success with praise for my solo coming from all sides, even from Mrs. Fanshawe who uses it but sparingly.

I regret my best slippers were quite worn through, so last Friday I was permitted to go into town with my friend Jane Willoughby and a governess called Miss Minns, and I was measured for more which will be ready next week and should not cost more than five shillings, unless they are beaded which means a shilling extra. They are stylish, with a narrow strap.

On our way home, who should we encounter but Mr. Mallory who brought us back in his carriage, much to Mrs. Fanshawe's annoyance since she says I have neither your permission nor yet that of Uncle Silas to drive with him! I pointed out that he is a business associate of Uncle Silas and reminded her that he escorted me to Mr. Foley's funeral. Her only reply was that *that* was an Unusual Circumstance, and was not best pleased when I said surely it was more unique than unusual since Mr. Foley was unlikely to have any more funerals! Miss Minns was in more disgrace even than I, and looked pink about the eyes for the rest of the day.

Please Papa, do write to Mrs. Fanshawe and tell her that Mr. Mallory is an old and trusted friend of the family and that I am not likely to come to any harm in his company.

The cloud appeared to be growing. Was Kit, then, to be the object of one of Emma's obsessions?

Inevitably she would be hurt, Dorcas told herself. That was the worrying thing; but then she wondered if she were being honest. Was it, perhaps, a simple case of jealousy? To read of riding in a carriage with Kit, going on parties, even sitting in church with him, was like a knife twisting in her ribs. And that, she told herself, was unworthy. On the other hand, *was*

Kit a trusted friend? Charming, plausible, devilishly attractive – yes, all of that. But trustworthy?

"You will not give this permission, surely Zack?" she asked.

Zachariah pursed his lips and puckered his face in the grimace that meant he was in two minds.

"I don't know, sweetheart," he said at last. "Surely there can be no harm in it? He is, after all, a friend of Silas and Fanny. We should, perhaps, be grateful that he takes an interest in our little girl."

"Zack, she is not a little girl! She is almost sixteen –"

"But young for her years."

"I have heard –" She hesitated, ill at ease, but went on resolutely. "I have heard it said that Mr. Mallory's reputation –"

"He is a gentleman!" Zachariah was looking as annoyed with her as she had ever seen. "Really, Dorcas, I am surprised that you are making a mountain out of a molehill in a way that is worthy of Mrs. Grimshaw."

"Well, thank you for that!" Dorcas said angrily, leaving the room before either of them could say more.

He had the imperfections of his virtues, Dorcas thought, as she walked alone on the beach. It had taken him months, if not years, to see the malevolence of Willis Trotman, to name but one example. He himself was innocent as a babe unborn and was constantly amazed that others could be so devious.

That so far Emma's relationship with Kit was one-sided and totally innocent, she had no doubt, but she was full of misgivings as his name figured more and more frequently in the pages of her letters. It could mean anything, or nothing, she told herself. After all, they all knew what Emma was like when in the grip of one of her obsessions; they dominated her thoughts and emotions, whether they were reciprocated or not – just as my thoughts and emotions were dominated, Dorcas thought; and not so long ago, either! It seemed no time at all since she, too, had longed to write his name or – still more – to speak it, just as if by doing so she could lend substance to his presence in her life.

He had responded by seducing her. No talk of love or misplaced letters or good intentions could alter the fact. She had been innocent, too, just as Emma was, while he, even then, had known exactly what he was doing. No, it was not jealousy that fuelled her unease, but fear for her stepdaughter.

She sank down on an outcrop of rock, and chin on her hand, gazed sightlessly out over the sea.

Do I really trust him so little? she asked herself. Why, then, does the thought of him still nag at me like an aching tooth?

When Fanny's letter arrived telling her that her grand-mother was ill she knew that a visit to Bermuda could not be delayed any further.

"I must go," she said to Zachariah. "I cannot leave everything to Fanny in this way, and should never forgive myself if I received a letter telling me of Grandmama's death before I had made an effort to see her."

This was undoubtedly true, but the problem of Emma weighed on her with almost equal urgency even though she said no more to Zachariah on the subject. Much as she disliked the prospect, it was a problem she knew she would have to tackle on her own.

The air in the sick-room was suffocating. There was a fire in the grate, even though the temperature soared outside, with blue sky visible through the half-closed shutters and dust motes dancing in the shaft of sunlight.

Mrs. Foley still lived, but already it seemed to Dorcas that the room smelled of death and putrefaction, with the addition of some sickly, musky perfume that had been sprinkled around to mask the worst of it yet only served to make the gorge rise chokingly in her throat.

There was nothing really wrong with her grandmother, the doctor said, nothing except her great age, which was a condition that would not respond to cupping, his most usual remedy. There was so little of the old lady that the bed-clothes were almost flat over her frail body, and the hands that plucked the sheet were like the claws of some small bird.

"Does the room need to be so hot?" Dorcas asked him.

"Yes, yes!" He was thin and sharp-featured, brusque in his manner, a far cry from dear old Dr. McClosky she remembered from her youth. He spoke with a kind of incisive sibilance that seemed to lend great authority to his words. "Most essential. *Most* essential! Even a breath of air could prove lethal."

But she's dying anyway, Dorcas thought helplessly, not daring to rebel.

"Dorcas?" the voice rose quaveringly from the bed, and she went over swiftly to the old woman's side. The doctor nodded towards her gravely and left the room with an air of one who has many calls upon his skills.

"It was good of you to come, dear," Mrs. Foley said, her voice little more than a thread of sound. "So good!"

Dorcas covered the frail hand with her own.

"I wanted to be with you," she said.

"So good," her grandmother repeated. She seemed to gather a little strength and the bonneted head moved on the pillow. "It was not always so," she said with a vestige of tartness. "You caused much – oh well!" The small burst of energy died and she sighed as if the memory of past troubles was too tiring to bear. "Never mind. It matters little now."

"I have very much regretted the pain I caused you," Dorcas said. It was a relief to have spoken the words, but even as she did so, she saw that the old lady had fallen asleep.

"For sure you caused de pain!" Hebe stepped out of the shadows; Hebe, who had served her grandmother for as long as she could remember. Hebe, who had stood between her mistress and anything that might trouble her like some brooding, bitter, avenging angel.

She smoothed the bed-clothes and bent tenderly over the old lady.

"Miss Fanny, she never cause no trouble to nobody – good as gold, she was; but you was diff'rent. May de good Lord forgive you for de pain you give dis good soul, you wid you' wild ways –"

"That will do, Hebe! That's all between my grandmother and me –"

"But it was Hebe dried de tears."

"I've made my peace with her."

Hebe folded her hands over her apron and said nothing, standing now beside the head of the bed as if she had no intention of being moved.

"You go git some air," she said after a moment, in a manner which suggested that Dorcas was incapable of sustaining the role of nurse.

For a moment Dorcas hesitated, then shrugged.

"Very well," she said. "There is, as it happens, an errand I want to perform."

Storm was staying at Cedarcroft. It had seemed sensible, for a house of sickness was no place for a noisy and high-spirited boy and Fanny had assured Dorcas that he would be no trouble to her.

Dorcas herself was sleeping in her old room at the family house in St. George's, the first time she had slept there since leaving Bermuda on her marriage. It was a strange experience, and one she did not particularly relish, but she felt that by doing so she was making clear to Fanny her commitment to her grandmother's care and her determination to give her sister a break from the burden she had borne for so long.

It had been a heavy one, and one that had exacted its price, for Fanny's health had suffered. For some months she had been plagued by an intermittent fever and admitted that she would indeed be thankful to give up – or at least reduce – her visits to St. George's.

"But you must have the carriage," she insisted. "With Silas in the Caribbean I shall not need it, I promise you. If you have it you can come and see us at Cedarcroft just as often as you can get away."

"How long will Silas be away? Are you sure he will not mind?"

"Three or four weeks, he said – and no, he will not mind in the least! In fact, I'm quite sure he would be delighted were he to hear of it, for he would know then that I am resting as instructed and not racketing all over the islands!"

Dorcas was appreciative of this gift of freedom, but it was not to Cedarcroft that she directed the coachman on this occasion. They drove towards Hamilton, but instead of taking the road which led beyond the town, they turned along Front Street and the quay where Tranton and Mallory had their office.

It was the ideal time, she told herself; it would be foolish to delay. With Silas away, it was logical to assume that Kit would be alone in the office and available for a private conversation. She would talk to him calmly, sensibly, one adult to another, assuming his innocence of any involvement with Emma. There would be no accusations or bitterness, merely the expression of a justifiable concern on behalf of an impressionable adolescent. And there would be no talk of the past either. That was a closed book. She would keep a tight rein on her emotions, give no hint that, even now, he had the power to excite.

All the way there she tried to plan what she was to say to

him. She would wrap the matter up, she decided. Thank him for his kind interest in Emma —

Oh, leave it! she told herself crossly. Why worry so? Who was Kit Mallory that he should throw her into this panic?

Finding herself twisting a handkerchief nervously between her fingers, she thrust it angrily inside her reticule, straightened her back and lifted her chin. She would be dignified. She was, after all, doing no more than any responsible parent would do — unless, of course, they happened to be blind and trusting innocents like Zachariah.

The office was over the ships' chandlery store that used to belong to Silas Tranton alone. Now the name of Tranton and Mallory was emblazoned everywhere and their shipping company plainly thriving.

A flight of wooden stairs outside the building led up to a narrow balcony and thence to an ante-room where a gangling youth on a high stool was writing in a ledger. His protruberant green eyes popped even further out of his head at the sight of Dorcas.

"Please wait a moment, ma'am," he said when she asked to see Mr. Mallory, and went backwards, as if in the presence of royalty, through the door which led to an inner office. Curiously Dorcas looked inside the room that was revealed, and saw him bend to speak to a shorter, fatter man who was in the act of unrolling a chart and spreading it on a table.

A breeze caught the door and it swung wide open. Now her view of the inner room was complete, even to the further door at the far end of it which, as she looked, was opened by Kit himself, smiling as he ushered in a familiar figure in a pale green dimity dress, a bonnet of chip straw on her head.

"Emma!" Dorcas took a step towards the door and breathed the name in a tone of shocked amazement. Why wasn't the girl at school? What could she — and Kit — be thinking of?

A sense of disbelief kept her from moving. Little though she trusted Kit, she had never thought him capable of compromising Emma to this extent. Now it appeared that this was not one of Emma's unreasoned passions, but a conspiracy between them; another of Kit's 'diversions'.

Sudden anger made her start towards them at the same moment as they became aware of her presence. She saw the happiness drain from Emma's face, saw it replaced by apprehension and bitterness.

"Why, Dorcas!" Kit's smiling confidence was unshaken. Had he no conscience? What a fool she had been to think him innocent in this case.

"What are you doing here?" Emma asked sulkily.

"I might well ask the same thing."

"Oh dear!" Kit gave a rueful laugh and looked from Dorcas to Emma and back again. "The fat's in the fire, young Emma. It's not only Mrs. Fanshawe who will require explanations, it seems."

He was as handsome as ever, Dorcas noted; made of different clay, it seemed, from the gangling, spotty clerk and the fat man with the chart. And the charm! It seemed to reach out and gather her towards him. No wonder he had turned Emma's head!

"You never change, do you, Kit?" Resolutely she refused to succumb and her voice was cold.

"Should I?" He twisted his lips and raised his eyebrows as she said nothing. "I think you'd best come inside, Dorcas. It seems to me that you're leaping to the wrong conclusions."

"I should like to think so."

Stony faced, she walked past them into the inner office, while Kit closed the door, shutting the three of them away from the curious glances of the clerks outside.

"Believe me," he said. "There is a perfectly innocent explanation."

"Do you think *she* would believe it?" Emma, now that she had accepted the fact of Dorcas's presence, wore an expression both of apprehension and triumph. Dorcas turned towards her.

"Please wait for me outside, Emma. I wish to have a private word with Mr. Mallory."

"I shall not! I'm not a child, to be dismissed while my elders discuss my behaviour. I wish to hear what you have to say."

"It's not your behaviour I wish to discuss. I want to talk to Mr. Mallory alone."

Emma took a step closer to her, her small face, so often shuttered and unreadable, suddenly coming to life.

"All you want is to spoil everything for me! When have you ever done anything else?"

Dorcas raised her hands in exasperation and let them fall again.

"Emma, you are a schoolgirl still, and in dangerous waters, believe me —"

166

"Wait!" Kit held up a hand to halt her. "Don't make too much of this, Dorcas. Emma came on a shopping trip and – somewhat inexplicably, I admit – became separated from her friends and therefore had no other course open but to come here, throw herself on my mercy and beg me to escort her back to school to plead her case with Mrs. Fanshawe who, by all accounts, is a dragon fierce enough to terrify the most fearless knight, never mind a defenceless maiden!"

He spoke dryly with an amused twist of his lips, plainly not believing a word of it and inviting Dorcas to share the joke. She remained unamused.

"And you were about to do as she asked? Did you not ask yourself *why* she concocted such a ridiculous tarradiddle? Surely you can see she is taking your attentions far more seriously than you can have intended? You have, after all, hurt others before her –"

As if in defiance and rejection of her elders, Emma had thrown herself down in one of the leather armchairs that stood before Kit's desk. Now she banged her clenched fists on the arms and sprang up, stamping her foot.

"I knew it, I knew it! You cannot bear for me to be loved by anyone – not my father nor my brother nor any man."

"Emma!"

Both Kit and Dorcas spoke together, but of the two of them it was Kit who sounded the more shocked. He went to the girl and took her by the shoulders.

"Now, Emma," he said. "You're letting your imagination run away with you. Your stepmother is right to be concerned."

"She spoils everything, always. She could not wait to come here and tell me I am too young to love you – yes, yes, *love*! I'm glad to have said it, glad you know my feelings!"

Her sobs filled the room as she bent her head, covering her face with her hands. Kit pulled a comical face in Dorcas's direction and ran an exasperated hand through his hair.

"Believe me, I didn't ask for this," he said.

Dorcas looked at him coldly. She moved to Emma and reached out to hold her, feeling her pain as her own now that it was not disguised by a show of defiance. Emma, however, shrugged away from her.

"Leave me alone," she said. "I want no sympathy from you. It's all your fault and always has been."

"Now see what you have done," Dorcas said to Kit bitterly. "Is there no end to your blindness and self-indulgence?"

"I fail to see how I can be blamed for the delusions of an hysterical girl." Kit's anger rose to meet hers and for a moment they glared speechlessly at each other, Emma's sobs the only sound to disturb the silence.

Distractedly Kit looked towards the girl, and he sighed, as if touched in spite of himself by this abject misery. Once more he took her by the shoulders, giving her a small shake.

"Emma, listen to me!"

She looked at him with streaming eyes.

"I know full well what you're going to say. You'll say I'm too young, no more than a child, not ready for love. Well, you're wrong."

"I see now that I am; still, it is as a child I've regarded you all these months."

"You liked me! You told me I was pretty and said you liked to hear me sing. You could listen all day — that's what you said to me."

"And all that was true! You're a pretty girl." He shook her again, charming and persuasive once more. Dorcas watched him. He has to charm, she thought cynically. He cannot bear to be out of favour.

"Listen to me," he said again. "I'm flattered you should think so much of me. On days when I feel old and worn, I shall think of your regard and become young again. Come, smile at me and tell me I'm forgiven for giving you the wrong impression."

Emma's eyes searched his face, desperate and appealing.

"You don't mean it," she whispered. "You're only saying it because *she* is here! I was certain you loved me. You *do* love me!"

He took his hands from her shoulders, clearly wearying of the scene. His voice, when he spoke, had lessened in sympathy.

"I have no wish to hurt you, Emma."

"*She's* making you say this. It would be different if we were alone. Please Kit — don't say such things — never mind that she is here."

Dorcas, her sympathy rebuffed so decidedly, had stayed silent, but she could not remain indifferent to such pathos. Surely, surely Kit must have seen the growth of this adoration? How could he have been so blind, so heartless, not to have put a stop to it months ago? The truth was that any female creature, no matter how young, had to be made to fall down and worship even though his interest might be non-existent.

"Come, Emma," she said gently, attempting once more to take her arm. "I have the Trantons' carriage outside. Come with me now and I shall explain to Mrs. Fanshawe that by happy chance we met in Hamilton and that I implored you to bear me company —"

"I shall go nowhere with you!" Violently Emma pulled away from her and turned towards Kit. "She has always hated me, always. She turned my father against me — yes you did, there is no need to deny it. There is no truth in her! She tricked my father into marriage by becoming pregnant — did you know that, Kit? It's a woman's oldest trick, Jane Willoughby told me. He would never have done it, else. We were happy as we were."

"Emma, be silent! That is enough." Dorcas had paled.

"It's true, it's true, no matter what you might say! I saw the dates in your own grandmother's family Bible. She was showing it to me, showing where she had written the date of Storm's birth, and Phillipa and Julia."

"My grandmother rambles, as you well know —"

"But this was true!" Emma was not shouting now, but was speaking very quietly and rapidly, her eyes bright with malice in her pale face. "Beside Aunt Fanny's name, the wedding date was written: 4th September, 1811. 'You've no record of Mama's wedding,' I said, just to please her. 'No more I have,' she said, all quavery and anxious; and then and there she wrote it in: Dorcas Foley and Zachariah Hardiman, married 15th January, 1811. I always knew that, of course, but I was young and stupid and never saw the significance, Storm being born but seven months later."

Dorcas was conscious of a sudden stillness as Emma fell silent; stillness from Kit, stillness from Emma, as if even she realised that she had said too much.

Kit was the first to speak.

"I think," he said, "we have heard enough for one day." He sounded strange and unlike himself, Dorcas thought; remote and impersonal and cold. "Wait for me here, Dorcas. Come, Emma."

Emma gave him a somewhat fearful glance, but this time she went unprotestingly as with a curt indication of his head he directed her through the door.

Dorcas knew that she, too, should make her escape but was trembling and needed a moment to compose herself.

By the time she had done so, Kit was back.

"I took the liberty of putting her into your carriage," he said. "She will have to make what explanation she can when she gets back to school." Dumbly Dorcas nodded in agreement. "Come through to my private rooms, please."

"I must leave," she said, paying no heed to this. "I am sorry you have been subjected —"

"*Come!*" He was remote no longer, but with eyes blazing with anger he grasped her arm and propelled her towards a door in the wall behind his desk. She gasped but did not resist. What had been said, had been said; she could neither erase it nor avoid its consequences.

Beyond the door was a passage with steps leading down to a square room, comfortably furnished, with a window overlooking the harbour.

"Now," he said, when with practised tact his slave withdrew on seeing that he had company. "Explain. Did Emma speak the truth?"

"About my tricking Zachariah? No, of course not."

"I mean about the date of your son's birth."

For a moment she hesitated, not meeting his eyes.

"Dorcas, answer me!"

She could not look at him. There was a picture of a sailing ship in a rough sea over the fireplace. She noticed a row of pipes, a carriage clock, a carved figure from some distant land.

"Will you answer me?"

His voice shook, and when she turned her eyes back to him she saw that all his smiling charm had fallen from him like a discarded cloak.

"Yes, it's true." Her voice emerged as a dry whisper. "Storm was born something under seven months after our marriage."

"Then he's *my* son!" Anger suffused his face and he smashed one balled fist into the palm of his hand. "Dammit, Dorcas, how could you? *My* son, masquerading as the son of a tuppeny-ha'penny nobody like Hardiman?"

Her anger flared too.

"He's a good man, and the best of fathers —"

"To *my* son?"

"Tell me, who is more the father of a child? The man who enjoys a brief moment of pleasure and runs away, or the man who for eight years loves and cares and devotes himself —"

"I would have cared for him, and for you."

"You showed precious little sign of it then!"

"You should have told me! You had no right —"

"How could I tell you? I neither knew nor could discover your whereabouts. I kept hoping and hoping to hear from you." Anger and the remembrance of past anguish had caused her eyes to brim with tears. "I nearly died when I did not."

"I wrote —"

"So you say! I saw no evidence of it." She dashed the tears away and gave a short laugh. "Is it any wonder that I at once fear for my stepdaughter when I hear of her attachment? Oh, Kit!" She sighed and turned from him, a look of despair on her face. "I have spent eight years — more — trying to gain her confidence, trying to be the sort of mother that Zachariah deserves for his children. Can't you see what you've done, simply because you had to charm that foolish girl, just as you charmed me, foolish girl that I was?"

"I loved you," he said.

"So I thought. My disillusionment was hard and painful."

She dared not look at him. She had to hold tightly to her remembrance of pain.

"You still refuse to believe that I wrote to you?"

She looked at him then, as if even now, in spite of her doubts, she longed for reassurance.

Wordlessly he reached for her.

"Believe this," he said, and angrily, without tenderness, his lips came down on hers and his arms imprisoned her.

For a moment she struggled against him; but his touch awakened longings she had done her utmost to suppress. She was flesh and blood with all the weakness that implied, and it was flesh and blood that she could feel now, hard and demanding, and ultimately irresistible.

Sanity returned, and she pushed him away.

"No, Kit. There must be none of that. All that is over and done with."

"Not quite." He spoke softly, all tenderness now. "Not quite, Dorcas. You're forgetting something, aren't you?" She looked at him enquiringly. "Aren't you, Dorcas?"

"I don't think so."

"You're forgetting my son."

"Why should you care about him? Until five minutes ago you had no idea of his existence."

"But now I know — and nothing can be the same again." He reached out to pull her close to him again. "Look at you, you're trembling! You still feel the same."

"No!"

"I'm the father of your child, Dorcas. We belong together. Didn't I tell you, the last time we met, there's never been another like you?" His voice was soft, insistent, ragged with emotion. "Believe me, when I came back and found you gone, it was like the end of the world, the end of everything I'd hoped for. All the time I was away, there was but one thought in my mind, to get back to you at the first opportunity. Yes, yes, I know what my mother told you! We've been through that and I readily admit that she was an ambitious woman, and malicious too, where your family is concerned. The same could be said for your father. Now both are dead, and where are we? Here, together, with a son that belongs to both of us and a lifetime still ahead of us. But for one lost letter, miscarried God knows in what manner –"

"Hebe." Dorcas spoke the name flatly. "Hebe could have destroyed it. She is, and always has been, devoted to my grandmother and disapproving of me. It is not outside the realms of possibility that she knew of our meetings and thought by taking the letter she was doing the right thing, forcing me into the right path. My grandmother was set on my marrying Mr. Amberley at that time."

Kit put a hand beneath her chin and tilted her face towards him.

"And you are content to let a slave keep us apart? Is that what you're saying to me?"

She looked at him wordlessly, knowing that all the longing she had denied for so long must be plain in her eyes.

"Please –" she whispered, not knowing for what she was pleading. Did she want him to turn away from her – to let her go, to stop looking at her in that way she remembered so well?

She closed her eyes as if to summon strength to withstand the tumult of emotion that he aroused. No strength came; only an urgent desire – forbidden, sinful, she knew, but she was powerless to withstand it. Her hands seemed to rise towards him of their own volition. The feeling of his arms about her seemed like the answer to a question that had tormented her for years, his lips on hers the natural conclusion of a thousand formless fantasies.

No rocky cranny in the cliff this time, but a wide bed, the door of the room locked against the outside world.

There was not much tenderness either, no gentleness, just

a wild and tearing hunger, hers equal to his, that left them both exhausted and bereft of thought or speech.

It was some time before Kit raised himself on one elbow to stroke her face, his mouth soft and smiling, his pleasure in her clear to see.

"You are lovely, lovely," he whispered. "You see, I was right. There is no one like you."

"Why Hardiman, of all people?" he asked a little later. "Did he marry you knowingly?"

"My father arranged it – and yes, he knew." The weight of her conscience, at the merest mention of Zachariah, was hardly to be borne. "He's been the best of husbands, Kit."

"A pleasant fellow, I always thought." Zachariah, it seemed, could be dismissed in half a dozen words. Kit threw back his head and laughed. "I never could understand how such an ill-matched couple came to be wed! You're like Beauty and the Beast!"

"He's a good man!"

"Oh, I'm sure of it." Good but comic, his expression said. "But it's to me you belong, my darling; you and the boy. Now and always."

"That simply isn't true, Kit. We can change nothing now."

Still smiling, he bent his head and covered her with small kisses.

"Listen to me, my love. We have many years ahead of us, and what we make of them is ours to decide. You know that Silas is in the Caribbean?"

Dorcas nodded, uncomprehending.

"We are negotiating new business links with Cuba. There are opportunities –" He seemed about to say more, but stopped abruptly. "That's by the way. The point of the matter is that I am to leave Bermuda to run our affairs in Havana, operating Cuban registered ships. We could go there, my darling – you and I and our son – and begin a whole new life."

"I am married, Kit."

"No one in Havana need know that."

He believed it, she saw. Because he willed it, he could see no impediment to his vision of a golden future in which they would be together.

"I know a splendid house we could buy, a sugar estate, with the house set on a hill." He was sitting up now, his handsome face alight with eagerness, his eyes brilliant with dreams. "The Spanish know how to live, Dorcas. There's music and opera there, and balls the like of which you can only imagine. Such a life we would have together!"

She saw, as in a dream, a picture of herself with Kit; finely dressed, receiving guests. As if divining her thoughts, he held her close, smiling and persuasive.

"Compare *that* with your little salt island! We belong together, darling. Like to like – you can't deny it. Hardiman will get over it. After all, he married you for money, say what you will –"

Her arms, which had reached up to circle his neck, slipped away and grew limp, and she blinked a little as the picture changed.

She saw a nut-brown face and dark eyes that were warm with love, and a comic pair of eyebrows that signalled the extremes of amusement and despair and bewilderment. She saw a short, barrel-chested, unheroic figure who walked with a seaman's roll, whose dark hair had touches of silver in it and who sang with the voice of an angel.

"Oh, Kit," she said helplessly. For a moment she could say no more, but lay against the pillows with her face turned from him.

"Dorcas, look at me. Can't you see how much I love you?"

She turned to look at him, at his handsome, smiling, confident face, and was frightened of the emotions he stirred in her. She wanted him as much as ever. They both knew it and it would have been fruitless to deny it.

"All will be well, my darling," Kit said, reaching out to hold her close. "We shall be happy together, believe me."

"Oh, Kit," she said again. "Nothing is as simple as you pretend."

Eleven

It bore no relationship to happiness. Sometimes Dorcas thought that the devastating longing that obsessed her was little more than a sickness, some mental disorder, that had taken hold of her and made her into a creature devoid of morality or decency, or even plain common sense; yet still she trembled at the merest thought of him.

Their opportunities to be together were limited. Sometimes she would put a lamp in the upstairs window, leaving the back door on the latch, as a signal that the coast was clear. Some nights he would slip in like a shadow for a brief hour or two – visits that left her full of guilt and self-loathing. Yet the nights when the lamp burned and he did not answer the signal, leaving her to watch and wait, jumping anxiously at the smallest sound, they were the worst nights of all. Where was he? How was he spending his time? What had happened to her, she asked herself miserably, that she could demean herself in this way?

A hundred times she vowed that she would finish the association once and for all; but at his step all her good resolutions melted away. Why, she asked herself, did she love him so? Why should trivial matters like the way a man's hair grew or the shape of his lips dictate a woman's response to him? Only in his absence did it seem nonsensical.

Fanny was worried about her.

"Dearest, I wish you would rest," she said one Sunday when Dorcas had gone to Cedarcroft for luncheon. "You are wearing yourself out. I swear you have lost weight and are as pale as a ghost! Grandmama herself would not wish it, and what Zachariah will think of us for not taking better care of you, I cannot imagine. You will make yourself ill if you do not take life more easily."

"I'm resting at this moment." Dorcas smiled at her sister, hoping that the smile would disguise the fact that she had slept for only two or three hours the night before. Kit had finally come, but late. He had fallen in with acquaintances at the tavern, he said.

"And I am an afterthought – to be kept waiting at your pleasure?"

"Hush, my darling! It was an opportunity to seek new contracts. Come and kiss me and say you forgive me."

She did both, and the night sky had been fading by the time he left her.

It was good now to breathe the sweet, fresh air at Cedarcroft and to sit back, happy in the knowledge that, for a few hours, no demands would be made of her, either from lover or sick-room. She enjoyed Storm's company, too. She missed him sorely and her spirits were always eased at the sight of him. His excited chatter about his friends, the Dickenson boys from next door whose lessons he shared, gave her more unclouded pleasure than anything else in her life at that moment.

"Mama, you should see Peter Dickenson dive! He stays under for hours and hours. Well," he amended, as Dorcas cocked an amused and sceptical eyebrow towards him, "minutes, anyway. He's teaching me and I'm *much* better than when we left home. I wish Papa could see. When will you come to the beach with us, Mama? Aunt Fanny says she will arrange a party soon. You will be able to come, won't you?"

"I shall certainly try."

Remorse prodded her with painful fingers. She had been guiltily obsessed with her own emotions, to the point of neglecting her son. She had told herself that he was happily occupied and for the moment did not need her; but *I* need *him*, she thought. Suddenly it seemed that he represented all that was normal and sane in her life.

"I have made a resolution," Fanny said. "I cannot let you take the brunt of caring for Grandmama any more. Now that I am so much recovered, we shall take turn and turn about in sleeping there."

"No, no, I shall not hear of it!" (But wouldn't that, after all, be the sensible solution – a way of forcing her own hand? No! She could not bear to face such a future.) "You have your home and your family to consider, Fanny, as well as your health."

Silas, who had returned from the Caribbean the previous week apparently highly satisfied with his negotiations there, looked at them both and shook his head in a resigned way as if he considered them mad.

"It would make a great deal more sense to bring the old lady here," he said.

"Oh, it would upset her quite dreadfully," Fanny said.

Dorcas agreed with her.

"She came to that room as a bride, Silas, and she's quite made up her mind that she will die there. She has moments of complete lucidity."

Silas shrugged his shoulders.

"On your own heads be it, then; however, I have to agree with Dorcas, Fanny. I cannot agree that your health would permit you to take up the burden again."

Thank God, Dorcas thought fervently. Thank God.

"Mama, you must come and see my new archery set." Storm was pulling at her sleeve. "Mr. Mallory gave it to me when he came up to see Uncle Silas the other day –"

"Mr. Mallory?" The name on Storm's lips came as a shock. Kit had said nothing.

"He came here the day after Silas came home," Fanny explained. "The bows and arrows had belonged to him as a boy, he said, and he thought Storm might appreciate them."

"How kind." Dorcas spoke stiffly. "However, such things can be dangerous, Storm. The little girls –"

"Oh Mama, I'm not a baby! Mr. Mallory showed me exactly how to use them and warned me over and over that I had to be careful."

"I hope you thanked him properly."

"Of course I did! I thanked him *and* wrote a note afterwards." Virtue shone from Storm's face. "He said he would take me fishing one day. I hope he remembers. He's a very nice gentleman, Mama."

"He seems to have taken quite a fancy to Storm." Fanny smiled at her sister, but found no answering smile of gratification on her face. She was hardly to know that a feeling of panic had Dorcas in its grip. What might Kit say to Storm? Surely he would give no hint of their relationship? She would have to speak to him – tell him to leave the boy alone.

"Of course, he ought to get married." Fanny, always ready for a gossip, pursued the subject of Kit. "One wonders why he has not! His name has been linked with one after another, but somehow it never comes to anything. Silas, why do you think Kit does not take a wife? It seems clear that he would like a family of his own, and goodness knows, there are enough young women in Bermuda who would jump at the chance to provide it."

"There you have it," Silas said, with a sardonic twitch of his lips. "It's always the unattainable that attracts Kit. He cares less than nothing for all the belles who swoon at his feet."

"How contrary of him!" Fanny said.

"It's a trait that makes him a good business partner," Silas went on. "He spares no effort to secure contracts that others might think impossible. One would think him hungry for advancement."

"I'm not sure," Fanny said consideringly, "if that is a very noble characteristic. What do you think, Dorcas?"

To her relief, Dorcas was saved the effort of replying by the announcement that luncheon was served.

"I've spoken to Silas," Kit said, "and all is prepared for my removal to Havana."

Restlessly, Dorcas moved her head on his bare shoulder.

"Kit —"

He stopped her mouth with kisses, not allowing her to speak.

"You'll come, Dorcas. I'm not going to lose you again."

"You know it's impossible."

"It's no such thing. Nothing is impossible, unless you wish it to be so. The choice is yours."

"I can do nothing while my grandmother lives."

She clung to this fact, welcoming the reprieve it gave her, knowing that the old lady was growing weaker by the day, the sands of life falling ever more quickly through the hour-glass. The reprieve, she knew, would only be short.

"I know that!" Kit's face was close to hers now; handsome, eager, vital. "But afterwards — darling, what more can I do to convince you that we belong together? I know why you hesitate, of course — you'll hurt Zachariah. But inevitably someone will be hurt. If not Hardiman, then it will be you and me; two against one! You're too young and lovely to be sacrificed on the altar of duty and convention."

"There is such a thing as morality —"

"Where is the morality in a forced marriage? In keeping a father away from his child? In denying the love we have for each other?"

In his presence, a magic future always seemed within her grasp. How do you define magnetism? she asked herself, watching him speak rather than listening to his words. It surely was not looks alone, though in Kit's case they played their part. There was pleasure in being the recipient of such a smile, a delight in being the one to kindle amusement and interest in his eyes.

Yet there were times when she felt she could dislike him. Take the matter of Hebe. He asked Dorcas one day if she had tackled the slave about the matter of the letter. Dorcas shook her head.

"No, of course not. Where would be the point? She would only deny it. Poor Hebe," she went on. "She is desolate at the thought of losing Grandmama. I cannot imagine how she will face life once she has gone. I shall ask Fanny if she might be given her freedom, though naturally, we shall continue to support her."

"*What?*" The face that Kit turned towards her was full of astonishment. "Give that old witch her freedom, after what she did to us? You must be mad, Dorcas! She should be beaten, not freed – and *would* be if I had my way."

"Kit, we don't know if she took the letter or not. And if she did, she must have thought she was acting for the best, doing what she thought to be right, and who can do more than that? Some of us," she said dully after a moment, looking away from him, "don't do as much."

Kit sighed with annoyance and left her shortly afterwards. It always exasperated him if she drew attention to her pangs of conscience – which was, as she told herself miserably afterwards, hardly to be wondered at. She should either turn to him joyfully and wholeheartedly, or not at all.

Could she go with him?

Such an outcome was not impossible, she recognised; not for this mad, bad, sensuous woman she had become, for surely she had changed beyond recognition the day Kit had taken her into his arms. She was no longer the same practical and dutiful wife who had settled for a second-best way of life on a barren salt island. She could almost feel herself changing, sloughing off the drab skin of her past.

On the other hand there was the fact that she was married to Zachariah – dear Zachariah, who had done no wrong, his only sin the blind and sometimes suffocating love that she had once accepted so gratefully. She received a letter from him.

My dearest Wife,
   The fine weather continues three bushels shipped this week but water low and there will be hardship soon I fear. I have crossed swords with Trotman on the subject of the water ration he seems to think slaves can live on a dewdrop how would he like it I ask him? The red hibiscus is flowering but the yellow looks to be in a bad way though Bathsheba makes certain it gets its share of dishwater each day. Also I have sung to it and scolded it to no good effect what are your instructions?
   My dearest I long for news of you and wish with all my heart that this was any other season of the year so that I could leave the salt and come to you. I pray that your poor grandmother's suffering will not be prolonged since it seems that there is little hope of recovery poor soul we all must come to it. I guess your spirits are low but remember there is one here who misses you and longs for your return me and the yellow hibiscus make quite a pair.

She could picture him clearly as he must have laboured over the composition of this letter, for such things did not come easily to him. He would have sat at the desk, smiling to himself as the thought about the hibiscus had come to him at the end, tapping the side of his nose with the quill.

How much easier it would be if only she could think of some grievous fault with which she could accuse him; something that would be sufficient to make her turn her back on him without regret or guilt.

"If your guilt is to love me, then it's no guilt at all," Kit said, when a few nights later she voiced this thought. "We were meant for each other. Storm is *my* son!"

"You've said nothing to him?" Dorcas spoke anxiously. "I don't want him told till I've made my decision."

"Haven't I promised to keep silence until you give me leave? I think he likes me, though."

Dorcas smiled ruefully at that and there was a dry note of resignation in her voice as she answered him.

"I'm sure he does," she said. "Show me anyone who can resist you."

* * *

Mrs. Foley died at four thirty in the morning of 16th August, 1819, and the funeral took place at St. Peter's Church two days later.

Dorcas felt weighed down, both by the heat and the dark clothes she wore, and also by the surroundings. She had avoided church as much as possible of recent weeks, for how could she kneel and make confession of her sins when she seemed incapable of renouncing them, given only a few moments of Kit's persuasive company? Now she looked around at the familiar walls of the old church, extended since she left Bermuda in 1811 but still basically the same with its cedar altar under the eastern window, and she felt a poignant longing for the lost innocence of childhood. How simple life had been then! How small the sins of omission and commission, seen from the position of an adulteress. Hideous word! She buried her face in her hands and wept, despising herself for the fact that others who saw her grief would no doubt respect it, attributing it to the loss of her grandmother.

Davey was looking at her anxiously. Scrubbed and shining and dressed in his best, he had come from school for the occasion, and he sat close beside her. He touched her arm and smiled at her anxiously.

"Mama?" he whispered. "Don't cry, Mama. She is at peace."

I wish to heaven that I were, Dorcas thought. She dabbed at her eyes and attempted to smile back at him, pierced to the heart by his likeness to Zachariah.

Emma sat beyond Davey. Her small, pale face was composed and expressionless, her neat ankles crossed, hands folded, head piously bent. Dorcas had seen her on two or three occasions at Cedarcroft, but they had hardly communicated since the scene in Kit's office. This was not from any lack of will on Dorcas's part; indeed, she had sought Emma out at the first opportunity with the intention of making her peace, speaking calmly and reasonably and suggesting that much had been said in the heat of the moment that was better forgotten.

Emma had looked at her coldly and said nothing, and since then they had treated each other with distant politeness whenever they were forced to meet, which had not been often.

Back at Cedarcroft, with Mrs. Foley interred in the family plot, family and friends gathered to express their condolences and remember the old lady in times past.

"Such a devoted mother and grandmother! What your poor, dear father would have done without her —"

"A true ornament to her sex, my dear Mrs. Hardiman. All our sympathies are with you."

"How she enjoyed her cards," said one elderly friend. "Almost to the end. She was kindness itself, and the soul of hospitality."

To all of which Dorcas, composed now, agreed gravely.

"She was indeed much loved," she said to Fanny when at one moment the sisters chanced to find themselves together. "Hebe is quite inconsolable. Which reminds me, have you had time to consider the matter I mentioned?"

Fanny looked flustered.

"I'm not at all sure it would be wise, Dorcas. Silas thinks not. It would create something of a precedent, would it not? I am quite certain Hebe herself has no thought of freedom."

"Are you?" Dorcas looked grimly amused. "Then she must be alone among her kind."

"You know how Silas feels about emancipation. He feels that this would be the thin end of the wedge."

"The decision is yours and mine to make. Hebe legally belongs to us now."

"I know, I know." Fanny looked more flustered than ever. "Pray, leave the subject, Dorcas. It is hard for me, with Silas setting his face so firmly against it."

"Please think about it a little more, Fanny, I beg you."

"Allow me to express my condolences, ladies."

Kit, solemn and correct, bowed over each hand, allowing only the flicker of a more intimate expression to creep into his eyes as he looked briefly at Dorcas. She wished he would go away. It was impossible for her to remain unaffected by his presence and she was terrified of revealing her true feelings by some unguarded word or expression.

"Excuse me," she said politely, seeing that he showed no sign of leaving her side. "I see Dr. McClosky across the room and must have a word with him; he so seldom appears in society these days."

Gravely amused, he bowed and watched her go. It did not matter; they would meet again before long, for Dorcas had resisted Fanny's pleas to come back to sleep at Cedarcroft forthwith, saying — rightly — that there was much that had to be sorted out at the house at St. George's.

He would have her, Kit thought, watching her slim and

shapely backview retreating from him while feigning absorption in Fanny's conversation. She *must* be forced to a decision soon. Somehow he would have to bring this ridiculous hesitation to a happy conclusion – the conclusion which was surely inevitable.

What, after all, had Hardiman to offer compared to the life that he could give her? She must be made to see that her husband would not die if she left him, and that the disapprobation of society would be fleeting and unimportant. Somehow he must convince her! After all, there was Storm to consider. His son. Didn't he merit a future less restrictive than that provided by a barren salt island and a clown like Hardiman?

He had seen the boy in church, sitting beside his mother, the Hardiman boy on her other hand. He could not have been alone in remarking the discrepancies between the two. They were like two different species. The Hardiman boy was bidding fair to grow into the image of his father; small, short-necked, ungainly – while Storm was a son any man could be proud of. He was intelligent and bright-faced, tall and handsome with red-gold hair and his mother's green eyes.

He looked round the room for the boy, Fanny having bustled off to carry out her duty elsewhere, but could not see him. Emma, however, caught his eye and stared at him coldly for a second in spite of the placatory smile he sent in her direction. Then, deliberately, she turned her back and spoke to a visiting Foley aunt.

Silas joined him, looking pained.

"There is only one thing worse," he said in a low voice, "than one's own relatives *en masse*, and that is one's wife's. I fear I am suffering from a surfeit of Foleys. Tell me –" He lowered his voice in a conspiratorial manner. "If I were to make some excuse to Fanny regarding business, could I not come down to your apartments after dinner? Her Aunt Clarissa Foley is to stay the night and quite honestly, I shall not be responsible for my actions if I am forced to listen to that woman quacking at me for an entire evening. In truth, there are some matters I should like to discuss with you – and if we chanced to crack a bottle or two in the process I should consider it no more than I deserve after the past few days."

"Nothing I should like more!"

Dorcas had already made it plain that she would not countenance a visit that night. It would not be seemly, she said; and he grinned inwardly at the memory of her words, for on reflection there seemed little that was seemly about the abandonment of her lovemaking. What a woman she was! Full of contradictions, yet more exciting than anyone he had known.

The mementoes of a long life filled box after box. Invitations, letters, dressmakers' bills; was it worth going through them all? Were it not for the fact that Dorcas knew, having been told by her grandmother, that she had in her possession old documents relating to the sale of one of the first plots of land ever settled in Bermuda, she would have burned the lot. As it was, she could not bear the thought that by so doing she could be destroying something that was of historical value.

It was trivia that predominated, however. She sighed wearily and rested her head on her hand for a moment, and it was in this attitude that Silas found her when Hebe ushered him in.

She looked up in some surprise. Silas did not habitually seek her out.

He smiled at her thinly, as neutrally polite as if she were a casual acquaintance.

"A sad task, no doubt."

"Yes, indeed." She collected herself rapidly and stood to receive him, ready to take this opportunity – whatever the cause of it – to do battle on Hebe's behalf.

"You look a little fatigued," he said. "I'm sure you must be relieved that you can now return home to your husband."

"Would you care for tea, Silas?" Dorcas made no comment on this observation. "Hebe was about to serve it, I'm sure."

"Thank you, no. What I have come to say will take little time. Please –" He gestured towards a chair. "Sit down, Dorcas."

She sat down, eyeing him warily. His was not a face that gave anything away, but she sensed hostility behind his expressionless exterior. Did he imagine that she was salting the more valuable items in the house away for her own use? Suspect her of helping herself to Grandmama's items of jewellery without reference to Fanny?

"I went to see Kit last night," Silas said suddenly. Dorcas was suddenly still, the hand that had been rearranging her skirt clenched on the thin silk.

"Yes?"

"We had business matters to discuss." He swung away from her, picked up a piece of porcelain from a small table, and appeared to study it meticulously. "One thing led to another." His voice was still remote and impersonal as he at last put the ornament down and looked at her coldly. "Kit is apt to grow confidential in his cups."

Dorcas said nothing, but her throat was suddenly dry.

"He told me that you were leaving with him to go to Havana."

"He – he had no right to say that."

"Come, Dorcas!" As if his anger and impatience could be contained no longer he sat down himself opposite her and grasping the edge of the table, leaned towards her with a face that was transformed by cold disgust. "From what he told me he has every right. You are lovers, are you not?"

Dorcas clasped trembling hands and rested them on the table before her, looked at them and removed them once more to her lap.

"Silas, I cannot expect you to understand –"

"I don't intend to try. I find the whole matter entirely contemptible."

"I imagine that you would. But Silas, I love him so! I have tried to deny my feelings, believe me, but I cannot. There is nothing you can say to me that I haven't said to myself. Truly I – I do not know how I could go on living without him."

"How touching!" Silas's expression had not altered. "So you are to throw convention to the wind, spit in the face of Church and society –"

"No – I don't know!" Agitatedly Dorcas got to her feet and took a few paces away from him. "I've made no decision."

"The fact that all decent people would revile you means nothing?"

"Of course it does. But if I'm prepared to take the consequences of my action –"

"And my wife – your sister? Suppose I tell you I am not prepared for *her* to take the consequences! You have seen how it is in Hamilton. We are respected here. We are leaders in this community. What will it do to her to have those who were her friends whispering behind their hands? It would be the ruin of her – and for what?" His thin lips curved downwards as if even speaking of the matter was distasteful. "For the sensual gratification of a lecherous woman. It is not," he went on, "as if you could expect happiness."

"Kit is convinced that all will be well."

"Then he deludes himself, and you, too." He gave a short laugh. "Have you not expounded to him your insane views on emancipation?"

Dorcas stared at him wordlessly, then shrugged.

"It's hardly a matter that has been in the forefront of our minds."

"I can believe it. Nevertheless, the matter is relevant. You must surely know Kit's opinion of slavery."

"I suspect it's no different from that of most others of his upbringing. Times are changing, though, whatever he thinks. Why should it be an issue?"

Silas smiled coldly, no humour in his eyes.

"You should have gone into his views a little more fully. Have you not asked yourself why we wish to register ships in Havana?"

"No." Dorcas looked bewildered. "Not specifically. I thought – the sugar trade, perhaps?"

"Not the sugar trade, Dorcas. Cuba happens to be among the few countries in the Caribbean where the slave trade is still legal. Britain, hypocritical to the end, allows the use of slaves but forbids their importation. Under Cuban law it was forbidden too, until two years ago. Now Spain has repealed that law and there's a great deal of money to be made. By us. It's not a trade that we expect to last long, but while it does we have every intention of being a part of it."

She stared at him.

"Kit knows this?"

Silas laughed briefly.

"Knows? He devised the whole operation. His first task will be to supervise the building of two new vessels. There have been certain formalities standing in our way until now, but on my recent visit I managed to grease a few palms, speak to the right people. So you see, my dear, your strongly held, stridently voiced views on emancipation are quite relevant. I doubt whether you would find happiness with a man who actually made money from blackbirding."

Slowly Dorcas turned from him and reached blindly for the back of a chair as if for support.

"Please go," she said.

"Very well. I have said all I came to say. I shall leave you now to reflect on the matter."

Picking up his hat and cane he rose to leave, but before he could go Dorcas whirled round to face him.

"Wait," she said. "Let me make sure I understand. You and Kit are to build slave ships to sail to Africa."

"The Gold Coast, actually —"

"There to buy — *buy* — human souls and transport them in chains, packed one above the other in stinking hell holes, with no room to breathe, so that you may sell them to the highest bidder."

"Oh, I think you overstate the horror," Silas said. "The survival rate is fairly high, I believe."

"Fairly high!" Dorcas repeated the words disgustedly. "Fairly high! I thought better of you, Silas."

He gave his thin cold smile, and shrugged.

"My dear Dorcas, we seem to be mutually disappointed in each other. I knew precisely what your reaction would be, which is the reason I told you of the scheme. The fact that I happen to disagree with your somewhat hysterical views is neither here nor there. Slavery has been with us since biblical times and no doubt will be with us for ever. Our entire economy depends on it. However, we have discussed such things sufficient times in the past for me to know that your mind is inflexible."

"I never thought that you would *trade* —"

He pressed his lips together and shook his head with grim amusement.

"Go back to your Zachariah, Dorcas. Your thoughts are more in tune with his, I'll warrant, than ever they would be with Kit Mallory."

"And Fanny?" Dorcas asked coldly. "What does she say of your — your new business venture?"

For the first time Silas looked less than sure of himself.

"I never discuss such things with Fanny. However, she is not the Abolitionist you are."

"Perhaps not. There are many well-meaning people who live with the system because it's an established fact and they feel an obligation to the slaves they own. Zachariah is one such. Trading is different. Fanny would be as repelled as I by what you propose to do."

"Then shall we strike a bargain? My silence about Kit Mallory for yours about my Cuban interests."

They looked at each other for a long moment, then Dorcas turned away.

"Please go," she said again. "Go, Silas."

Her self-control was at an end, and he had barely left the room before she slumped into an armchair, covered her face with her hands, and wept bitter tears for the dream that he had destroyed, the fairy tale that she had never, in her heart, believed could come true.

She wept, but beyond the tears there was a relief that could not be denied; beyond the tears there was sanity and peace, and a profound thankfulness that this decision had been made for her.

Beyond the grief there was the knowledge that Zachariah waited for her return, as loving and dependable as ever. She would delay her journey no longer.

The voyage was punishing for the first few days, the sea rougher than she had ever experienced. Somehow it seemed entirely appropriate that she should feel so ill, so incapable of thinking of anything beyond her own physical misery.

"Poor Mama!" Storm said, his sympathy perfunctory, for there seemed something within him that rose in exultation at the fury of the elements. "Captain Reed says the glass is rising, so there's no real danger. Do you want me to stay with you – because I will if you want."

The offer was made while he stood on one leg, half in and half out of the cabin, and he rushed off almost before Dorcas had uttered her plea for solitude, not hearing her strictures about taking care and keeping away from the rail.

She was glad to be alone. Her parting with Kit had not been an easy one and the taste of it was still bitter in her mouth.

So much anger! She could not have believed that he could change so. Even his face had altered, becoming narrower and sharper. He had called her a cheat and hypocrite and a thief.

"You've stolen my son from me – and for what? For a few slaves that matter neither here nor there. For a principle, dreamed up by men who know nothing of the true situation."

Dorcas, all tears spent, had pressed her hand to her throbbing temples.

"God knows," she had said, "I've cheated and lied, though not to you. But a hypocrite? No! Don't you see that's why I can't allow myself to be kept by the proceeds of slavery? Can't you see it for the evil it is?"

"Don't preach to me! I need no sermons, least of all from

you. Go back to your mealy-mouthed peasant, and when he claims his marital rights, think of the nights we have shared, and *would* have shared —"

"There's more to married life than shared nights. The stigma would last us all our days —"

"You never meant to come with me, did you? This is just an excuse. If it had not been slavery, you would have found some other good reason for taking my son away a second time —"

"Your son, your son!" Dorcas's anger had flared. "Precious little you cared for the result of that shared night all those years ago. I'm thankful — yes, thankful! — that the man he knows as his father is decent and kind. He's better off without you, Kit Mallory. I shall pray fervently that he shows no taint of your blood, as long as he lives."

How could she say such things after all they had been to each other, no matter what the provocation? She had wept again and reached out a hand towards him as if she would take back the words if she could, but she had seen from his expression that it was too late. His face was cold and set, his eyes glittering behind half-closed lids.

"You bitch!" he had said harshly. "You'll regret saying that."

She had whitened at his vehemence.

"I spoke in the heat of the moment. I'm sorry."

"I shan't forget."

Helplessly she had looked at him; at the sharpness of his features, at the mouth that had thinned and grown bitter. She had been reminded of another face, another crisis in her life.

"You look just like your mother," she had said.

And he had done, she remembered, lying miserable and sea-sick in her bunk aboard the tossing brig that was taking her back to Grand Cay. The easy charm, the heart-stopping smile; all his indefinable magic had gone, to be replaced by that expression of cold, vindictive spite that she remembered so well.

"If the belles of Bermuda could see you now," she had said to him, with bitter humour.

Was it truly over, then? Physically she felt so wretched that it was almost impossible to determine where one pain ended and another began. She could only pray that once the physical misery was at an end, her mind, too, would find rest.

* * *

Zachariah sailed out to meet her in the lighter, his face bright with joy, and later, at home, Bathsheba was equally joyful.

"Welcome home, Miz Dorcas," she said. And as she unpacked while Dorcas washed: "Hear de Master whistle? He don't raise a note, all de time you away. No ma'am, he don't sing no more'n a roach."

After darkness fell and Storm had gone to bed, recounting his experiences to Zachariah as he went, they sat on the porch. The night was full of the murmurous sound of the sea, contrarily tranquil now that the travellers were safely on shore. Their chairs were pulled close so that Zachariah could hold her hand in his.

"Thank you for coming back," he said.

Dorcas laughed a little breathlessly and turned to look at the familiar, comforting bulk of him.

"Why would I not come back?" she asked lightly. "This is where I belong."

He pressed her hand to his lips, sudden emotion threatening to overcome him.

"There was such a distance between us," he said. "And I'm such a poor hand with the pen. There was so much I longed to say, so many nights when I sat here and thought of you. It seemed – I don't know – unreal, somehow, that you should be married to me. For the life of me, I couldn't see why you should come back."

"Zack, you're far too humble! You must know I love you."

In the silence that followed, the realisation that her words were true, and that she had finally broken the bonds that had kept her in thrall – not only during these past weeks in Bermuda but throughout the whole of her marriage – sifted through her like a shaft of light. She was free of Kit at last.

It was like a burden falling from her shoulders, like reaching a safe harbour. Turning, she clasped Zachariah's hand in both of hers.

"Never have such thoughts again," she said.

It was too dark to see his expression, but she sensed that he trembled on the edge of tears.

"My sweetheart," he said gruffly. "My Dorcas."

Twelve

Tamarind Villa,
Grand Cay,
Turks and Caicos Islands
4th December, 1821.

My dearest Fanny,

Yours of 20th November to hand, and I praise God that you are safely delivered of a darling son and pray that you will shortly be restored to full health. Zachariah joins me in sending felicitations to you and Silas. On the whole, I find I must agree with your husband that the name 'Nicholas' is to be preferred to 'Josiah', though I know that by so doing I may be showing a want of filial respect. Our father, though to be admired in some respects (not least his love of country and devotion to public service) was nevertheless not a man who demonstrated understanding of his fellows nor yet the enjoyment of life which must surely be our wish for this precious newcomer.

Zachariah and I have both considered carefully your suggestions regarding Emma. Your many kindnesses both to her and Davey over the years can seldom have found an equal, and already we are much in your debt. I confess myself in something of a quandary on the matter you raise! The relationship between Emma and myself has ever been a difficult one, as you well know, and added to this she has made it clear over the past months that she little relishes the thought of returning to this poor island and the limited social life it offers.

For both these reasons, the proposal that she should stay with you as governess and companion to your children has indeed fallen on receptive ears. It must also be said that her chances of finding a suitable husband must perforce be increased should she remain in Bermuda, and this is a matter which has been weighing heavily on Zachariah's mind of late.

However, my dearest Fanny, much as this arrangement would suit *us*, I am not convinced that it would suit *you*, for I feel I must remind you that though Emma is fond of young children there is something in her nature that renders her incapable of the good-humoured give-and-take which surely must be the corner-stone of untroubled relationships. It would go against my conscience if I did not urge you to reflect most carefully on this head.

But if, having reflected, you still wish her to reside as a member of your family at Cedarcroft then I for one will be overjoyed, knowing that she will have a home second to none, among those who will show her nothing but kindness and understanding.

Dorcas paused to re-read the words she had written, shook her head doubtfully over them, and sighed a little. She could not feel optimistic about the eventual outcome, no matter what immediate answer to Fanny's domestic problems Emma might appear to provide.

Her gloomy thoughts were interrupted by the sound of shouts and laughter from the beach outside, and her expression lightened. Storm and Aaron, the son of Joe and Bathsheba, were clearly enjoying themselves.

Gone now were the days when shouts would be the result of squabbles between Emma and Davey or Emma and Storm. Though she regretted the fact that Storm had few friends to play with, for he was the oldest of the settler boys on the island, she could do no other than be thankful that he had Aaron. Though two years younger than Storm, in common-sense matters he was in some ways more mature.

She heard more laughter. For a moment she was tempted to leave her letter and go out to watch them in their play, but she resisted the idea. She could imagine the scene well enough; the crescent of white sand with its fringe of casuarina trees, crabs scuttling along the shore-line, and the stone breakwater built by Zachariah thrusting its bony finger into the turquoise sea. She knew exactly how the sun-dappled water would shoot upwards like a handful of diamonds at the impact of the boys' bodies. Lucky Storm, to be young and male and free to dive and race about the island barefoot! He had grown tall in the last year and his face had lost the roundness of extreme youth. He was, it was clear, going to have the Foley nose, and his hair had darkened a little, making it nearer her own in colour than it had been when he was small. Only a certain clean-limbed strength reminded her of Kit.

She *must* return to her letter!

All is well here. You remember, I am sure, Marcia's son, Dr. Bettany, who was visiting the island at the same time as you were (oh, so long ago!). On further acquaintance I find him not near so intimidating, and can only admire his dedication to his calling. He has made it his life's work to study the problems attendant upon childbirth and has come to some interesting conclusions regarding childbed fever – so tragic, and alas, so common. Cleanliness is, of course, all important; yet he assures us that there are many lying-in hospitals where it is all but unheeded, and he has received nothing but scorn from midwives who refuse to concern themselves unduly on the matter.

But his most controversial contention is that the incidence of childbed fever is increased where doctors and students attendant upon the lying-in come straight to the mother from the dissecting room. His assertions have led him into much argument and indeed have caused his dismissal from the hospital in Charleston to which he has devoted so much time and energy. He is taking a rest from controversy here on the island and has proved to be an interesting and entertaining companion, particularly to Storm who hangs upon his every word. He, it seems, is less concerned with the benefits Dr. Bettany bestows upon humanity than his amazing ability to name every bird that shows itself here, not to mention his skill with rod and line!

We shall all miss him when he goes back to America. He is to join a more enlightened and less hostile hospital in Boston on his return, and Marcia is going with him to settle him into his new home. I pray heaven that she is not tempted to stay there! I cannot imagine what life here would be like without her stimulating friendship. There is no other with whom I can experience true communion and no other who can reduce the annoyances caused by the Grimshaws and Trotmans of this world to nothing more than an opportunity for amusement.

Alas, even her wit cannot induce me to see the funny side of Willis Trotman at this moment. He makes it his business to oppose Zachariah at every turn at meetings of the Assembly, with such a degree of animosity and sheer bile that rational discussion of Zachariah's plans for the island's future is all but impossible. It is quite maddening, since Zachariah has the good of the island at heart, whereas Trotman seeks merely to feather his own nest; however, he and Mr. Grimshaw appear to have formed an unholy alliance which is well-nigh impregnable. The other Representatives from Grand Cay are weak individuals who seek only Mr. Grimshaw's favour, and those from the other islands have differing interests and axes to grind.

Forgive me, dearest Fanny, for troubling you with such matters, which must seem so trivial to you. You must be the happiest woman alive at this moment as you hold your long-awaited son in your arms. How I wish I could be with you to join in your delight! Be assured I think of you constantly –

And not without a certain amount of envy, Dorcas admitted to herself with a sigh, her thoughts going off on a tangent once more. *Why* had she not conceived? Her longing for a child was as fierce as it had ever been – more so, in fact. A child for Zachariah would be a love-gift, some small recompense for the betrayal she had perpetrated. Still her hopes came to nothing.

Marcia had urged her to talk to her son, who had made a study of women's matters, but she had been unable to bring herself to do so. It would have been easier to approach a stranger. In any case, Zachariah was uneasy about the idea of taking such things further, fearful that by interfering with God's will her own life might somehow be put in danger.

"We have Storm, sweetheart," he said. "Let us be content. He is the finest son any man could wish."

"And soon must go away to school."

"Ay, I suppose so; but not yet. Not yet."

Dorcas agreed with him. She could not bear to think of the time when the boy would leave home. These years were so short and flew so fast. So recently, it seemed, Davey had been a small, stocky, merry little boy. Now he was a midshipman aboard a frigate, somewhere in the Mediterranean.

Inevitably the time would come for Storm to continue his education elsewhere, but meantime it was as if the island were some giant pleasure ground designed for his use. Together he and Aaron sailed and swam and fished, going out with Joe for nights at a time, exploring the outlying islands, growing tough and confident and full of seaman's knowledge.

"He's learning more here than ever he would at some niminy-piminy school," Zachariah said.

"I agree! But he needs book-learning too, Zack."

"He gets book-learning. I never knew such a boy for reading."

That was true, too. Together with some items of furniture – now gracing the parlour and turning it into a more elegant room than the first Mrs. Hardiman could ever have dreamed of – Dorcas had brought back from Bermuda a considerable number of books from her father's library; heavy tomes for the most part, but included in their number a surprising selection of novels which cast an amusing sidelight on Josiah Foley's nature.

"The old fox!" Dorcas said to Zachariah. "When I think of the times he retired to his study while all the rest of the household walked on tip-toe lest he should be disturbed in his contemplation of weighty matters of state! None of us had the slightest suspicion that in reality he was closeted with Fielding and Walpole and Smollett. Why, he gave us to understand that all works of fiction were far too trivial to engage his attention! We thought that in his lighter moments – if any such occurred – he turned to volumes of collected sermons."

Whatever his grandfather's reading tastes, Storm was working his way through novels and sermons alike, the written word in whatever form exercising a fascination for him.

"Do you understand that?" Zachariah had asked him incredulously one day, finding him lost in *Tristram Shandy*.

"Not a word," Storm admitted cheerfully. "But I still like reading it."

At which Zachariah had shrugged his shoulders and shaken his head in bewilderment, but also with a certain amount of awe. He, who had been trying to read *Pilgrim's Progress* for the past few years, was both impressed and perplexed by such an apparent contradiction.

Enough wool-gathering! This letter to Fanny would never be finished at this rate. Determinedly she returned to it.

The season has been a good one for salt and we still have a considerable quantity to be shipped, mainly to the Cahill Company who have taken a goodly proportion of the raking this year, being delighted with the quality. There is no doubt that thorough attention to the preparation and cleaning of the salt ponds has had its reward, for not only has Mr. Cahill professed himself thoroughly satisfied but has recommended Zachariah's salt to others, thus increasing the volume of our exports.

In spite of all, we have more time for entertainment and recreation now than during the summer months, and the fund for our proposed new church grows apace. Only last night Zachariah sang at a concert in aid of this cause and was gratified to be called back no less than three times by the audience.

In all it was a delightful evening. Dr. Bettany professed himself astonished at the standard of the musical offerings – higher, I must confess than on some occasions in the past, for we have had some welcome additions to our small community. The wife of the new Collector of Customs plays the pianoforte with considerable skill and two brothers from Puerto Plata who have taken up residence here play several instruments. They are contemplating setting up as music teachers! So you see, we are becoming very cultivated in this little backwater.

The time draws on when I must bring this long letter to a close, but I cannot do so without once more returning to the subject of Emma. Do, I beg you, give this matter your most serious consideration, dearest Fanny. I feel I must urge you to do so, yet at the same time I am anxious that my own difficulties with her, which are, perhaps, inherent in the relationship between us, should not in any way cast a shadow on her future. Only you and Silas can make the final decision.

I pray that we shall soon meet. Write, soon, I beg you, and tell me of the dear baby's progress. I long to have word of you all.

She finished the letter, signed her name, folded the several sheets and sealed them. She looked towards the pretty French clock on top of the bureau that had once had pride of place in her grandmother's bedroom. Time yet to write a brief letter to Davey. How strange to think that he was seeing peoples and places that she had never seen; and disquieting, too, the signs of envy that she had detected in Storm.

Davey, she was convinced, was lost to them. A life at sea

had always been his aim, and though there were hardships to be borne, he seemed content to undergo anything in order to fulfil his ambitions. He would never come back to the island other than for a short visit.

Storm had always seemed different. He was a child of the island, knowing every inch of it and as involved as Zachariah in plans for its future. From the first he had been allowed to play with Aaron and other children of the black community, both slave and free, and was as happy sharing a meal of grits with them as sitting down to a roast dinner with his own family.

Still, it was natural that he should long to see the sights and events that were now part of Davey's experience. Didn't she long to see them herself? Dorcas quieted her fears. The time would come when he would satisfy his curiosity about the rest of the world, and having done so, would return to the island. This was where he belonged, where he would settle and bring up a family in his turn. The thought of living out her life on this island without him was something she could not bear to contemplate.

There were those who criticised his upbringing.

"Really, I wash my hands of those Hardimans," Mrs. Grimshaw had been heard to say more than once. "They simply have no sense of the fitness of things. That boy is allowed to mix with *anyone*! What his future will be, I simply cannot imagine. My heart bleeds for him! Running wild like that, mixing with every Tom, Dick or Harry – he'll grow up to be nothing more than a savage, mark my words. Mind you –" and here she was inclined to lower her voice confidentially and flare her rocking-horse nostrils still further – "there was always something strange about the Hardimans. I said it from the first. Look at their friendship with Mrs. Bettany, a woman lost to decency if ever I saw one. Out and about by herself in all the worst areas, passing on heaven alone knows what ridiculous ideas to the slaves, speaking up in public just as if she were a man! No one would give her the time of day in Nassau, of that I can assure you. And that so-called doctor son of hers – did you hear he was forced to leave a hospital in Charleston? I had it on good authority. It's to be hoped he takes his mother back to America with him and keeps her there. This place would be the better for it, I can tell you."

*　　*　　*

"You won't keep her away, will you?"

Hugh Bettany had walked into town on his final day and had called into Tamarind Villa to say his farewells. He had found Dorcas alone, Zachariah not yet returned from an inspection of his holdings to the south of the island, and had sat drinking tea with her on the veranda.

They had conversed easily but superficially. Dorcas was always too conscious of the one matter she longed to, but dared not, discuss to do anything more. Now, however, he was aware that she was looking at him with a very real expression of appeal in her eyes.

He smiled at her reassuringly.

"Nothing keeps her away from the island for long. On the contrary, she's been trying to persuade me to stay."

"Oh!" Dorcas sighed as she set down her cup. "How wonderful that would be! What peace of mind to know that we had a medical man here in Grand Cay. But no – it wouldn't be right. You have so much to offer the world."

He laughed at that.

"I wish my late employers in Charleston could hear you say so!"

"It will be better in Boston. May I give you more tea?" She took his cup and refilled it in silence. "You deserve a far wider audience than we can provide," she said, as she handed it back to him.

"I don't ask for acclaim. That's not the point of my work."

He spoke impatiently, his face suddenly stern, not smiling any more.

"I didn't mean –" Dorcas began; but before she could finish he was leaning forward apologetically.

"Forgive me! I shouldn't have bitten your head off in that way. It was unforgivable of me."

"I expressed myself clumsily. I merely meant that our small world here was too restricted for you."

"How strange." He was smiling again, but his eyes were intent. "I have often thought the same thing of you. Yet you seem happy. Serene. Don't you long for other fields to conquer?"

She smiled back at him slowly, an enigmatic look in her green eyes, and he blinked as if the force of her beauty was something that had not fully struck him until that moment. This was untrue. It struck him afresh every time he looked at her, but always with that same original impact.

"Conquests, Dr. Bettany," she said, looking away from him as she picked up her cup again, "do not necessarily mean happiness."

"Tell me what does, then." He spoke with deceptive casualness. "Tell me how you manage it, Dorcas. Tell me how you came to this place."

Suddenly there seemed a new dimension to their conversation, as if they were on the brink of some unchartered country which might promise untold riches but which could also be dangerous. In the silence which followed his request, she was thankful to hear the sound of the buggy trundling over the potholes of the track which led to their door.

"Here comes Zachariah," she said, conscious that the atmosphere was rapidly returning to normal at the mere mention of his name, horrified at how close she had come to telling this man secrets that not even her husband was aware of.

It was as well, she thought, that he left for Boston so soon; the island would, after all, be a safer place without him.

The letter from Boston had taken weeks to arrive. Dorcas looked at it with a sense of foreboding. Hugh Bettany had said that his mother wouldn't be able to keep away from the island, but it was not something on which she would have cared to wager any substantial amount of money.

She hardly dared to break the seal. The loss of a friend is an unhappy business in any circumstances; in those prevailing on the island, it would have been a disaster.

"If this is to say Marcia isn't coming back –"

"Open it," Zachariah urged her. "It probably says nothing of the kind, but there's only one way you'll find out for sure."

With growing astonishment Dorcas read the letter.

"Zack, you will never guess! She is to be married."

"So she *is* staying in Boston?"

"No, no – not at all. Already she and her husband are on their way here." Smiling now, Dorcas hastily turned to the next page. "Oh, such a surprise! He is, she says, an unusual man – well, he *must* be, mustn't he? A Renaissance man, she says –"

"Renaissance?" Zack frowned at that. "What part of the world does he come from, then?"

"She means he's a cultivated man, with many interests. He has a fortune of his own, she says, but is delighted to give over his large house in Boston to his son so that he may live out his life in the sun. He cannot wait to study the flora and fauna of Grand Cay and to have all the time he wishes to paint and to read and to fish –"

Zachariah, whose face had been furrowed in perplexity, brightened a little at the last word.

"Perhaps he may not be so bad," he said.

"Oh Zack, according to Marcia, he is not bad at all. His name is Thomas Redfern. Isn't this the most astonishing news? I can't wait to meet him."

Neither could the rest of Grand Cay.

Zachariah was not alone in harbouring doubts. Inevitably there were ribald remarks in all the saloons in Backsalina, for few of the customers could imagine the kind of man who would contemplate living happily with a woman of such strong and peculiar opinions.

"He'll wear the skirt, I reckon," Oliver Porrit said. "And she'll wear the trousers."

"Ay, that's a fact! He'll need to be a saint to put up with it."

"Word is that he's black," said Jamie McGregor, one of the small-time salt proprietors.

"Ay!" Another, thin-faced man was quick to agree. "Zack Hardiman told Gilligan, he's a Reenaysince man. Ain't that one o' them Frenchie islands in the Caribbean?"

"French he may be, but not even that harpy would bring a black man home."

Opinion, however, remained uneasy, and there was a general sigh of relief when Thomas Redfern proved to be a small, spry man with snow-white hair and a neat, pointed beard, and bright blue eyes that sparkled with merriment and interest. He was slightly shorter than his wife, and for a while the sight of them walking together was the cause of amusement to the general populace, for Thomas – who from the beginning affected a wide, flat sombrero – always seemed to be a pace or two behind his forceful wife. He was for ever stopping to examine a curious fragment of stone picked up from the road, or a beetle under a leaf, while Marcia proceeded swiftly about her business, which meant that more often than not he seemed to be scurrying along to catch her up.

As the years passed, however, and their contentment was plain to everyone, they ceased to be objects of interest, and people forgot that there had been a time when Marcia had lived alone at Treasure Bluff. Thomas Redfern was accepted.

"I cannot get over my good fortune," Marcia said to Dorcas. "Seldom have I found any human being – still less a man! – whose thoughts chime so perfectly with mine. Which isn't to say that we don't argue! Still, on all the important issues we are at one."

"Doesn't he miss Boston?"

"Not at all. He says he is more than content to live here, in peace and tranquillity."

"Peace and tranquillity? You with all your crusading zeal?" Dorcas laughed, teasing her. "There's precious little peace wherever you are to be found. Unless marriage has changed you, of course."

"Mellowed me, perhaps," Marcia admitted.

Maybe the years mellow all of us, Dorcas thought. For good or ill, the island was her world now, and Hugh Bettany had not been so wide of the mark when he described her as serene and happy. That terrible time in Bermuda had been put behind her completely. All life, she told herself firmly, was a matter of compromise, and she had much to be thankful for. If sometimes she was irked by the narrow confines of the island, she could console herself by thinking that she had a husband who adored her and who had a secure livelihood, thanks largely to the Cahill contract. And though she might dream of a more glamorous life somewhere far from this flat little island, there was no gainsaying that here she had her place. Here she was known and respected (by most, if not by all). Here she belonged.

Undoubtedly the addition of Thomas Redfern to the small community had made it a far more pleasurable circle to belong to.

His influence was indefinable. She could not put a finger on the time she realised that, thanks to him, everything had changed. She merely became aware, quite gradually, over the years, that he gave their narrow existence an added dimension, for Zachariah and Storm just as much as for her. To Zachariah, a little uneasy in his presence at first, he became a trusted friend; to Storm, a source of knowledge, a companion, a sounding board, someone quite unique in his life.

Treasure Bluff, always a refuge, became a place which on Grand Cay had no equal; a place where conversation was not confined to salt or the style of Mrs. Grimshaw's new bonnet, or even to the wider issues of slavery and emancipation which had seemed so revolutionary when Dorcas had first met Marcia.

Politics to Dorcas had meant the politics of Bermuda or, at its widest, the actions of Britain towards her colonies. Now for the first time she became aware of a vast world where ideas were changing — where craftsmen were banding together into trades unions, where the paddle steamer was being introduced into waterways where only sailing craft had been seen before; a world where new machinery was forcing traditional workers into unemployment or the mastering of new skills; a world where unrest was growing at governments dominated entirely by the landowning classes.

Books and papers flooded into Treasure Bluff.

"I think Mr. Redfern knows *everything*!" Storm said, full of admiration.

"I rather think he would be the last one to claim that," Dorcas replied. "He's interested in everything, that's where his strength lies. If he knew everything, Storm, why would he spend the better part of yesterday lying on his belly with you, watching an iguana? He didn't know, but he was determined to find out, that's the difference between him and most others."

"Do you know, Mama," Storm said on another occasion. "Mr. Redfern is quite sure that Christopher Columbus made his first landfall here on Grand Cay, and not on Watling Island at all."

"Now, how would he make that out?" Dorcas, hemming a sheet, looked up with a fleeting smile.

"There are lots of reasons. First, it says in Columbus's log that the island he discovered had an inland body of water, just as we have. And he says that he circumnavigated the island in the forenoon, and he could never have done that if he had been at Watling Island, for it's too big. And then it says that Columbus saw a whole lot of other islands from where he had anchored, and you know very well that from Hawkes Nest, that's just what he would have seen."

"It's an interesting theory."

"And what's more," Storm continued triumphantly, "Mr. Redfern found a letter in a bottle on the East Beach, and it came from Portugal which proves that the currents brought it all the way to Grand Cay, just as they brought the *Santa Maria*."

"I'm beginning to agree with you that he hardly needs to go to school," Dorcas said to Zachariah. "Thomas is an education in himself."

But she was not speaking seriously. The break would have to come, and she knew it, but somehow the thought of sending him to Bermuda caused tremors of disquiet – irrational though she recognised them to be.

Kit, by all accounts, was still in Havana and surely unlikely to pose any threat to the boy or to her. Months would pass without her giving him a thought; then the merest expression or gesture of Storm's would force her to recognise that Kit was his father, and she would remember the manner of their parting and his threat that he would never forgive her repudiation of him, and would make her regret it.

It had been said in the heat of the moment, she told herself; but as a kind of insurance policy she suggested that perhaps Storm might prefer to go to school in Jamaica, or even America. Both Storm and Zachariah were astonished and refuted such a suggestion absolutely.

"I want to see Peter Dickenson again," Storm said. "We arranged that I would."

"Surely you will be glad to have Fanny keeping an eye on him?" Zachariah asked. "Far better to let him go to a familiar place, sweetheart."

"I'll write to Fanny," Dorcas said resignedly.

In reply, Fanny wrote that they would, naturally, be delighted to have Storm in Bermuda and would greatly enjoy seeing him at Cedarcroft for weekends.

His cousins will be overjoyed [she wrote]. And Emma, too – on which head I am so pleased to report that she continues to give invaluable help. Little Nicholas is particularly devoted to her, and she to him, though of course her main function is to give the girls their lessons.

We see to it that she enjoys a pleasurable social life. There is a young surveyor, newly arrived from London to report upon the provision of roads, who has been particularly attentive. I cannot say with any truth that she appears much interested in him, but it is early days yet and he seems an agreeable fellow. Meantime she was squired to a ball last week by young Cousin Josiah (now quite the dandy) and looked charming in pink figured silk, newly made for her by Mademoiselle Lafitte. I feel sure I can say that she is

growing up to be both amiable and attractive and that all
the troubles you have endured are at an end . . .

Dorcas missed Storm sorely after he left for Bermuda and
counted the weeks until he would be home again, but she was
far from discontented.

"How things have changed since I first came here," she
remarked to Marcia one day as together they walked home
from the room they had established as a clinic. "Having a
proper church provides a focal point, don't you agree?"

"I guess so." Marcia sounded a little half-hearted in her
agreement. "But why only a *gallery* to hold the negroes? I
thought all were equal in the sight of God!"

"Well, the Methodists would agree with you there."

"They would, indeed. They make the black inhabitants
their first priority. For that I honour them, but I could wish for
less hysteria in their worship – less hell fire and damnation."

"It brings drama into their lives," Dorcas said. "Bathsheba
loves it all."

"I suppose we all need a little drama. I tell myself so every
time I hear the latest piece of embroidered gossip said to
originate with Mrs. Grimshaw. Apparently I deny Thomas a
proper diet, forcing him to live entirely on vegetables for some
strange purpose of my own – scientific experiment is, I believe,
supposed to be my motive. If only Mrs. Grimshaw knew how
fervently Thomas tries to convert me to his long-held views
on the avoidance of meat."

"Oh, take no notice of the wretched woman," Dorcas
advised, laughing. "She'll find fault with heaven, if she ever
gets there."

In her opinion, Treasure Bluff, with its long, low house set
on a small knoll that caught every breeze, its surrounding
palm trees and the wide expanse of ocean, provided the ideal
escape from the claustrophobic little community that had
grown up around the harbour. Marcia and Thomas had
created there a very special atmosphere of their own and
Dorcas loved nothing better than to enjoy the ideas and
conversation that took wing in their company.

Tamarind Villa became a more urban off-shoot of this
ambience, the kind of house where unexpected visitors knew
they would find a welcome and a place at the table. A visiting
sea-captain would know, as he dropped anchor, that the
Hardimans would greet him as if he were the one person they

longed to see, while to those who lived nearer at hand, an evening stroll was as likely as not to include a few minutes spent on the Hardimans' porch.

"There's something not quite nice about it," Mrs. Grimshaw said to her cronies. "It's not as if the house is always tidy — and does Mrs. Hardiman care? No, she does not! Horace and I called there on Sunday evening; it was not *my* wish, I assure you, but Horace had to see Mr. Hardiman on some matter of business and I went along for the exercise. There were no less than *three* strangers there, off schooners the lot of them, and what do you imagine they had been doing on the Lord's day? Reading the papers, that's what! Oh, she made the excuse that the seamen had been starved for news and that the papers had just been passed on to them from Treasure Bluff, but there they were strewn all about the place and I thought it showed a slovenliness that could only be condemned. I'd never tolerate it in my house, I can tell you. And she was very free with them, I thought. Well, you know Mrs. Hardiman — always ready to talk and laugh with any man! *I* was brought up to think that a woman should behave modestly and with discretion, particularly on the Lord's day."

Dorcas only laughed when such criticisms filtered back to her, as inevitably they did. She was happier in these years than she could ever have imagined; certainly, she told herself, she was happier than she deserved, and was thankful that Zachariah seemed equally contented. Her infidelity became only an intermittent, if troublesome memory.

Inevitably, perhaps, she thought of confession. There were times when she was so close to Zachariah — times when they sailed together to some uninhabited island or walked at dusk on the beach with only the stiff-legged little shore birds and the scuttling crabs for company, when the words were so ready on her tongue that she felt she had only to part her lips for them to speak themselves. But always she held back. Confession, she knew, might bring ease to her own conscience but would only cause heartache for Zachariah. Would it not be sheer self-indulgence to burden him with the secrets of a past that was over and done with? Better to concentrate on atoning in the present; better to ensure that from this moment on she would seek only his happiness.

Into this serene existence came a letter from Fanny, disturbing their tranquillity like a stone flung into a pond.

I regret that, though I have not mentioned it before this for fear of worrying you, things here have not been satisfactory for the past six months. I am sure that it is partially Phillipa's fault, for she can at times be difficult; an adolescent girl is not the easiest person to deal with. However, matters have deteriorated to such a pitch that the continued presence of Emma is playing on all our nerves and Silas is adamant that we can no longer keep her here.

In many ways I feel sorry for her. She has a curious manner which seems to deter any young man from pursuing an acquaintance with her, much though she herself desires friendship. The young surveyor whom I believe I mentioned to you some time ago, has recently become engaged to Miss Granger, an event which seems to have brought home to Emma that such a happy outcome is, for her, as far-distant as ever. In vain have I tried to convince her that at four and twenty years of age she has by no means lost her chance of marriage. Still she seems to have retreated into herself and has become bitter and withdrawn, constantly at odds with Phillipa and as possessive with little Nicholas as ever she was with Storm when he was young.

So great is my love and high my regard both for you and for Zachariah that it is only with the greatest difficulty I can bring myself to write this letter, and perhaps would not have done so were it not for the fact that Silas has other problems which are causing quite sufficient trouble without the additional burden of domestic discord. Kit Mallory is to quit the partnership which has been so fruitful all these years! He has met and married none other than the daughter of Mr. Cyrus Webberley, the owner of the Gold Star Shipping Line and a most wealthy gentleman to boot. Mr. Webberley, it seems, sailed to Havana with his daughter and met Kit at an Embassy ball, whereupon both members of the family appear to have succumbed to the Mallory charm!

For the moment the happy pair are to remain in Cuba looking after the considerable interests of the Gold Star Line, but it seems certain that eventually Kit will go to London. Silas is very upset . . .

And I am delighted, Dorcas thought joyfully, this second piece of news taking momentary precedence over the previous item. She need worry no more about Kit and his intentions towards

Storm. He had married an heiress (making his mother's predic-tion come true at last) and would no doubt shortly set about founding a family of his own. Storm must soon be forgotten.

Zachariah, however, was little concerned about this part of the letter. The part about Emma he read through with a beetling of his brows and a twisting of his mouth, and he sighed as he laid the paper down, and shook his head despondently.

"What ails that girl, Dorcas? She seems to sow discord wherever she goes. Her mother had a strange, dark streak, it's true, but never like this. She was never at odds with the world, as Emma seems to be."

"She seems," Dorcas said, "to be one of those individuals about whom it can be truly said, she is her own worst enemy. Still, in all fairness Zack, we have not heard her side of it."

"Fanny couldn't be other than kind. Why, they've treated her as their own daughter – entertained her friends, taken her about with them, bought her fine clothes –"

"I know; but Fanny admits that Phillipa is difficult, and now that Silas is worried about Kit's defection, it could be that his temper is unpredictable." Dorcas sighed. "If only she could meet the right man – have babies of her own that she can love and care for."

"We'll have to see what we can do for her here," said Zachariah.

"My brief," Dorcas said to Marcia, "is to find her a husband."

"Perhaps she will find herself one."

"Well, I hope so. Still, I can give her some help along the way – and so must you, Marcia, I beg you! We shall embark on a campaign of parties and balls in our search for an eligible male. No stone must be left unturned or avenue unexplored. Think, now; what bachelors do we have on the island?"

"Gilligan? Willis Trotman?"

"Oh, really!"

"Well, Mr. Grimshaw has a new clerk."

"No more than seventeen years of age, I swear. Captain Bell from the *Sea Goose* brought his First Officer to the house last night, and I thought him most agreeable – but what are the use of First Officers? They're here today and gone tomorrow." She pulled a horrified face. "Goodness me, Marcia, I'm beginning to sound like my own grandmother!"

"At least you sound reasonably cheerful at the prospect of having your stepdaughter home."

"Needs must." Nothing seemed to worry her, now that the looming shadow of Kit had been removed. "I'm determined that somehow we shall live together in a civilised manner, no matter what our past difficulties have been. I'm having her old room repainted and some new curtains made, and Zachariah has ordered a larger wardrobe to be made for her."

Even after these improvements, the room still looked a little bare, Dorcas thought. She moved in a small secretaire and an upholstered chair that had been downstairs, and made another journey to the new shop opened to stock linen and clothing, and managed to find a lace bedcover to replace the worn and threadbare quilt that had been in use before.

"There!" She looked with pleasure at the complete picture. "That looks very nice, don't you think, Sheba?"

"Maybe Miz Emma like it, maybe she don't." Bathsheba had been singularly lacking in enthusiasm when she had been told about the impending arrival of the daughter of the house. "You don't never know what Miz Emma's goin' to like, and dat's for true."

"I want her to feel welcome. I want to get off on the right foot."

Bathsheba continued to look sceptical.

"Sometimes dere ain't no right foot where Miz Emma is," she said. "Sometimes every foot is de left foot."

"We must give her a chance, Sheba. She may have changed. She's an adult now, not a child; and Fanny was so pleased with her at first . . ."

No one knew exactly when she would be arriving. She was expected on the next packet, but there had been rough seas around Bermuda and she could have been delayed. As the days went by without any sign of her, Dorcas found herself unable to settle to any of the activities that normally occupied her happily, and she returned again and again to Emma's room as if to satisfy herself beyond all possible doubt that she had done all she could to make the girl comfortable.

It was, she realised, a feeling of guilt that made her do it. That awful scene in Kit's office! Could either of them ever forget it? How much better it would have been if she had never gone there to remonstrate with him! But she'd acted for the best, from the best of motives. Surely now that she was older, Emma would understand?

When finally she came, Dorcas recognised with a sinking of the heart that it would take more than a new cupboard, fresh paint and a pretty bed cover to effect much change in her. She was neat and tidy in spite of an exhausting voyage, and greeted her father and Dorcas coolly, dismissing her unexpected departure from Cedarcroft with indifference, as if the whole matter had been no more than a foolish whim on Fanny's part.

"It wasn't *my* fault, I assure you," she said off-handedly when Zachariah broached the subject. "I do not consider myself the least bit to blame. If both Phillipa and Aunt Fanny take it into their heads to be jealous of me, quite without cause, then that is their concern and their misfortune."

"But they've shown you nothing but kindness," Zachariah began, before subsiding into silence as Dorcas shot him a warning glance.

"Tell me, have you seen Storm recently?" she asked Emma, determined that these first few moments should pass off peaceably. "The wretched boy writes so seldom, and I long for news of him."

They were at this moment riding down the bumpy strip of road leading beside the sea towards Tamarind Villa, with Emma glancing about her at all the development that had taken place since she was last on the island but not by a flicker of an eyelash making any comment on it. Her lips curved into a small, tight smile at Dorcas's question.

"Storm? Oh, he's well enough. He'll always be well enough!"

"Does he visit Cedarcroft often?"

"Not so much recently. They are very dull! Nobody visits much just now, with Uncle Silas in such an ill-humour. Aunt Fanny thinks him overdone, you know, and greatly blames Mr. Mallory for leaving him in the lurch."

Emma looked at Dorcas as she mentioned Kit's name, her eyes hard and challenging, and Dorcas knew with a sinking of the heart that Emma had forgotten nothing and forgiven nothing. Kit stood between them still.

Later, when she went with Emma to her room, she attempted to exorcise the past.

"For all our sakes, Emma, let us forget all that happened and be friends," she said.

Emma, who had been surveying the changed room in silence, looked at her with raised eyebrows.

"You truly believe that to be possible?" she asked.

"Why not? We're both adults now. You're old enough to understand why I was concerned for you when you were young and vulnerable."

Emma sat down in front of her mirror and began to take down her hair. Heavy and black, it fell on to her shoulders. She did not speak, and Dorcas looked at her, exasperated by her lack of response.

"In any case," she continued after a moment's silence, "we have to live together and might as well do it amicably. Tell me –" She deliberately lightened her tone. "Do you like your new furnishings? I hoped they would show how much we welcomed your homecoming."

"How very kind." Emma remained dryly unimpressed. "They are very pretty – if, perhaps, more suited to a dewy-eyed young girl than an old maid such as I."

"Emma, what nonsense! You're no old maid."

"No?" Emma did not look at Dorcas but went on brushing her hair, her lips still curved in their bitter little smile. "All the girls I went to school with are married. Jane Willoughby married a lawyer last year and went to live in America. I, it seems, am doomed to remain single."

"I never heard such rubbish!" Dorcas sat down on a small chair, angling it so that she could see Emma. Leaning forward, she spoke eagerly. "With the winter coming on, there are any number of parties and dances being planned. You'll have the time of your life. We're bidden to the Cliffords on Salt Cay for the whole weekend, and Marcia and Thomas are having a ball next month. They've asked some American settlers from the Caicos, so a whole new circle of acquaintances might be opened up. I thought that we ourselves could have a ball soon after, then if there happened to be any of them you liked particularly we could quite naturally offer them an invitation –"

"American settlers from the Caicos? Failed cotton planters?" Emma gave a short laugh. "None of them has a penny to bless themselves with. Jane has a beautiful house in Atlanta with two carriages and any number of slaves, and as many dresses as she chooses."

"Obviously she has been very fortunate." It was with an effort that Dorcas kept her temper, but her voice showed no sign of it. "The Caicos settlers have fallen on bad times, it's true, but they are gentlefolk from good families."

Emma laid down her brush.

"And an old maid cannot ask for the moon," she said flatly. "I must say, Dorcas – oh!" She stopped short and looked at her stepmother with raised eyebrows. "You don't mind if I call you Dorcas? Even Father seems to have realised the foolishness of trying to make me call you 'Mother', and to continue with 'Miss Dorcas' –"

Dorcas made a dismissive gesture.

"Pray, call me what you wish. Dorcas will do very well."

"I must say, Dorcas," Emma continued, "that you show a very agreeable determination to find me a husband, though whether it is for my benefit or for yours I am not sure."

Dorcas sighed as she looked at Emma, and sat back in her chair as if conscious of defeat.

"Your interests have always come first with me, Emma," she said wearily. "I know you find it difficult to believe, but I assure you it is so. I have always tried to do what is best."

"Yes." Emma turned back to the mirror. "Yes, I remember. Sometimes it meant being cruel to be kind, did it not?" Still her face wore that little half-smile, though the words were bitter. "Sometimes your concern made it necessary to inflict pain. I cannot forget, Dorcas, nor ever will, the way you contrived the humiliation of a girl whose only crime was to fall in love."

Dorcas recoiled at the venom in Emma's voice.

"*Contrived*? Was it I who willed your presence in that office?" She leaned forward again. "Don't you realise I *hated* seeing you hurt? If you want to blame anyone apart from yourself, blame Kit Mallory who was too blind to see what he was doing to you. Believe me, that occasion gave me no pleasure."

"Of course not." Emma's voice plainly mirrored her disbelief. "I'm sure it must have pained you deeply."

For a moment Dorcas said nothing. She raised her hands helplessly, palms upwards, then let them fall to her lap before she got to her feet.

"Well, Emma," she said. "The choice is yours. We may live together amicably, or we need not. For my part, I should like an untroubled existence and I ask you to provide it, for your father's sake, if not for mine. One thing I have learned over the years," she went on, turning by the door. "You only damage yourself by clinging to past bitterness. I ask you most earnestly to cast all that away and make a new beginning."

Emma said nothing as Dorcas left the room. For a moment she sat as if turned to stone, her eyes downcast, her lips fixed in their mirthless smile. Then she looked up to study her reflection, and the smile faded.

It was a round, pale face that looked back at her; small, regular features, a pinched little mouth. Not ugly, she told herself; not ugly at all – just not pretty, not noticeable. Her brows were too thick, her eyes too small. Even her hair, once such a source of pride, seemed to have lost much of its life and lustre. It hung down on each side of her face, dull and heavy.

For a moment she contemplated herself, chewing at her lip, her brows drawn together; then, as if in sudden pain, she closed her eyes and the tears spilled over. She picked up the brush in a hurried, fumbling gesture and swept it forcefully through her hair, again and again and again, as the tears ran unchecked down her cheeks.

Thirteen

Willis Trotman had been a witness to Emma's arrival and had stood idly watching, sucking thoughtfully on a tooth as Dorcas and Zachariah greeted her and took her back to Tamarind Villa. It was not that the girl interested him sexually. His taste did not run to thin, pale, flat-chested females with faces that would turn the milk sour. Still he watched with an expressionless curiosity, as if the sight of the Hardiman family was something he wished to store away in the recesses of his mind.

Later he went back to the wharf, to watch as an army of slaves loaded salt aboard the brig which had brought Emma Hardiman back to the island. He stood quite still, arms folded across his chest, thick lips twisted with envy and resentment. This was Hardiman salt that was being taken out by the lighter; Hardiman salt, bound for Cahills in Nova Scotia, shipped by a vessel belonging to Tranton and Mallory.

Family connections and privilege! Jealousy was a sour taste on his tongue. It was November now, with winter squalls marking the end of a good season. There would be no more raking this year and few ships calling to collect the remaining two hundred thousand bushels waiting for shipment, white pyramid beyond white pyramid. He had a good ninety-six thousand bushels of his own waiting there, but whether they could be got away before the winter rains ruined them was a moot point.

It was different for Zachariah Hardiman. Feather-bedded by the Cahill contract, given preferential treatment by Trantons, he prospered where others failed. Some said Hardiman's salt was cleaner than most, his workforce more willing, but Trotman spat into the dust at his feet to show his opinion of that theory. No, it was privilege and privilege alone that Hardiman had to thank for his good fortune.

"The luck o' the de'il," a voice said in his ear. Trotman glanced sideways and saw that he had been joined by Jamie McGregor, but he uttered no word of greeting. If anything, his expression of distaste deepened. McGregor was an unimpressive-looking man, small and dusty, a fraying straw hat pulled down over a low and sun-peeled brow. To Trotman he seemed to personify the unimportant, insignificant type of drifter who would be here today and gone tomorrow, doomed for ever to be poor and unsuccessful and a failure in every venture to which he put his inefficient hand.

"Will ye look at that," McGregor went on, his Glaswegian accent tuned to register resentment. "The rest of us put together will be lucky if we ship the half of it."

Trotman's silence continued but his lips twisted a little more, as if to register his total repudiation of the implied alliance with McGregor and others of his ilk. Unaware of his contempt, the Scotsman lifted his nose, bent in some long-forgotten bar-room brawl, and sniffed the wind.

"They're getting that lot away just in time," he said. "We're in for rain, if you ask me. I've still got seven thousand bushels waiting."

"Seven thousand!" Trotman gave a short and scornful laugh. "Is that all?"

"It's a lot to me." McGregor's resentment was turned against the man at his side now. "What's amiss with you, Trotty? Too much grog last night, or did the harlots shut the door agin ye?"

"Hold your jaw!"

McGregor swallowed with difficulty at the sight of the face that Trotman turned upon him, licked his lips and attempted a smile. He lifted a placatory hand and sidled away.

"No offence, Trotty. No offence. Just m' wee joke."

Trotman hardly noticed his departure. The luck of the devil, he thought, McGregor's earlier words repeating themselves in his mind.

One day things would be different. One day this island would be his particular kingdom, he was determined on that. Let others find wider worlds to conquer; he would be content to reign here, a big fish in the smallest of pools.

Here he had authority. He owned as many shares in the pond as Hardiman now and almost as many as Grimshaw. Porrit and Everard and McGregor and Lester – he dismissed them contemptuously. They were fly-by-nights who had come when things had begun to pick up after the disastrous hurricane of 1815 and had managed to hang on by their fingernails ever since. The next natural disaster would be the finish of them. They had no significance except for their ability to vote him in or out of office.

That they continued to elect him was no measure of their friendship. It all boiled down to power, which was the only thing that interested him; power to control people and events. No, the voters of Grand Cay had no liking for him, and he asked for none. They believed him to be a hard man, but a man who would safeguard their long-term interests. A man who provided a necessary balance to Zack Hardiman's tendency to be too soft towards the slaves. Their future, they thought, was safe in Trotman's hands.

In this they were deluded. The only interests Trotman served were his own. He despised the small men who raked their limited shares, lived from hand to mouth and would never aspire to anything more; and he despised, too, those owners who had family connections and were able to ship their salt when the rest was left stockpiled on the ground beyond the wharf.

He was accused of being hard on his slaves. He knew it and he cared nothing for such accusations. It was all right for those others, those privileged ones. Everything he owned was solely because of his own efforts, his own native wit, his own thrift, allied to relentless ambition and constant vigilance. He was accused of being mean with his money, and he cared nothing for that, either.

One day he would own a fleet of ships – then his accusers would laugh the other side of their faces. His eyes focused again on the brig and the bile rose in his stomach. Though he could think of no one on the island he liked particularly, he reserved a special kind of bitterness and loathing for Zachariah Hardiman and for that high and mighty whore of a wife of his who would laugh and flirt with any man on the island – even Gilligan, for God's sake – but had always treated him as if he were some kind of leper, lower than the lowest vermin.

He had this recurring fantasy of Dorcas Hardiman, kneeling to him, her bodice torn and slipped from her shoulder, her hair wild, imploring him to take her, do with her what he willed. He narrowed his eyes as he thought of it now, and unconsciously he licked his fleshy lips.

Why she thought so highly of herself, God alone knew. She had married a common seaman, when all was said and done – and there was more to that marriage, he would swear, than met the eye! The Foleys were, after all, an old and proud

Bermudian family. One day he would get to the bottom of it.

Privilege! It was enough to make an ambitious man without connections choke on his own bitterness. Before God, he swore to himself as he turned from the sight of the brig and walked back towards the road and the salt that waited, probably in vain, for vessels to take it away – before God, he'd see to it that he never had another year like this.

Ted Palmer who was on his way down to the wharf tipped his hat to Trotman in passing and wished him good evening, but received no reply.

He grimaced and lifted his eyebrows as he went on his way. God help Trotman's enemies, he thought. His expression alone was sufficient to kill.

Both Dorcas and Emma were busy in their separate rooms. Emma had been on the island a month now but during that time Dorcas had heard no word from Fanny and the letter she was writing was somewhat anxious in tone.

My fervent prayer is that you remain in good health [she wrote] and that the children and Silas are likewise blessed. It is indeed easy to imagine any amount of misfortunes without the benefit of communication – as I have said to dear Storm more than once, though he takes little heed of it!

I long to hear from you that the unfortunate affair with Emma has raised no barrier between us. I am persuaded that this cannot be so, my dearest sister, for the love between us is something that surely will survive any misfortune, and though I am aware that your patience must have been sorely tried you must know that none could regret the unhappy turn of events more than Zachariah and myself.

I am thankful to report that Emma appears to be enjoying the social events which have marked our life in a quite unprecedented way since her return. At least, I think and hope she is enjoying them, though she waxes enthusiastic about very little and shows a marked want of *animation* which is, I am persuaded, the greatest obstacle to her receiving the admiration that would be of such great benefit to her. She has had several new dresses made up for her by a Spanish dressmaker recently come from Puerto Plata, all most becoming in my opinion, and at Marcia's party she looked as well as I have ever seen her.

It was a grand ball at Treasure Bluff and everyone of any consequence was there, including the Carwardines and Mortimers from Providenciales – families of American origin who seldom visit Grand Cay; indeed it was the first occasion on which I have met Mrs. Carwardine who proved to be a lady of the greatest refinement.

Simon Carwardine seemed quite taken with Emma. He is a young man of four or five and twenty; not handsome, perhaps, but not ill-looking either and with his mother's pleasant manner. I have taken the step of asking the Carwardines to the party which we are to hold at Christmas and they seemed pleased to accept, which leads me to think they would not look unfavourably upon a match between the two young people.

It is, of course, far too early to speculate and nothing may come of it. However, I beg you to add your prayers to mine that Emma will find someone (if not young Mr. Carwardine) with whom she may achieve lasting happiness. I am persuaded that she could yet prove to be as loving and agreeable as anyone else were she to be held in high regard by that person she most loves. It is Marcia's belief that it is a feeling of deep inadequacy that renders her difficult to live with, and now that she has drawn this to my attention I can see that she is probably right.

Seated at the secretaire that Dorcas had placed in her room, Emma took up her pen to write to her friend, once Jane Willoughby, now Mrs. Robert Leonard of Atlanta, Georgia, despite the fact that no less than three previous letters had received no reply.

It was the capricious nature of the mails that was to blame, of course. Jane would have written – of course she would! Emma would not believe – could not allow herself to believe – that their friendship had meant so little that it had been abandoned the moment Jane had found more absorbing interests. Why, had she not written the moment she returned from her honeymoon to describe her house and clothes and carriage? Of course she was still the same friend, and would always remain so. Firmly Emma squashed the small maggot of doubt that wriggled in the recesses of her mind.

Her eagerness to be rid of me would be laughable if it were not so contemptible [she wrote]. This Mr. Carwardine who is being thrust upon me is small of stature and has those pale lashes which I recall you found so laughable in that young sub-lieutenant who was so smitten with you and whose name I cannot now recall. That my father appears to acquiesce in her schemes is a great sadness to me and proof positive that she has succeeded in turning him against me, for how would he otherwise contemplate the possibility of my marrying a man of no fortune and of being banished to Providenciales? Even if I had not given my heart to another many years ago, the prospect is one that would fill me with despair.

I look at her sometimes and wonder if her conscience ever troubles her when she remembers the dreadful wrong she did in coming between me and my only true love when the passion between us was like a tender green shoot, about to unfold but then blighted by the winter of her cold scorn and dislike of me. Still I bear the scars and ever will. Even though he has married another, I remain convinced that I alone am the one woman who could make him truly happy,

My dearest Jane, you have ever been my good friend and I give thanks to heaven for your happiness. Wanting good fortune on my own account, it is a blessing to be able to rejoice in yours.

What the future of your friend will be, I cannot tell. A loveless marriage or a life of loneliness? Sometimes the years to come appear to stretch before me without light and without hope, a vale of tears through which I am doomed to wander without love or understanding. Perhaps there is some religious order that would accept me . . .

She broke off, pen poised, as she considered the not unattractive alternative of going into a decline. It was satisfying to think of her remorseful family gathered around her deathbed, and it was only with reluctance that she dismissed the idea, remembering that an essential requirement was her own absence from the scene.

She sighed and continued with her letter.

Now that Christmas is but three weeks distant, all the talk is of the dance we are to hold here, to which everyone on the island has been invited and many from other islands, too. Would that I could approach the event with the same frivolous enthusiasm as my stepmother! There is, I fear, little chance that I shall enjoy the occasion, though I am saving a new rose-pink figured silk for it and shall hope not to cut too poor a figure. Heaven send that it does not rain! My father says that it *never* rains when he gives a party . . .

"It's a bonny night," Zachariah said, looking up at the black velvet sky ablaze with stars. "Oh, a bonny night! Give us a bonny tune to match it, lads!" This last instruction was shouted through cupped hands in the direction of the da Costa brothers who were setting up their music stands and taking their instruments from velvet-lined cases.

"They'll be overworked before the night is out," Dorcas said, laughing at his eagerness.

It was as calm as summer outside. Beyond the circle of light they could see the edge of gentle waves creaming against the beach, and only the smallest breeze stirred the casuarina trees.

As was his habit on festive occasions, Zachariah had strung lanterns in their branches and the foliage of the hibiscus and oleander and frangipani, so carefully nurtured by Dorcas over the years, had taken on a new and dramatic appearance in the light of more lanterns set beneath them.

Zachariah, however, was gazing with admiration at his wife.

"You look as beautiful as ever, sweetheart," he said; but she was in no mood for compliments.

"I wonder if I have forgotten anything?" she mused. "I cannot think that I have, but one can never be certain."

"There's sufficient food?"

"Oh Zack, of course! And enough wine to sink a frigate."

"Then there's no cause to worry."

"I hope you're right."

Dorcas was conscious of a small, nagging feeling of unease, however, and identified it as stemming from Emma's behaviour at the meal they had eaten together earlier in the evening. Always quiet and withdrawn she had seemed even less responsive than usual, showing no interest whatsoever in the preparations for the party that were going on all around them.

"Did you think," she said now, "that Emma seemed a little – well, odd, at dinner?"

"Odd?" Zachariah considered the matter, pulling the kind of faces that indicated he was reflecting deeply. He shook his head. "No more odd than usual, sweetheart. She was quiet,

I'll admit, but I put it down to nervousness. It wouldn't surprise me if something came of it between her and young Carwardine –"

"Oh Zack, I beg you not to count your chickens." Anxiously Dorcas glanced up at the window of Emma's room where a lamp burned. "I do wish she would hurry. She should be here with us to greet the guests."

It would be just like her to stay in her room and sulk, she thought; but dutifully Emma came down in time to welcome Marcia and Thomas who brought with them the Mortimers and the Carwardines. She looked flushed and almost pretty in her new pink dress and seemed to have thrown off her dark mood of earlier in the evening. Dorcas allowed herself to hope a little. Simon Carwardine seemed attentive and Emma appeared to be putting herself out to make pleasant conversation.

Soon all the guests had arrived and the strains of music vied with the babel of conversation – conversation no less animated because its participants had met a dozen times during the past few days. Still there was much to say, compliments to be paid, the season's greetings to be conveyed. Dorcas and Zachariah moved among their guests with ease and enjoyment, knowing that long after the round of Christmas parties was over, this was one that would stay in the memories of those that were present.

The da Costa brothers retired exhausted soon after midnight, and it was then that Zachariah took over, the music becoming livelier and flagging spirits rallying. Sets were re-formed and the dancing continued until the small hours.

It was three thirty before the last coach drove away. Flushed and laughing, Dorcas leaned against Zachariah, hugging his arm.

"Wasn't it a lovely party?" she demanded. "Didn't you enjoy it, Zack? Oh, I don't think I've ever danced quite so much. Has Emma gone to bed? She looked so pretty tonight, didn't she? Somehow I'm so much more hopeful about young Mr. Carwardine, aren't you? Oh!" She yawned and stretched luxuriously. "Come to bed, Zack, or I shall fall asleep where I stand. Heaven alone knows how we shall wake up in the morning."

"It's all right for you young things," Zachariah said. "Think of me, poor old man that I am."

For all that, he was up and away to his office by the time

that Dorcas came downstairs next day. Of Emma there was no sign.

"Let her sleep," Dorcas said to Nola who enquired if she should take coffee upstairs. "She's had so many late nights recently."

For herself, she attended to the clearing up of the house, directing the slaves in their labours, and had just collapsed wearily upon the rocking chair on the porch when a bare-foot little boy arrived carrying a letter addressed to Emma.

She took the letter and sent the boy around to the kitchen for refreshment, for he'd had a long walk if he had come all the way from Treasure Bluff. The letter was, of course, from Simon Carwardine. She put it in her pocket, laughing at herself a little, for in spite of everything she was aware of a warm and sentimental glow at the thought of love-letters passing between the two young people. Heaven send that this was the begining of real happiness for Emma.

She looked at the clock and saw that it was eleven o'clock – not too early now for coffee, she thought; and she took the letter inside so that Nola could take it up on the tray.

In a matter of minutes Nola was downstairs, the tray still in her hands and a look of alarm and astonishment on her face.

"Miz Emma ain't there, ma'am," she said.

"Not there?" Dorcas looked at her uncomprehendingly.

"She ain't slept in her bed, ma'am. Don't look like she been there all night."

"You must surely be mistaken!" Dorcas went upstairs without delay, however, and stood on the threshold of Emma's room looking about her with total disbelief and bewilderment.

The room was unnaturally tidy. Anyone would think she had vacated it completely, Dorcas thought, and went to a small three-drawered commode that stood under the window. The moment she looked inside it she knew that wherever Emma had gone, she intended to be away for some time. Underwear was missing; shifts, stockings, drawers, night-gowns.

She went to the wardrobe. Some dresses still hung inside, but others had gone.

Simon Carwardine – an elopement; no, that made no sense, for why would he have written to her?

Dorcas went downstairs and looked at the letter, in two

minds as to whether she should open it or not. Where could the wretched girl have gone? She had no friends on the island. Had she returned to Bermuda or run off to see her friend Jane in Atlanta? It was possible, but hardly likely for to her knowledge no vessel of any size had left Grand Cay that morning.

And why such secrecy? Zachariah was an indulgent father and would have helped her to do whatever she wished. It would upset him, this departure without a word of explanation. Oh, *damn* the girl, Dorcas thought angrily. Why could she never act like a rational human being?

"Miz Dorcas?" Bathsheba had come into the room, alarmed, no doubt, by Nola's report of Emma's empty room. "Miz Dorcas? You all right?"

"Sheba, she's gone. There isn't any doubt. She's taken most of her clothes."

Bathsheba's face seemed to tighten with disapproval.

"Where she go, that bad girl?" she asked crossly.

"Goodness knows! Perhaps there's some explanation I haven't thought of. Sheba, send someone for the Master, will you please? Say that I need him urgently –"

But before Bathsheba had moved, Zachariah had stormed into the house, his face contorted with fury, a paper in his hands. He thrust it towards Dorcas.

"Read it," he said, and turned from her as if he could not trust himself to say more.

Dorcas looked at him anxiously, but did as he told her.

Dear Father, [the letter said]. By the time you read this I shall be far away with the man I love. I little thought that I should meet such a man on this island being wholly persuaded that having loved once I should never do so again, but I praise Heaven that I was wrong.

Dorcas looked up from the letter.

"Simon Carwardine?" she said in astonishment. "I can hardly believe he would –"

"Read it," Zachariah grated.

Secrecy has been essential since your enmity for him is so great that we both know you would do all in your power to prevent our marriage. Pursuit is useless for I cannot tell you in which direction we sail. Nassau? Jamaica? Havana?

Puerto Plata? I do not know and am too happy to care, just so long as a priest can be found to tie the knot which will bind us. In any case, you would be powerless to prevent the marriage, for I am of age and no longer a child to be dictated to, even though there are those who do not appear to realise the fact.

By the time we meet again I shall be Mrs. Willis Trotman. I am sorry for the shock that this will undoubtedly cause you but am persuaded that your wife will take but a little time to convince you that this is no tragedy since it has been all too clear to me from the time of my return that her only concern has been to find me a husband who will remove me from your roof. Tell her I regret to have thwarted her scheme regarding Mr. Carwardine, but compared to Mr. Trotman he is little more than a callow youth.

When Dorcas looked up again her expression was as horrified as Zachariah's own.

"How could she?" she whispered. "How *could* she? How could she be so wicked and misguided?"

"God alone knows." Distractedly Zachariah ran his hand through his thick, greying hair, shaking his head as if the blow Emma had dealt him had been a physical one. "Trotman, of all people! She loves him, she says!"

"Because I said once I had never met a man I held in such low esteem," Dorcas said bitterly. "Equally, I was misguided enough to say I liked young Mr. Carwardine. I should have known better! How she hates me still. Zack, what's to be done?"

"Done?" He looked at her dazedly. "There's nothing to be done. Even if I knew where to start looking, they've had a good six-hour start – perhaps more. We don't know when she left. She paid someone to deliver the letter to me after eleven o'clock. He knew nothing."

"But *Trotman*!" Still Dorcas could hardly take in the fact of this marriage. "Zack, there must be something –"

"Nay." Wearily he sat down and sat staring helplessly before him, hands dangling between his knees. "The girl is right in one particular. If marry him she will, she's of age and there's naught I can do about it. She's made her bed –"

"And must lie upon it," Dorcas finished for him sadly, wondering as she did so how many times and about how many people such a statement had been made.

She sat down beside Zachariah and put her arms around him, cradling him close, bitterly angry with the daughter that could have dealt him such a blow. No man deserved it less.

Trotman! Involuntarily she shuddered, seeing the fleshy lips and the hot, cruel little eyes. Angry as she was with Emma, there was beneath the anger a flicker of pity for her. Wicked and misguided she might have been, but the bed she had made would be a hard one, of that Dorcas had no doubt.

She remembered the previous letter that had arrived, and mentioned it to Zachariah. He took it and opened it; read it in silence and handed it to her.

My dear Miss Hardiman,

I venture to write for I must leave Grand Cay for Providenciales this day. Please bear this circumstance in mind and do not think me over bold. I cannot leave without seeing you. I have thought of nothing and no one but you since we danced last night. I cannot express my feelings in writing but would convince you of my undying love and my good intentions if we could but meet. I shall be on the beach to the south of the wharf at midday, and beg that you will meet me there.

Hoping that you will not disappoint me, I remain, my dear Miss Hardiman, ever your devoted,

Simon Carwardine.

"Oh, the pity of it," Dorcas said, in a low voice.

Zachariah could not reply. With his head turned from her, face shielded by his hand, silently he wept.

Dorcas had never known him so low in spirits, or so implacable.

Emma and Willis Trotman were away from the island for two weeks, during which he refused to speak his daughter's name. After they returned, a brief wedding ceremony having taken place in Nassau, still he insisted that his home should be barred both to Emma and to her husband. The man had proved his vile nature for all to see, he said in justification to Dorcas, and as for Emma – when had he behaved in a way that deserved such deceit? No, he could not receive them; *would* not receive them. That the decision was one that went against the grain was plain by his unhappiness and uncharacteristic silences. Dorcas suggested a holiday.

"Could we not go to Bermuda?" she asked, happy to contemplate the possibility now that Kit was in Havana and safely married. "It would do us good to leave the island."

"You're right." Zachariah seemed to brighten. "There are times when this place can seem very small."

The idea grew and developed in his mind. By the time he returned home that evening he had recovered something of his old bounce and vigour.

"Sweetheart, I've had an idea," he said, taking both her hands in his. "Why stop at Bermuda? We could go to America! I've long wanted to see Charleston; I sailed with a fellow once who talked of little else."

"America!" Dorcas looked at him with dawning delight. "Zack, you have neither the time nor the money."

"Nonsense. I can take a month at this time of the year, and as for money – well, last year was a good one. And let us be honest." He sobered for a moment. "Had Emma married in a more conventional manner it would have cost us a pretty penny. It's an ill wind, sweetheart. Let us at least reap a little benefit from the unhappy affair."

"Oh Zack!" Dorcas's eyes were sparkling now. "Is it really possible? You cannot imagine how I have longed to go."

"It *is* possible, and we *will* do it! Oh, such a time we'll have, my lass. I feel ten years younger at the very thought."

Unable to sit still he sprang up and paced the room, full of plans and dreams.

"I wonder when there will be a suitable vessel? We'll take ship as soon as we can and sail up the coast – Charleston, Baltimore, Philadelphia, New York. Then home via Bermuda to see Storm – maybe bring him home with us for a few weeks. That would cheer him, wouldn't it?"

"You know it would! But Zack –" The light had gone a little from her face, and he looked at her questioningly. "Zack, when we come back, the situation with Emma will be just the same. You don't think, perhaps, that a small attempt at conciliation might ease our return? God knows I have no wish to have Trotman behaving as a member of the family, but you're hurting yourself as much as Emma by cutting her off in this way. I've seen how it troubles you."

"Ay." He spoke heavily and once more sat down beside her. "Ay, you're right. Perhaps it's time for the olive branch."

*   *   *

It was known simply as the Trotman House. There were no trees close by to soften its outline, no flowers outside, no attempt made to beautify it.

Other houses were adorned with dormer windows and balconies, white picket fences, neat paths edged with conch shells. The Trotman House had dormer windows high under its roof, but they were always shuttered like eyes that were blind, and no path led from the track over the sandy, cactus-strewn waste that surrounded it.

It was not a small house. Willis Trotman had built it when he managed to acquire most of the shares in the salt ponds close by South Creek, and he had been determined to make of it something that others would admire and envy, something suited to his new status. The basics were there; the rooms were spacious and lofty, but having constructed them he had seemed at a loss to know what to do with them. He had picked up some pieces of furniture when the McGoverns left the island and had bought a bed from a settler in the Caicos who was returning to South Carolina, but all of his purchases had seen their best days long before he acquired them and had in recent years deteriorated still further in the humid, salty air, lacking any kind of care or maintenance.

"The place lacks a woman's touch," he had said to Emma, that first time he had seen her wandering around the creek and had invited her on to the porch for a cooling drink.

He had never considered her as a woman. She was too small, too childishly built. He liked his women tall and long-limbed, with deep bosoms and some kind of spark to them, not quiet and passive. But seeing her on his porch, noticing that after all her waist had quite a curve to it, bringing a blush to those pale cheeks with a lightly paid compliment, the sneer behind it carefully hidden, made him think that after all there might be something to be gained by pursuing her. He had weighed up the possibilities carefully, and the more he thought about it, the more promising the situation seemed.

But by God, he hadn't needed to pursue her, not after that first time.

It had been the back end of the year, the slack period when there was little to be done at the ponds, the time he was accustomed to devote to poring over his account books. He had no office in town and worked at home. Scarcely a day had passed without a sight of that small, girlish figure apparently absorbed in sketching the flora and fauna of the island.

226

How, secretly, he had laughed at the pretence! She couldn't sketch worth a damn. It was a man she wanted, like every other whore; the feeling of strong arms around her and a man's body pressed to hers.

"Young men are so callow!" she had said. He mimicked her cruelly after she had gone, laughing to himself at his version of her precise, childish voice. "I have always been attracted to older men, Mr. Trotman."

She was attracted, all right. There was, he thought, never a girl who came to hand so readily. However, he cautioned himself to wait. He could have had her at any moment – well, perhaps not that first time, but maybe the second and certainly the third. It was not sensitivity or diffidence or concern for her reputation that held him back, but rather the need to plot his future carefully.

He was thirty-seven and he needed a woman; more precisely, he needed a wife who would give him an heir. The idea was one he had dallied with recently, but it had come to nothing since there was, until Emma's appearance, no suitable single woman on the island. He had all but made up his mind to look for one the next time he went to Jamaica.

Now here was Hardiman's daughter throwing herself at him! If he couldn't make some kind of capital out of that, then he wasn't the man he took himself for.

There had to be a show of love, of course. Innocents like Emma Hardiman demanded it, even though it was crystal clear to him that beneath her professed attraction to him was a rock-hard determination to spite her stepmother who, it appeared, had other plans for her.

Well, that was good enough motivation, too. In fact it created a warm glow inside him to think what it would do to Zachariah and Dorcas Hardiman if he should carry Emma off from under their noses.

The slaves heard their master laughing inside the bleak, barely furnished house that week before Christmas, and they looked at each other in astonishment.

There had never been much laughter in the Trotman House.

"You want I bring broth, Miz Trotman?"

The slight, black figure hovered beside the bed like a mosquito, Emma thought. Insubstantial but persistent. Weakly she shook her head.

"Just leave me, Becky," she said.

"You don't eat, you grow weak. Dere's a potful of chowder on de fire."

"Leave me, I said. Are you deaf! All I want to do is rest."

Emma opened her eyes a fraction, just sufficient to see the girl pick up a dressing-gown from where it had fallen by the foot of the bed and hang it upon a wooden peg behind the door. She turned and took some stockings from a chair, smoothing and folding them.

"I said *go*!" Emma lifted her head from the pillow and glared balefully at the girl who hunched her shoulders defensively.

"Cookie done tol' me, straighten Miz Trotman's room, Cookie say."

"Well, *I* tell you to go! I just want to be left alone." By this time Emma's voice was little short of a wail of despair.

Oh, how fervently did she want to be left alone! It wasn't fair, she thought, as the door closed behind the slave girl. Dorcas had told her that love was natural and not to be feared. She would have said differently if she had been a proper mother. A proper mother would have warned her that love between a man and a woman was horrible and brutal, a violation that had to be suffered and endured over and over and over again.

She could never have imagined it! Willis had seemed kind before they were married; kind and patient and sympathetic to her plight, letting her talk for hours about her misfortunes and the way no one at home understood her. He had agreed that Dorcas could not be trusted. He was tall and strong and powerful and had sworn that he loved her and needed her and would protect her.

How swiftly that love had turned to contempt! It was not her fault — no, it was *not* her fault! Someone should have warned her, prepared her, made her understand that she was ruining her life.

No one had said, either, that being pregnant made one feel so ill. She'd heard people speak of morning sickness, of course, but had never realised that sometimes it lasted all day. She had a weaker stomach than most, that's what it was. More sensitive. Willis ought to realise it and make allowances, not force himself upon her night after night, thrusting his thick, muscular body into her as if he hated her and wanted nothing more than to spear her to death.

She only felt safe when he was out of the house. What was

she to do? Go home? What was the use? Even her father had turned his back upon her, and even if he relented and she went home, Willis would find her within the hour and bring her back. She belonged to him now. Besides, the thought of giving Dorcas the satisfaction of knowing what a mistake she had made was too humiliating to consider.

At least she was having a baby of her own. She cheered considerably at the thought. She had always loved babies. You knew where you were with babies. You could hold them in your arms and cuddle them, and they were soft and warm and loved you uncritically.

She heard a shout from downstairs and stiffened in horror. What was Willis doing home at this time of day? He was going down to Hawkes Nest, he had said, and wouldn't be back until four at the earliest, and here it was no more than eleven thirty.

She knew he would be angry to find her still in bed, and she was right. He stormed into the bedroom and called her a lazy slut and asked if she thought she was the first woman in the world to have a baby.

"Still," he said, his teeth bared in a grin, his hands going to the buckle on his belt. "Since I find you so conveniently in bed –"

"No, Willis, please! Not now!" She cowered away from him, and he laughed, taking her dressing-gown from its peg and throwing it towards her. It had been a feint, no more; a joke of the unpleasant kind he delighted in.

"Get up," he said. "Try to make yourself look respectable, for once, and I'll give you some news."

"What is it?" she asked as she tied the sash around her waist and smoothed her hair. She would not have dreamed of disobeying him.

"Make a guess!"

"I can't, Willis. Tell me! Stop being such a tease." It must surely be good news, she thought, for he was in unusually high spirits.

"It's your father." He sat on the bed, lounging back on his elbows, smiling at her. "He's capitulated."

"Capitulated?" She stared at him as if the word was new to her.

"Given in," Willis said impatiently. "Decided to acknowledge us. Doesn't that please you? I told him he was to become a grandfather and he told me that he and the Divine Dorcas

229

are off on some jaunt to America. We are to visit them before they leave. I knew he would climb down in time. Well —" as Emma still stood, dumbly staring — "aren't you pleased?"

Slowly Emma sank down on the bed beside him, her eyes fixed upon him.

"I don't know," she said. "It will be difficult."

"Rubbish! Of course you're pleased. I certainly am." In the highest of humours he reached for her, and only laughed when she slid away and made some pretence of looking for something in her wardrobe. "It's only right that we should be one happy family, for families stick together, isn't that so? When your father sees how contented we are together —"

"Contented?" Emma abandoned her search in the wardrobe and turned to look at him in astonishment.

"I wish you'd stop repeating every word I say! Contented I said, and contented I meant."

He pushed himself off the bed and came towards her, reaching out a hand to pull her close.

"When we visit them, Emma my sweet," he said, his voice soft and deceptively gentle, "there will be no complaints, no whining, no cries of how hardly you are used, is that understood?"

In silence she looked at him, her breathing rapid and shallow.

"Then you must treat me well," she said at last, greatly daring. "If you hurt me, they will know."

His thick lips with their exaggerated Cupid's bow flattened in a smile and his voice grew softer still.

"How will they know, sweet wife of mine?" he asked. "Who knows what goes on in the bedroom, once the door is shut?"

For a moment they both stood in silence, his pale eyes fixed upon her, bright with malice and amusement. Then he laughed contemptuously, pushed her away, and strode from the room.

Fourteen

"Will you take a little more chicken, Mr. Trotman?" Dorcas asked.

"Thank you. The white meat, if you would be so kind."

See how he lounges in his chair, Dorcas thought bitterly. How he is gloating over all of this! The desire to speak sharply to him was almost too much to be borne. How wonderful if she could say, "Sit up straight, Mr. Trotman, and either behave like a gentleman or leave my table!"

Instead she spoke with icy politeness and smiled with her lips only and suffered for Zachariah, whose daughter it was who had been guilty of the gross stupidity which had brought this man to their house.

It was, after all, far worse for him. Over the years she had made sure that she came into contact with Trotman as little as possible and had been relatively unaffected by him, but Zachariah had been forced into associating with him, much as he disliked the man. No, she corrected herself. Dislike was too small a word. Trotman, as Zachariah saw it, had been guilty of insulting his wife and to him there was no greater crime. All the other disagreements they had suffered over the years, both in and out of the Assembly, paled into insignificance beside it. She looked at her husband now and in spite of everything could not suppress a small twinge of amusement. Always transparently honest, never able to hide his true feelings, his face was going through the contortions he invariably found necessary when some dissembling was called for.

It was right, though, that they should both try to put the past behind them for the sake of the coming child. What monster would they breed between them, she wondered – and then felt ashamed of the thought. Whatever the sins of the parents, the child was innocent. For his sake, if for no other, they should remain part of Emma's life, ready if needed to give love and stability. Zachariah had been a far happier man since accepting that fact.

"I'm sure you must find plenty to occupy you in your large house, Emma," she said now, her voice carefully conversational. "To make a garden in that spot will certainly be a challenge."

"We don't have water to waste on that sort of thing," Trotman said.

"We none of us have water to waste, Mr. Trotman. I use naught but dishwater and my flowers do quite well, as you can see. I could give you a few cuttings, Emma, if you would like them."

"Thank you."

Emma's voice was low, her whole bearing subdued. She scarcely raised her eyes from her plate to look either at her father or Dorcas. Perhaps she was repentant at the manner of her elopement and regretted the shoddy treatment she had meted out to her father. Certainly there seemed little else to cause it, for much as Dorcas disliked Trotman, she could not fault his behaviour towards his wife, which was solicitous and affectionate in the extreme. He smiled down at Emma and pulled her hand through his arm as they left the table and made their way to the porch, fussily settling her into a comfortable chair, making sure there was a cushion behind her back in just the right position.

"I have to take care of her well," he said to Zachariah. "She is doubly precious to me now."

"Ay," Zachariah agreed awkwardly. He cleared his throat and rocked back and forth upon his heels, as if feeling that something should be said to mark the occasion and conscious that as yet he had not said it. "Well now," he began at last. "I'll not pretend I was happy about this marriage – how could any father be so, with his daughter stealing away like a thief in the night?"

"I'm sorry, Papa," Emma whispered.

"Sorry for the manner of it, perhaps." Trotman reached for her hand and smiled at her tenderly. "But not, surely, for the fact that we are married, sweetheart?"

"Oh no, Willis," she said quickly.

Zachariah cleared his throat again.

"We've had our differences, Trotman," he continued.

"Hence the need for secrecy!"

"You do me an injustice. If Emma had come to me and told me that she truly loved you –"

"You would have done your best to change her mind."

"Well –" Zachariah did not deny the charge. He rocked a little more, pulled a few faces and beetled his brows. "Well, what's done is done, and can't be undone. All I want – all I have ever wanted – is my daughter's happiness, and now there's the child to think of. I shall welcome a grandchild."

"I'm sure that you will." Trotman's voice was bland with no edge to it, but Dorcas could sense the satisfaction behind the words. Questions chased themselves in her mind. Why did he want this alliance with the Hardiman family when he had never made any secret of his contempt for Zachariah? No matter how he smiled on Emma, there was no power on earth that could convince her he was truly in love.

He was a devious man. No one had ever been able to explain the sudden wealth that had enabled him to make his start in the salt ponds, not with a few shares but with enough to set him immediately among the larger owners. Few did not suspect some clever manipulation of the McGovern brothers' books, and equally there were few that did not believe him guilty of bribery and intimidation when it came to the purchase of the unwanted shares that were for sale after the annual distribution.

Nothing illegal could, however, be laid with any certainty at his door. Yes, she thought now as she looked at him bending his head towards Emma with every appearance of solicitude, devious was the word. Personally she would not trust him the fraction of an inch.

"You're looking very well, Emma," she said, with a sudden uprush of unexpected sympathy for the girl.

She spoke nothing but the truth. With her body a little more rounded, with even her face a little fuller, she did look well.

"And why shouldn't she?" Trotman beamed upon his wife. "Happiness is the greatest beauty treatment of all, I've heard said. Motherhood is supposed to be the happy event which must crown every woman's life."

"I do feel better now," Emma said. "At first I felt very nauseous."

"No man can understand how wretched one feels! I'm glad that stage is over."

"It will be happiness all the way now." Trotman still smiled at Emma, the very epitome of a devoted husband. "I shall see to it, I assure you."

"Emma, I have baby clothes upstairs which you may have if you wish. They belonged to Storm. I kept them —"

Dorcas broke off suddenly and gave all her attention to pouring coffee. She had kept the small garments in hope and recognised that to part with them would signify that hope had been relinquished. Well, there was little point in being other than realistic.

"I should like you to have them," she said.

"Thank you." Emma's whisper came only after she had glanced towards her husband as if for approval.

"We shall go and look them out directly." Dorcas's voice was firm. She was determined that she would rid herself of the things this very day, before she changed her mind: besides, she would also be glad of the opportunity to have a talk with Emma alone. She felt puzzled by this strangely timid, subdued young woman who seemed like a stranger. Emma had often been difficult, sometimes sulky, but she had never held back from expressing her opinions. Now she gave the impression of being almost too cowed to speak.

The men made no protest as she bore Emma away upstairs, though Zachariah caught her eye with an appealing look as if to beg her not to leave them alone for too long.

Trotman, on the other hand, looked pleased with himself, as if events were shaping themselves exactly as he would have wished.

"I'm glad to have a chance to talk to you alone," he said to Zachariah, smiling somewhat enigmatically as he looked down into the depths of his coffee cup. "In fact I would have sought the opportunity had it not been presented by you. I've been wanting a word."

"Oh?" Zachariah raised his eyebrows.

Trotman looked up coldly.

"About the Cahill contract," he said.

Zachariah's expressive eyebrows climbed still higher.

"That's hardly your concern."

"Ah!" Trotman permitted himself a smile, lounged back in his chair, and crossed one leg over the other, perfectly at his ease. "That's the very point I wished to make. You see, I propose to make it my concern."

Zachariah stared at him, his face expressing a mixture of bewilderment and suspicion, laced with a lingering determination that he would do and say nothing that would spoil this new atmosphere of reconciliation.

"You'd best tell me what you mean," he said at last.

"Gladly." Trotman smiled at him. "It's simply told. You have the Cahill contract; I want it."

"Ha!" Zachariah put his coffee cup down on the table with a bang. "Well, I'm afraid that want must be your master, as my mother used to say."

"I don't think so." Still Trotman smiled. "I think you are going to pass it over to me as a marriage settlement."

"I've never heard —" At a loss for words, Zachariah moved his head from side to side, a look of outrage on his face. "You must be out of your mind, Trotman! My arrangement with Cahill goes back years —"

"The contract calls for salt of the highest quality, isn't that right? Such a pity you will have to write to tell them that your next crop is polluted and you are unable to supply their requirements. However, you will say, your son-in-law's salt is quite unaffected by the bacteria which has wrought such havoc in your ponds —"

"You're mad!" Zachariah sat rigid in his chair, his face scarlet with anger. "There's nothing wrong with my salt! It's the cleanest of any on the island and there's no man can gainsay that."

"Then think of some other reason why you should default."

"I'll do no such thing. Why should I?"

At his raised voice, Trotman held up his hand.

"Hush! Let's not alarm the ladies."

"My God, I'll alarm you before I'm through." Zachariah was out of his chair, pacing up and down the porch, arms flailing. "I've never known such bloody effrontery! Wedding settlement! What right have you to come here —" Words failed him again and he paced for a moment in silence, coming to a halt before Trotman, his forefinger pointed towards him.

"Listen to me," he said, making an effort to keep his voice low. "I have to accept you as my son-in-law because there's nothing I can do about it, but I don't have to like it — and I don't have to stand for insolent demands, either. I'll stick to my contract and supply salt to Cahill, come hell or high water."

"Even at the risk of having your wife's name dragged through the mud?" Trotman's voice was pleasantly conversational, unemphatic, but it had the effect of making Zachariah, who had been walking away, whirl to face him, suddenly still.

235

"What has my wife to do with this?" His flush was gone and he was now quite pale, his black eyebrows standing out more dramatically than ever.

"That son of yours – or hers, I should say. Storm. He bears little resemblance to you, wouldn't you say?"

Trotman's eyes were watchful. No flicker of emotion on Zachariah's expressive face was lost on him.

"Get out!" This was a Zachariah Hardiman that few would have recognised, a man whose voice was hoarse with suppressed rage. Trotman, however, did not move from his chair, but smiled scornfully.

"I have to wait for my wife," he said. "My wife – your daughter. She knows a lot more about Storm's origins than you give her credit for."

"There is nothing for her to know."

"Really? She knows that Storm was born less than seven months after you and the lovely Dorcas were married. She knows that the wedding was a hasty matter, arranged to prevent a scandal in the Foley family. Did you do it for love, Hardiman, or were you paid?"

Zachariah charged towards him, his hand upraised, but powerful as he was, Trotman was taller by more than a head, and as solid as a stone wall. He towered above Zachariah, caught his wrist, and after a moment's struggle succeeded in forcing him back.

There was a triumphant glint in his pale eyes. He had always been a master of bluff – a good poker player. His only solid fact was the date of the wedding. The rest was pure conjecture, a pretence of knowledge based on nothing more than observation and deduction. Now he knew that it had been very firmly based indeed.

"Who was the father, Hardiman?" he asked conversationally. "Or did she keep you in the dark about that? Perhaps she didn't know. Perhaps she was spoiled for choice, as the saying goes. Oh come, no brawling," as Zachariah charged towards him again. "What would the ladies think?"

"Shut your filthy mouth." Breathing heavily, fists clenched, Zachariah stopped short of attacking the man. "There's no truth in any of this; do you hear me? No truth at all."

"No?" Trotman gave a short laugh. "Well, there'll be plenty who want to believe it. Human nature's like that. Show people a beautiful woman and they'll do their best to prove she's a whore."

"You bastard." Zachariah groped for a chair and sat down, not taking his eyes from the man opposite him. "You filthy, contemptible bastard."

Trotman laughed again.

"You're not so far wide of the mark. My mother was a whore, too – but at least she didn't try to pass herself off as a lady."

"Shut your mouth," Zachariah said again, trembling with the force of his anger and knowing his own impotence in the face of Trotman's superior strength and his own unwillingness to brawl within earshot of his wife and daughter. "You'll not say one word against Dorcas – not one word, do you hear? There's such a thing as slander, you know. Spread your lies and the law will hear of it –"

He broke off as the sound of Dorcas's voice could be heard as the two women approached through the inner room. He got to his feet and stood, shoulders hunched, hands deep in his pockets, facing out towards the sea so that his back was towards his wife and daughter. Dorcas must not see his emotion, must never know of this.

"Just think of it," Trotman said, quietly and quickly. "It would be worth it, wouldn't it? My silence in return for the Cahill contract?"

"Zack, just look at these," Dorcas said as she came through to the porch. "I had forgotten how very tiny new babies are. Can you really believe that Storm ever fitted into them? How foolish I have been to keep them so long, but at least now they will be useful. Ring the bell, Emma, and we'll ask Nola to find a basket to hold them."

"Pray don't trouble." Trotman stood up. "We can carry them just as they are, and must leave now in any case. Fetch your hat, Emma."

Emma darted a nervous glance at him and scurried off to do as he told her, leaving Dorcas at something of a loss. The atmosphere on the porch was one that could be cut with a knife. She might have known, she told herself, that it would take only a few moments for Trotman and Zachariah to be at each other's throats. She went over to Zachariah and took his arm as if to demonstrate on which side of the fence she stood.

"I have told Emma she must come to visit us often," she said.

237

Zachariah nodded, without speaking, while Trotman bowed towards her.

"Too kind," he said.

Why, Dorcas wondered, did he always have to look so scornful. What had she said to deserve such a derisive sneer?

"A woman needs a friend at a time like this," she said.

"She has me, Mrs. Hardiman. Isn't that so, dearest heart?" This last remark he directed towards Emma as she re-entered the room. "We are all in all to each other, my little wife and I."

Zachariah was strangely silent as farewells were said. Once they were alone, Dorcas looked at him inquiringly.

"Something's wrong, isn't it? What did that wretched man say to upset you?"

Zachariah shrugged and drew his mouth down.

"How can I be other than upset to see my daughter married to such a creature?"

"No more than that?" Dorcas studied him closely.

"No more." Zachariah turned and walked heavily back from the gate to the porch. "What man needs more?" he said, almost to himself.

He's getting old, Dorcas thought with a sudden clutch of fear, seeing how the vitality had drained from his face. Was he ill, in pain? She had never known him so subdued.

"I'm perfectly well," he said with uncharacteristic testiness when she tackled him about it one morning at breakfast. "This trip will set me up."

"You're certain you feel up to it?"

"Good heavens, woman," he exploded with a welcome return to his old manner. "I'm not in my dotage yet. I'm fifty-four next birthday."

"Then I shall stop feeling sorry for you and begin to get angry! Why are you going around looking as if you've lost a guinea and found a farthing? You must come to terms with the fact of Emma's marriage, Zack — or is it something else that's worrying you? I wish you would tell me."

But muttering and pulling faces he stamped off to the salinas, leaving her curiosity unsatisfied. Thank heaven, she thought, that in only a few short weeks they were to sail away from Grand Cay and all the problems it contained. A holiday would give them a new perspective.

* * *

Charleston, she decided, was in every way the most delightful of cities, with its harbour and fine buildings; until, that is, she saw Baltimore which seemed to her to have attractions she had seen nowhere else. The domed cathedral, the statue of George Washington, the marble fountains, all seemed of a magnificence that must surely surpass everything.

Philadelphia, too, she enjoyed greatly, especially its theatres and in particular a production of *Romeo and Juliet*, where the last act found her in floods of tears, weak with emotion.

"Oh, imagine living in a city where one could experience such joy every week of one's life," she said, mopping her eyes. "But I must say," she went on, taking a somewhat calmer view, "I do consider that Friar Lawrence was most misguided, don't you, Zack? I can't feel that he acted at all sensibly and was much to blame for the final tragedy."

She was still brooding on the intricacies of the plot as later she sat before her dressing table and brushed her hair, reliving every dramatic moment.

"How foolish young girls can be," she said thoughtfully. "But who could blame Juliet, when all is said and done? The gentleman who took the part of Romeo was quite devastatingly handsome —"

"I'll be your Romeo." Zachariah, clad in nothing but a nightshirt, dropped theatrically to one knee and held out his arms to her, as unromantic a figure as it was possible to imagine.

Hairbrush uplifted, Dorcas advanced towards him across the hotel bedroom.

"Romeo, Romeo, wherefore art thou Romeo?" she implored dramatically, eyes cast heavenwards. "Deny thy father —"

"Mind what you're doing with that hairbrush!" Zachariah, rubbing his shoulder, glared at her from his lowly position and scrambled to his feet. "Juliet was never supposed to set about her lover —"

"Oh, I'm sorry!" Laughing, Dorcas fell into his arms. "I was merely making a dramatic gesture. Oh Zack, it's good to see you playing the fool again. You were right about this holiday. It has done us good."

He held her close and said nothing, but later as they lay in the dark, she was conscious of his restlessness.

"What is it, Zack?" she asked at last. "What's troubling you?"

He pushed himself upright and fumbled with the flint to light the lamp so that he could turn and look at her.

"There's something I must tell you," he said. "I must get it off my chest before we get to Bermuda and see Silas. It's about the Cahill contract."

Dorcas pushed herself up against the pillows and frowned at him uncomprehendingly.

"What about the Cahill contract, Zack?"

"Silas is bound to ask how it goes." He was looking away from her, not answering her directly. "He knows Mr. Cahill and was instrumental in securing it for me, but you must be the first to know I have had to withdraw. The fact is, Dorcas, my salt's not up to it. I've been forced to tell them so – tell them I can't fulfil my part of the bargain." He talked down her startled comment, lifting a hand to silence her. "I've suggested that Willis Trotman should take on my commitments and I've no reason to think they won't agree. Why shouldn't they? We've had a long and honourable association. They trust my word."

Dorcas would keep silent no longer.

"Zack, what foolishness is this? I've heard nothing against your salt –"

"Allow me to know my own business best."

She could not remember him speaking to her with such harshness, and stared at him in astonishment. He sighed, lifted a hand towards her, then let it fall again.

"I'm sorry, sweetheart. You've every right to question me, but believe me, I'd little choice in the matter. This seemed to me a fitting wedding present."

"But the Cahill contract is our bread and butter!"

"We'll not starve without it."

"Is there really something wrong with your salt – and if so, *why*?"

Zachariah shrugged, not meeting her eye.

"It's a question of bacteria, I'm told. Sometimes one pond is affected, another escapes. I daresay it will pass muster for a buyer not quite so particular as Cahill."

"We should never have come on this holiday! Next year might be a lean one."

"Nay, nay, don't make things out to be worse than they are. Last year was a good one and I've money in the bank."

"I don't understand." She lay back against the pillows and

looked at him narrowly. "How can you know at this stage that next year's salt will be affected?"

"I must do as I think right." He turned to extinguish the lamp, not able to look at her. "Say no more on the subject, Dorcas."

She did as he told her, but was far from sleep as she lay beside him in the darkness, trying to make sense of this development, and failing utterly. How many times had Zack congratulated himself on the purity of his salt, and the industry of his workers that meant it was often so much cleaner than others? Trotman, he had said many times, never got the best from his labour and the product suffered accordingly. How many times had Zack said, 'Thank God for Cahill,' knowing that though other markets fluctuated, this one remained constant? How could this make sense?

He was generous, of course; she had always known it. However, a sizeable cheque would have answered the need for some kind of gift to the newly-weds, particularly in the circumstances in which the wedding had taken place. No, none of it made any sense to her – or to Zachariah, if she summed up the situation correctly. There had been something strange in his manner.

Beside her, equally far from sleep, she heard Zachariah sigh and felt him toss restlessly.

Damn Trotman, she thought bitterly. Damn him, damn him.

How he fitted into all this she had no idea, but she felt certain that he was at the back of Zachariah's unease. Nothing had been the same since he married Emma.

"It sounds the most wonderful trip," Fanny said, a little absently, sewing a small white garment with neat stitches. She was pregnant again, plump and complacent, and not – as Dorcas realised – much interested in her sister's impressions of Philadelphia or anywhere else.

"I've talked enough," she said. "Tell me of your doings, Fanny. You are looking exceedingly well – and so, I may say, is Silas."

"Yes, thank God, we are all in good health. Young Nicholas is growing out of all his clothes – and my dear, what *did* you think of Storm when you saw him?"

Dorcas laughed.

"I hardly recognised him. He must have grown twenty inches, I swear."

"And so handsome, too! Everyone says he is the very image of you, Dorcas. One thing I know, he's already turning heads among the opposite sex, though to give him credit he still seems devoted to his studies."

"I'm glad of that. At sixteen there's plenty of time for other things. He's still a boy, however tall he might be."

"You need have no worries about him. He has a good head on his shoulders, Dorcas. Why, only last week Kit Mallory said —"

"Kit Mallory?" Dorcas echoed the name in astonishment, almost dropping the cup she had in her hands. "Isn't he in Havana?"

"Oh, did I not tell you?" Fanny was threading a needle, her attention only half with Dorcas and the news she was imparting. "Kit and his wife arrived in Bermuda two weeks ago, or thereabouts. They've left Havana."

"Are Kit and Silas on terms, then? I gained the impression that Silas was displeased —"

"Oh, that's a thing of the past." Dismissively Fanny shrugged her shoulders. "It was not so much the severance of the partnership that vexed Silas as the manner of it, for it was all so sudden with no proper discussion of how it was all to be resolved. Pray don't ask me what arrangements they have now made, for those things go over my head as you well know! Silas tells me nothing, which is just as well for I am sure I should be none the wiser if he did. However, the long and the short of it is —"

Dorcas could hear the voice going on and on, but took in nothing apart from the disturbing fact of Kit's presence on the island. Storm, she thought. *Storm*!

"Is he here to stay?" she asked abruptly.

Fanny, apparently talking now of Silas's new business partner, stared at her.

"I mean Kit," Dorcas said. "Is this merely a visit."

"Oh yes, of course. He and Isobel are here simply so that he can show her his old home. She had never before been to Bermuda and seems quite taken with it. They are off to London soon, for Kit is to take up some immensely high position in the Gold Star Line; apparently Mr. Cyrus Webber-ley has already bought a grand house for them in a place called Portman Square which Isobel tells me is quite one of the most fashionable places to live."

"He appears to have done well for himself."

"Well, you know Kit! Silas always did say that when he married, he would take care to marry money. He was ever one of the most ambitious men I've met, but even without a fortune Isobel must have dazzled him. Wait until you see her, Dorcas! I've never seen such skin! One hears of the English rose complexion but never have I seen such a perfect example of it."

"She's young, no doubt," Dorcas said dryly.

"Not more than eighteen, I swear. What a dog he is, isn't he?" Fanny snipped at her thread, and fussed with needle and pincushion.

"How long are they to stay?"

"My dear, never fear – you shall have a chance to see them for we have invited the world and his wife here on Saturday, both in your honour and in honour of the Mallorys. Everyone wants to meet them – and you, too, of course. Word has gone out of Isobel's beauty and you know what it's like in a small place! The talk is of little else."

"I can well imagine."

"If only Kit's mother and father could have lived to see this day! Wouldn't Mrs. Mallory have been delighted? She was so certain that Kit would marry well and now here he is, having carried off the prize of the year. She really is a most enchanting girl, with such pretty manners."

"But no family yet?"

"I hear she miscarried a few months back. But time is on her side. I've no doubt she will produce a quiverful of perfectly beautiful children, for they are indeed a handsome pair."

"I hope," Dorcas said, "that she has half a dozen sons."

And never, she thought privately, have I expressed a more heart-felt wish than that, her only other desire being to remove herself and Storm well away from Hamilton and the Bermudas until Kit and his beautiful wife had sailed for England. This she knew to be an impossible dream. She and Kit would meet, would converse politely and say how delighted they were to see each other again, playing out the inevitable charade no matter what their hidden feelings might be.

Heaven send that he was truly in love with this paragon that Fanny had described with such fulsome praise. Heaven send that she did indeed produce son after son, so that never again would he cast covetous eyes on Storm.

"Tell me of Emma," Fanny said, suddenly changing the subject. "I was not in the least surprised to hear that Zachariah has softened towards the wretched couple. He was ever the most generous of men."

Dorcas compressed her lips in a rueful smile. Fanny, she thought, didn't know the half of it.

"For the sake of the coming child we felt we should restore relations," she said.

"But to entertain the unspeakable Trotman! How can you bear it?"

"It's not an easy matter," Dorcas admitted.

"Can she really be in love? No, I cannot believe it, not after all you have told me about him. What do you think, Dorcas? Does she see something in him that is hidden from the rest of the world?"

It was almost with relief that Dorcas turned her mind to the thorny subject of her stepdaughter. Almost anything was better than thinking of Kit as she had last seen him, coldly angry and vowing revenge.

"Hardiman, my dear fellow!"

Kit's smile, Dorcas noted, was as open and charming as it had ever been, the warmth of his manner towards Zachariah revealing no indication of the fact that nine years before he had done his utmost to bring heartbreak to the man whose hand he now shook so effusively.

"And your dear wife, too." Kit bent over Dorcas's hand. "How delightful that our visits should coincide in this way. A happy chance, wouldn't you agree?"

"Indeed," Dorcas said politely.

"You must meet Isobel." Kit looked over his shoulder and laughed to see that already his wife had been surrounded by a group of sycophantic matrons, almost as if she were royalty. "I shall rescue her," he said. "I think everyone has fallen in love with her quite as desperately as I."

Dorcas smiled non-committally and inclined her head, waiting until he had gone before turning to Zachariah.

"Come and talk to my Paget cousins, Zack," she said. "It's years since I saw Cousin Sarah. Is something wrong?" Her arm through his, she paused and looked at him questioningly. "You don't look enthusiastic at the prospect."

"Silas is with them. He's not best pleased with me at the moment."

"You told him about the Cahill contract?"

"It came up in conversation. It's not his business and I told him so, but it might be prudent to allow him time to recover his temper."

"That may take some time," Dorcas said. "Speaking as one who has yet to reach that happy state!"

"Sweetheart –" Zachariah's voice was pleading, and almost against her will, Dorcas smiled at him.

"What am I to do with you?" she asked.

"Trust me," he said. "Love me."

"Both of which I do, gladly."

"Good evening, Mother – Father." Storm stood before them, more than a head taller than Zachariah, glowing with health and vitality, his hair burnished to the colour of old mahogany.

"My, how smart you look!" Dorcas said. "I wonder you can turn your head with such a high stock."

"I must have tied it a dozen times, but I think it's right now, don't you? Cousin Josiah came with me to the tailors. He's the last word! He said waistcoats like this were all the thing."

"I don't advise sitting down in those trews," Zachariah said. "They'd split from here to kingdom come –"

"Take no notice of him! You look very fine and we're proud of you, aren't we Zack?"

"Certainly we are –"

"Mr. and Mrs. Hardiman, may I present my wife?" Kit had joined them again. "Isobel, meet old friends of mine, Mr. and Mrs. Zachariah Hardiman."

"Enchanted – delighted – a pleasure to make your acquaintance –"

The civil words flew from one side to the other and Dorcas saw that, if anything, Fanny's glowing description of Mrs. Kit Mallory had erred on the conservative side. She was of a slim and graceful build with perfect features, as delicate as if they had been made of Dresden china, her skin smooth as a flower's petal, her wide eyes the most vivid and unusual shade of deep blue. Her hair was pale gold, elaborately plaited on her crown, ringlets hanging on each side of her face, and everything about her, from the diamonds that hung from her ears to the silver kid slippers on her feet, seemed to add to the air of glamour and opulence that surrounded her.

"And this," Kit said, with a certain note in his voice that only Dorcas detected, "is Storm."

"Your son?" Isobel smiled at Dorcas as she extended her

hand to Storm. "I can see the likeness. How do you do, Mr. Hardiman?"

Storm bowed over her hand murmuring something incomprehensible, and in spite of her discomfort at the whole situation Dorcas could not avoid a feeling of amused affection for him. Two minutes before he had been preening himself before them, the very model of fashion, delighted with himself and his new grown-up clothes. Now, suddenly, he was a bashful boy again, none too sure what to do with his hands or his feet.

"He has changed a good deal since I last saw him nine years ago," Kit said.

Dorcas looked at him and her amusement died. He smiled still, but there was a look in his eye that was both cold and challenging.

Zachariah was speaking – something about looking forward to having Storm with him now that he had so nearly approached man's estate. The time would not be long delayed, he was saying; Storm's schooldays would be over soon. Kit was nodding as if in agreement, nodding and smiling, assenting to the idea that a man would be glad to have his son going into business with him. His eyes, however, were still on Dorcas, steely and inimical, giving a totally different message. Nothing has changed, she thought with dread. His marriage has made no difference at all. Still he wants vengeance.

For a moment she returned his look, but it struck such a chill in her that she wavered and looked away, towards the son who stood so innocently and unknowingly beside his father. He, she saw at once, was quite oblivious to Zachariah, Kit, or indeed any other of the fifty or more people who filled the room with colour and movement and conversation.

His eyes were only for Isobel and in them was an expression which she recognised easily enough.

Aged sixteen, at eight of the clock, on a warm June evening in 1828, in the residence of Mr. and Mrs. Silas Tranton of Hamilton, Bermuda, Storm had fallen in love.

Fifteen

Before the evening was out, Kit had proposed a beach party for the following week, to which the Hardiman family was cordially invited.

"How very kind," Dorcas said, with an icy smile. "Alas, we are already engaged —"

"I think not, my dear," Zachariah interrupted in his ingenuous way. "You must surely have mistook the date."

"Oh, please Mother!" Storm's voice, long since settled into a manly baritone, seemed to revert to the more uncertain pitch of previous years. "Surely it could be arranged?"

Dorcas had no alternative but to accept the invitation gracefully, but afterwards she took Zachariah to task.

"Could you not see I had no wish to go?" she asked crossly.

"By why, sweetheart?" Zachariah looked astonished. "You are not normally so unsocial! I thought you genuinely mistaken, and could see how disappointed Storm was that we couldn't accept."

"Storm is better kept away from the Mallorys." Dorcas was removing her jewellery and in her agitation found difficulty with the clasp of her necklace. "Oh, drat this thing! Zack, please help me —"

Please help me, please help me. Can't you see my need?

The words seemed to echo inside her head as she waited, neck bent as if in submission, for Zachariah's thick, stubby fingers to deal with the delicate clasp. But she knew there was no help anywhere. The time had passed for confession and absolution. She had a hopeless feeling that events were moving beyond her control and only disaster would result.

"Why should Storm be kept away from them?" Zachariah asked.

"Did you not see the way he looked at Mrs. Mallory?"

"A cat may look at a king," Zachariah said with an indulgent chuckle. "There, my love. That's done it. Take care it

247

doesn't tangle in your hair. No, no, sweetheart!" He moved away, still laughing quietly. "Let the boy look his fill. He'll get a chance to do naught else, I'll swear."

There was no answering smile on Dorcas's lips.

"He'll be hurt. I feel it in my bones."

"Nonsense, my love!" Zachariah sat on the edge of the bed, hands on his knees. "Be reasonable, Dorcas. You worry too much. Oh!" he waved a finger as she began to speak. "He'll sigh over the girl – heaven knows she's worth a few sighs! – but haven't we all sighed and all survived? He's coming back to the island with us in little more than a week and the Mallorys will be long gone to England by the time he returns here. Mark my words, Isobel Mallory will be forgotten in no time."

"Perhaps."

Nevertheless her apprehension persisted.

They joined the party after all, in the absence of any real reason why they should not, and Fanny and Silas also came – though not without a great deal of doubt and indecision on Fanny's part, for she felt disinclined to make the long descent to the beach. It was Dorcas who persuaded her to come, feeling the need of moral support, and afterwards Fanny thanked her for doing so, pronouncing the occasion a great success.

"Though I cannot believe Mrs. Mallory would agree," Fanny said. "She did little but sit beneath her parasol, as immobile as I."

"How beautiful she is," Phillipa breathed, of an age to yearn. "And such clothes!"

"It is ill-bred to make such personal remarks," Fanny said severely.

"But Mama, they are nothing but the truth! Oh, how I wish we could go to London to see some of the things she told me about! The great new shops in Regent Street and Oxford Street, and the Vauxhall Gardens. It sounds too wonderful for words."

"The sooner the Mallorys leave, the better," Fanny remarked privately to Dorcas. "I consider Mrs. Mallory an unsettling influence on Phillipa. She is so impressionable!"

Dorcas could only agree with her desire to see the couple gone. However, it was not Storm's rather touching and wholly innocent adoration of Isobel that caused her to lie sleepless in her bed on the night after the beach party, but rather the picture of Kit as he had been that day, with all his formidable charm channelled in one direction; towards Storm.

With the consummate skill that came naturally to him he had somehow made it appear, with no word spoken, that he and Storm stood together, bonded by an understanding, a daring, an impetuosity, not shared by any of the others in the party. Apparently unmarked by the years, which had left him as lithe and lean as ever, he had outswum Storm and had balanced equally surely on an outcrop of rock, and when others had counselled caution, he had given the boy a smile of complicity, as if to say, 'Let the killjoys speak; you and I are two of a kind!'

No, Dorcas had longed to shout. You are *not* two of a kind! Storm is gentle and kind and would never willingly hurt a living soul.

Sleepless, she sighed and turned her head restlessly on the pillow. Was she being unfair? A dog in a manger? Kit was, after all, the boy's father, however much she disliked acknowledging the fact, and perhaps she should not grudge him this fleeting moment of communion with his son; and *would* not, she told herself, except for the gleam of malicious triumph in his eyes when he looked towards her, and the memory of that long-ago threat.

There was little he could do, however. With his wife's fortune at stake, his incentive to keep silent about his past must surely be overwhelming. She disliked intensely his manipulation of Storm — obvious to her if to no one else — and she distrusted his motives, but looking at the matter practically there was surely no real cause for alarm.

Soon they would all go their separate ways, and never again need their paths cross. Soon, thank heaven, the whole episode would be behind them.

They had been back on Grand Cay no more than two weeks before another brig from Bermuda brought a surprise which drove all thoughts of the Mallorys from Dorcas's mind. Even Storm, who had shown a marked tendency to drift off on solitary walks, a volume of one of the romantic poets in a back pocket, shed his love-sick melancholy and reverted to his normal, high-spirited self. Davey had come home on furlough.

"I could hardly believe my ears," he said, "when I turned

up at Cedarcroft to find I had missed you only by a matter of days. I had no idea you'd been in Hamilton."

"I wrote," Dorcas told him. "I said that we were going to America and would end the trip in Bermuda."

"I've had no news since – oh, since Emma's marriage! Lord, what a surprise that was!"

"To all of us," Dorcas said dryly. "To think of all my fine words doing no more than entertain the fishes! Really, it's not to be borne! But do tell us – how long can you stay?"

"I'm to be back in Bermuda by the end of July to be in time to sail on the *Blenheim*, bound for Jamaica. I'm posted to Port Royal to join Captain Merriman's new command as lieutenant."

"Lieutenant! Zack, did you hear that? Davey has promotion!"

"Captain Merriman asked for me in particular," Davey said with pardonable pleasure. "He said when he left his old command last year that I should join him if it were at all possible, and so it's transpired. I'm delighted, for I never met a captain I liked more."

"Such a difference a good captain makes to a ship," Zachariah said reminiscently. "And a good boatswain, too. A bad one can make life a living hell! There was one aboard the *Merry Monarch* when I was a lad I'll not forget if I live to be a hundred. A hard man, he was, who could think up more reasons for a taste of the rope's end than I've had hot dinners."

"Davey, where have you been? You must have seen such places!"

Storm was eager, impatient for news of the seafaring life, and he listened entranced as the magic names were mentioned: Genoa, Brindisi, Athens, Gibraltar.

"And Alexandria?" Zachariah asked. "I mind once, sailing into Alex –" and

"Davey, did you ever touch Valetta?" and

"I must tell you about the time when we were caught by a storm in the Bay of Biscay –"

Dorcas, no less interested, looked at the two of them exchanging travellers' tales and was happy to see that Davey had matured into a man who succeeded in combining his father's warmth with an indefinable air of authority. There was a twinkle in his eye and a ready joke on his lips, but she guessed that there were few men who would dismiss his opinions as unworthy of serious consideration.

"You can be proud of him, Zack," she said the next day when Davey and Storm had left the house to sail beyond the reef as in past years.

"Ay, I am," Zachariah replied with satisfaction. "And how much he owes to you, sweetheart. He's a gentleman, through and through, for all he looks like me."

"He owes more than his looks to you," Dorcas said. "Isn't it wonderful that he should come just now to bear Storm company and raise his spirits? It was truly providential. Of course," she added, "we must arrange for Emma to come and see him – and the Unspeakable Trotman, I suppose. Perhaps on Sunday. Does that suit, Zack?"

"What? Sunday?" Zachariah's smile had died and had been replaced by a scowl at the mention of Willis Trotman. Still scowling, he sighed. "Ay, I suppose so – though if I'm to be honest, I can think of no day that suits where he's concerned. Still, the boy must see his sister and as I cannot see any invitations being issued from the Trotman household, I imagine it's up to us. Sunday will do as well as any other day."

"What on earth has happened to her?" Davey asked in bewilderment when the luncheon party was over and Emma and Trotman gone. "She seems as if she hardly dares breathe without his permission. I almost longed to provoke one of our famous childhood battles, just to see if she has any spirit left."

"Yet he speaks to her in a kindly way," Dorcas pointed out, struggling to be fair to the man she instinctively distrusted.

"There's a feeling of violence about him," Storm said. "I don't mind telling you he puts the fear of the devil into me – he always has done, since I was little. A long time ago when Aaron and I were very young and Trotman was building that house of his out at South Creek, we happened to be in the area, just exploring the way we used to do. The builders had left the house for some reason and there seemed no one about, so we went over to look at it. It was sheer curiosity – we were doing no harm – but suddenly there was Trotman, rising up with a face like thunder, shouting and swearing and charging at us with a stave in his hands, just as if we were a band of marauding cut-throats instead of two extremely frightened small boys. I can tell you we took to our heels and didn't stop running until we got to Palm Grove!"

"He reminds me of a master-at-arms on the *Jupiter*," Davey

said. "To the captain he spoke as if he'd just swallowed a jar of honey, so smooth and sweet you'd imagine no gentler man ever lived; but to the men he was the devil incarnate."

"And what happened to him?" Dorcas asked idly.

Davey looked at her and shrugged as if he rather wished he had never mentioned the man.

"He was hanged," he said. "He killed a man in a fit of temper one night when he was ashore."

Dorcas shivered.

"What dreadful things you have seen, Davey," she said, "out there in the big, wide world. And we so sheltered here on our little island."

The short time that Davey spent with them went quickly, and all too soon the day came when he had to sail back to Bermuda.

"But Jamaica is not so far distant," Dorcas said, with an attempt at cheerfulness. "Perhaps you can come again."

"Ay," Zachariah agreed. "Tell that Captain Merriman to sail his frigate in this direction."

"Stranger things have happened."

"Look after yourself, son."

"Yes, Davey – guard your health."

Dorcas had learned by this time that Port Royal was one of the most feared posts in the Navy, many sailors going there to die in the fever-ridden climate.

"I shall be right as rain," Davey assured them. "After all, I'm no stranger to a hot climate."

"Davey always could take care of himself," Emma remarked, as if she found this more a matter for complaint rather than a consolation.

Rather unexpectedly, for she had shown remarkably little interest in her brother during his short stay, Emma had come down to the wharf to see him go, and though she said a cool farewell to him, Dorcas thought there was a touch of wistfulness in her face as she stood and watched the ship sail away on the morning tide, its sheets filling with the strong wind and the waves creaming white around its hull. What was she thinking? Did she, too, long to sail away?

"No doubt you will welcome a holiday away from the island once the baby has been born," Dorcas said. "Perhaps Willis will take you to Bermuda."

"Bermuda?" Emma gave a short laugh. "I wouldn't give a thank you for it, I promise you. I was too ill-used there to think of it kindly."

And that, madam, thought Dorcas, is a matter I refuse to comment on!

"Well, it's good to know you're quite contented here," she said evenly. Emma gave her a sharp look.

"Why wouldn't I be contented? There's my baby to look forward to."

"Yes, indeed. Emma, why not come home to have luncheon with us? You've seen so little of Storm. Wouldn't that be a good idea, Zack?"

Both Zachariah and Storm heartily endorsed the invitation, but Emma shook her head.

"Willis will expect to see me at home," she said. "He doesn't care for it if I am not there."

"We can send a message so that he will know your where-abouts."

"No, no!" Emma seemed poised to run at her insistence. "No, I must go home."

"Then at least let Storm take you in the buggy," Dorcas said. "The walk is far too long for you in the heat of the day. Storm, you'll take your sister, won't you?"

Storm professed himself delighted, Emma climbed into the buggy, and together they drove off, the wheels kicking up puffs of choking dust for there had been no rain for many weeks and the heat was intense.

"Perhaps she may confide to Storm where she would hesitate with us," Dorcas said.

"Ay." Zachariah was looking after them with a troubled frown on his face. "She seems — I don't know — unnatural. Not herself. But then —" He took Dorcas's arm and pulled it through his own as they began to walk towards Tamarind Villa. "But then, do I know my daughter any more? She seems a stranger to me. Lord knows," he went on, "she was always difficult, always at odds with others, but she was normally affectionate with me. Now, well, she's gone from me, Dorcas, and I am sad for it and worried about the girl, for though Trotman keeps assuring us of the love that's between them, still I find it hard to believe and can't imagine she is happy with him."

"She's happy about the baby, at least."

"Ay, ay." He cheered a little. "A baby of her own! She'll

be glad of that. Will we be invited to their home, d'you think, when we have a grandchild to visit?"

It rankled with him that neither he nor Dorcas had ever been asked across the threshold of the Trotman House, and he made little secret of the fact.

"Perhaps she will show Storm a little more hospitality than she has shown us," Dorcas suggested.

However, when Storm returned home he reported that Emma had acted most strangely, appearing ill-at-ease and answering him only in monosyllables.

"In fact she seemed to be sitting on the edge of her seat the entire way," he said, "and she scuttled indoors like a scared rabbit the moment we arrived without offering me so much as a cup of cold water. I had the feeling that she expected Trotman back at any moment and expected him to be angry because she was in my company."

Baffled, Dorcas shook her head.

"I don't understand any of it," she said.

"Storm Hardiman came here? You let him drive you back?"

"It was so hot, Willis, and I get so tired. And after all, he is my brother."

"I wonder!"

"I will always think of him as a brother, whatever you might say."

"But why Storm? Why didn't they send you with one of the slaves?"

"No slave was there! Storm had driven Papa and Davey and Dorcas to the wharf."

"What did you tell him?"

"Tell him?" At this unhelpful response he turned angrily towards her and she cringed away from him. "I told him nothing, Willis. Truly! What could I tell him? He did most of the talking – all about Davey and the wonderful places he had seen and how he would like to travel one day –"

"And what about the Divine Dorcas? No doubt you gabbled your complaints to her?"

"We spoke very little. Everyone was taken up with Davey."

"No complaints?" Trotman affected astonishment. "I can hardly believe it!"

"Quite the reverse! I told Dorcas I was contented."

"Why?" About to pour himself a tot of rum, he put the bottle down and reached to hold her tightly by the shoulders,

254

looking at her narrowly. "Did she question you? Did she suspect that you might not be contented? Ask if I treated you well?"

"No, no – it wasn't a bit like that! I said I had no wish to go to Bermuda and Dorcas said she was glad I was contented here, that's all. Willis, I swear that was all! Leave go, do. You're hurting me!"

Slowly he relaxed his hold on her, never taking his eyes from her face.

"I'll not have any whining," he said.

"I didn't whine! I never whine!"

For a moment he looked at her in astonishment; then he laughed, his laughter long and loud and full of mockery as he turned back to the rum bottle.

With Davey gone, Dorcas watched Storm warily, fearing a return to his previous love-lorn state; however, he seemed happy enough, spending his days and some of his nights fishing with Joe and Aaron, visiting Treasure Bluff to debate affairs of the day with Marcia and Thomas Redfern, and discussing the production of salt with Zachariah.

Word that the latest London papers had arrived sent him up to Treasure Bluff one afternoon, and he returned full of news.

"The talk in the Houses of Parliament is all of Abolition," he told Dorcas. "For a change, it's the island of Mauritius that's accused of brutal treatment of its slaves. Wilberforce and his followers are up in arms."

"More power to him," Dorcas said. "There's a man whose name will live in history."

"Uncle Silas says that hanging's too good for him."

"Uncle Silas's views are at variance with mine, as you well know."

Storm laughed.

"Well yes, it has been brought to my attention."

"And you?" Dorcas asked after a moment. "Where do you stand?"

"Oh, I'm with you," Storm replied with no hesitation. "How could I be otherwise, brought up the way I have been? No matter how benevolent the master, surely it cannot be right to own another individual – and where slaves are treated cruelly, as all too often they are, then it's nothing short of a sin against the Holy Ghost."

"When Abolition comes, for come it will, both employer and employed will feel the pinch."

"I've spoken of it with Aaron. He says any sacrifice is worth it, and I'm inclined to agree. Mr. Redfern believes that Whitehall will eventually set a date and that the slave-owning colonies will be given several years to set their houses in order. I think it will be a challenge. I'm willing to wager I'll make a success of producing salt, even with a free labour force."

Dorcas smiled at him.

"So Davey hasn't dazzled you with his tales into wanting to join the Navy?"

"What's the Navy but another form of slavery? All those brutal punishments! No thanks, it's not for me. Though I must say," he added, "I should like to travel the world. In my own time, and in the best cabin, of course!"

Their conversation was ended abruptly by a summons for Dorcas from the kitchen, but she went on her way feeling cheered, both that Storm was on the side of the angels in the ever-continuing debate about slavery, and that apparently he was still content to come back to the island.

"Ay, we've plans for the future, the two of us," Zachariah said when she recounted Storm's words. "We've talked about it. Just one more year and we'll be managing things together."

"What did he say about the loss of the Cahill contract?"

Zachariah pulled a few faces and did not answer her directly.

"This is proving a good year, sweetheart. We'll not miss it."

"It's in the bad years we'll need Cahill," Dorcas said dryly, and Zachariah said nothing, knowing that she was right.

The summer passed and September came with its oppressive heat and gun-metal skies, and there were a few storms too, with rain lashing down in sudden, tumultuous torrents which flooded the unpaved roads and turned them into quagmires, leaving puddles to steam in the sun once the storm was over. None was near hurricane force, however, and though some of the salt was adulterated, for the most part the deposits dried out quickly enough.

In October, when all threat of hurricanes was over, Storm sailed back to Bermuda for his final year at school, the brig that was to take him there bringing mail which included a letter from Fanny, the first for several months, dated 16th September.

Dorcas tore it open anxiously, fearing that the long silence had been caused by illness or some other disaster, but her fears were soon put at rest.

My dearest Dorcas [Fanny wrote],

I beg your forgiveness for not writing before this, but my silence has been occasioned by pressure of visitors, including Silas's sister, Jane Braithwaite, and her four children. With my own baby due in less than two months, you can imagine that I was less than delighted with this arrangement! However, she had been promising a visit for some time, and since their house in Boston has needed extensive rebuilding, this seemed as good an occasion as any. When I tell you that the bed of lilies before the house has been entirely trampled, one window broken by a shuttlecock and Silas's best fishing rod snapped in two, you will understand that I am not sorry to see the entire family returned home – regarding which, I must tell you before I forget that Jane is acquainted with your Dr. Bettany – or more accurately, with his superior, a Dr. Wilde, who resides in the house next door (and for that must surely deserve our sympathy!). She tells me that Dr. Bettany is once more at odds with the authorities, who consider his ideas quite nonsensical, and has been forbidden the hospital!

How very sad this is, to be sure, for I am persuaded by you that his only sin is to be in advance of his time, and that his devotion to duty is beyond reproach.

For myself, I confess I am perfectly happy with Dr. Duncan. Old fashioned he may be, but reliable for all that! He pronounces himself equally satisfied with me and assures me there is no reason in the world why I should not have a trouble-free confinement. I am not the only one to think well of him, for Isobel Mallory assures me she could not have had better attention in London. I have only this moment realised that it is so long since I wrote to you that you are probably not aware that Isobel and Kit are still with us. As soon as her condition became known they decided to winter here in view of her past history of miscarriage, and have taken a lease on Ibbot's Folly, that rather grand old house on the way to Tucker's Town.

We so look forward to Storm's return. He is a dear boy, so much loved and admired by his cousins.

"I wish they had gone back," Dorcas said to Zachariah.

"The Mallorys?" He raised his eyebrows and laughed at her. "You're not still worrying about Isobel and Storm?"

Dorcas did not reply. She was conscious of a feeling of apprehension; a certainty that somehow, in some way, Kit would not fail to take advantage of Storm's presence on the island, to wean him away from her. It was all very well for Zachariah to tell her that he was a sensible boy, unlikely to be hurt by his calf-love for Isobel. How could she tell him it was Kit's influence she feared?

She waited for Storm's first letter and when it finally came, the name 'Mallory' seemed to leap from the page.

Expecting to find them left long since it was the greatest surprise to me to meet Mr. Mallory at Cedarcroft and to learn that he and his wife are settled at Ibbot's Folly. He was kindness itself and invited me there for the following Sunday. It appears that though Mrs. Mallory has withdrawn from society to a great extent, she grows dull without young company. I cannot imagine anyone growing dull when Mr. Mallory is present, for he seems to me the most likeable and amusing man it is possible to meet! I enjoyed a most entertaining time there on Sunday and have been assured by them both of a welcome any time I choose to call.

"I hope," Dorcas said to Zachariah, "that he is not spending too much time with the Mallorys. It will surely interfere with his studies."

Zachariah pulled a face at her, mocking her severity.

"All work and no play," he said. "The boy must have some enjoyment, sweetheart. You should be pleased he has found congenial company! Many lads of his age might be engaged in plenty worse."

"I feel —" Dorcas struggled for words to express the inexpressible. "I feel no good will come of it."

But Zachariah only laughed and shook his head at her.

"You were always down on Kit Mallory," he said. "And he so agreeable! I can't understand your aversion. Remember when Emma was at school —"

"Yes," Dorcas said stiffly, cutting short his reminiscences. "Yes, I remember."

You would not recognise Ibbot's Folly for the house it was [Storm wrote during November]. Mrs. Mallory has exquisite taste and cannot bear not to be surrounded by beautiful things, so new hangings and furnishings have been shipped in, for all they are to occupy the house but six months.

I am teaching Mrs. Mallory to read! Not literally, of course, for she learned her letters as well as the rest of us, but she has never found any enjoyment in books and this is an omission I am determined to rectify. With what should I entice her, Mama? I wish you would advise me. I have tried her with Jane Austen, but she finds her somewhat difficult . . .

"She finds Jane Austen too difficult, if you please," Dorcas told Marcia, stabbing her needle into the canvas of her tapestry as if she would prefer to be stabbing it into soft flesh.

Marcia looked across at her and laughed.

"Well, it's not a hanging offence, you know. Hardly grounds for banishing Storm from her company. Really, I think you are taking this too seriously, Dorcas! What harm can she do the boy, bearing in mind that she is seven months pregnant and her husband, apparently, is ever-present."

"Exactly," Dorcas said obscurely, and sighed.

"You worry too much." Marcia smiled comfortingly at her friend. "Trust to Storm's common sense. He has a good head on his shoulders."

So Mr. Mallory took me with him to the boatyard owned by his brother [Storm wrote at the beginning of December]. And we spent almost the whole morning looking round it and seeing several different craft in the course of construction. It was most interesting and instructive. Father will like to know that I saw a sloop which I thought would serve us well, if he were to think of enlarging our fleet(!)

We then went aboard a large brigantine anchored in the harbour, owned by a friend of Mr. Mallory's, and we were entertained to luncheon. There was much talk of the Gold Star Line and its possible expansion. Uncle Silas says that Mr. Mallory has fallen on his feet, as he always does. He is, of course, referring to his marriage to the only daughter of a wealthy ship-owner, but it is my opinion that Mr. Webberley is the fortunate one, for he has surely acquired a son-in-law without equal. I admire Mr. Mallory more than I can say, and it is clear that the gentlemen aboard the brigantine felt likewise, for we were treated as if we were royalty – he the King, and I the Crown Prince!

If there had ever been any doubt in Dorcas's mind, it was gone now. There was a battle in progress – a battle for Storm's heart and mind, and it was a battle that Kit would clearly stop at nothing to win.

Trust Storm's common sense! When, she demanded of herself, did common sense have anything to do with it? The boy was dazzled by so much glamour, and who could blame him? When Kit set himself out to charm, then he was a formidable force; add a young wife as ethereally beautiful as Isobel and the contest was surely over before it had begun. All Dorcas could do was continue to write affectionate letters to remind him of home, and this she did, forcing herself to say nothing that might push Storm into taking sides.

The month passed, and there was no word from Bermuda. Fanny had given birth to a baby boy at the beginning of November, and though well, she had been much occupied and letters from her had been few. Now Christmas was upon them, and with it a flurry of letters both from Fanny and Storm. He was, it seemed, to spend the holiday at Ibbot's Folly rather than at Cedarcroft as in previous years.

We shall be sorry not to have his company [Fanny wrote], but it seems that he amuses Mrs. Mallory and Kit is anxious that nothing should upset her at this time. He begged for our understanding which we, of course, were glad to give. It seems that his wife's time must be very near now. Kit is anxious, he tells us, to have a son . . .

. . . a daughter [Storm wrote at the end of January], to be called Catherine, but who has already been re-christened Kate. Mrs. Mallory is very well and her spirits are high – as well she might be, for just before the birth, who should arrive but her father, Mr. Webberley himself, in his 'admiral's barge' (a snow furnished and equipped with every luxury for his particular use). He is excessively fond of his daughter and says he could no longer keep away from her, so anxious was he to see her state of health for himself.

260

Mr. Webberley is a somewhat terrifying old gentleman with the aspect of an elderly pirate, but I stood up straight, held my quaking knees steady, and answered up when spoken to. Mr. Mallory reports that he was taken with me and pronounces me 'the finest kind of Colonial youth', so I pray you will bear this in mind on those occasions when you are less than pleased with me!

How I wish Father could see the snow (the *Stella Maris* by name – all Gold Star vessels are called after some species of heavenly body) though I daresay he would say it was a whole lot too fancy for his taste.

"I suppose," Dorcas said to Zachariah dryly as she broke the seal on yet another letter which arrived from Storm towards the end of February, "this will contain the next thrilling instalment of the Mallory saga! How they seem between them, to have bewitched –"

She broke off, the colour draining from her face as she saw what the letter contained.

"Read it, read it," she said, in reply to Zachariah's agitated query, thrusting the first page towards him and turning to the second.

It is only for a year or so [Storm had written]. During which time I shall sail with Mr. Mallory, acting as his assistant and secretary while he studies the feasability of further routes for the Gold Star Line, mainly in the Orient. Much of our time will be spent in London, but our travels, when they take place, will be aboard the *Stella Maris*. I cannot express the excitement I feel! It means that I shall have to leave school before the year is up, but I beg you for your permission to do so since this is the kind of opportunity I have always dreamed of.

"You must forbid it, Zack!"

"Forbid it?" Zachariah's expression was a caricature of consternation. "Sweetheart, the boy would never forgive us! This is a chance not to be missed."

"He must finish his schooling."

"He's bored to death with that school, and has learned all he can from it, I'm sure of that. Think what an education this would be."

"I don't want him to go."

261

Zachariah put the two sheets of paper down on the table beside him and for a moment seemed to be concentrating on smoothing out the creases made by the folds in the thick vellum.

"Sweetheart," he said at last, his voice gentle, and his face as serious as she had ever known it. "Sweetheart, you know full well that I would do anything in the world to please you; but in this matter I cannot. We must not hold Storm back. It's not for ever, after all. A year, he says."

"A year – *or so*! That can mean anything! Zack, you want him home as much as I do – you have plans for him –"

"Remember the birds? The tighter you hold, the more they struggle to be free? We must let the boy go, Dorcas. He'll come back."

With an angry movement she rose from the table and walked swiftly away from him, out through the porch, setting the rocking chair swinging emptily as she passed it. She walked away from the house, towards the trees and the beach and the sea, stained now with all the colours of the dying day.

Zachariah, she knew, was close behind her, concerned and comforting, but she did not look at him as he came to stand beside her at the water's edge. Instead she stared at the horizon and the half-circle of the sun as it slowly slipped away out of sight while all around it the sky flamed crimson.

"Sweetheart, don't grieve so," he said coaxingly, taking her arm.

She stared directly ahead and said nothing, conscious of only one thing: Kit had won the battle.

"He'll come back," Zachariah said again.

"I wonder."

She turned to look at him then, and he was shocked by the look of hopelessness on her face.

"Just pray, Zack, that you're not mistaken. For myself –"

For a few more long moments she continued to stare at the sunset without speaking, and then she sighed.

"I should not care to put money on it," she said.

Sixteen

"Ain't no use frettin', Miz Dorcas." Bathsheba, almost as wide as she was tall, moved her bulk around the kitchen with surprising agility as she made preparations for cooking dinner. "Our chile come back when he good and ready."

"Our child is a child no longer." Dorcas stepped out of her way. "It will be his twenty-first birthday in August."

"Don't I know it? I done count every one. Master Storm, he like one of my own."

"A year or so," Dorcas said bitterly. "That's what he said when he went away. I knew then it would be longer. If only one could be sure that letters reached him!"

"He come back, Miz Dorcas. Every night, I pray to de Lord —"

"So do I, Sheba. So do I."

Eggs were cracked into a basin and whisked vigorously.

"Martha, you ready wid dat water?" Bathsheba called to her ten-year-old daughter who was filling a pitcher from the tank outside. "Mary, you go help yo' sister, now —"

"You're the lucky one, Sheba." Smilingly Dorcas drew aside for the eight-year-old Mary to scamper outside. "Six children and all on the island."

"De Lord done shower me wid blessin's, dat for true. Dat de reason Joe and me done get saved. Dat de reason we done wash in de blood of de Lamb."

Dorcas shuddered.

"Why do you Methodists find it necessary to be so gory?" she asked.

"Gory?" Bathsheba stopped in mid-action, bowl in one hand, whisk in the other. "I cain't understand 'gory', Miz Dorcas. *Glory*, dat I know. We all headin' for de Glory Land, and dat for sure."

"Yes, well, perhaps —"

"'Perhaps' don't make no never mind! Mr. Winklow done tell us —"

"Yes, yes, Sheba! I know what Mr. Winklow done told you."

Dorcas was weary with Mr. Winklow. She had welcomed his arrival warmly enough; had invited him to dinner and even thrown her sitting-room open for a series of prayer meetings and Bible studies, sympathetic with the work that the Methodists were performing in the Caribbean while the established Church of England had been lamentably slow in extending their missions to include the slave population.

Zachariah, too, had co-operated with the man, often fighting his battles in a largely hostile Assembly, always supporting his own long-held belief that contrary to popular white opinion, the slaves had every right to hear the Word of God.

Mr. Winklow, however, was not an easy man to like. In appearance thin and undersized with sparse hair and a veritable snow-storm of dandruff on his drooping shoulders, his self-esteem was in inverse proportion to his stature. No trace of doubt or appreciation of another point of view ever appeared to enter his unprepossessing head. He knew, without any question, what was right; right for the slaves, right for their owners. His solutions to the problems of the West Indies were simplistic and ill-thought-out, his condemnation of harmless pleasures equally swift.

Even the past year's Christmas celebrations had been ruined by a thunderous denunciation on his part of a society which allowed slaves to dance and sing on the anniversary of Christ's birth, and Zachariah's mild defence – that this was a custom enjoyed by the slaves who had little else to look forward to throughout the year – met with a harangue which implied that Zachariah and those like him were doomed to eternal damnation at the very least.

Mr. Winklow saw sin in everything and prided himself on speaking his mind at great length, dwelling on the hereafter as if he had intimate and irrefutable knowledge of what was in store; the untold glories that awaited the élite that were saved, the eternal agonies that were the lot of the heedless (i.e. those who did not attend his church. Even the Anglicans, he implied, were in danger of sizzling upon the devil's grill).

Both Dorcas and Zachariah not only disliked him as a man but were made profoundly uneasy by the hysteria whipped up by his frenzied exhortations. For once Zachariah found himself sympathising with Willis Trotman who had always opposed the influence of the missionaries; however, as a

264

matter of principle, he continued to support Winklow's presence and the right of anyone who so desired to attend his meetings. Winklow would not last for ever, went his argument. Other more congenial missionaries would take his place. It would be wrong to curtail the freedom of worship simply because this particular man was not immediately likeable.

Bathsheba and Joe were founder members of the Methodist church on the island and something of a power in the land. All the family lived together in a wooden shack at the extremity of the Hardiman plot, a shack that was kept spotless and was surrounded by flowering hibiscus and oleander. No queen was more proud of her palace than Bathsheba of this small dwelling. She might still come to work for her Miz Dorcas, but she did so because she wanted to; she was a free woman, and the choice was hers.

Joe earned a little by selling his fish and caring for the ketch, and he grew a small amount of guinea corn behind the shack. He, too, was a happy man, for his children had been born free. Aaron still fished with his father but was also working in a boatyard that had recently begun expanding its business, and his younger brother – always known as Little Joe – worked with him. Martha had begun to work in the house with her mother and showed a remarkable talent with her needle. Ruthie, next in line, spent much of her time looking after the baby, two-year-old Sim, while Mary tried very hard to be useful in the kitchen but more often than not managed to spill or drop or trip over whatever item was nearest to hand, exasperating her mother but being forgiven by all, for she had a bewitching smile that seemed to say life would always be a little easier for her than for others.

They had taken the name of Brewer, since Joe had been brought up in the household of a man of this name long years ago in Bermuda. Scrubbed within an inch of their lives and dressed in their best, the Brewer family made an impressive pew-full, Sunday by Sunday, while Dorcas and Zachariah, risking eternal damnation, went across the salinas to St. Thomas's where the Book of Common Prayer was followed diligently and the threat of hell fire given no more than passing reference.

"How long is it since we saw Emma at church?" Zachariah remarked as they drove home one Sunday, the salinas to the right and left of them already forming their crust, the start of the raking season only a few weeks away.

"No doubt Trotman disapproves."

Zachariah snorted, but said nothing. He could hardly bring himself to mention the fellow's name. His salt ponds bid fair to produce a good crop that year and the thought of his lost Cahill contract was something he tried to put behind him. He had found new markets, but nothing that could compensate, nothing that provided the year-by-year assurance he had enjoyed before.

"He's doing his best to get rid of the Methodists, Bathsheba says."

"There's naught he can do to them – you tell her. The law's the law."

"When did Trotman bother about the law?"

Zachariah made no reply. There was, after all, little he could say.

Kit Mallory, a little plumper and sleeker, with a few silver hairs at last beginning to show at his temples, smiled to himself with the greatest satisfaction.

"Mallory always falls on his feet," people said. He had heard them – Silas Tranton in particular.

Now as he looked down the length of his dinner table in the comfortable London residence with its fashionable address, seeing the gleaming crystal and silver and hot-house flowers, Silas's oft-repeated words seemed to echo most pleasantly in his mind. Good old Silas, dry-as-dust old Silas, cautious old Silas! Where would he be at the moment if it were not for his, Kit Mallory's, flair? Presiding over a faltering, down-at-heel family brokerage firm, that's where he would be.

Flair! That's what it took to make a success of life. Not breeding, nor education, nor even a title (though there were a few of those around his table that night) but *flair* – the instinctive knowledge of when to move and in what direction.

Silas would never have gone into Cuba without his insistence, though he was happy enough to embrace the idea once he had investigated all the possibilities for himself and found that the opportunities for profit existed in abundance – and how those profits had poured in! It amused Kit to think that both he and his illustrious father-in-law laid the foundations of their personal wealth in circumstances that were dubious to say the least. No wonder they had immediately recognised a certain kinship! It had taken Cyrus Webberley a very short time indeed to realise that he and the man his daughter wished to marry spoke the same language.

It had not been slave- but gun-running that made Cyrus Webberley wealthy. He had seen his opportunity in the 1790s when the mulattos of the Caribbean were struggling against the oppressive laws of the Paris Assembly. He had seized the chance to expand his modest ships' brokerage business by trading in arms and had prospered mightily.

Afterwards the whole of the Caribbean had erupted in war and his operations had, perforce, to come to an end; but not before he had amassed a sufficient amount of capital to found the Gold Star Shipping Line.

He had been too busy making money to marry until late in life, he told Kit. He had then taken a wife much younger than himself, a distant relation whom he realised, quite suddenly, had blossomed from a pretty child to a beautiful woman. She, orphaned and forced to earn her living as a governess, had married him gratefully enough despite their difference in ages, but had died shortly afterwards in childbirth, survived by the exquisite, doll-like baby girl he had christened Isobel.

Isobel! Pretty, pampered, Isobel, who resembled her mother and was adored by her father; she looked like an angel, with golden hair and a flawless skin and eyes like violets. Spoilt, wilful Isobel, whose perfectly shaped lips uttered nothing but platitudes, who had no humour in her make-up and whose brain must surely be no larger than a pea.

She represented the one area in Kit's life with which he was dissatisfied. It was not even, he reflected bitterly, as if she were at all rewarding in bed. On the ever-diminishing occasions when he made love to her, he always had the feeling that he was embracing some inanimate lay-figure, a china doll who could never warm to his touch however skilfully he exerted himself. And she had not even given him an heir! Two girls only inhabited the nursery – Kate and Marianne – pretty children, both of them; he loved them dearly, but they were hardly of the same worth as a male descendant to carry on the name.

He looked towards the end of the table where, lovely as ever, Isobel bent her graceful head towards Sir Anthony Trundle. A sapphire pendant gleamed enticingly in the hollow between her breasts, revealed by her low-cut blue dress with its deep, lacy frill. Sir Anthony looked suitably enraptured. Was he thinking that Kit Mallory was a deuced lucky fellow to be married to such a creature? It seemed likely.

There was that, at least, to be said for her. Other men admired her and envied him, not for one moment guessing how bored he was with her. He was even more bored with her than he was with the diminutive Lady Trundle who perched at his right hand like some over-bred lap-dog, all snuffles and wrinkles, and a high, earnest voice that yapped on and on and on. At least he was not called upon to do more than look attentive and smile his charming smile at her, nodding from time to time as if to show his interest. Hastily he adjusted his expression, realising that she had embarked on a dissertation on the evils of slavery. He smiled no longer, but contrived to look suitably concerned. Yes, yes, he agreed. It was indeed barbarous. The sooner it was brought to an end the better.

It was quicker to agree; more fashionable, too, and with luck would keep her occupied for a little longer until he could decently turn to little Mrs. Mountjoy on his left who had already given him a smiling look before turning to the guest on her further side, and who looked a far more entertaining proposition.

"The Reform Bill?" (How had she made that leap from slavery to the franchise? He neither knew nor cared.) "How fascinating and instructive, Lady Trundle, to hear the views of an intelligent woman!"

She was off again. He helped himself to turbot in wine sauce from a dish offered by one of the maids, female acolytes to the two liveried footmen who circled the table under the direction of Saunders, the butler. (Nice little girl, he thought in passing, with a brief smile towards her. Neat figure, amusing little face. New, perhaps. Must be. He would have noticed her if she had served him before.)

Abstractedly he nodded and smiled at Lady Trundle as in agreement, and thus encouraged she continued her dissertation. Storm, Kit noticed, was faring better. He could see his dark red-brown head bent towards the blonde ringlets of the woman on his left, apparently both of them engaged in animated conversation.

How the boy had developed in the past three years! Physically he had filled out. He had grown from lanky youth to well-proportioned manhood and was now someone that any woman would look at twice – and then again, Kit thought with satisfaction. Just like his father.

The changes went deeper than that, however. Three or four years ago he had been eager, but shy and diffident, distrustful of his own judgement. Now there was an impressive confidence about him.

The year spent as purser aboard the new Gold Star packets across the Atlantic had done that. He had been forced to deal with people both rich and poor, had seen life at first hand. Admittedly this had led to a few differences between them, particularly regarding the conditions for steerage passengers; but he was proud of the fact that Storm had fought his corner so valiantly, and had developed a respect for the way he stood up for his principles, however misguided he thought those principles to be. His arguments had, in the end, led to a few minimal improvements. Gold Star could afford them. Poverty at home meant that more and more people were leaving England to make a new life in the Colonies and America.

Kit would have given much to acknowledge Storm as his son. Perhaps one day he would be able to do so, but not while the old man lived. Cyrus Webberley was still the power behind Gold Star even if he now left the day-to-day management to Kit and treated him in every way as the heir apparent, and he still adored his beautiful daughter scarcely this side of idolatory. A new will could be drawn up at any time. It would be the height of folly for Kit to draw attention to past indiscretions. Or present ones, he thought, with a brief and troubled recollection of a certain lady who was growing somewhat tiresome and would have to be shed without delay.

Returning to Storm, he was not going to let the boy go, however, even if the relationship between them remained unacknowledged. Storm still spoke of his eventual return to the Turks Islands, but so far had allowed himself to be diverted. He had, Kit knew, enjoyed the time they had spent travelling the East together, and if the year he had spent as purser were no holiday, at least he had relished the challenge and had learned the business through and through.

After that it had been easy to persuade him to stay yet another year in the London office, putting his knowledge and experience to work – and there was no one alive who could convince him that Storm was not enjoying himself! He seemed to embrace eagerly everything that London had to offer. He dressed in the height of fashion, talked his head off in the city coffee houses where most of his brokerage business was done, frequented theatres, danced the night away in all the best houses thanks to his and Isobel's patronage. Was it likely that he would give all this up to go back to that scrubby little island? It hardly seemed probable!

A wife was what he needed; some wealthy English girl who would ensure that he stayed to enjoy this civilised life. He would give his mind to the matter. There surely must be someone suitable, though not the usual bread-and-butter miss, that was certain. Storm made no secret of his amusement at the affectations of most of the well-brought-up young ladies in society. He needed someone of spirit, Kit thought, looking at him thoughtfully.

God, the boy was like his mother! Kit saw him laugh and move his head and it was as if a knife twisted in his gut.

It angered him, that thinking of Dorcas was still as painful as this. Well, it was some consolation to know that she was suffering, too. He'd succeeded in taking away Storm from her; let her brood on that, those nights when she lay beside that ill-educated, grinning baboon of a husband. How could she have gone back to him? How could she have said that he was a better father?

Silence from Lady Trundle. She was looking at him oddly – and no wonder, for he had lost the thread of her discourse long ago.

"Tell me," he said hastily. "Have you managed to see the latest offering at Drury Lane?"

"Indeed I have, Mr. Mallory –"

Yap, yap, she was off again, and he smiled and nodded, hearing one word in ten.

"Oh, I do so agree, Lady Trundle. A most interesting interpretation."

Gad, that new maid had a fascinating look about her. You'd think she was someone of breeding, with that straight little nose and fine skin. And as for those eyes . . .

Look at him, Storm thought, taking time out from laughing with young Mrs. Craven. He can't keep his eyes away from that maid. The old bastard.

She was worth looking at, he'd admit that. New, surely? Anyway, he hadn't seen her before, and he visited Portman Square often enough.

Kit liked them young. Liked to think of himself as young,

which was why he had stopped Storm calling him Mr. Mallory in short order once they were on the *Stella Maris* together.

It had taken some time for the scales to fall from Storm's eyes. My God, he thought amusedly now; what an innocent I was! How I hero-worshipped the old devil.

Still do, in a way, he admitted ruefully. Can't imagine why, but there it is — there's something about him; a vitality that attracts and charms and makes one forgive and forgive and forgive. And what's more, makes one *believe* the old humbug even when it's perfectly obvious that he's lying through his teeth. Never was there anyone so perfect in the art of manufacturing a plausible tale in order to extricate himself from trouble. Sometimes he gave the impression of believing his own flights of fancy.

What were the chances of the new maid staying out of his clutches? About nine to four against, going on past form.

How frightful to be Isobel; but then, it must be pretty frightful to be married to Isobel, too. She really was the most stultifyingly boring woman in the world — and to think how he had mooned over her as a love-sick adolescent! Even written poetry to her, God help him.

Thank heaven he had insisted on taking lodgings in Black-friars! The constant company of Isobel with her obsession regarding social advancement and her tedious little coterie would have been too frightful to be borne, though he appreciated that it was kind of both Kit and Isobel to press him to live with them in Portman Square.

Their kindness to him had always been phenomenal and for this reason there was much he would do to avoid hurting them, but on this matter he had been adamant. He had thanked them warmly, but had gone his own independent way, so that he could live his own life and have his own friends — some of whom, he was aware, would make the Mallorys' hair stand on end.

Perhaps it was because of his unconventional upbringing, the way he had been allowed to run wild and mix with every stratum of society on the island, that he found it so difficult to conform in adulthood. Both Isobel and Kit valued people for their position or what they were able to offer. What they would make of, say, Peter Roman, he could not imagine. Peter Roman was one of his closest friends, a bookseller who had risked imprisonment by selling pamphlets campaigning for a free press. Then there was the journalist William Cawley, who wrote what Kit would undoubtedly consider inflammatory articles about the inequalities of life in contemporary Britain.

Many an evening had he spent with both men, exulting in their enthusiasm for argument, their commitment to reform, their passionate beliefs and biting wit. He loved the thought that he was here at the centre of the world, present at the birth of new ideas and new aspirations.

He had been bowled over at first by the sheer size of London, and was appalled by the poverty of much of it – the crowded courts and alleys of St. Giles where the Irish immigrants congregated, by Whitechapel and St. George's in the east. He saw misery as he had never envisaged it; children undersized and pale as ghosts, heaps of sickening rags that on closer inspection turned out to be old men and women, too battered by life and adversity to do more than wait for death in the shadows.

Set against this was all the teeming life of the docks, with their East Indiamen and tea clippers, whalers and schooners and brigs; Chinamen with pigtails, wealthy merchants, Lascars, slop shops, tally shops, the sound of scraping fiddles and screeching parrots. It had become the breath of life to him.

There was excitement here in the narrow streets and a feeling that great things were about to happen – were happening already. London was growing, pushing outwards away from the river, and the new streets were wide and elegant, lined with grand houses.

Sometimes he wondered if he would ever be able to leave it, but at other moments he could see with his inward eye a golden beach and a sea of surpassing clarity, and blinding white, glittering salt ponds waiting for the rakers. Waiting for him.

At those moments he knew that he would go back. Not quite yet, but one day. He would, he felt sure, know the time when it came.

That new little maid was something to see! What was it that made her stand out so? Normally maids were little more than a pair of hands, hardly noticeable unless they did something frightful like pouring soup down one's shirtfront or breaking the best Waterford, but this girl was different.

Her small, heart-shaped face was serious and her eyes – such eyes! – were intent on her duties, looking always to Mr. Saunders for silent instruction. A slight inclination of his head (or rather the nose, Storm corrected himself, for this organ was of a size and colour to make all other features insignificant) sent her scurrying to the end of the table, underlip caught between her teeth, to proffer a dish yet again to Sir Anthony.

She looked up and saw that she was the subject of Storm's scrutiny. Her eyes were clear grey, fringed with black lashes, and for a moment she returned his look, unabashed – even a little amused, before lowering them once more to the dish she held in her hands.

A smile would be worth witnessing, he thought. He wondered if it would be possible to provoke one, but dismissed the idea instantly. It would not be fair on her. Maids were regarded with disfavour if they showed any emotion in public, and Saunders was a formidable disciplinarian who would make her life not worth the living if she disgraced herself. He had been told a few things about Saunders by Frank, the under-footman, with whom he had shared the odd drink at the Lamb and Flag, a nearby public house – another association which would have caused Kit and Isobel to raise their hands in horror. Whoever heard of drinking with a footman? Storm, however, had found the revelations of life below stairs instructive and fascinating. Saunders, he had concluded, had much in common with some of the less humane boatswains of which his father had spoken in the past.

"Do tell me," Mrs. Craven said to him, turning in his direction once again. "Where is it you say you come from? I confess I have never heard of such an island and feel quite certain you have fabricated the whole story! Come now – admit that this Grand Cay, or whatever you call it, is no more than a figment of your imagination."

"Madam," Storm said, "I assure you it's no figment. The merest pinprick on the map it may be, but it exists. Blue sea surrounds it, and there are white beaches of finest sand –"

Mrs. Craven opened blue eyes wide.

"How *wonderful*," she breathed. "It sounds like Paradise."

"When I am rich," Dorcas said, "which is not likely to be in the foreseeable future, I shall leave this island on the first day of July and not come back until the end of October. I shall go to some cooler clime; Halifax, perhaps, or Boston."

She could have bitten her tongue out. Why mention Boston, the place where poor Dr. Bettany had once again been so shamefully treated? She laid her sewing down and looked at him apologetically.

"Oh Hugh, how wretchedly tactless I am! Forgive me, I beg you. It was but a slip of the tongue, for I declare after its treatment of you I am as unwilling to honour Boston with my presence as you must be. The heat has a numbing effect on my brain."

Hugh Bettany laughed.

"The time will come, no doubt, when I'll feel less bitter against the place. It's a fine city, no one can gainsay that. If you have never been, then certainly you should go – but alas, minds there seemed as closed to new ideas as anywhere else."

"Well," Dorcas picked up her sewing again. "It's an ill wind. We've gained from Boston's folly."

It was no empty politeness on her part. The thought that there was, at last, a medical man on the island was a comfort that was quite impossible to express.

"At least I feel I shall be of real use here," he said. "The worst thing was being banned the hospital and the lying-in wards where there was so much that needed to be done. The frustration was quite maddening."

His face had thinned and aged, Dorcas saw. Marcia had told her that still he did not sleep well, pacing restlessly on the beach and returning again and again to his studies. It would, perhaps, be good for him to immerse himself in matters such as broken bones and cut fingers, childish epidemics and ageing, arthritic limbs, as well as in the delivery of babies.

"Do you think," she asked lightly, in an attempt to amuse him, "that intense heat truly does affect the brain? I swear there are more dramas, more brawls, more umbrage taken during the summer months than at any other time of the year, particularly when it's as hot and still as it is at the moment."

"It would be more surprising if there were not! Tempers are naturally shorter."

"Small issues seem to loom so large. Take Mrs. Grimshaw, for example. She has taken to her bed, I understand, and refuses to speak to a soul simply because she was not bidden to Waterloo to meet some visiting scion of the Misick family. And Mrs. Porrit made a point of coming up to me in the street to say that I was not on any account to think she was hurt, though her expression was dark as night, but did I realise that she and *not* Mrs. Everard had been in charge of the preserves stall at the church fête for the past three years and why, therefore, had I transferred her to the fancy needlework stall as a mere assistant! In vain did I explain that the fancy needlework stall was twice as important. She had decided to be offended, and offended she was. Then, of course, there's all the controversy surrounding the Revival."

"Revival? What Revival is this?"

"Have you not heard? Then I shall tell you quickly before Zachariah comes in, for he has banned any mention of it and I can hardly blame the poor man, for he is beset on all sides."

"This is a religious Revival, I take it? They abound in Boston in certain quarters."

"Would that America had kept the idea to itself! Our Mr. Winklow is, thank heaven, about to leave us – but for one whole week we shall be honoured by the presence of not one but two Methodist missionaries on the island. A Revival is to be the outcome; a whole week when the Methodists wallow in prayers and repentance and are washed in the blood of the Lamb. Forgive me, I sound most dreadfully irreligious and truly I do not mean to be so, but I have been subjected to such a bombardment on the subject! Bathsheba is in her seventh heaven."

"Such occasions are a great source of drama."

"I have always said so; but surely when drama merges into hysteria, should we not then become concerned? Both Zachariah and I believe we should."

"Then Zachariah is against it?"

"No, no – this is his dilemma! He has fought long and hard for the principle of freedom of worship for the slaves. As you well know, there are many against it, and his battle has been far from easy. Though he deplores some of their excesses, he will defend to the death the right of the Methodists to hold whatever meetings they wish. He donated quite a substantial amount to the building of their church and has never subscribed to the theory that their missionaries preach sedition. However, Mr. Winklow and the whole idea of this Revival disturb him somewhat."

"Is there nothing that can be done to prevent it?"

"Nothing that wouldn't cause much ill-will and resentment – unless you could lace all the drinking water with a powerful sleeping draught, so that all the members of the congregation snore in their pews instead of screaming and shouting and beating their breasts."

"Easier, perhaps, to slip senna into Mr. Winklow's tea. That might, one imagines, give him something else to think about."

They laughed together.

"Oh, if only you could!" Despite her amusement, Dorcas sounded genuinely regretful. "Alas, I can think of nothing else that would suffice. It is, in fact, against the law to forbid such meetings, whatever Willis Trotman says."

"He would stop it if he could, of course. Dorcas, while on the subject of Trotman —"

Hugh hesitated for a moment and Dorcas saw that some deeper concern was troubling him.

"What is it?" she prompted, as his silence lengthened.

"It's Emma I'm worried about. I was called to see their little boy, Daniel; he has a troublesome cough. Nothing serious, you understand, but I understand her concern. It's impossible to be too careful in a climate like this."

"She's a good mother to those children, whatever else one might think of her."

"She seemed —" again he hesitated. "I hardly know how to put it. Distrait, I suppose. Disorientated."

Dorcas frowned.

"Mentally disturbed, you mean?"

He brushed this aside with a gesture of his hand.

"She suffered a miscarriage quite recently, I understand. It could be a case of simple melancholy — if melancholy is ever simple! She has a right to mourn."

"And no doubt mourns alone," Dorcas said. "I can't believe that Trotman is of any comfort to her, for all his fawning affection in company. To be honest, Hugh, I have long been worried about her. Three babies and two miscarriages in four and a half years of marriage is too much for any woman!"

"I agree. She must be allowed a respite. Is it any use asking Zachariah to speak to Trotman?"

Dorcas gave a short laugh.

"He'd listen to nothing that Zack says. Poor Emma! I could try having a word with her, perhaps, but she usually makes it clear that she wishes to discuss nothing with me."

"I'm not at all sure that she's in a fit state to discuss anything. I tried myself to suggest, tactfully I hope, that a longer period of recovery might be in order next time before embarking on another pregnancy, but it was plain she had no wish to speak of the matter. I'm to see Daniel again tomorrow, so will make another effort to speak to her of her own health."

"You're quite sure there's nothing really wrong with Daniel? He's a lovely little boy! He reminds me so much of

276

Davey — and Zack too, of course. And speaking of angels, here he comes."

She looked towards the door with such an expression on her face, that Hugh Bettany felt as a child must feel when excluded from a birthday party.

Envy is one of the seven deadly sins, he reminded himself; and immediately remembered the other sins he had lately been charged with, back in Boston. Arrogance, pride, want of respect. How it had hurt, how empty he had felt when he had been forced to abandon the work that had driven and obsessed him all the days of his adult life.

Perhaps even turning his back on this would lose its bitterness if there was someone like Dorcas waiting —

Stop it, he cautioned himself. Be thankful for friendship.

He rose to clasp Zachariah's hand.

Emma listened to the child crying in the night. Cautiously she sat up, looked down at her husband for a moment, then, reassured that he was asleep, tried with the minimum of disturbance to slip from the bed.

"Where do you think you're going?"

She had been wrong. He was not asleep, and he shot out a hand with a grip like iron the moment she made a move, imprisoning her and jerking her back to the bed.

"It's Daniel, Willis. He's crying."

"You think I can't hear him? Leave him! He'll be quiet soon enough. He'll learn to hold his noise if you don't go running to him every minute."

"He's not well. You know he's not well."

"I knew you'd make a milksop of him."

"Willis, he's only a baby — not three years old yet! Besides, he'll wake the others."

"I'll make him stop." He had pushed her back on the pillow and was already getting out of bed himself. "I'll not take any nonsense from him."

"No Willis — let me go. Please don't hurt him, whatever you do —"

He was standing now, and looming over her, the moonlight that came in through the uncurtained window making his shadow monstrous on the bedroom wall. She made another effort to rise, but once more was pushed back.

"You can hold your noise, too," he said.

"Willis, *please*! I beg you —"

277

She wriggled from the bed and pattered over bare boards as he turned to leave the room, but the door was slammed in her face. For a few moments she stood with her head resting against it, shivering slightly in the air in which there was no hint of chill. There was a weakness in her limbs, a roaring in her head. She should be there with her child, she thought with rising desperation, but she seemed unable to move.

After a while the crying stopped. She raised her head and listened to the silence. What did it mean? What had Willis done to achieve it? With dragging, uncertain footsteps she stumbled back to bed.

"You see?"

Willis was back, a note of satisfaction in his voice as he climbed into bed beside her. "You're a fool. It's firmness the boy needs. You make a rod for your own back."

"He's sick," Emma said, but faintly and hopelessly. Her husband was a huge, threatening, suffocating presence beside her. Of late she had noticed this strange phenomenon. When he was close to her like this, she often found it difficult to breathe. She held herself rigid as far away from him as possible, her breathing shallow, her eyes tightly shut.

She heard him laugh, heard the bed creak and felt it sag as he moved towards her. She cringed as she felt his hot breath on her cheek.

"No, Willis," she said, but with as little conviction as before. "No, please Willis. I'm so tired."

"You're always tired. Tired, tired!" His hands were rough as they seized her nightdress, his weight insupportable. "God, what a wife I landed myself with."

The rushing in her head grew louder and louder, and when finally his weight was lifted and the intolerable pounding was done, she lay without sound or movement, feeling in some strange way as if her mind had left her poor, violated body and was looking down on her from some other place.

For a long time she lay sleepless, incapable of thought, conscious only of a misery that could have no possible end.

Yet surely, it must end some time, she thought at last. Everything ended eventually. And on the heels of this came another thought.

Death was the end. He'd not stop until he had killed her.

"Praise be to God," Gilligan said one day towards the end of September. "For once a shipment has come in at the right time and I've silks and satins in stock the like of which ye've never seen, and bonnets as well. Now, wouldn't ye be wanting a bonnet for the Revival, Mrs. Hardiman, ma'am? I'm tellin' ye, the world and his wife will be dressed up to the nines for the occasion."

"I'm not at all sure I'll be going."

Gilligan, a little more wrinkled, a little more rum-soaked than when she had first made his acquaintance, shook his head sympathetically.

"And I'd not be blamin' ye for that, ma'am — no, indeed I would not."

"You're not going yourself, I take it?"

"Sure, what would a good Catholic like me be doing among all those Methodies? Will I show ye the bonnets, Mrs. Hardiman? Never mind the Revival — a lovely lady like you needs a new bonnet every now and again. Tell ye the truth, there'll not be too many among the gentry that put in an attendance for the place will be crowded with slaves and rakers galore, but I've shifted a bonnet or two on the strength of it! Will you look at them, now? Did ye ever see the like of them? And look at these fans! Carved ivory, they are, just off the boat from New York. Did ye ever see workmanship like it?"

Dorcas, who had intended to buy buttons and thread and nothing more, was diverted in spite of herself, and picked up the fan he produced from its box.

"It's lovely," she said. "My grandmother had one much the same. Chinese, isn't it?"

"Now, haven't ye hit the nail plumb on the head? It came from New York, right enough, but the sailors were telling me there's a place called Chinatown there where you'd be forgiven for thinking you were in the heart of Shanghai, for never a Christian face do ye see there. You've travelled yourself, Mrs. Hardiman. You've likely seen it."

"No," Dorcas admitted. "I haven't seen it, but I have heard of it."

"A heathenish place it sounds, right enough, with the New Year falling in February. Can ye see the sense of that, now?"

"Different places have different customs, Gilligan."

"Never a truer word, Mrs. Hardiman, ma'am. So ye'll not be taking a fan, nor a bonnet either?"

"Not just at the moment, thank you. Just the thread and

these bone buttons. You'll not be making your fortune from me!"

"I'd not know what to do if I had one, ma'am, and that's the plain truth of it." He grinned at her as he wrapped up her purchases. "All I ask is a steady trade and a quiet life – and the Lord alone knows if I'm to be granted it, or anyone else for that matter." He leaned forward across the counter and lowered his voice. "Have ye heard the rumours, Mrs. Hardiman?"

"Rumours?" Dorcas laughed. "I gave up listening to those long ago. There are more rumours than salt on this island."

"Isn't that the truth, now?" Gilligan, however, was not to be thwarted. "It's that Haitian woman from Backsalina, ma'am," he said. "It was said in the saloon last night that she's prophesying disaster if the Methodies go ahead with this Revival. She's saying the whole place will be struck by a thunderbolt sent from heaven –"

"Oh, really!" Dorcas looked at him with exasperation as she took her goods from him. "You shouldn't repeat such things, Gilligan, for you know as well as I do they are started by those who are against the Methodists."

"Well now, ma'am, you may have the right of it there, for it was Mr. Trotman himself who told me of it and the Lord alone knows he'd do anything to stop them in their tracks. But there were sailors in the saloon who said such things had been known –"

"Sailors are full of stories, as you well know! Gilligan, I do beg you not to repeat this for emotions are quite high enough without the stimulus of malicious rumours."

Despite Gilligan's assurances that henceforth his lips would be sealed, it became clear to Dorcas that the rumour had already received credence in some circles, for it was told to her as a matter of gospel truth no less than three times during the next ten minutes.

"I don't like it at all," she said later to Zachariah. "When or where this thunderbolt is supposed to strike is not clear, but plainly the whole purpose is to create panic in the minds of the slaves. Gilligan admitted that he was told it by Trotman. It would not surprise me in the least to know that the Haitian woman knows nothing of it, and that Trotman fabricated it to keep the slaves away from the meetings."

Zachariah admitted wearily that certainly such a ploy would not be beyond Willis Trotman.

"I am tired to death of the arguments surrounding this whole occasion," he said. "A religious service is one thing, but this is being turned into a three-ringed circus. All through the week there are to be services at the slave barracks, with the climax at the church on Saturday evening."

"If you ask me," Dorcas said, "Gilligan is likely to be the main beneficiary. He is apparently doing a brisk trade in new bonnets! He told me, though, that not many of the 'gentry' appeared to be going, so I trust that will include us."

"Oh my dear, I think I must go." Zachariah took her hand between both of his, his expressive face clearly demonstrating that duty warred with inclination. "I've argued so long and so heatedly for the Methodists' right to preach to the slaves that if I turn my back on them it will seem as if all my arguments were so many empty words. No, I fear that it will be my duty to go, but naturally you need not –"

"If you go," Dorcas said, "then I go with you. In any case, Bathsheba would be disappointed if I did not. Martha and Mary and Ruthie are having brand new dresses for the occasion – and *I*," she added, as if a happy thought had just struck her, "I shall, perhaps, buy a new bonnet after all."

Seventeen

The latest vessel in the Gold Star fleet was the *Southern Cross*, a packet of some five hundred tons, built on the Thames for the express purpose of taking migrants to Van Diemen's Land, for it was not only convicts who were now making a new life on the far side of the world.

"How many years before such a ship is powered by steam?" Storm asked Kit. "It won't be long, in my opinion."

"I wonder." Kit looked dubious. "A paddle steamer across the Channel is one thing, but to go such distances – why, where would one put the passengers, with so much fuel to carry? I can't see it coming in my time, Storm, but perhaps when you have the running of Gold Star things may be different."

When *he* had the running of it? Storm noted the form of words, but made no comment, assuming they were spoken lightly and should be taken equally lightly. In any case, he had never made any secret of his intention to return to the Turks Islands sooner or later.

The *Southern Cross* was now being commissioned and for the whole of that week, Storm had hardly set foot in the office in Leadenhall Street, being much occupied with the engagement of the crew and the provisioning of the ship. It was on the dockside that Kit's scrawled note was brought to him.

Far too long since we have seen you [he had written]. If you've nothing better to do, dine with us tonight. An early arrival will please the children – we'll forgive your lack of dress if it suits to come straight from the dock, for it's nothing formal. Just myself and Isobel.

Storm took the paddle steamer to Westminster when his work was finished and walked from there. Life, he thought as he strode up Regent Street, was full of diversity; last night a helping of eel pie in a tavern by the river, washed down with ale and a heady brew of fighting talk from Peter Roman and Will Cawley and others of their persuasion. Tonight, one of Mrs. Pratt's delicious dinners in Portman Square and some – he profoundly hoped – of Kit's excellent claret.

He would welcome a chance to see the little girls. Kate was a bright child of four, Marianne only eighteen months younger. He often went out of his way to spend some time with them. It was necessary to go out of his way, for they were seldom seen outside the nursery. Isobel played with them for a few moments in the afternoon if she chanced to be at home and was otherwise unoccupied, but normally they were left to the care of their nursemaid.

He consulted his watch, and slowed down a little. The hour was earlier than he had thought; not yet four thirty. The dullness of the day, allied to the fact that he had been down at the dock since six o'clock that morning, had made him lose count of time and think it much later. Perhaps he ought, after all, to take a cab back to Blackfriars, wash himself and change his clothes. A day spent in warehouses as well as on board the *Southern Cross* had made him feel considerably less than immaculate.

But Kit had said come early, never mind dress. He would go on now that he had come so far, he decided. No doubt someone would be ready enough to provide him with soap and water; it would not be the first time that he had made himself at home in Portman Square.

He pulled the bell at the side of the colonnaded door and was surprised when it was opened to him, not by Saunders the butler, but by the maid he had first noticed during the dinner party earlier in the year. She was, he thought, even prettier than he remembered.

"No Saunders?" he asked with a smile as he handed her his hat.

"No, sir. Mr. Saunders is indisposed."

Her mouth was determinedly grave, but her brilliant, black-fringed eyes seemed to sparkle as if laughter were only just beneath the surface.

"Really? Nothing serious, I hope?"

"He was stung by a wasp. Mrs. Pratt is putting the blue-bag on him now."

She was biting her lip, eyelids lowered. What was the accent? Storm asked himself. Whatever it was, it was enchanting.

"Dare I ask," he said, "where this intrepid wasp had the temerity to bite our good Saunders?"

"On his nose, sir." She looked up then, no longer able to control the illicit mirth, and clapped a hand over her mouth. "Oh, 'tis wrong to laugh, sir!"

But Storm was laughing too, for even if the incident was more tragic than comic, certainly to Saunders, there was something inherently risible in the picture of a blue-bag being applied to the formidable proboscis: and underneath the amusement there was sheer delight at the sight of the girl, so fresh and young and artless. I knew she would look like that when she smiled, he thought. I knew it!

"We ought to think shame," she said. "Laughing at the poor man."

"So we should. Poor Saunders!"

"Poor wasp," she said, and giggled again.

He could have looked at her for a long time, but suddenly she sobered as if remembering her duties.

"Mrs. Mallory 'ent at home, sir. She's at Mrs. Mountjoy's, but the Master mentioned to Saunders as you'd very likely be here early and said we was – *were* – to show you upstairs to the yellow room to wash yourself, like, seeing you was – *were* – come straight from the dock. If you'd wait one minute, sir, I'll fetch hot water."

He watched her retreating form with pleasure as she went towards the kitchen regions. She was rounded where she should be rounded, slim where she should be slim. Her dark hair was a little unruly and escaped from her frilled cap in small tendrils around the back of her neck. What part of the country did she come from? Her voice had a country burr that was unfamiliar to him: a softness which sounded alien in London.

In a few moments she was back holding a brass can, and he followed her up the wide staircase as she led the way to the room that had been set aside for his use.

"Are you happy here?" he asked her, more to give himself an opportunity to hear her voice once more than for any other reason.

"Oh yes, sir. Mr. Saunders is a bit strict, like, and the work is hard, but all in all it en't – *isn't* – too bad."

"You come from the country, don't you?"

Unexpectedly she turned round and wrinkled her delightful nose at him.

"You'm making mock of the way I speak!" Untroubled, she laughed at him over her shoulder. "Well, laugh away, sir. Violet – Mrs. Mallory's maid – is teaching me to speak proper, and soon you'll take me for a lady."

"I take you for a lady now."

"Go on with you! I'm naught but a country bumpkin – a Cousin Jenny."

The way she said it, the laughter in her voice, made it clear that this, whatever it was, was nothing to be ashamed of.

"Who or what is a Cousin Jenny?" Storm asked.

"Cousin Jacks and Cousin Jennys – that's what they call the Cornish."

"And what's your real name, Cousin Jenny?"

"Daisy, sir."

They had reached the top stair and for a moment she hesitated, looked back at him doubtfully as if she were about to say more, then went on without speaking further, along a corridor to the second door on the left. She went inside and set the can down on the wash-stand.

"There's towels and all made ready, sir."

"Thank you, Daisy."

She smiled at him again, but guardedly this time, as if she had something on her mind. She half-turned to leave the room, but stopped and looked towards him again, giving the impression of indecision. Storm looked at her enquiringly.

"My name en't really Daisy," she said.

"No? Then why –"

"It's the mistress, sir. She says that's what they all must call me, for Loveday's too fancy a name for a maidservant. 'Tis not that I mind, sir, not exactly, just that sometimes I feel as if – as if –" She shook her head helplessly. "As if Loveday en't there any more."

"Loveday!" Storm had moved a little closer to her. "It's a lovely name! Why shouldn't you have a fancy name?"

She looked up at him, her eyes wide and earnest.

"Tidn't that fancy, sir. Not really. 'Tis a Cornish name, see."

"I shall call you Loveday."

"No, no, you mustn't!" The grey eyes widened still further, this time with alarm. "The mistress would know I'd been talking to you, and she'd be some mad with me."

"Very well. But whenever I say 'Daisy', you'll know that in my heart I'm calling you 'Loveday'. Then you'll know that

Loveday is there, all right. Loveday, if I may say so, is very beautiful."

The colour rushed to her cheeks, but though confused she smiled at him shyly. There was a small indentation that came and went at the corner of her mouth, he noticed. The urge to touch it was almost irresistible.

"Thank you, sir," she said. "I s'pose I'm some foolish to worry about what I'm called."

"I don't think so. My name's Storm and that's fancy and foolish enough for anyone, but I'd be horrified if anyone decided to call me James or John. Tell me, what brings you to London?"

"My auntie, sir. My mother and father and brother all died of the cholera. Ever so many in our village died. She's kind, my auntie. She'd married and left the village by the time the cholera came. Her husband, my Uncle Will, couldn't find work so he came up to London, and because I was the only one left they brought me, too. He found work at the docks, as a lighterman with Gold Star —"

"I see, I see! So it's all in the family."

"In a manner of speaking, sir."

She smelled clean and faintly sweet, like honey. For a moment they looked at each other without speaking — assessing, seeking, wondering. A formidable gulf of class and position divided them, but in spite of it there was something in each that reached out to the other. Storm saw her frown a little as if she were troubled by something beyond her understanding.

"Mr. Saunders said you'd likely be having tea in the nursery," she said. "I'd best get back to work downstairs."

He smiled and nodded, but spoke her name before she reached the door so that she turned round once more.

"Yes, sir?"

He lifted his hands and let them fall again.

"I don't know. Forgive me! I simply wanted to say your name again and see you smile at me."

She did smile, but it was a small, dutiful affair and the look she gave him was wary and measuring as if she had suddenly realised that if the gulf were to be bridged at all, she was bound to be the loser.

"If you've all you want, then," she said, and left the room before finishing the sentence.

Storm stood where she had left him for a few moments,

making no move towards the warm water she had provided. Fool, fool, he berated himself. It was one thing to admire a maidservant's looks and quite another to flirt with her in a way that might make her think –

What would she think? What did he think? Was he, in the last analysis, any more virtuous than Kit?

Slowly he took off his jacket, unbuttoned his cuffs and turned them back so that he could wash his hands. In spite of his confusion, he smiled to himself, remembering her smile and the eyes and the delectable shape of her.

Loveday, he thought. Loveday.

"My dear boy, it's the coup of the decade," Kit said exultantly.

He had come home in the highest of spirits, cock-a-hoop with success. Over dinner he had explained the reason for his elation. He had that day negotiated a contract with a Mr. Gresham Earnshaw who owned a large cotton mill in Lancashire.

"We're to ship all his exports," Kit said. "Every last yard of cloth."

"I don't understand. Why, with Liverpool on his doorstep, would he ship from London?"

Kit tapped the side of his nose.

"Never underestimate a good salesman, my boy. I have a silver tongue, didn't you know?"

Storm continued to look puzzled.

"There must be more to it than that," he said. "I've always understood that northerners were hard-headed businessmen."

"It makes good business sense as well." Kit gestured to the footman to refill the glasses around the table. "The truth is that Earnshaw was looking for a change. He's been let down a couple of times by the Black Ball Line, goods left overlong in warehouses, that kind of thing. Added to which he sends a vast amount of goods south on the canals for sale in London. What more reasonable than sending the whole of his production by the same means and shipping from here, by the best line in Britain at advantageous rates? So damned advantageous, if the truth be known, that we'll take a loss this year and even next, but in the end the arrangement should pay us hand over fist."

Isobel yawned ostentatiously behind her hand.

"I might have known it would be naught but business that was spoken of tonight," she said. "There was a time, Storm, when your visits were entertaining, but you've become so dull of late."

Storm apologised hastily and begged her to tell him the latest gossip of the drawing-room, since there was no other subject he could think of on the spur of the moment that was likely to interest her.

"We have been invited to Almacks at last," she said, melting towards him. "Did Kit not tell you? Oh, how like him, when it is all I have thought about for so long!"

"The matter did not loom large in my life, my dear."

Isobel shot her husband an irritated look.

"I cannot see how you can dismiss it so. Anyone knows that one might as well be *dead* as live in London and be excluded from the Wednesday balls."

"They say," Kit said in a humorous aside to Storm, "that naught but bread and butter is served and the whole exercise is one of acute tedium."

"As if that matters!" Isobel was shrill with exasperation. "One goes to see and be seen."

"And perhaps," Storm suggested, "to be able to say to one's friends afterwards how bored one has been."

"At any rate, I am having a new ball gown for the occasion. In fact, since winter will be upon us soon, I shall need at least two for I haven't a rag to wear that hasn't been seen a hundred times before. Serena Mountjoy was telling me of a wonderful mantua-maker –"

"Engage her by all means. You well know I've never grudged you a new dress in your life. Which reminds me – Mr. Earnshaw has his wife and daughter with him in London and they, it seems, are of the same mind as you. Life will be insupportable for them without new gowns and bonnets and heaven knows what gewgaws. It would be a kindness if you were to give them the benefit of your advice, for I gained the impression they were not familiar with London."

"Oh, Kit! Such a bore." Isobel pouted. "I have better things to do."

"Nevertheless," Kit said smoothly, "so that we can ensure the continued flow of new ball gowns, you will grant me this small favour, surely?"

"What on earth will I have to say to a pair of rustics?"

"You do them an injustice. Mrs. Earnshaw seemed a pleasant woman when I met her at the hotel, and as for her daughter –" He paused and smiled as he thought of Dorothy Earnshaw – "you will find her amusing, I think."

For once in his life he had assessed the girl with a view to Storm's preferences rather than his own, and had not found her wanting. She had a fresh, artless prettiness and a forthright, unaffected manner that he felt sure would appeal to Storm. Add to this the fact that Gresham Earnshaw was one of the wealthiest men in Lancashire, and it seemed to him that a meeting between the two young people was highly desirable, to say the least. Subtlety was needed, however. He knew Storm well enough by now to know that he bolted like a stag at the barest hint of coercion.

"Where," he asked, feeling that he had said enough on the subject of the Earnshaws for the moment, "is the estimable Saunders tonight?"

"He is indisposed," Isobel told him.

It was Frank, the footman, who had served their dinner, but Storm had been conscious throughout the meal of the trim figure flitting in and out of the shadows at the periphery of his vision carrying the dishes in from the kitchen and handing them to Frank. At this remark he could not resist a quick glance to see Loveday's reaction, and was gratified to note that those clear grey eyes flashed briefly towards him as if in secret acknowledgment of their shared laughter.

"Pour a little more wine, Frank," Kit said. "We've something to celebrate tonight. Do you know, Storm, that cotton constituted two-thirds of the country's exports? I've calculated that this Earnshaw contract could add to our volume of business by forty per cent!"

"It's excellent news," Storm agreed. "But I'm still surprised that he finds it worth his while."

"Whatever happens, his goods must be shipped with the utmost efficiency and despatch. How is the commissioning of the *Southern Cross* progressing?"

"Very well. I'm most impressed with the master –"

"Excuse me, gentlemen." Isobel rose to her feet. "If all you intend is to talk of Gold Star matters, then I shall retire. No, pray do not concern yourselves! I have plenty to occupy me and should not dream of troubling you by demanding that you pay heed to me."

"I feel ashamed," Storm said guiltily when she had gone. "She has every right to feel slighted. It was ill-mannered to exclude her."

Kit, however, waved such considerations aside.

"My dear boy, Isobel is bored by anything I have to say and will be far happier reading a worthless novel. This is, after all, a special occasion for us. I have the feeling that this Earnshaw contract marks an important stage in the company's affairs. Earnshaw is a powerful man, pillar of his community. A little short on pedigree, perhaps, but who are we to cavil at that? He's one of the new industrialists who are certain to wield more and more influence in the years to come, mark my words. Thanks to him, his home town of Garbridge has a fine Town Hall, and they're building a Poor House too, solely endowed by him."

"A public benefactor, then."

"Much respected locally," Kit grinned. "I have his own word on that! Modesty is not one of Mr. Earnshaw's virtues! He talks loud and long of his humble beginnings, but those are left far behind, I promise you. He's built himself a fine house in the hills above Garbridge and it would never surprise me to find he has his sights set on Westminster. Yes, a worthy man is Earnshaw. The salt of the earth, the kind of chap who's pulling England out of the doldrums and making it great, the very backbone of the country."

They sat over the Stilton and the port, Kit growing visibly more mellow as the evening progressed. Coffee and brandy were served, cigars lighted.

"Life has dealt me a good hand, on the whole." Kit lounged back in his chair, exhaling lazily. "There's little I would change if I could have my time over again." He smiled reminiscently, as if he were seeing the past through a haze of brandy fumes – a haze which softened the rough edges, smoothed out irritations. "Oh, there have been disappointments, I'll not deny it, but we can only live one life. If I had married –" He caught himself up, gestured vaguely with his cigar. "If I had chosen another wife, then I should not have had all that I have now. Yes, I've lived a good, full life and most of it I have enjoyed. I've seen the world; had my share of wine, women and song. And now –" He waved his cigar again, indicating the room with its pictures and luxurious furniture. "I have all the material comforts a man could wish for. I even have the most beautiful woman in London for my wife! The fact that she has the intellect of a day-old chick doesn't prevent other men looking at her and envying me."

"Kit, I think perhaps –"

"No, no, don't go, old chap. You've not finished your brandy yet. It's good to talk like this – and we have, after all, something to celebrate." Thoughtfully he drew on his cigar, still smiling.

"Yes," he went on after a moment. "I'm a lucky fellow, there's no doubt of that. I pass my days in an occupation that brings me excitement and satisfaction as well as monetary reward. And I have you, in every way as close to me as any son could be."

Storm looked surprised and a little embarrassed. It was not like Kit to be sentimental.

"It's good of you to say so," he said.

"Words come cheap. It's deeds that matter."

"Well, as to that," Storm said. "You've been good to me in many practical ways, too. You and Isobel have shown me nothing but kindness."

"Kindness? No, no!" Again Kit gestured with his cigar, but negatively this time, dismissing Storm's gratitude. "You've worked your passage, my boy. You've shown remarkable aptitude for this line of business. Webberley is delighted with you. There's naught to stop you taking over from me when the time comes."

"That's very gratifying. But as to the future –"

"We'll not talk of it yet. It will be many a long year before I'm thinking of handing over to a successor, but when I do there is no one I would rather see follow in my footsteps. Haven't I told you I regard you as a son?"

"But Kit, grateful as I am, I've never made any secret of the fact that one day I'll go back –"

"Nonsense, nonsense, I'll not hear of it! Go back to the islands? They're naught but a joke, my boy, with nothing to offer someone such as you."

Storm opened his mouth to argue, but closed it again. It was quite clear that it was the wine talking – Kit's voice, manner, appearance all proclaimed the fact. Tomorrow, no doubt, the whole subject would be forgotten. He got to his feet.

"Kit, it's been a delightful evening, but I have to be up betimes in the morning –"

"One more drink! Don't go just yet."

He groped for a bell to ring, failed to locate it and shouted for Frank instead.

It was not Frank who appeared, however, but Loveday,

pale after her long day's work, her eyes ringed with exhaustion.

"If you please, sir, Frank has gone to his bed on account of the fact that he has to be in Islington to catch the coach at three of the morning. It's his mother's funeral in Colchester tomorrow –"

"Well, I'll not complain at the substitution, will you, Storm? Frank's not near so pretty!"

But Storm was still refusing a last drink.

"It's very late, Kit. It's time we were all abed."

"Nonsense, nonsense! On this night of all nights. Fetch us another brandy, there's a good girl – Daisy, isn't it? Aptly named, wouldn't you say, Storm? She's fresh and pretty as any flower. Sit down, boy, do, I've more to say to you yet."

Unwillingly Storm retook his seat, glancing apologetically at Loveday as he did so. This time she did not meet his eye for her attention was wholly directed towards Kit. She had placed the decanter on the table beside him but as she turned to leave he had caught her apron in his hand and pulled her closer.

"Don't run off, my dear. Let me look at you. Did anyone ever tell you that you have the kind of eyes that would charm the heart out of a man? Is she not lovely, Storm?"

"Indeed she is," Storm agreed. "And very tired too, if I'm not mistaken."

"Is that so, Daisy? Are you tired?"

"Yes, sir." Loveday's answer was barely audible.

"But not too tired to serve your master, surely?"

His tone was flirtatious, jocular, but there was no answering smile on Loveday's face, and the expression in her eyes was veiled by her dark lashes.

Kit laughed as he tugged at her apron.

"Well, I suppose we'll have to let you go, pity though it is to part with you. Run off and get your beauty sleep, Daisy – though I swear you need it less than most."

"Yes, sir. Thank you, sir."

Smilingly Kit watched her go.

"She gives me ideas, that wench," he said, while she was still within earshot. "Ideas below the waist. There's a sort of question in those eyes that any red-blooded man yearns to answer. What do you say?"

The door closed behind her, but still Storm remained silent. Kit's smile died.

"Do I detect disapproval? Dammit, I sent the girl off to bed, didn't I?"

"Hardly before time." Storm's tone was mild, hiding the strength of his feelings. "Have you any idea of the hours your servants work? I've no doubt that girl rises at five to begin her duties at five thirty – and hard duties they are, for the most part."

"All the more reason to enliven her day with a little appreciation. She's not the usual kind of drab we get here, is she? There's something about her – a distinction in her features. She's a girl of spirit, I'll wager. She'd be good between the sheets."

Storm was conscious of a red-hot, whirling core of anger situated somewhere in his diaphragm, but he reminded himself of Kit's condition and fought to contain it. His voice, however, sounded strained and harsh when he spoke.

"I do beg you –" he stopped in mid-sentence as if not knowing how to carry on. Kit raised amused eyebrows at him.

"What do you beg of me, boy?"

"To leave the girl alone. She's very young and innocent. A country girl."

Kit burst out laughing.

"It's you who's the innocent one! Country girls are the most knowing. You'd be surprised at what goes on within the most harmless-looking hay stack. Believe me, a wench such as our Daisy knows what life is all about. So, my lad, it's every man for himself, and may the best man win." Mischievously he shook his cigar towards Storm like an admonitory finger. "But I warn you, my boy, I'm putting my mark on that one."

"No!" The word burst from Storm and caused Kit to look at him with quizzical surprise.

"You have your own plans for her, is that it?"

"No," Storm said again, but this time with less aggression and with a certain amount of secret guilt. The girl did appeal to him greatly, and he could not deny it, yet he felt repelled by the implications of Kit's type of *droit de seigneur* seduction.

Kit continued to regard him with some amusement.

"Surely you're not growing priggish in your old age? If so, I shall remind you of certain nights in Bali –"

"I hope I'm not priggish." Storm spoke stiffly. "It's merely that it seems grossly unfair to assume that a maidservant is fair game. It puts her in an impossible position. Whatever she does, she's bound to come out of it the loser."

"I think you underestimate my talents! I've not had any complaints to date."

"Not even from — what was her name? That red-headed maid who left very suddenly. Polly, wasn't it? I don't suppose she was able to find work again, with Isobel refusing her a reference."

Kit's face had thinned and grown cold as it always did at the barest hint of criticism.

"What a humbug you are, Storm!"

"I'm sorry you should think so." Storm rose again. "I really think I should go. It's not my place to be critical —"

"That, certainly, is true." Not only cold, but icy now, Storm thought. Where was all the expansive *bonhomie* of earlier in the evening? It was the wine talking, he told himself. The sooner he took himself off the better. No doubt all would be forgotten in the morning.

"It's the way I was brought up, I suppose," he said, in an attempt to lighten the atmosphere. "You know my father! He always ties himself in knots in his attempt to see the other fellow's point of view. I'm the first to admit it can be infuriating at times."

"I'm sure," Kit said unsmilingly, "that your father is everything that is excellent."

"He is a little hard to live up to at times." Storm was blissfully unaware of any sarcasm. "There's a kind of simple goodness about him that affects people, in spite of themselves. His standards are such that they are bound to form a yardstick —"

Abruptly Kit got to his feet, brandy glass in hand.

"You'd better leave," he said. "Just get out. I've had enough of your sanctimonious platitudes."

He swung away towards the dying fire, leaving Storm to stand uncertainly for a moment.

"I'm sorry to have offended you, Kit," he said at last. "The truth of it is we've both had too much to drink. You cannot surely think I have anything but the warmest regard and gratitude —"

"Did you not hear me? Get out, I said."

Helplessly Storm looked at his averted back, sighed and shrugged.

"Good night, Kit," he said quietly, and left as he had been ordered.

There was no one now to see the look of cold and relentless anger on Kit's face, though the expression was one that Dorcas might have recognised.

Was he never to get the better of that goddamned peasant? he asked himself. Was that smiling, capering little ape to haunt him all his days? By all that was holy, hadn't he just laid the whole world at Storm's feet?

With what result? He'd had Hardiman thrown in his face once again, held up as a shining example, revered as some kind of plaster saint.

In his anger he clasped his glass so convulsively that the stem broke and with an oath he hurled it into the depths of the fire so that briefly the dregs of spirit flared and died. And with that bright flame his determination was rekindled.

Hardiman would not win. The final victory would be his. One day Storm would, of his own free will, renounce the dubious life that the islands had to offer and would take his place as Kit's son; unacknowledged, perhaps, but still his son for all practical purposes.

It would be a sweet victory – and it would come, it would come; he had no doubt of it. There was, after all, still a card or two to play.

Still the community in Grand Cay waited and still the missionary did not come. There were rumours of storms around Jamaica.

"May the Good Lord keep him safe," Bathsheba said earnestly as she went about her work.

Dorcas's prayer was somewhat different. She wished the man no harm, but prayed that somehow he might be delayed until Mr. Winklow had left the island. With any luck the new man might be more moderate, less of an orator, more wary of whipping up the emotion so beloved of Mr. Winklow. She was persuaded by Bathsheba into attending one of his special services and had been horrified by the evidence of mass hysteria she had seen, brought about by the almost loving detail with which the man described the torments in store for the sinful.

"The Revival will mean the same, only much more of it," she said anxiously to Zachariah. "It cannot be good for simple folk to have their fears preyed on in this way."

The heat continued unabated and salt was being shipped every day, bushel after bushel. Vessels came and went in the harbour. Trotman looked very pleased with himself these days – a cat with the cream – as well he might, Dorcas thought, with Cahills apparently enlarging their order. She wondered what he did with his money. Emma appeared to spend very little and always looked drab and ill-dressed, while the house was as dilapidated as ever.

Thankfully Daniel seemed quite restored to health, his cough completely gone, but Emma still gave cause for worry. There seemed little that Dorcas could do, however. It was only occasionally that Emma responded to any invitation to Tamarind Villa though she was often asked to bring the children to visit, and never had Dorcas and Zachariah been invited over the threshold of the Trotman House.

"Is all well with you, Emma?" Dorcas asked one morning when they met in the street and Emma had rejected her plea that she should call into Tamarind Villa for a cup of tea. She was struck by Emma's vague manner and the emptiness of the gaze that was turned upon her.

She made no reply, but gave a brief and meaningless laugh.

"If there is aught I can do –" Dorcas began; but already Emma was edging away.

"No, no, there is nothing. All is perfectly well."

"Then let us meet again when you have more time –"

But Emma had scuttled off with a fleeting glance over her shoulder as if she expected to be pursued, leaving Dorcas to continue on her way feeling far from easy about her stepdaughter.

The day dawned at last when the new missionary arrived.

"Praise de Lord, Miz Dorcas," Bathsheba cried, lifting her eyes and hands to heaven. "Mr. Short done come. Now we have de Revival."

September was all but finished, the temperature was high, the air oppressive still.

"This is the worst possible time for it," Dorcas said to Zachariah. "Emotions run so high when it's as hot as this."

"Sweetheart, if I've told you once, I've told you many times. You need not come! It's only a cussed sense of duty that tells me I ought to be present. Believe me, I'd give much to spend Saturday evening sitting on the porch with you, a glass of rum in my hands."

"And I've told *you* that if you go, I go."

"Why haven't I been blessed with one of those biddable wives who do what they're told?" Zachariah demanded of heaven.

"If that's what you wanted, then you should have thought of it a little earlier."

The new missionary was a Mr. Short, and contrary to what might have been expected, towered over Mr. Winklow and was far superior to him in appearance. He was dark-haired and dark-eyed and had a smile that seemed to reveal far more than his fair quota of teeth.

"He pray like an angel," Bathsheba reported. "You jes' wait, Miz Dorcas. He pray like you don' never hear before."

The word went swiftly around the island. Mr. Winklow was handing his baton over to a man who was more, not less, inclined to incite hysteria, and Dorcas's heart sank accordingly.

All through the week of the Revival stories were told of men falling down in trances, of women sobbing and fainting, even of speaking in tongues. A charged stillness seemed to hang over the island, manifesting itself in steely skies and a flat, oily sea. In Backsalina, where the poorer white people lived, brother fought with brother, small differences suddenly taking on a significance far beyond their worth, and in the slave barracks there was a feeling of sullen resentment, of uneasy calm of the type that precedes a hurricane.

Dorcas greeted Saturday, the day of the final and most important meeting, with a sense of relief. Soon the island would settle down into its accustomed calm. The cooler weather would surely be with them before long, bringing with it a drop in heightened emotions.

"You're really going?" Marcia asked her on the morning of the meeting.

"I feel I must, to support Zachariah. I gather we're practically alone among the salt proprietors to promise attendance."

"Hugh speaks of putting in an appearance through sheer curiosity – and who knows? He could be useful! The Haitian woman is still said to be prophesying doom. It's to be a thunderbolt from on high, I understand. Tonight is its last chance of putting in an appearance."

Dorcas laughed.

"I've always discounted that rumour. You know it was merely put about by Trotman to discourage the slaves from attending. He's had small success, it seems. Bathsheba says there are dozens turned away each night."

"I'll be interested to hear Hugh's report of it – and yours too, of course." Marcia smiled wickedly. "Come and see me when you're washed clean."

The church was packed to suffocation by the time Dorcas and Zachariah arrived there, both the ground floor and the upper gallery. She looked round for Hugh, but could not see him. Either he had changed his mind about coming or was sitting in some position where he was not visible to her. The sun had gone down by the time the service began, but lamps had been lit and the pulpit area and the platform on which it stood was brightly illuminated.

Behind the platform there were hangings of red from floor to ceiling, and before them stood Mr. Winklow and Mr. Short, clad in black, hands solemnly clasped before them, faces expressionless as they watched the congregation shuffle and jockey for places. The only animation Mr. Winklow showed was soon after Dorcas and Zachariah entered the building when there seemed to be a risk of a fight breaking out at the door.

The two men conferred as the Hardimans were shown to the seats that had been reserved for them somewhere about the middle of the church, then Mr. Winklow nodded importantly as if in agreement with Mr. Short, and set off down the central aisle towards the crowd at the back.

There was room for no more, it seemed, and the doors must be barred to prevent a surge from the people who still wished to come in. A pity, Dorcas thought, on a night so warm, but she saw that the windows were open as wide as they would go. They were tall and narrow and she was a little amused that the Methodists had seen fit to build a church with windows set so high in the wall that it was impossible to see out of them even when one was standing up. Were they so afraid that their congregation's attention would be diverted from the sermon?

Mr. Winklow began the service with a prayer in his usual extravagant style and then a hymn was sung, during which Mr. Short retired to the rear of the platform. With his back to the congregation he was apparently engaged in prayer on his own account, no doubt preparing himself for the oration he was about to deliver.

At the end of the hymn he turned, and for a long, hushed

moment he stared with his dark and hypnotic eyes at those who sat dumbly before him. Not a fan fluttered; hardly, it seemed, a breath was drawn. Then in a voice charged with emotion he announced dramatically:

"We are on the brink of the pit. From the moment of our birth we are dying. From the moment of our birth the pit comes ever nearer and there is not one of us who knows when the trumpet will sound. For some death will be swift and merciful, but others will linger on the brink of decay and decomposition in mortal agony, their agonies made the more unendurable by the recollection of past sins."

Mr. Short, it seemed, had an even more intimate knowledge of hell than Mr. Winklow and could describe it in even greater detail, the smallest of which was not spared on that airless evening. It was not long before there were sobs and low moans from the congregation, and cries of 'Save me, Lord', 'Jesus, help dis sinner', and 'Oh, save me, save me!'

"This is horrible," Dorcas said quietly to Zachariah, who looked over his shoulder to see if there was any way they could leave. The door, however, was still shut and a crowd stood in front of it. Even the centre aisle was full of people, many down on their knees and weeping openly.

"It can't last for ever," Zachariah said as the sobs and moans rose to a crescendo, Mr. Short having arrived at some of the more refined tortures awaiting those sinners who failed to repent.

The hysteria mounting from the congregation seemed like a tangible force. Dorcas could see a young white girl, daughter of the saloon keeper, sobbing into her handkerchief, while beside her, a black girl of about the same age whom she recognised as the daughter of a free carpenter, moaned softly, her mouth squared in horror.

Her attention was momentarily diverted by a vague impression of something flying through the air, but by the time she turned her head there was nothing to be seen. Almost before she had time to wonder if so much emotion had caused her to hallucinate, there was a bang and a flash, then bang after bang after bang, and almost every woman in the place was screaming, high pitched and piercing, and the men were shouting, too, and the whole congregation had turned towards the barred doors and were running, pushing, clambering over pews, fighting to get out while the two preachers stood aghast, impotent in the face of this mass panic.

Zachariah stood his ground and shouted to those around him.

"Stop! Keep still! Stay where you are!"

Dorcas clung to his arm, buffeted this way and that by those from the front of the church who stampeded past them.

"Hold on to the pew," he bellowed in her ear, and freed himself from her grip, climbing up so that he could better be heard, cupping his hands to his mouth and shouting again.

"Stay where you are! Stand still!"

The screams were those of pain now as figures fell down into the crowd and were trampled underfoot. One hand clenched tight to the pew, the other pressed to her mouth, eyes wide with horror, Dorcas stood and watched helplessly.

Some at the front of the church had refused to panic and, like Zachariah, were urging others to be calm, pulling at their arms and shoulders in an attempt to persuade them to return to their senses. By far the vast majority, however, were beyond reason.

And still the doors at the back were closed, while Mr. Winklow wrung his hands from his grandstand position on the platform.

"Zack, Zack, there's Martha —"

Desperately Dorcas pointed far into the crowd where Bathsheba's daughter in her new pink dress was clearly visible for a moment as the crowd parted, then she, too, fell down as others pushed forward on top of her.

Zachariah rushed in like a terrier, hurling back men twice his size, shouting at hysterical women to get back, fighting his way to the point where Martha had dropped from sight.

Dorcas wept as she watched. It was as horrifying as any vision of hell conjured up by Mr. Short. They had descended to the level of beasts, their only thought that of self-preservation.

Suddenly the doors at the back gave and the mob surged out into the night, and the rush of cooler air seemed to bring with it a return to sense and decency.

The church emptied, and the scene was like a battle-ground, with pews battered and broken, groaning figures prone on the floor, and others silent, unconscious, limbs twisted in unnatural attitudes. Others were simply winded, frightened and angry.

Wildly Dorcas looked around for Zachariah.

"Where did he go?" she asked Bathsheba who had come

down, sobbing, from the gallery. "Did you see him? Did he get out? He went to get Martha."

She edged around a broken pew and looked with pity upon a young girl who lay sobbing, blood pouring from an ugly wound in her head.

"Oh, you poor thing," she cried, dropping to her knees. "Bathsheba, someone must run for Dr. Bettany. There are people injured down here behind the pews."

"Mrs. Hardiman!" Mr. Winklow was beside her, taking her arm, but angrily she shook him off.

"Just see what you've done," she said furiously. "See the havoc you caused, stirring up hysteria in that wicked way." She had folded a jacket beneath the head of the girl on the floor and now stood up to face him. "Not to mention your criminal foolishness in locking the door."

"Mrs. Hardiman —" again she shook him off.

"I must find my husband," she said. "I've no wish to speak to you."

Joe was beside her.

"It was something done come t'rough de window. You cain't blame Mr. Winklow."

"Mrs. Hardiman." Again Mr. Winklow was trying to make himself heard. "Mrs. Hardiman, your husband is over here."

He pulled her gently towards the side of the church, and she broke away from him, stepping over the legs of a man who was nursing a broken ankle, picking her way through a litter of hymn books.

"Where?" she asked desperately. "Where? I don't see him?"

Then, suddenly, she did. He lay slumped between two pews, quite still, brown eyes staring blankly at the ceiling. Beside him was Martha, limp and lifeless, arms wrapped around herself in futile protection.

Mr. Short was bending over Zachariah as she fought her way as close to him as possible, doing her best in the confined space to kneel beside him and take him in her arms.

"It's no use, my dear sister," Mr. Short said sadly. "He has gone to his eternal rest, he and the little girl alike."

"No, no!" Angrily Dorcas pushed him away. "Fetch the doctor. He's unconscious, nothing more. Dr. Bettany will save him. He is here, somewhere."

Bathsheba's weeping filled the ruined church, and blindly, gropingly, Dorcas turned towards her.

"Sheba?" Dorcas's voice was uncertain and tremulous. "Sheba, don't cry. Dr. Bettany will come —"

"I'm here, Dorcas."

Hugh was there, standing beside her, and he put an arm beneath her elbow to help her to her feet.

"Hugh, you can save Zack, can't you? He's badly injured —" She faltered into silence at the expression on his face.

"You and Bathsheba must comfort each other," he said gently.

Eighteen

Several days elapsed before Storm and Kit met again for there was still much to be done at the docks and Storm was present only infrequently at the office in Leadenhall Street.

By the time they came face to face once more, it was as if the quarrel had never been. Indeed, Kit seemed determined to make amends handsomely and insisted on taking Storm to lunch – not to the chop house round the corner which was always filled with ship brokers and merchants and men from Lloyd's, but to his club in St. James's where they could converse in comfort.

"All is going well with the Earnshaw deal, I hope?" Storm asked.

"More than well – in fact it's on that head I particularly want to speak to you. Earnshaw has had to go back to Lancashire."

"Not before signing the contract, surely?"

"Alas, yes! The documents were not drawn up in time, but Earnshaw assured me there was no possible slip. He's one of those bluff north-countrymen –" Kit drew his brows together and adopted an exaggerated accent. "'My word's as good as my bond, Mr. Mallory' – you know the type! Not that I was best pleased with Simkins and Lotterby for not producing the contract for him to sign before leaving London. Still, the blame was not entirely theirs and there's nothing we can do about it now. Mrs. Earnshaw took a sudden whim to go home and nothing would prevent her."

"When will it be signed, then?"

"When you take it to Garbridge Hall." Kit laughed at Storm's expression. "Don't look so horrified! A breath of country air will do you the world of good. Earnshaw was kind enough to invite Isobel and myself for a visit, but as you can imagine, no power on earth would drag Isobel away from London just now when she has at last been invited to Almacks. Besides, there's a big society wedding coming up; the Trundles' daughter."

"Surely he'll not take kindly to my taking your place!"

"On the contrary. I explained your importance to the firm and the part you'll be playing in years to come and he expressed the strongest desire to entertain you."

Storm opened his mouth to protest; to say once more that he had every intention of leaving London at some time. Kit, however, was speaking with all the charm and persuasion of which he was capable.

"I'd be glad if you'd go, Storm. It's a question of diplomacy as well as security. I'll have the assurance of knowing that the contract reaches its destination safely, while you will have the opportunity to establish good relations with a man who will be one of our most important clients – if not *the* most important."

Storm stifled his protests which, on reflection, seemed of little importance. When the time was right, he would go – that was all there was to it. Meanwhile it was pleasant to be back in Kit's good graces, and after all, the thought of an excursion to the north was not unpleasant.

"Well, if you put it that way." He smiled at Kit, and smiled inwardly at himself, too. How impossible it was not to be beguiled by the old rogue! "I've not been far out of London yet, it's true."

"And I'll put a coach and pair at your disposal – and old Turner, who's the best coachman I ever employed. You'll enjoy yourself, my boy. Earnshaw has promised a tour of his mill. With luck he may even show you the foundations of the Poor House."

"With such pleasures in store, how can I refuse?"

Kit sat back in his chair and sipped his wine, his look of satisfaction and pleasure clear on his face.

I've done my best for you, Miss Earnshaw, he thought. The rest is up to you.

The boy who had once written poems to Isobel Mallory was not so far from the man Storm had now become.

The coach rattled over rutted lanes and splashed through fords, but any discomfort passed unnoticed. The serene and smiling countryside basking in the glory of an Indian summer, was so pleasing to him that he found himself groping for words that would adequately describe his feelings of delight.

The words, however, would not come and he smiled ruefully to himself. He was no poet, never had been, despite those long-ago verses which even now caused him to squirm with embarrassment.

It would be good, though, to be able to share his joy and satisfaction at all this beauty he journeyed through. A companion would make everything perfect – someone to whom he could say: just look at the curve of that hillside, and that church in the valley, and that cottage garden ablaze with chrysanthemums and michaelmas daisies.

Loveday, he thought; and felt a special kind of happiness as he remembered her eyes and her smile. Kit had been right. For all his denials, he did have designs on her. She was constantly in his thoughts.

He wanted to know more of her; to talk to her, find out what went on in her mind, hear of her dreams and aspirations. What did she think of when she was serving at table? Did she respect or despise those who considered themselves her betters?

She was quick and bright, that much was obvious. He remembered the way she had hastened to correct her speech, and found it endearing. He thought of the family she had lost and was moved with compassion, and admiration too, for in spite of her misfortunes she gave no sign of self-pity.

All the long hours of that trip, Loveday was his companion. Did she ever think of him, he wondered? And if so, did she think of him kindly, or was he tarred with the same brush as Kit? He hoped not.

He wished with all his heart that Kit were different, at least in this one respect, for the attitude he showed towards women was one that he had never been able to admire. He should have married another kind of woman altogether, Storm thought, with all the sagacity of his twenty-one years. Someone who was more of a match for him, who would have kept him amused and intrigued. Poor Isobel! Once one had grown used to her startling physical beauty, she had pitifully little to offer.

No one could say that of Loveday. There was spirit and humour in her face, and instinct told him that to know her well would be a rewarding experience.

It was towards noon on his second day out of London that he realised the character of the land was changing. He passed clusters of buildings around a mine's winding gear and the coach clattered through grey, depressing little towns where houses gave the appearance of being thrown up in a hurry for the benefit of the workers in these gaunt mills whose tall chimneys belched smoke and covered every surface with grime.

This, then, was the industrial north he had heard about; still beautiful when the towns were left behind, with country much grander and wilder than in the south. Bare hillsides swept to immense distances. It had, he thought, an uncomfortable kind of beauty, as if the vastness of it served to underline man's unimportance.

The weather had changed too, a prolonged shower of rain being followed by largely grey skies with only an intermittent, watery sun to lighten the gloom.

He wished profoundly that this long journey would end, for his enthusiasm had waned as his weariness increased. Surely the gates of Garbridge Hall would appear soon. Instead, the landscape seemed to grow more bleak with every passing mile and there seemed few habitations of any kind.

Ahead were crossroads, windswept moorland stretching in all directions, relieved only by isolated clumps of stunted bushes. A signpost pointed the way to Garbridge and Storm's spirits rose, only to fall again when a few yards further on the road divided and there was no indication which fork would take them to their destination.

Irresolutely the coach halted. Storm put his head through the window and engaged in a brief but inconclusive discussion with the coachman.

"I'll go and investigate," Storm said finally. "Wait here – the lane's too narrow to turn if we should choose the wrong way."

It was a relief to get out and stretch his legs. There was a keen wind blowing, but the rain had held off and the sun seemed to be gaining ascendancy over the clouds so that the river that he could see winding through the valley below glinted like a mirror.

It took him only a short time to decide he had taken the wrong road, for it grew rougher and narrower. Yet it appeared to lead downwards towards the cluster of buildings at the far end of the valley, which he assumed must be the town of Garbridge. His information was that Garbridge Hall was situated on the hills above the town, but so far he could see no sign of it.

He could, however, see a movement a few yards down the track, a flash of colour only partially concealed by a clump of bushes growing above and beyond him. He heard the whinny of a horse and thankfully set off towards the sound, glad to find proof at last that there were others alive in this desolate world.

The moment he saw them he knew he had interrupted a moment of importance. The rider of the horse was a girl of, perhaps, eighteen or nineteen, fashionably dressed in a green habit with a high, hard hat set at a jaunty angle, brown hair caught in a snood beneath it.

Standing beside her, holding the horse's bridle, was a young man. He was dark-haired, powerfully built, hatless with his shirt open at the neck, his moleskin jacket hanging open. A gipsy, Storm thought immediately – then corrected himself. There was no reason other than an impression of a kind of untamed wildness why he should think so. The man was probably a perfectly respectable farm-worker.

Both faces were turned towards him as he appeared on the track below them and both expressed wariness and surprise, frozen into immobility as if they were performers in a tableau. Time, for one moment, stood still.

"Good day to you – I wonder if you can help me!" Storm spoke, and time moved on. The black horse with its white blaze tossed its head and the girl put out a gloved hand to gentle it. The man moved his shoulders, pushed his windswept hair out of his eyes.

"Are you lost?" It was the girl who spoke. She was smiling now and looking friendly; which was, Storm thought, more than could be said for her companion who continued to regard him with a lowering look of deep suspicion.

"Yes. I'm looking for Garbridge Hall. Do you happen to know where to find it?"

"None better."

She looked down at the young man and touched him briefly on the shoulder with her riding crop in such a way that the touch took on the character of a caress. They exchanged a few words that were inaudible to Storm; then the man nodded and stood aside, watching as her horse picked its way down the steep hillside. So little said, Storm thought; yet so much drama. The air seemed to tingle with it, as with frost on a winter's morning.

"You have some sort of conveyance?" she asked as she joined Storm on the track. "Or did you drop from the heavens?"

Storm returned her smile. She spoke rapidly and directly, without shyness. Her widely spaced blue eyes surveyed him with interest but with no trace of coquetry, and her mouth seemed to twitch with some private amusement.

"My coach is up by the crossroads," he said. "I'm a stranger in this area."

"I can't imagine," she said, "why you wish to visit Garbridge Hall. Are you not aware that the wild northerners who reside there eat poor southerners alive?"

"I had hoped," Storm replied gravely, "that one look would convince them I should prove uncomfortably indigestible."

She laughed at that.

"Well said, Mr. Hardiman – for you are Mr. Hardiman, are you not? I am Dorothy Earnshaw, so am well qualified to guide you to the Hall. It's not far, but difficult to find if you don't know the area."

"What a happy chance that I saw you!"

She raised her eyebrows at that and gave her private smile, as if she was less than convinced of the happiness of the situation, but she said nothing until they had almost reached the coach. Then she reined in her horse and came to a halt so that he had little alternative but to do the same.

"Mr. Hardiman," she said. "Perhaps you will agree that one good turn deserves another. I wonder if I may ask you a most enormous favour?"

Her eyes were solemn now, wide and pleading.

"Of course. Ask away."

"I should be most obliged if you would refrain from mentioning to my father the circumstances in which we met. He has a most unreasoning dislike of Robby – Robby Holroyd, the gentleman I was speaking to."

Gentleman? Somehow Storm doubted it, but the matter was no concern of his.

"I shall say nothing," he said. "Except that I was delighted to come across you on my lonely way."

Relieved, she smiled again.

"Then I am sure we shall get on together very well," she said.

"You know, of course, that this whole visit of yours was a conspiracy between my father and your Mr. Mallory, don't you?" she asked the next day when they were riding together. "You and I are supposed to fall violently in love. I thought it best to warn you from the outset that this is quite impossible."

They had stopped on a bare hillside so that Dorothy could point out various landmarks that were worthy of his attention, but having exhausted their possibilities, she turned to him and delivered this bombshell.

"But – but –" Storm stuttered, while she laughed at him. Twenty-four hours had not accustomed him to her forthright manner, though he had realised the previous night over dinner that it was not only her blunt nose and chin she had inherited from her father. It was clear that they shared a certain forcefulness in the expression of their strongly held opinions and more than once Mrs. Earnshaw had been compelled to exercise considerable diplomatic skills to restore an atmosphere of calm.

"You surely must be mistaken," he managed to say at last. "Mr. Mallory wanted a certain document delivered in person –"

"And my father was kind enough to invite you to stay and see his mill and enjoy some country air! I saw through it at once. He is for ever dangling eligible gentlemen before me, quite without effect, for my affections are already engaged."

"By Robby Holroyd?"

She had been looking down, fidgeting with her reins, but at this she looked at him with a defiant expression.

"Yes, Robby Holroyd. They have forbidden me to see him, so I'm forced to go against their wishes. My parents, Mr. Hardiman, are people who are aware only of material values. They are hypocrites, nothing more." Her eyes flashed angrily. "On the one hand, my father prides himself on being the son of a man who pulled himself up by his own boot-straps – and on the other, he tries to tell me that Robby isn't good enough for me. One would think us royalty, to hear the fuss he makes. I have no time for such snobbery!"

"I've little time for it myself," Storm agreed. "Still, fathers are always protective towards their daughters, aren't they? They want nothing but the best for them."

"Robby *is* the best! Oh, I know he looks like a gipsy, but he has the soul of a poet and one day the whole world will recognise it and acclaim him." She kicked her horse into motion and slowly they walked side by side along the track. Her face under its stylish, mannish hat was set and determined.

"It's not only Robby's lack of worldly goods that my

309

parents object to," she went on, "but his political ideas also. He espouses the cause of the common man, you see. Have you any *idea*, Mr. Hardiman, how horrific is the lot of the poor peasant? The country has never been wealthier, my father says. Ha! Tell that to the agricultural labourer who has lost his grazing rights, and to the artisans who have no place in the world now that machines produce goods quicker and cheaper."

"I'm very much aware that there's a great deal of in-equality."

"Tell me –" She reined in her horse again and with a change of manner that he was coming to regard as typical, went chasing off after another conversational hare. "Do you like your Mr. Mallory, Mr. Hardiman?"

"Like him?" Storm looked nonplussed. "Yes, of course."

"Ha!" She gave her short, scornful laugh again, and once more set her horse in motion. Storm looked at her, amused and puzzled.

"I take it you differ," he said. "Which is strange in itself. He's usually a great success with the ladies."

"I could tell that from his manner. Oh, how I dislike that kind of man! He looked at me as if he were stripping every item of clothing from my body – and as if I should think myself flattered by it!"

"I've no doubt he thought you attractive."

She laughed at that.

"Oh, I smiled at him and fluttered my lashes and generally acted like the type of brainless ninny young ladies are sup-posed to be. The only difference is that with me it's naught but a game. If he had only been aware of the acidity of my thoughts below my sweet exterior, he would have been horrified! Men like that make my blood boil! We are supposed to be nothing more than decorative handmaidens with not a thought in our heads."

"Believe me, he has many good qualities."

She looked at him with pursed lips and an exasperated expression.

"Well, you'd have to say that, wouldn't you? Come on – this is a good place for a gallop."

She was off, flying across the expanse of grass as fearless and daring in this as in the expression of her opinions.

An extraordinary girl, Storm thought, galloping in her wake – but in many ways a girl who seemed like a breath of fresh moorland air after the coy little coquettes he was more accustomed to. London was full of that kind.

However, if she were right about the conspiracy between Kit and her father, then their hopes were doomed to disappointment. Even without Robby Holroyd in the picture – and heaven alone knew what conflicts that relationship would bring her! – the plan would never have succeeded, for much as Storm was inclined to like her, he felt no stirring of physical attraction to her – any more, apparently, than she felt for him.

The thought that Kit was attempting to arrange his life was irritating, but it was an irritation he shrugged off easily enough. What did it matter? Tomorrow was earmarked as the day he would visit the mill with Mr. Earnshaw, and the day after he would set out on his return journey -- never, probably, to know the end of the story of the heiress and the gipsy, as he had dubbed Dorothy Earnshaw and her wild-looking lover.

He was looking forward to his visit to the mill, for the growth of the cotton industry since mechanisation was the talk of the country.

"You'll not have seen anything like it," Dorothy said to him over breakfast. He thought he detected a dry note in her voice, but could not be sure, since her head was bent demurely over her oatmeal.

"Ay, that's right." Mr. Earnshaw was quick to agree. "We've the latest in machinery, Mr. Hardiman."

"I shall be glad to hear your impressions on your return." His daughter's voice was innocent and wholly devoid of expression, but Mr. Earnshaw replied with more than a touch of defensiveness.

"He'll find nought to criticise. Our volume of production speaks for itself."

Storm had the feeling that he was listening to some other, unspoken argument and it puzzled him a little, but it was soon forgotten as they drove down the hill towards the town.

It was a fine morning and the countryside looked at its best, the trees surrounding Garbridge Hall glowing gold in the autumn sunshine. The small town had come into existence as a centre for local farmers, and it retained the square and the cross where a market was still held each week.

The centre looked clean and prosperous, despite Dorothy's

words regarding the plight of country people, and Mr. Earnshaw pointed out the Town Hall with great pride.

"They'd not have had that without me," he said.

"It's a fine building," Storm agreed politely.

It stood on one side of the square opposite the church of St. Michael's and All Angels' and close to the Bull's Head Inn where even now passengers were boarding a mail coach bound for Manchester.

Storm looked about him with interest.

"I've not seen much of rural life since I've been in England," he said.

"Garbridge is a fine place. I'd not want to live anywhere else." Bluff, blunt-featured, Mr. Earnshaw looked to left and right with satisfaction. "Give me the good fresh moorlands and the friendliness of a small town where a man is known and respected."

"I can see it has much to recommend it," Storm agreed. But even as he spoke he saw that as they left the square behind them and rattled over cobblestones towards the river, the charm of Garbridge diminished appreciably.

The road narrowed and from it led dark alleys with mean, shabby dwellings overhanging them, plaster peeling, broken windows stuffed with paper, and over all the pervasive smell of an open sewer.

Mr. Earnshaw appeared to notice nothing amiss and gestured with the silver-topped cane he carried in his hand.

"Most of these folk work for me. My father started from nothing, you know. Pulled himself up by his own boot-straps. I often wish he'd lived to see his son a Justice of the Peace and one of the most respected men in town, owner of all this property and a cotton mill second to none. It would have given him a deal of pleasure, would that."

Storm gave a polite murmur and was called upon to do no more for they had arrived at the river, beside which stood the vast and forbidding edifice that was Earnshaw's Mill, four floors of ugliness which seemed to throb with the force of the power looms housed within.

Inside, the noise was indescribable. Storm felt assaulted and dazed by it and for a few moments could take in little. The atmosphere was thick with steam and the stench of oil, and the heat was intense.

Earnshaw bellowed information into his ear.

"One hundred looms on each floor, steam driven." Storm

nodded in acknowledgment. "We have to maintain a humid atmosphere or the thread breaks." He nodded again. "These machines are known as 'throstle-frames' – they spin the warp. Over there are the mules for the weft."

Storm nodded again, feeling as if he had entered some vast devil's kitchen, an inferno which bore no relation to anything he had ever seen or imagined. To think of working here, day after day!

It was then that he noticed them – small, wizened children, reddened eyes set in bone-white faces, dressed in little but rags. They darted under the great, clacking machines and appeared to hover dangerously close to unguarded moving parts, galvanised into ever more frenzied activity at Mr. Earnshaw's approach.

The mill-owner laughed at his expression.

"They're used to it," he bellowed.

"But how old –?" There were laws governing the employment of children, Storm knew.

"None under nine years of age." Earnshaw winked at him. Rubbish, was Storm's instant reaction. That one there – boy or girl, it was impossible to tell – could not possibly be more than six.

The hands at the end of stick-like arms were bleeding and the child looked down at them, idle for a moment, until one of the women tending the loom saw the idleness and slapped him briskly about the legs.

Unmoved, Mr. Earnshaw passed up the mill and with mounting horror Storm followed him. The misery of that one child was duplicated over and over, in every direction in which it was possible to look. How could anyone view it with equanimity?

The silver-topped cane lashed out towards a small boy swaying wearily towards a loom and for a moment the child knuckled his eyes and snivelled until another lash sent him scampering away to retrieve a bobbin. Storm caught at Earnshaw's arm.

"He'd 've been in that loom in a trice," Earnshaw shouted. "They have to keep awake."

At least the incessant noise prevented conversation, and Storm was thankful for that. His overwhelming emotions were those of disgust and disbelief. How could any man sleep soundly in his bed at nights, knowing himself responsible for this pathetic, stunted army of gnomes, these pale, misshapen dwarfs who coughed in the foul atmosphere, tired and re-signed like little old men and women at the end of a long, hard life rather than at the beginning?

And grew up, he noted as he looked around him — those that grew up at all — into pale, misshapen adults.

He reminded himself that Earnshaw was his host. He reminded himself of the importance Kit attached to this contract. Though his instinct was to seize that silver-topped cane and slash and slash and slash again at Earnshaw's self-satisfied face, he gritted his teeth and did nothing; and despised himself for his diplomatic restraint.

Earnshaw appeared to take his silence for admiration, continuing to bellow self-congratulatory information into his ear. They went to the floor where the scutching machines opened the raw cotton and where, in an atmosphere thick with cotton fibre, more of the pathetic army swept up the waste.

"We'll not linger here," Earnshaw shouted, banging his chest with his fist. "The fibres choke my lungs."

"What of the children?"

"Eh?" Earnshaw looked at him without comprehension.

Downstairs again, a foreman was engaged in beating a boy for some transgression that could only be guessed at, and though Earnshaw lingered to see the punishment carried out, Storm strode outside and grasping the edge of a low wall beside the river, stood with lowered head as he breathed and struggled for control.

"Was t' noise too mooch, sir?" a voice asked him.

He looked over his shoulder and saw a bent, hawk-nosed man with wispy grey hair who had paused for a moment in his task of stacking boxes. Storm nodded.

"Yes," he said. "That, and other things. Tell me," he added quickly as the man turned away to continue his work. "Those children — how many hours a day are they employed?"

The man hesitated, glanced fearfully over his shoulder towards the mill, and took a step closer to Storm.

"Sixteen hours, sir, unless t' river be low — and they nowt but babbies, some of 'em. Five, six — Earnshaw don't care."

"But the law says nine, surely —"

"Get about your business, Crowther." Earnshaw had come from the mill and the old man did as he was ordered, but slowly and with a look in his eye that was far from the respect his master had boasted of.

"He's a trouble-maker, that one," Earnshaw said, standing and watching him for a moment. "I only employ him out of the goodness of my heart. His father and my father worked together when they were young; hand-loom weavers the pair of them. Well —" He gave the wall a sharp rap with his cane. "We make our own fortunes, I always say. Some go up and some go down."

Storm said nothing, and Earnshaw shot him a glance that was half-amused, half-scornful.

"Did you not care for the noise and the heat?" he asked. "Most visitors feel the same, but to us who are brought up to it, it means nothing."

Storm opened his mouth to speak, counted ten, and closed it again.

"As for the children," Earnshaw continued, walking slowly towards the coach that waited for them. "They're free labour, sent by their parents. In my father's time we had foundling children sent from Liverpool and London. That building there —" He pointed beyond the mill with his cane — "That's where they were housed and fed. It was a good system from our point of view, but it's against the law now."

"Speaking of the law —" Storm began diffidently.

"You're thinking they're under age." Earnshaw winked again. "Well, between us, I'll admit it. The smaller they are, the easier they get under the machines. The inspectors can usually be persuaded to turn a blind eye. It's a matter of competition, you see. If one mill-owner does it, what are others to do? I have to make a profit, after all."

And we, Storm thought with a deep feeling of depression, will profit from your profit; but still he said nothing.

He managed to maintain the appearance of polite, if silent, attention during the journey back to Garbridge Hall as Earnshaw spoke of marketing and exporting his goods, but his thoughts were miles away. He was thinking of his own childhood, of running barefoot on a sandy beach, of diving into warm, sparkling water, of the feel of the sun on his face as he sat on his father's shoulders, happy and secure as he grasped a handful of thick, black hair between his fingers. And at the contrast, he could have wept.

"Well!" Dorothy arrived back at the Hall almost at the same moment as they did, and she reined in her horse beside them. Was she ever out of the saddle, Storm wondered? "What did you think of it all, Mr. Hardiman?"

Storm hesitated only a fraction of a second.

"It was very – instructive," he said.

She laughed at him, head thrown back, a look in her eyes that seemed to say that she saw right through him and was amused by his dilemma.

Storm was thankful to have got away without committing himself further, but at luncheon she returned to the subject.

"Are not the children of Garbridge fortunate, Mr. Hardiman, to have the opportunity of such congenial work?" she asked with apparent innocence, and laughed again at Storm's discomfiture. "Don't tell me you have doubts on the matter? It is so good for them, you know, to be kept short of sleep. It stirs up their dear little intellects, encourages early maturity –"

"That's enough, Dorothy." Earnshaw's bluff smile was unaltered, but his voice was steely and unamused.

"Of course, they're not all appreciative of the benefits," she went on, unaffected by the fury in his eyes. "They have to be beaten frequently to keep them awake – but after all, it's for their own good. It keeps them nimble and on their toes, avoiding the machinery that would mangle and crush –"

"I said that's enough!" His anger undisguised now, her father crashed his fist down on the table. "There's not a child there that isn't sent by his own parents."

"That's very true, Dorothy," Mrs. Earnshaw said. "You should listen to your father."

It was as if she had never spoken.

"They're sent by their parents to augment pathetic wages that barely keep the family above starvation level."

"They're thankful for the chance."

"Thankful?" Dorothy gave a bitter laugh as she turned to Storm. "Do you think they are thankful, Mr. Hardiman? Would you be thankful if you were their parents, seeing your own children mutilated by the machinery or ruined in health by breathing the fibres and foul air?"

"How dare you speak to your father so! Leave the table, miss." Mrs. Earnshaw fairly quivered with outrage.

"Ignore her," her father said, shovelling rabbit pie into his mouth. "She's happy enough to enjoy the benefits provided by the mill. Mr. Hardiman and I understand each other."

"Is that right, Mr. Hardiman?"

Storm looked across the table at Dorothy Earnshaw. She was not smiling now, but her clear and uncompromising gaze seemed to pose the question he had been avoiding all morning.

He switched his gaze to Mr. Earnshaw. He had stopped masticating and was regarding him with an expression that was hard to read. He seemed suddenly on his guard, waiting warily.

Remember your manners, he cautioned himself. This man is your host. Then, violently – to *hell* with manners!

"I confess to being appalled by the conditions suffered by such small children," he said, and heard his voice tremble.

"Oh?" Earnshaw had laid down his fork and was staring at him with eyes that were as hard and bright as marbles. "Oh? Children don't work in London, is that it?"

"Yes, yes – of course they do!" It was a fact of life, children of the poor worked, but never like this. "Never, though, have I seen such pathetic specimens. Those in your mill looked hardly human."

"Are you criticising me?" Earnshaw's face had grown red and his voice sounded hoarse, as if he were being strangled. "You know nothing of my trade, nothing of local conditions, and you come here with your high and mighty London ways, telling me how to run my business –"

"I wouldn't dream –"

"I don't need a young whipper-snapper laying the law down to me. My father built up this mill from nothing – *nothing*, do you hear me?"

"Pulled himself up by his own boot-straps," Dorothy put in impudently.

Earnshaw shot her a quelling glance, recognising her sarcasm and angered by it.

"Exactly," he said harshly. "I've nothing to apologise for, not to you nor anyone else, so you know what you can do with your criticisms. Keep silent about matters you don't understand."

"Certainly, sir." Storm's voice was punctilious in its politeness. "I would never dream of telling you how to run your mill. All I question is the need to exploit tiny children to the detriment of their health and in defiance of the law."

"Oh, well done, Mr. Hardiman, " Dorothy said softly.

"It's not well done at all, miss!" Mrs. Earnshaw's voice trembled with anger. "Mr. Hardiman has abused our hospitality."

Earnshaw smiled with a kind of grim satisfaction.

"He's done more than that," he said, his voice quieter now, more controlled. "He's cut off his nose to spite his face, that's what Mr. Hardiman has done. You can go back to London, young man, and you can tell Mr. Mallory I'm signing no contract with Gold Star. The Black Ball Line will continue to have my business. At least they read me no sermons."

Storm felt slightly sick.

"Sir," he said. "You must, of course, do as you think fit, but if I may remind you, you chose Gold Star because our terms were advantageous. For aught I know," he added with an attempt at humour, "you may disapprove of the captain's politics or the way he ties his stock, but still his ship will carry your goods cheaper —"

"I'll not have it!" Earnshaw said harshly, not allowing him to finish. "I'll not accept criticism from a jumped-up shipping clerk who thinks he knows all there is to know, and you can tell Mallory so. Perhaps it will teach him not to send a boy to do a man's job."

"*I* think Mr. Hardiman is a man, and a courageous one," Dorothy said defiantly.

Storm looked at her with grim amusement.

"Thank you, Miss Earnshaw," he said with heavy irony. "Thank you very much. I hope that sentiment will do much to comfort me in the troubled times that lie ahead."

He left that afternoon, not before Mr. Earnshaw had made a great show of tearing the unsigned contract into pieces and throwing it into the fire.

He put up for the night in Manchester and set off for London early the next morning, the country once more bathed in autumn sunshine, golden trees outlined against a cloudless sky. It was warm for the time of year, which did not prevent a feeling of dread gripping him like an icy hand.

What on earth would Kit say? Unhappily Storm remembered his euphoria at bringing off such an unlikely coup and he knew that he had every reason for doubting that much understanding or sympathy would come his way.

Kit, under the same circumstances, would have been as horrified as Storm at those poor, pale, wizened children, but he would have looked at the matter philosophically and would have lied unblushingly when his opinion was sought. He would have appreciated his own inability to change matters, done a few sums in his head, and in answer to Dorothy Earnshaw would have murmured some platitude that might have left her unsatisfied but would have ruffled none of his host's feathers.

But it's vile, an obscenity, Storm thought, smiting his knee with his fist. Profit at the expense of children's lives! Surely Kit would understand his emotions, and how impossible it had been to keep silent, in the end? After all, he had tried. He had bitten his tongue, hidden his initial shock. If it had not been for Dorothy Earnshaw, insistent and probing –

Perhaps he should thank God for Dorothy Earnshaw. What, after all, was of more importance? The integrity of one's own beliefs or an ability to accommodate the most heinous practices for the sake of a profit?

Perhaps he was doing Kit an injustice. Perhaps he would understand.

Though the hour was late Storm went direct to Portman Square for he knew he would not rest until the weight of confession was off his mind. Kit, he knew, was unlikely to be in bed.

An added incentive was the possibility of catching a glimpse of Loveday. Though on his homeward journey other considerations had dimmed the bright, clear thought of her that had enlivened his trip north, the recollection of her could still cheer him. He told himself he was being foolish. She had probably wasted no time at all in thoughts of him. Logic and common sense, however, had little to do with the matter. Somehow she seemed to represent all the eternal and unshifting joys that would remain long after Mr. Earnshaw and all his works were forgotten.

There was no sign of her when he arrived, however, and he was shown into the drawing-room by Frank. Kit and Isobel had been entertaining friends, now on the point of leaving, but at Storm's arrival they delayed their departure. He was much embarrassed by the warmth of Kit's welcome and the expansiveness of his greeting.

"Just look on this fellow," he cried, clapping a hand on Storm's shoulder. "My trusted emissary! He may be young, but he's performed a great service for Gold Star, I can tell you."

"Kit, I –" Storm hesitated. This, perhaps, was no moment for revelations such as those he had to offer, hard though it was to be hailed as a returning hero.

"Such a modest expression!" Kit was laughing at him, with affection.

"I can see the future of Gold Star is in excellent hands." This was Sir Carrington Babcock, a close neighbour and a Minister of the Crown, red-faced and hearty and full of good cheer.

"Indeed, Sir Carrington," Kit said. "Indeed it is."

"Storm, do you need refreshment?" Isobel asked. "Such a prodigious journey! You must be exhausted."

"I am a little tired," Storm confessed, "but thank you, I have no need for anything to eat." Or ability to eat it if produced, he added silently, his dread increasing with every moment. "I felt that I wanted to make a report to Kit before the night was out."

The departing guests made their farewells and with thanks and compliments were shown from the house. Isobel, too, said goodnight and retired to bed. Storm and Kit were at last alone.

Now, Storm thought, his heart sinking still further.

"I'm afraid," he said, "the news is bad. Earnshaw refused to sign."

Kit, about to light a cigar in the fire, straightened and stared at him.

"*What*? Why not? What happened, in God's name? The old devil swore —"

"He took me to the mill. He's breaking the law, Kit. He's employing tiny, under-age children for up to fifteen and sixteen hours a day in the most horrific conditions you could imagine —"

Kit's smile had died, his mouth thinning into an unfamiliar shape, his whole face growing sharp and wary, poised on the brink of wrath.

"And you pointed out the error of his ways, no doubt," he said icily.

"Not at first. It wasn't like that. I was appalled, but I kept silent, for I knew how much was at stake. It was later, back at the house, when Miss Earnshaw asked me what I thought and insisted on an answer. It was impossible to lie —"

Kit's eyes were two glittering points. He tossed the forgotten cigar into the fire with a dismissive flick of his fingers.

"My God," he said softly. "You insufferable little prig. What, may I ask, did you hope to achieve? Did you suppose that Earnshaw would touch his forelock and apologise and swear never to employ another child again?" His voice grew harder and angrier. "Is it going to prevent him shipping one bloody bail of cloth? *Someone* will ship it if we don't, so for the sake of your pathetic little conscience we've lost a contract worth God alone knows how many thousands. But it doesn't matter, does it? *You* will sleep easy!"

"Kit, believe me, it wasn't like that. I was driven into a corner – but it was truly frightful, I assure you, the sight of those poor children. It was like a glimpse of hell. In a way I was ashamed of keeping silent so long."

Kit said nothing for a moment, but the hand that lit his fresh cigar shook.

"Should I make a check of every exporter to ensure that his morals are up to your standard? Should we get it in writing, that he's good to children and old ladies and never lays a whip upon his horse?" His voice rose, harsh and violent as his anger spilled over. "Should I mount a personal crusade to ensure none of our ships that sails to the West Indies brings back anything from estates where slaves have been flogged this past year? God! The hypocrisy of it!"

He turned from Storm and paced agitatedly up and down the room, his steps rapid and jerky.

"You!" he said, stabbing his cigar towards Storm. "Still wet behind the ears, but still able to teach your elders how to manage their affairs. You know it all, don't you? You know the answers to everything!"

"I don't have answers," Storm said stiffly. "I just have questions."

"I'll not be put in the wrong by your high-minded posturing! You're more like your mother than I realised. She was always one to strike moral attitudes."

The last remark was made in a tone of such bitterness that Storm stared at him.

"If I'm like her, then I'm proud of it," he said.

"Proud of it you may be." His pacing over, Kit stood on the hearth-rug, feet apart, arms folded. "But it makes you useless to me. This is a hard, competitive world. There are fortunes to be made in shipping, and I intend to make mine several times over – and I won't be held back by pious, mealy-mouthed considerations like a few pauper children whose lot is changed not one iota whether we ship or whether we don't. Is that clearly understood?"

Storm took a deep breath.

"Clearly," he said.

"Then think it over. I'll expect you in my office at eight in the morning, when we can discuss whether you intend to play the game by my rules or if you'd rather get out. Now I should be thankful if you'd take yourself off."

Storm, however, stood his ground.

"Kit, believe me, I'm sorry to have let you down. I cannot think, though, that had you been there to see for yourself –"

"For God's sake, *go* –" Kit turned to tug at the bell. "Show yourself out. As for myself, I need a drink."

Storm left the room, almost colliding with Frank as he came in to answer Kit's summons, and in spite of an overpowering desire to get to his own rooms to lick his wounds, he dallied a little in the fastening of his overcoat until the footman had emerged once more.

"Are you on duty alone tonight?" he asked conversationally.

"There's a coupla maids in the kitchen a-clearin' up the dishes," Frank said. "There's been company tonight."

"Yes, of course. I saw them."

"That Sir Carrington, a caution 'e is and no mistake!"

"Frank –" Desperately Storm took a step towards him as the footman made to go about his duties. "Frank, is Daisy about?"

"'Aven't you 'eard about Daisy?" Frank stopped again. He came close, looked over his shoulder, gave a wink and inclined his head confidentially.

"Thought you might 'ave been told," he said. "Seein' it caused such a rumpus. The mistress gave Daisy 'er marchin' orders. She's gawn, sir."

"Gone? Gone where?"

Frank shrugged his shoulders and turned his eyes up to heaven.

"Gawd alone knows, sir," he said, and went on his way.

Nineteen

Treasure Bluff had, for once, failed to work its magic on Dorcas. There was no place for her here, or anywhere.

"I should have persuaded him to keep away from the meeting," she said distractedly, sitting with Marcia. "Perhaps if I had not been so ready to accompany him, he would not have gone. I had this strange premonition of disaster – did I not tell you so, Marcia? I'm sure that I must have done, for it seemed to me that the whole island was strange at that time, as if not only I were uneasy but that others were aware of the atmosphere, too. If only I had begged him not to go!"

Marcia looked at her with compassion, and let her talk. Five weeks after the dreadful events in the church, still she seemed dazed with shock, still she went over every incident. Never, Marcia thought, would I have believed that Dorcas could look colourless. It was as if Zachariah's death had drained the spirit from her, quenched the light that made her stand out from the crowd.

She covered Dorcas's hand with her own.

"He thought it his duty to go to the church that day. You mustn't blame yourself for supporting him! When did you ever do anything else?"

Dorcas made an attempt to smile at her.

"As, indeed, you support me. Dear Marcia! What would I do without you? I must be a sore trial to you."

"We've been through good times and bad times together. How is Bathsheba?"

"Coping far better than I. She has such faith!"

"She has Joe, too, and her other children. They must be a comfort to her."

"There is no bitterness in her." Dorcas sighed. "Oh, what a dreadful thing it was, Marcia. Five innocents dead and a dozen injured. Thank heaven we at least have a doctor on the island now."

"Hugh's certainly not been idle. I gather there are still no definite clues to point to the culprit?"

Dorcas shook her head.

"Nothing definite, no. There are plenty of suspicions, though. Most think it was a prank that went disastrously wrong, instigated by Trotman even though he himself didn't throw the fire-cracker and has a dozen witnesses to prove it. It was he who carefully spread the rumour about God sending a thunderbolt to punish the slaves who attended, after all — and there's something else I've remembered, Marcia. At night, when I lie awake unable to sleep, I go over every detail, every remark, and last night I suddenly remembered something that Gilligan said some time ago. He said that he was drinking in the saloon with sailors from an American ship out of New York. They talked of Chinatown, he told me, and how the Chinese celebrate New Year."

"With fire-crackers!"

"To the best of my recollection he mentioned no such matter, but he did say that the Chinese and their customs were talked of and how strange it was that their New Year fell in February. That I remember quite clearly."

"Was Trotman present?"

"I'm sure that he must have been, for that occasion was the first time that I heard of the stupid rumour he was spreading about the Haitian woman. The sailors could have given him fire-crackers, couldn't they? Quite innocently, I mean, thinking it likely he wanted to play a joke."

"It could have happened like that," Marcia agreed. "And a joke was, I am sure, all he intended. Even Trotman could not have been evil enough to plan such a disaster, though the kind of stupidity that would do anything to create panic in such a confined space defies belief!"

"He wasn't to know that Winklow would close the door so that no one could get out. Oh!" Unable to sit still, Dorcas rose and went to the front of the porch, then as swiftly returned. "Oh, what a combination of wickedness and folly. Marcia, how am I to live with it?" Dry-eyed, she stood with the back of her hand pressed to her mouth. "I am inconsolable!"

"My dear!" Swiftly Marcia was at her side and with her arm about her led her back to her chair. "We shall have tea without waiting for Thomas or Hugh." She gave a laugh that was almost a sob. "Such a tiny remedy for so great a grief! Tell me, Dorcas, has Emma been any comfort to you?"

"Poor Emma," Dorcas said, shaking her head. "Her

troubles are worse than mine. She's pregnant again, you know, and far from well."

"Who's far from well?" Hugh Bettany, his approach unheard, joined them on the porch and greeted Dorcas. "On second thoughts," he went on. "Pray don't tell me for I fear it could be the last straw that breaks this poor camel's back. I've just come from a visit to the Trotman household."

"Not Emma?" Dorcas asked. "It was she we spoke of."

"Emma is —" Hugh appeared to hesitate, then shrugged. "She is well enough, I suppose, for the moment. I ventured to speak to Trotman about her general health but was told to mind my own business — so for Emma's own sake I said no more in case he should forbid me the house altogether. I'm a little concerned about Daniel, so didn't want to risk banishment."

"What's wrong with Daniel?"

Fear for the little boy had penetrated her pain, Hugh could tell. Well, perhaps that was no bad thing. She would have to come to life again sooner or later.

"He has a slight fever — nothing serious, I feel sure, but he'll bear watching for a day or two. Children's temperatures go up and down very quickly, as you well know. I'll keep my eye on him, you can be certain."

"I'm sure you will, Hugh."

He saw she had retreated again; indeed, it was only a short while before she stood abruptly and said that she must return home.

"Do stay a little longer," Marcia begged. "Why, Hugh has had no chance to speak to you and Thomas will miss you altogether."

"I'm poor company, Marcia," Dorcas said, and although Hugh added his voice to his mother's, urging her to stay, she could not be persuaded. Marcia watched her driving away from Treasure Bluff, and was shaking her head doubtfully as she returned to Hugh.

"I don't know," she said. "Perhaps I should have gone with her."

"I think she wanted to be alone," Hugh replied. "She knows we're here when needed. She must work through this in her own way."

"I hate to think of her going back to an empty house."

"Still no word from Davey or Storm?"

"No — but then there's hardly been time. I feel sure Storm

will come when he hears the news, but Davey's duties may well not permit him."

Hugh sighed and lay back for a moment in his chair, his eyes closed.

"Has it been a hard day?" his mother asked.

"Not really." He was silent for a moment as if recalling certain details of it, but roused himself to take a cup of tea from her. "Those Trotmans! They're a strange couple. There's something about them and the entire atmosphere of their house that depresses me beyond measure."

"Trotman is enough to depress anyone," Marcia said. "He's a brute!"

"And Emma is a pathetic creature without, apparently, the will or the ability to stand up to him." He sighed again. "It would help matters if she were different."

At that Marcia gave a short laugh.

"My dear Hugh," she said. "Haven't we all been saying that for the past twenty years?"

Culturally the Lamb and Flag Tavern was many miles from Portman Square, but geographically it lay only a few short streets away. It was full of smoke and the smell of unwashed bodies and damp clothes on that wet autumn night, and Storm, having spent the better part of three evenings there, was heartily sick of the place.

He was waiting for Frank. Sooner or later he would put in an appearance, he felt sure, and then he would be able to question him further about Loveday. *Someone* in that house must know what had happened and where she could be found.

He was almost ready to give up hope of seeing him that night and was gloomily contemplating the prospect of a fourth visit to the tavern when at last his patience was rewarded and he saw the footman pushing his way through the knot of people close to the door. At once he got up, pint pot in hand, and went towards him.

"Frank," he said. "You're just the man I want to see."

"Lord love us, it's Mr. Storm." Frank grinned with surprise at the sight of him. "A little bird told me you wasn't likely to be around these parts again."

"I'd like a quick word with you, Frank. But first, a drink —"

"I need one, sir, and that's a fact and no lie. 'Ammer and tongs it's been tonight, I can tell you. S'welp me, it's enough to make Nelson and Old Boney take a back seat! Master and Mistress argifying in the dinin'-room, Mr. Saunders and Mrs. Pratt goin' at each other in the kitchen. There's been nothing but trouble in that 'ouse the past two weeks. 'Ere – " He grabbed Storm's arm. "If you've something to ask me you'd better ask it quick. I got to get back – Mr. Saunders'd string me up if he knew I was out at all."

Storm bought him a mug of ale and drew him over to a settle in the corner where they could talk in comparative privacy.

"I'll come straight to the point," he said. "I want to know about Daisy. What happened, and where is she now?"

Frank looked uncomfortable. His eyes slid away and he shifted in his seat.

"I dunno where she is," he said. "And as to what 'appened – you'd better ask the Master that."

Storm was suddenly so angry that he could hardly breathe. "Did he seduce her?"

Frank looked sideways at Storm. There seemed more than a trace of hostility in his expression.

"He'd 've liked to. It was a shame, sir, you ask me. She was a good girl, Daisy was. She didn't want no truck with the Master. It ain't 'er fault she's pretty as a picture. 'E never could keep 'is 'ands to 'isself, the Master couldn't."

"What happened exactly?" It was hard for Storm to keep his voice quiet and controlled. He held his mug in his two hands on the table in front of him and kept his eyes fixed on it as if only by doing so could he keep his anger in check.

"The Mistress came across them in that passage between the dining-room and the pantry. Master 'ad 'er by the arm, a-pullin' 'er close, like, and though Daisy swore she was tryin' to get away, Mistress would 'ave it it was all 'er fault." Frank pursed his lips, put his head on one side and mimicked Isobel's voice in a high falsetto. "'Your behaviour is *pro*-vocative, my girl', she says, and that was poor Daisy out without a character, just like Polly before 'er."

"But not in the same condition?"

"I'm tellin' you, Daisy's a good girl. It upset 'er, the way 'e was always a-touchin' of 'er arm and passin' remarks. Can't you speak to Mistress, sir, bein' a friend, like?"

Storm gave a short laugh and shook his head.

"It seems I'm a friend no longer, Frank."

He thought briefly of the scene with Kit in the office, when, his temper cooled a little over night, Kit had fractionally extended an olive branch. All would be forgiven, it seemed, if Storm would mend his ways and learn to think only of profits. The matter of Earnshaw and his mill would be forgotten. After all, said Kit, such disagreements happened in the best regulated families, and this chestnut could yet be pulled from the fire. He himself intended to travel to Lancashire to see Mr. Earnshaw in a few days.

Storm had thanked him politely but had said that, having thought the matter over, he felt very strongly that the time had come for him to return home.

"I can't thank you enough for all that you've done for me," he said. "But I have, after all, a job waiting for me in the islands. This has been a wonderful interlude –"

For some reason it was this word that had enraged Kit.

"Interlude!" he repeated with astonished anger. "Interlude!"

"I've always thought of it as such," Storm said.

The blood rushed to Kit's face at this and he had hammered the desk with his fist.

"You idiot, are you mad?" he shouted. "Don't you know what you're throwing away?"

This was Storm's life, he told him angrily. This was where he belonged, where he would have a brilliant and successful future if he could only stop trying to behave like some latter-day Sir Galahad.

And then, as Storm stuck to his guns, repeatedly thanking him but saying that nevertheless he would be glad to leave at the end of November, Kit had become cold and vindictive, calling him stupid and stubborn and ungrateful, telling him that there was no need to wait until the end of November, he could go now, *now*, this minute –

Storm put the memory behind him. He had gone from the office, but not from London. He was determined that he would see Loveday before he left the country, even if it were only to say goodbye. The thought of her cast off because of Kit's selfish pursuit of pleasure was too much to bear. He had spent days looking for her, but with no success.

"You must know where's she's gone, Frank," he said. "She had a relative working for Gold Star, didn't she? An uncle, I believe. Do you know his name?"

Frank shook his head.

"No, sir. I never heard."

"Or where she lives? You must know that!"

Again Frank shook his head and again Storm detected a faintly hostile wariness about him.

"No, sir. Beggin' your pardon, sir, but what is it you want 'er for? You're not the man Mr. Mallory is, I knows that, but it ain't fair on the likes of Daisy to be a-pickin' of 'er up and a puttin' of 'er down."

"Believe me, I'd never harm her. My intentions are of the best. I just feel I must —"

He hesitated. What must he do? See her again? Talk to her? What other intentions could he possibly have? Perhaps, after all, it would be best to sail away and forget her, but he knew it to be impossible. He would have to go on trying to find her as long as he was able.

"I want to help her," he said. "Surely Mrs. Pratt knows where she lives?"

"No, sir, that she doesn't. She was gone that quick! 'Pack your bags and go,' Madam said, and go she did — and Mrs. Pratt don't know where, I knows that for sure, for we found a kerchief belonging to 'er in the wash-house, and I says, tell me where to take it and I'll take it, I says. And Mrs. Pratt says, I've no idea where she's gone, no more than Tom Noddy, she says — and she dassent ask Mistress, she says, on account of 'er bein' in such a state about the lass."

Sadly Storm nodded, reached in his pocket and produced a handful of coins.

"Thank you for talking to me, Frank," he said. "Buy yourself a drink, and remember me kindly, for I doubt we'll meet again. I'm going back home in a little while — back to the West Indies."

"You'll surely be round to Portman Square to say good-bye?"

Storm shrugged and sighed.

"Perhaps," he said. "Perhaps."

Did duty demand it, he wondered, after all that had been said? There had been kindness in the past, that was unde-niable; and admiration and real affection. All that, however, was overlaid now by Kit's anger and his own distaste. A graceful letter to Isobel, perhaps, would suffice — though even she was guilty of inhumane behaviour towards Loveday. No one who had lived with Kit as long as she had could surely be in any doubt where the blame must lie.

Call me a prig, Kit Mallory, he thought, as he turned up

his collar against the drizzle and walked towards the gas lamps of Oxford Street. Call me what you like. I'm sick to death of the pair of you.

Dorcas was at her desk writing to Fanny when, unheralded and unannounced, Willis Trotman stood upon the porch and knocked on the door-jamb, the door itself standing open to admit the breeze.

She looked up in disbelief.

"*You* come *here*?" she asked.

"I must say I've received warmer welcomes. May I come in?"

"You may not." She laid down her pen. "I cannot imagine under what circumstances you and I could possibly have anything to say to each other. Please go."

She stood up hastily, as he stepped into the room, totally ignoring her words.

"A pleasant room," he said, looking around him. "I have always thought so."

"I asked you to go, Mr. Trotman."

"My dear Dorcas –"

"Don't call me that!"

He bowed.

"Mrs. Hardiman, then. I know you blame me for Zachariah's tragic death and seem unaffected by the fact that I have a dozen witnesses to say I was in Venner's Tavern at the time –"

"You were behind it, and nothing you can say will convince me otherwise."

"Be careful of slander, Mrs. Hardiman."

"I know it as sure as I know the sun will rise in the east."

He gave his unpleasant smile.

"Then I'll waste no time in denying it. There is naught so obstinate as a woman with her mind made up."

"I asked you to leave."

"I have something of importance to say to you. Permit me five minutes."

Emma? Daniel? The thought of them and their ill-health flashed into her mind and caused her resolution to waver. Daniel's fever would bear watching, Hugh had said –

"Five minutes," she said. "But not here. Come outside to the porch."

She would not, could not, allow him inside, she was determined on that. He gave a private, sneering smile as if her niceties amused him, and with a mock-gallant gesture stood aside as she went out to the porch.

"Well?" she asked stonily, neither sitting nor inviting him to do so.

"I am concerned about your future," he said. "Plainly you are no longer interested in your holdings."

"That's not true!"

"No work has been done."

"This is not the raking season."

"There's always maintenance to be carried out. Your slaves are idle – and you not even aware of it!"

"I have an overseer, Mr. Trotman."

"McMurtree?" Trotman laughed harshly. "He's a fool."

"My husband thought a great deal of him –"

"And monitored his work constantly! McMurtree, my dear Dorcas – I beg your pardon! Mrs. Hardiman! – is an overseer who needs overseeing. Without supervision he is useless, and so are your salt ponds."

"How kind of you to be concerned," she said icily. "I am touched, but would beg you to attend to your own business and leave mine alone."

"The fact is," Trotman said, lounging against the wall of the house with his arms folded. "You have no interest at all in the ponds. You've always been too damned good for this island, haven't you? In your own estimation, I hasten to say."

"Get out," Dorcas said, her teeth clenched with anger.

"No! *You* get out! I will give you a fair price for all your assets as they stand; house, land, office and shop, slaves, barracks and horses, plus a small amount for the unexpired weeks of your lease of the ponds – which in view of the fact that the next allocation is little more than eight weeks away is more than generous. I will have it all valued by an independent –"

"Get out." Dorcas could hardly contain her fury.

"I don't think you understand. You would be able to live in comfort close to your family in Bermuda. I would pay in cash. I've saved –"

"I don't doubt it. God knows you've not spent on anything all the years I've known you. You even grudge your wife and children the price of a bolt of cloth to make new clothes, even though you must have plenty, having swindled my husband out of the Cahill contract –"

"Hold on." Trotman stood straight and put his arms down by his sides. "That was a gift, freely given."

"I doubt that. Zachariah was always evasive about it – but that's beside the point. I don't know yet what I'm going to do with myself or where I'm going to live out the rest of my life, but let me make one thing clear, Mr. Trotman. Never, never, will you get your hands on one iota of my property. Sell our slaves to you?" She laughed harshly. "I would die first – and as for this house, I'd set fire to it myself rather than let you set a foot in it."

He had watched her apparently unmoved throughout this speech, his mouth drawn down in a bitter smile, and he continued to watch her when she fell silent. He said nothing for a moment, then with his eyes still holding hers, he reached out and pulled her close to him.

"Listen to me," he said, very quietly. "I thought you might feel that way. There's just one thing you haven't taken into consideration." Contemptuously he let her go, pushing her away from him. "You see, my divine Dorcas, I know about you. I know that Zachariah took money to give a name to your bastard. I know you were false, I know you played the whore. I know you tricked him and lied to him."

"I see." Dorcas had paled and her voice was barely audible, but she looked at him directly and her eyes were hard and bright. "I see. So that's how it was done! It's all clear now. You blackmailed Zachariah into handing Cahill over to you, didn't you? I knew there was nothing in that cock-and-bull story about his salt being below standard."

"He saw sense." Trotman smiled at her. "He didn't want your name dragged through the mud. The way I see it, you owe it to his memory to do the same, to do what he would want. You don't want people whispering, wondering, laughing at him and at you –"

Dorcas was shaking. She reached out and with a hand placed firmly in the middle of his chest, shoved so hard that he was taken by surprise and staggered off balance a little.

"Get out," she said again. "And take your poisonous little schemes with you. You're getting none of what's mine – never, never, never! And as for your pathetic, despicable attempt at blackmail, you can do and say precisely what you like, do you understand? Nothing you can say or do can spoil the happiness I had with Zachariah, and if you imagine I am concerned in the smallest degree by the opinions of others, then you are wrong. Get this into your head, Mr. Trotman, and pray remember it: *I do not care*! That, perhaps, is the one benefit bestowed by tragedy. It directs the mind to what is important and what is not. You, Mr. Trotman, are not important, and I ask you once more to leave my house and never come back to it."

She watched him go, still trembling with the force of her anger and outrage and disgust.

I really don't care, she thought with a sudden stirring of pleasurable liberation; and there was pleasure, too, in knowing that at last she had told Trotman exactly what she thought of him.

I left him in no doubt, she said to the spirit of Zachariah who was never far from her. I told him, didn't I?

But he was right, conscience told her, about the neglect of your business interests.

"You goin' out, Miz Dorcas?" Bathsheba asked, seeing her five minutes later with her hat and parasol.

"Yes I am, Sheba," she said. "I feel it's time I had a few words with Mr. McMurtree."

Emma ventured out very little these days. She had no energy or interest in going into the tiny township and there seemed little point in dragging herself through the dust merely to walk in the inhospitable area in which Willis had sited the house.

She played with the children, but was already intimidated by her first-born, Howard, who was self-willed, violent and noisy. Daniel was different. Daniel was a dark, merry little boy, smiling and affectionate. She could have cuddled him all day, but he was too active to submit happily to that. The baby, who might have been expected to be more amenable to such treatment, had never appealed to her much. He seemed all angles and flailing fists and squared mouth − not at all the little dream-baby she had longed for.

Most days she could not be bothered to dress and come downstairs, and now that she was pregnant again and Dr. Bettany had told her to take care of herself, she had the perfect excuse to wear a loose wrapper all day and sit at the window of her bedroom with the shutters thrown open, looking out on the bleak, scrubby landscape, with the trees of South Creek beyond and the glint of the ocean in the distance. She could see the children playing from this vantage point, a painful pleasure. She did not care that Mollie was so much better with Howard than she was, but it hurt when she saw Daniel clambering on her knee and laughing in play.

When she felt better, she said to herself: when this strange fog of inertia lifted, then everything would be different. Meantime she was comforted by the thought that unlike Howard, Daniel sometimes looked towards her window and waved his plump arms and called to her.

"Look at me, Mama. See me hop, Mama. Watch me throw, Mama."

She would wave back, and nod and smile, though she felt close to tears because she felt so ill and could not play with him as often as she would have liked.

The baby, Robert, was too young to care. She was glad, as she looked down, that it was Mollie who had to chase after him as he crawled determinedly away from the patch of shade in which she attempted to keep him, pacifying him as he screamed with belligerent fury each time he was brought back.

She sewed a great deal, partly through necessity – they all, Willis included, wore garments that were patched and darned, with turned collars and cuffs – and partly because she liked it. It was something she could do, her one talent.

People had said, once upon a time, that she could sing. She remembered, as from a different life, that she had received compliments about her voice, had stood on a stage and been applauded. But Willis had hated it, had told her that she made a laughing stock of herself, and now she had lost the ability to string two notes together, and forgotten the words of all the songs her father had taught her.

It was strange how her memory failed her these days. Sometimes she would stand for minutes at a time in the middle of the room, not able to remember just what action she had been about to perform. Sometimes, as with the singing, a faint whisper of the past would come to her and she would ask herself; did this happen to me? Or did someone tell me of it? Or was it, perhaps, a dream?

She was sewing a little yellow shirt for Daniel the morning when the whisper came, and at intervals during the afternoon it teased at her consciousness. At some time in the past she had sewn a small yellow garment and had been praised for it. When, and by whom? She could not remember.

It was only when she picked up her scissors – thin, elegant, pointed scissors, finely chased and razor sharp, a present from

334

her father many years before — did she recall the incident fully. The doll's dress, she remembered, slashed to ribbons to spite Willis. No — she frowned. That was wrong. She had done it to spite Dorcas, not Willis.

But Willis had been there. She saw it all quite clearly now, as if the sun had come out to dispel the mist. She saw herself and Davey walking with Dorcas towards her father and Willis; saw her father stretch out his arms to receive their hurtling bodies, heard him chuckle with delight, felt his comforting arms around her, holding her safe and secure, as if no harm or sadness could ever come her way.

Tears poured down her cheeks. She had loved him so! Willis didn't understand, had shown no sympathy or tenderness since the dreadful accident in the church.

"I hope you cry as much for me," he had said harshly.

But she wouldn't! Life with him was insupportable. If it were not for Daniel she would do away with herself. Even now — she stared at the silver scissors in her hand, shuddered and put them down.

I'll get better, she thought. When I've had this baby, I shall feel quite different. Perhaps it will be a girl this time. A girl would be nice.

And after that?

She leant her head on her hand and wept again. After that, another baby and another and another, until quite legally, Willis had killed her. That would be the end of it. She knew it without any doubt at all. He was sick to death of her, she knew. Whatever his purpose had been in marrying her, he had long since repented of it.

Howard was yelling down below.

She wiped her eyes and looked down. He only had the baby to tease that particular day, for Daniel was sick, and he was taking out his frustration on Mollie, belabouring her with a stick. Well, she was big enough to look after herself. Just so long as Daniel didn't wake.

Please God, don't let him be ill — really ill. Dr. Bettany had said it probably wasn't anything very much. Oh God, please let him be better tomorrow. He had been quite unlike himself today; miserable, and unusually prone to tears.

Howard *had* wakened him! She could hear the boy stirring in the next room, whimpering as if he were in pain.

She went and brought him back to where she was sitting close to the window, cuddling him on her lap.

The whimpering ceased. He sucked his thumb, burrowed his head into her breast for comfort, and slept again. His weight was a joyous burden. Utterly dependent, devoid of any wish to escape from her arms, this was how Emma loved her children.

For the moment, she was wholly contented.

"If you please, sir –" Mrs. Cummings, the widow who owned the house in which Storm had taken rooms, pitched her voice low in deference to his bereavement.

"What is it?" Storm turned from the window to face her, pale and unshaven. His face was drawn, the carelessness of his dress demonstrating without a doubt that the news of his father's death had been a cruel blow.

"A smarter, cleaner young gentleman I have never had in my house, Mrs. Cook," she said frequently to her neighbour. "And always a kind word and a smile, with not a trace of haughtiness like some you meet."

It grieved her now to see how his condition had changed.

"There's a young lady to see you, sir," she said. "I told her as you wasn't receiving, but she begged for a word with you. It's a Miss Loveday Treleaven –"

"Loveday!" Storm was shocked out of the apathy into which his grief had plunged him, and he looked around wildly as for the first time realising that for two days no one had cleared the room and that both it and he were equally dishevelled.

He ran a hand through his hair, reached for the coat that hung over the back of a chair, swept papers from a sofa underneath a cushion.

"Take that tray out, Mrs. Cummings, if you please," he said. "And show her up."

Loveday! After all this time of fruitless searching! How on earth – ?

She was there, in the doorway before he could make up the fire or straighten the room further. It was raining outside, and the hair beneath the little round hat she wore was bedraggled, her brown dress muddied at the hem, the shawl about her shoulders beaded with moisture.

"Excuse me, sir." Nervously she stood on the threshold. "I don't want to trouble –" She stopped short as if taken aback by her first real glimpse of his face. "Oh, sir," she said after a moment's shocked silence. "Oh sir, whatever is it?"

"Come in, come close to the fire." Storm went across the room to greet her. "I can't tell you how pleased I am to see you – but come in, do! You're all wet."

Still she looked at him without moving, her eyes searching his face. Her expression was full of surprised concern and it was clear that whatever it was that had brought her to see him so unexpectedly, it had nothing to do with the news of his father.

"Come in," Storm said again. "Shut the door and get warm."

She did as he told her, coming closer both to him and the fire.

"What is it, sir?" she asked again softly. "Something's happened!"

"It's my father." Storm turned and put more coal on the fire, suddenly finding, now that he was exposed to her sympathy, that the control he thought he had achieved was more tenuous than he had believed. He paid great attention to his task before standing up and brushing his hands together briskly as if this matter had wholly occupied him. "I heard yesterday morning that he was dead – killed in some stupid, senseless accident two months ago."

"Oh, my lor'!" Instinctively Loveday stretched out a hand towards him, then let it fall again. "That Mrs. Cummings should have said! Oh sir, I'm some sorry, truly I am. I know what 'tis like to lose someone dear. Oh, what a day to choose to tell my troubles! I'd best be off –"

"No, no – please! Don't go! It's wonderful to see you. I've looked for you everywhere. Didn't you know I was looking for you?"

"No, sir." Loveday looked mystified.

"Take off your shawl. We can put it on this chair to dry."

He angled the sofa towards the fire, shook up a cushion, and primly she sat down, her back straight, her reticule clasped between her two hands on her knee.

"Thank you, sir," she said. "I'll stay a few minutes, then. A body d' need company at a time like this."

"Believe me, there's no company I'd rather have! I tried to find out your aunt's address, but no one knew it, then I sent someone looking for all Cornish lightermen with Gold Star. I found no less than four, but not one who'd ever heard of you."

"I never said my Uncle Will was Cornish! My auntie is,

sure enough, but she married a foreigner over to Plymouth. A Devon man is Uncle Will, and one who keeps himself to himself. He's got few friends among the lightermen or anywhere. He said I'd be a fool to come to see you, but 'twas my auntie who found out where you lived and said I should come. She said you sounded as if you weren't like the others."

She bit her lip and looked away from him, as if conscious she had said too much.

"You had told your aunt of me?"

"I told her about everything that happened at Portman Square. All the parties and dinners and the important people that came to the house. She liked to hear about it."

"What did you say about me?"

"Not much!" Loveday forgot momentarily that she was shy and he bereaved, and flashed him one of her enchanting smiles. "She would've said I was being proper daft, and that you'd not notice me in a month of Sundays."

The implications of this statement took Storm's breath away. He went to sit beside her on the sofa.

"You're wrong, Loveday," he said. "Oh, how wrong you are! But tell me what brings you here?"

"Never mind me." She had sobered again and was looking at him with clear, grey, sympathetic eyes. "Tell me about your dada. Was he like you to look at?"

"No, not at all." Storm turned from her and leaned back in the corner of the sofa, looking into the fire as if he could see pictures in it. He smiled as if they were happy images he could see there. "He was a short man. Stocky, with very dark hair – thick and black and strong. My earliest memory is of being carried on his shoulders. He used to gallop about and sing songs to make me laugh."

"He sounds kind."

"Oh, he was; as kind and loving as any father could be – and so generous! Not just with material things, but generous with his time and attention. He gave of himself –"

Loveday let him talk.

"I'm boring you," Storm said from time to time, but always she shook her head.

"No," she said. "It's like a story, all those tales of foreign parts, and your father sounds a lovely man. I wish I'd known him."

"If only –" Storm began, but turned his head away from her suddenly, unable to continue. "Forgive me. I don't want

to embarrass you with womanish tears. It's just that, all at
once, I realised afresh that I should never see him or speak to
him again. The thought is one that's hard to bear. God, I'm
sorry –"

She took him in her arms, simply and naturally, conscious
of an undeniable feeling of happiness at his need of her. Was
it wrong to feel happy at the sensation of his hair beneath her
fingers, the warmth of his flesh against hers, when he himself
was so sad? Perhaps; but it was a feeling she could not deny.

"My handsome," she said softly, as she had longed to do
from the first moment she had seen him. "There, there, my
handsome. Tidn't nothing to be shamed of, tears for someone
you love."

A knock at the door caused them to spring apart, to
straighten hair and dress.

"I thought you'd like tea," Mrs. Cummings said; and it
was the right thing, Loveday thought practically, much as she
had enjoyed that brief and wholly innocent embrace. There
was nothing like tea for restoring normality to any situation.

Storm watched her pour it, feeling suddenly calm and at
peace. The sadness was there, but was not now so unbearable.

"Now it's your turn to talk," he said. "Tell me, what made
you seek me out? You spoke of troubles –"

"It's they Mallorys." Loveday put down the teapot with a
thump. "They turned me off without a character, Mr. Storm,
though I'd done nothing wrong and well Mr. Mallory knew
it. He never spoke up for me, not when Mrs. Mallory was
saying all manner of things against me."

"I'm sorry. I'm ashamed for both of them."

"It's like I said to you before – Loveday wasn't a person at
all. She didn't matter. 'Twas as if I didn't exist, had never
been born."

"You matter to me."

"Then give me a character – that's all I ask. Give me a
character and I'll trouble you no more. I'll never get another
place, else."

Storm laughed briefly.

"Loveday, my dear girl! Naturally I'll do whatever I can to
help, but do you really think a reference from me will carry
any weight?"

"It'll serve, sir." Her eyes were wide and pleading. "P'raps
not for a lady here in London, but I've other plans. I can't
stay on with my auntie. They've troubles enough, with a big

family and no money to speak of, and Uncle Will wondering aloud how long I'll be a burden to them. So I thought of a scheme."

"And what's that?"

"I've always longed to see foreign parts, sir. My father was the same. He always used to say we came from a long line of Spanish sailors, and maybe we did, but right or wrong there's something in my heart that won't be satisfied till I've seen something of the world. So when I saw the notice asking for girls for Van Diemen's Land —"

"Van Diemen's Land!" Storm sat up in his seat and looked at her in horror.

"'Tidn't only convicts as go, sir. Not now. They want servants and all sorts."

"'All sorts' is right!" Storm spoke dryly. "What does your auntie have to say?"

"She says, good luck to me. She says she'd go too if she was younger and not tied down."

Storm took both her hands in his own.

"Loveday, don't go," he said.

"But, sir —"

"What did you call me just now, before Mrs. Cummings interrupted us? You remember!"

She laughed and blushed and Storm watched for the tiny indentation beside her mouth that he longed to kiss.

"My handsome," she whispered, lashes lowered on her cheeks. "'Tidn't nothing! Everyone's 'my handsome' in Cornwall."

"Then listen to me, my handsome." The lashes lifted and he looked into the depths of her lovely eyes. "I don't want you to go to Van Diemen's Land, not to be a servant, nor yet an 'all sort'. I want you to come back to the Turks Islands with me, as my wife."

She stared at him without speaking, eyes wide, lips parted, such a look of astonishment on her face that he laughed as he reached for her and held her close against his shoulder.

"I'll make you happy," he said softly. "I swear it! I love you. I seem to have loved you for so long. Look at me, darling Loveday."

She did so, wonderingly, and for a while he held her face between his hands, and looked and looked as if even now he could not believe that she was there, so close and so compliant.

"I love you," he said again, and his voice shook a little. He bent to kiss the tiny mark that had driven him mad before finally, joyously, his lips moved to seek hers.

Twenty

Daniel was crying; not in a demanding, full-blooded roar as Howard would have done, but gaspingly, almost apologetically, his tiny whimpers interspersed with calls for his mother.

"That child," Willis said savagely, throwing a boot to the corner of the room as he undressed for bed, "is more trouble than the others combined."

Emma, already in bed but climbing out to go to Daniel, found the spirit to argue with this injustice.

"That's not true! He's sick. You're never fair to him, just because he favours my side of the family."

Swiftly he lashed out, hitting her in the face and sending her cowering back against the pillows once more.

"Leave him, you fool," he said.

"He's *sick*, Willis! The doctor said he must have plenty of liquids."

"And that's another thing. I'll not have that mealy-mouthed bastard Bettany sniffing around here, telling me what to do with my own wife." The other boot followed the first, and he stood up, bare-chested, hands on hips, looking down at her, an expression of contempt on his face. "Look at you, you pathetic little whey-faced —"

He turned from her in disgust and made for the door.

"You're good for only one thing as far as I'm concerned, and I'm not having Bettany taking that away from me. I'll be with you in a minute — but first I'll shut that child up."

"Don't hurt him, Willis. Give him a drink." Emma's voice was weak and quavered like an old woman's. She had little hope that he would heed her.

She began to cry. Willis wouldn't care if Daniel died, just so long as he had Howard. Howard was a small facsimile of himself, twice as noisy, twice as troublesome as Daniel, but though the boy came in for his share of cuffs, Willis was proud of him, as if his aggression were proof of his masculinity.

"Mama, Mama!"

She could hear Daniel from the next room, louder now,

more desperate. She threw off the covering and ran across to the door, opening it in defiance of her husband, anxious to see what was going on. By the light of the lamp which Willis had carried into the room with him, she saw that he stood over Daniel's bed, one large hand holding the child down. She ran to his side and ineffectually pulled at his arm.

"What are you doing, Willis? You'll hurt him! Give him water."

"He's had water."

"Then let me come to him. He's sick. Let me hold him."

"He'll stay in this bed if I have to hold him down all night. Stop snivelling, for the love of God – you're helping nobody. Get back to bed! The child must learn I mean what I say."

"I'll stay with him, Willis. I'll see he stays in bed. Just let me stay with him. Look, I'll sit on this chair beside him. I won't take him out of bed, I promise."

Willis laughed scornfully, and from Howard's bed came his childish treble, echoing that scorn.

"Mama would only cuddle him."

"See – even Howard has your measure."

"Why shouldn't I cuddle him? He's little and he's sick."

With his free hand Willis reached out and pushed her away.

"Get back to bed." He laughed again. "Try showing some affection for your husband, for a change."

The push had sent her cannoning into the edge of the open door and for a moment she closed her eyes against the pain. She knew that she should try again to reach Daniel, but knew, too, that she could not win. She had never won against Willis, never once.

She went back to the bedroom, closed the door and leaned against it. There was no sound now from Daniel. He was frightened into silence too, just as she was, equally at the mercy of the monster she had married.

Who would look after him when she was dead? As soon she would be – she had little doubt of that. Willis would destroy her body as he had destroyed her spirit.

She placed her two hands on her stomach. The swelling was barely noticeable yet, but just the same, another life was there within. Was it a Howard or a Daniel? Suppose it was a girl – a tiny, pretty little girl?

Willis would destroy her, too, one way or another.

There had to be an escape; there had to be. Somehow this nightmare must be brought to an end. Meantime, Willis would soon be back, brutal as ever, intent on proving that he was the master.

In the same moment as she wearily pushed herself away from the door the moon broke through the clouds. She could see the honeycomb pattern on the white cover and the brass bed-knobs gleaming in the sudden shaft of light. There was the little yellow shirt where she had left it on her work table by the window, and beside the shirt, shining even brighter than the brass knobs, lay the silver scissors.

Emma stood in the centre of the room and looked at them. She could feel them in her hands; comfortable, familiar, a tool of which – for once – she was the master.

Convulsively the fingers of her right hand moved; open, shut, open, shut. Then dazedly she looked around the room again. She had been about to do something, she thought, eyes clouded and brows drawn together. But what?

Her gaze settled on the bed. That was it, of course. She had been about to go to bed. That was all. Nothing more.

To wait for Willis! She closed her eyes, weak with revulsion, sickened by the certainty of pain, of delicate membranes bruised and assaulted, of the violation of mind and spirit. Get back to bed, Willis had said. Those had been his orders. Very well, she thought. I will get back to bed and I will wait for him there; and for the first time for many months, she gave one of those small and secret smiles that had always irritated Dorcas so greatly.

It was early, with the sky still pale in colour and sea as calm as oiled silk; a sudden lull in the round of winter storms that had been lashing the island.

Dorcas, unable to sleep, rose from her bed and occupied herself by writing to Fanny.

I began writing to you yesterday in reply to your kind letter [she wrote], but was interrupted by none other than Trotman, who had the effrontery to come here and offer to buy me out; house, slaves, everything!

I know I have no need to dwell on my emotions. My detestation of the man is such that the very sight of him induces a feeling of physical sickness within me. But for his wickedness, Zachariah would be with me today and no amount of witnesses will convince me differently. Naturally I informed him in no uncertain manner that I would never sell to him; and not only to him, dearest Fanny, I am not yet in a position to sell at all.

This does not mean I am not grateful for your loving, generous offer of the house in St. George's, which I appreciate would mean a substantial loss of income to you were you to allow me to live in it at such an advantageous rent. When Silas purchased my share of it after Grandmama's death it was, as I recall, to effect an investment beneficial to you and your children for years to come. Grateful as I am, I cannot feel it right to take advantage of your generosity. It is not always wise to enter into such business arrangements with one's nearest and dearest and I could foresee a time when my occupation of the house could be a burden – if not to you and Silas, then to your children and *their* husbands – still unknown quantities!

Besides, I am reluctant to leave Grand Cay at this point. I know that you tell me Kit Mallory's letters to Silas imply that Storm will stay with Gold Star and has no intention of returning home (and pray do not think I am not gratified that he is so highly thought of), but I have yet to hear from him direct that he has abandoned all idea of returning here. Marcia wrote to him immediately after Zachariah's death to acquaint him with the news and I have written twice since, but so far there has been no reply. This, I am convinced, is entirely due to the unreliability of the mails, always so unpredictable and liable to delay or miscarriage. Soon there will be word from him and I will better be able to plan my future.

My instinct is to continue Zachariah's work. The letter I started yesterday was full of doubt, self-pity and indecision, but since then I have spoken to the overseer, young Mr. McMurtree, who is a pleasant enough fellow, knowledgeable about the salt business, but seemingly incapable of making decisions. Together I feel we might make a fair fist of running affairs until Storm comes to take command, or even longer if he tells me this is not his wish –

At that point she became aware of the sound of horses' hooves and a wheeled vehicle approaching the house. Curiously she looked up from her letter, her head cocked, pen still in her hand. It was too early for a social call and she knew of no business matters which could bring anyone out to see her at that time.

She went out to the porch and saw that it was Hugh who had arrived.

"Thank God you're up and dressed," he called without dismounting, dispensing with a formal greeting. "There seems to be trouble at the Trotman House."

"I'll come. Give me one moment."

Dorcas ran inside for her hat, called briefly to Nola to tell her she was going out, and in a few moments they were jolting over potholes on their way to South Creek.

"It's not Daniel, is it?" she asked anxiously, looking at his worried expression.

"No, not Daniel. I hardly know what to expect, Dorcas, but if the messenger who rode over to me is to be understood – and God knows he was incoherent enough – there's been some terrible accident. Trotman's dead and Emma's out of her mind, or so the man said."

"Oh, God in heaven!" Momentarily Dorcas squeezed her eyes shut as if to ward off the horror. "What happened? What kind of accident?"

"We shall know soon enough. 'Blood everywhere' he kept saying. 'Blood everywhere, blood everwhere.'"

Silent, unseeing, Dorcas stared straight before her at the track that twisted through the thorny scrub, remembering Emma as she had been so often these days; vague, disorientated, diminished. And she thought of Trotman and shuddered.

"I have been so blind," she said.

Emma did it, of course. How she did it was yet to be revealed, but Dorcas had no doubt that, goaded beyond endurance, she had somehow contrived to kill him.

"Was it a gunshot?" she asked – foolishly, she knew, for Hugh had no more knowledge of the incident than she had. "He could have had a gun. Zachariah was issued with a blunderbuss when he was in the militia and only recently found it and handed it back."

"It's possible," Hugh admitted.

"Emma –"

"Is not responsible. Whatever happened." He spoke decisively with a savage glint in his eye and a twist to his lips. "In my view, Trotman was a brutal psychopath who's all but destroyed her. She's going to need your help, Dorcas."

Dorcas said nothing. She thought of Emma – the unresponsive child growing into the sulkily defiant girl and the hostile woman; always possessive, always difficult. It was impossible to avoid a sinking of the heart.

"I don't know that she'll accept help from me," she said. "We'll see."

After the worst that her imagination could envisage, Dorcas was relieved and surprised to find that downstairs there was no evidence of tragedy. The house was comfortless with an air of neglect about it, but she guessed that this was possibly no worse than usual. The children were in the kitchen, Howard and Daniel unusually quiet, the baby grizzling with his face covered in gruel. One glance assured her that, for the time being anyway, Mollie was coping adequately.

Hugh had gone directly upstairs, and having satisfied herself that the children were unharmed, Dorcas joined him.

Trotman lay sprawled on the bed, face down, and there was indeed blood everywhere, soaking through the bedding, splashed over every quarter of the white honeycomb spread, staining the floor boards and painted in handprints on the pale wall close to the bed.

Blood everywhere; and evil, too. Dorcas could feel its presence, smell its sickly odour, and she shuddered uncontrollably, longing to flee from it, stifled by its creeping, enveloping miasma.

"Where's Emma?" She found it hard to breathe, to speak.

"I don't know." Hugh was occupied with Trotman. "Can you find her?"

Thankfully Dorcas escaped. She looked in the two other upstairs rooms, called Emma's name, but received no response.

"Missis done gone," one of the slaves told her when she returned downstairs.

"Gone where?" Dorcas's tone was sharp. The girl was slatternly, with an air of sly enjoyment. "Did you see her leave?"

"She act real strange, ma'am. I tell her she still in her night clo'es, but she act like she don' hear."

"Which way did she go?"

"I guess she go south, ma'am. She go north, you and de doctor see her."

South Creek, with its mangroves and stillness and clouded water. It was like a nightmare, Dorcas thought, the inevitable end to a long-felt dread that had persisted in haunting her from the first moment she had seen the place. It was all too easy to imagine a pale face and long black hair drifting lazily in the green depths.

Visions of horror seemed to press in on her as she hurried down the path that led to the creek. The vegetation was thick on each side, head-high and oppressive, sea-grape and cactus and dense thorn trees. All was silent, the only movement the flashing wings of a bird as it skimmed across the path in front of her.

There was no sign of life at the creek itself. She halted and looked around.

"Emma," she called. "Emma!"

It seemed as if her loud voice was an intrusion in this quiet place. An osprey, preening on a dead branch which raised gaunt arms from the water, lifted its head and was still, as if waiting for another cry that would send it fleeing in fright.

The sun was warmer now, and she could feel the heat of it on her back. She shaded her eyes to look across the creek; and then, from somewhere to the side, she was conscious of a movement. Quickly she turned her head and saw Emma. She was walking towards her, idly and apparently aimlessly, her attention concentrated on the twig in her hand and the leaves she was stripping from it.

There was blood on her nightgown, and her hair hung about her face, lank and dishevelled. She paused and seemed to be looking down at something that had caught her attention on the ground.

Slowly, casually, Dorcas walked towards her.

"Hallo, Emma," she said quietly, when she was close.

"Look." Emma pointed to the ground. A small, furry animal, a mouse or shrew, was lying dead, part consumed by maggots that wove themselves in and out and over in a heaving, enveloping mass. "Poor little thing!"

She sighed, but she did not seem unhappy as she looked up at Dorcas and showed no surprise at seeing her. In fact, Dorcas thought, she looked peaceful and untroubled.

"Come, Emma," she said.

"Did Papa send you?" Emma asked.

Dorcas hesitated, then seeing the blankness, the innocent enquiry in her eyes, hesitated no longer.

"In a way," she said, as she took Emma's arm. "Yes, in a way he did. He wants me to look after you. Come. Let's go home together."

*   *   *

348

Still no word from Storm. With each ship that called, her hopes rose, only to be dashed time after time. In the hours before dawn when she could not sleep, it was all too easy to believe that she would never hear; that Kit had at last broken his silence and had told Storm that the father he had lost had been no father at all, and that in disgust and revulsion Storm had turned from her and from the island and everything else that reminded him of his childhood.

Daylight brought more rational thoughts. Distances were great and the risks to shipping incalculable. She would hear soon; she felt quite sure of it.

Meantime, sadness seemed to be a tangible weight, with many layers. The loss of Zachariah was, of course, the worst, made even more heavy by her seeming inability to remember that he had gone. So often she thought of something she would say to him the moment he returned home; so often she reached out towards him during those vulnerable night hours. Once, she even poured a cup of tea for him. Such lapses only served to add yet another layer to the core of anguish inside her.

She was sad, too, that he had seen so few of his dreams come true. Still North Creek was closed to the sea; still there were few buildings of any substance on the island, no overall plan of development. Revenue continued to be paid to the Government of the Bahamas, which gave little or nothing in return.

Davey was far away, long gone from Jamaica and unable to come home just yet, even for a short holiday. Emma lived in a world of her own, childish and utterly dependent. All knew that it was by her hand Willis Trotman had died and there was a period of intense concern while the authorities debated what was to be done with her, but the outcome was never seriously in doubt.

They had no facilities or precedent for dealing with a crime like hers. The prison on the island was primitive, intended only for the dregs of humanity, and hospital facilities were of the most basic kind. After due discussion, those who sat in judgement were only too ready to solve the problem by releasing Emma to Dorcas's custody, convinced by Hugh that she had acted under intense provocation while the balance of her mind was disturbed.

There were some on the island who spoke bitterly of privilege – of one law for the poor and one for the rich. If one of Trotman's slaves had stabbed him, they said, he would have been strung up before nightfall! There were, however, few who could imagine that the pathetic, pale, waif-like Emma posed any threat to the community. She would recover completely, Hugh said, given peace and care and freedom from anxiety, and all of this Dorcas did her best to provide.

The house rang again with the voices of children; not always harmoniously, it was true, but at least Tamarind Villa lived again.

One day Dorcas walked alone on the beach, and saw a metal ring protruding from the sand at the water's edge. Curiously she bent down to inspect it, hooked a finger round it and pulled it out, finding that she held in her hand a rusted fragment of iron, broken and battered, but still recognisable. It was part of a manacle or leg iron. Her lips had a bitter twist as she hurled it from her, back into the waves.

Another sadness, she thought – and perhaps this guilt and not Zachariah's death, grievous though that had been, lay at the root of her melancholy.

It was of little comfort to tell herself that she had always opposed slavery, that she and Zachariah had freed many slaves, not only Joe and Bathsheba, but others throughout the years. It was of little comfort to think that it was a sense of responsibility that had, in the main, led them to retain others less able to stand on their own feet.

The guilt went deeper than that, and far wider than this small island. The whole of the West Indies, far back in history, was nurtured by the tears and the sweat of generations of slaves, thousands of miles from their homelands, denied freedom and dignity. It seemed, in that one moment of clear-sightedness, that her tears mingled wth theirs, her sadness no more than part of the tide of misery that lapped the shores of all the islands, lush or barren, volcanic or coral, bleak or beautiful. In this, if in no other way, all the islands were alike.

She stood for a moment and looked at the water. The sea was not clear today, even in the shallows, but green and clouded by the sand stirred up by the rough waves.

Far out in the Caicos channel a schooner was riding high, only to plunge almost out of sight as the waves tossed it unmercifully, while towards the wharf she could see small craft straining at their moorings.

Beyond them a larger brig was unloading, and in spite of herself, she felt the stirrings of hope. Perhaps this would be the ship that brought her word from Storm. How resilient is the human heart, she thought with rueful amusement, as she turned her steps towards home. Why am I so resolutely optimistic?

Slowly she walked back, stopping now and again to watch the flight of a bird or pick up a shell.

It was only gradually she became aware of the figure coming down the beach towards her. She stopped in her tracks, conscious of the sudden hammering of her heart.

The man began to run, ploughing with difficulty through the sand, feet sinking at every step. But still he ran, and still she stood, incapable of movement.

He was taller and his hair had darkened. His shoulders were wider than those of the youth she had last seen as she waved farewell, but still there was no mistaking him. What mother could forget her son's smile or the sound of his voice?

Still she could not move but it did not matter, for he had reached her, had enveloped her in a hug, had lifted her off her feet.

The tears that poured down her cheeks were tears of sadness for Zachariah, for herself, for lost dreams and past sins; but they were tears of joy, too.

Her optimism had been justified. Storm had come home.

"This," Dorcas said to Loveday, "is my favourite place in all the island."

The girl looked at the cliffs and the rocks and the breaking sea.

"'Tis lovely," she said. "It reminds me of home." At once she corrected herself. "Oh, I'm a great silly! This is home."

"You may find it hard and unfamiliar at first," Dorcas warned, remembering her own feelings during the early days on the island.

Loveday shook her head.

"No," she said. "I won't. I'm quite sure of it."

"It's a far cry from London."

"I never belonged there, no more than Storm did. There was always something different about him, I knew it from the first. He wasn't like the others, unfeeling and uncaring. This is his place, he says, and now it's mine. He has such plans! I only hope –"

She broke off and looked at Dorcas as if attacked by sudden doubt and uncertainty. She looked out to sea again, to where the ranks of white-capped waves raced towards the shore.

"What is it, Loveday? What do you hope?"

For a moment the girl did not answer, and when she did her voice was almost inaudible.

"That loving him is enough," she said.

"Loveday!" Smiling, Dorcas turned the girl to face her. How fortunate, she thought; how very fortunate that Storm had been sensible enough to recognise pure gold when he stumbled across it. "I do wish," she said, "that you could have known my husband. I have the feeling that you and he would have been good friends. He would have been so pleased that Storm married you."

"Would he?" Loveday's uncertainty seemed to dissolve in the warmth of Dorcas's approval, and she smiled in return, all doubt dispelled from her clear grey eyes.

And as she smiled, Dorcas had the strangest feeling that somewhere not too far away, a stocky, nut-brown man was at that instant tucking a fiddle beneath his chin.

The melody that he was about to play would be one to set the feet dancing, she felt quite sure of that.